SERAPHYMPIRE
The EDGE *of*
APOCALYPSE

The Guardians of the Gateways Series.

Seraphympire ~ Guardians of the Gateways.

Seraphympire ~ Keeper of the Key.

Seraphympire ~ The Edge of Apocalypse.

SERAPHYMPIRE
The EDGE *of*
APOCALYPSE

RENEE
SPYROU

BOOK 3.

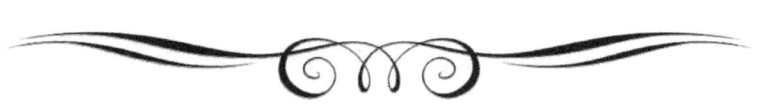

For my beautiful daughter Eleyna.

ACKNOWLEDGMENTS.

I'd like to thank the usual suspects; my husband who never lets me down and always comes through for me no matter what. I couldn't write my stories without your endless support, love and patience. Funnily enough, my banter about my books still make your eyes glaze over. I think the next book I write will have to be about fishing. Yeah, no, never.

I'd also like to thank my gorgeous daughter, whose belief in me and my stories keeps me from giving up when the inner critique just wants to trash talk and bring me down. I love our brain-storming sessions and all the character videos you've done for my books.

A huge thank you goes out to my editor, Abigail Nathan of Bothersome Words, who never fails to ask the right questions. Your attention to detail, thoroughness and professionalism are always spot on. You make my words sing.

Also, a special thank you goes out to my parents and the rest of my extended family and friends who never fail to make me laugh.

Last but not least, a big thank you to all my wonderful readers, for making what I do worth all the hard work, sweat and tears. And a special thank you to those of you who always come and say hi when I'm doing my book signings, you know who you are, my book signing events are even more special because of you. I love catching up. I'm sure I'll see you at my next book signing lining up for this book. Thank you all again and happy reading.

Fate whispers to the warrior,
"You cannot withstand the storm."
The warrior whispers back,
"I am the storm."

Unknown

PROLOGUE.

Autumn

31st of October

1307

Voices echoed throughout the town centre. The villagers no longer insisted the witch be burned at the stake. Instead, they chanted, *'The Golden One. . . The Golden One.'* How fickle humans were. Alexander's heart pounded in his chest, the loud beat echoing in his ears. His eyes trailed after Lazarus as he wove a jagged path through the chanting crowd towards Makayla and Salomae. Everything inside him screamed to follow. He exhaled then gasped in oxygen, his lungs burning as he took each breath. His nostrils flared as the smell of wood smoke and unwashed bodies blanketed him. He swallowed the awful taste in his mouth, wishing he could go with them.

Alexander looked at the mud coating his boots and took a step forward . . . then another. Bugger the consequences. There was nothing left for him. She was leaving him for another man – one he was yet to become. Leaving to save a future he could not comprehend – *their* future. It was ridiculous – unbelievable, yet he had seen the evidence for himself. A future seven hundred years ahead in time; the 21st century.

How the hell was he going to survive seven hundred years without her touch – without seeing her smile or hearing her laughter? Alexander clenched his fists; his knuckles popped, cracking with the pressure. Six days was all he'd had with her, his wife, the woman he'd spent millennia searching for. The woman he'd been born to love and protect. His destiny. Six days; three of which he'd wasted.

He looked up again, his eyes finding Makayla's.

"Alexander, I pledge my love to you and only you, forevermore!" Makayla yelled across the courtyard.

"And I you, Makayla!" he yelled back. *"And I you,"* he murmured again, watching Lazarus climb the burning wood pyre. The vampire's silhouette shimmered with rippling waves of iridescent light. A magical shield protecting his body from the flames. Alexander held his breath as Salomae lowered her head and Lazarus jumped onto her back.

Makayla smiled across at his stepmother, Lilian, the woman his father had wed not long after his mother's death. He wondered if the warlord Bulan Tzul had killed his mother like his cousin Tyron had implied. He suspected Lilian, the scheming bitch standing across the courtyard, was the one responsible. Tyron was her protector and confidante, and did her bidding. It was more likely to have been Tyron, not the warlord, who murdered his mother. His cousin was far more devious than Alexander had imagined and a vampire no less. What a fool he'd been.

Makayla unsheathed one of her daggers and sliced it across her palm. Blood gushed from the wound and snaked a red, glistening path down her wrist. Alexander watched her use the same bleeding hand to grasp the ruby Trinian gem that was hanging about her neck. The moment she touched the gem the village courtyard was immersed in red light. A giant translucent, red orb fragmented about Makayla, Salomae and Lazarus. Tunnelling winds buffeted them, growing stronger with every passing minute. Sparkling light orbited the red sphere, which pulsated like a giant, beating heart. It expanded and grew brighter with every shuddering beat.

Alexander swallowed the lump in his throat. His eyes burned as he swiped a trembling hand across his forehead. He wanted to cry out, to scream for her not to leave. Instead, he bit down the words on the tip of his tongue, his jaw clenching. He knew she could not stay, for she already existed in the 14th century. She would not forsake him – not in the past nor the future. He was a dead man if she did.

He shook his head and stared back at Makayla as she gazed

up at the heavens, her glorious hair spiralling above her. She glanced towards him one last time, her hair catching in her mouth. He heard her voice in his head as she mouthed, *'I love you, I'll find you; this is not goodbye.'* A sad smile swept across her face as she looked back up at the darkening sky. A vortex opened above her, shooting a red conduit up into space. Cyclonic winds circled Makayla and her companions. It blasted down over them before being sucked back up into the maelstrom.

Alexander looked up at what appeared to be a gateway into heaven. A loud boom rent the sky and the unmistakable odour of a lightning strike permeated the air. Makayla, Lazarus, and the Terrin disappeared in a brilliant flash of red. The vortex imploded and all that remained was a red beam of light shooting up into the sky.

She was gone.

Alexander looked at his feet, his shoulders sagging. He glanced back up at the crowd, watching as pyre ash rained down over them. They continued staring up into the heavens. No longer chanting their mantra. Not even the children made a sound. The silence seemed so loud.

Alexander turned towards the podium where Lilian and her daughter Abby, Tyron, Zack and Beltizare, as well the Cardinal and the Grand Inquisitor perched. He saw their demonic faces clearly now; their teeth were sharp elongated fangs and their eyes were black and soulless. Dark-purple veins covered their faces, pulsating beneath their translucent skin as the blood pumped through their bodies. His bond with Makayla had changed him and now he could see what lay beneath the subterfuge Lilian and her companions projected. He would have his revenge. He wove his way towards the podium, the squelching of his boots as he trudged through the mud lost to the growing roar in his ears. He smiled when he noticed Lilian's frown. It was small recompense for what she had stolen from him but he would see her squirm this day. Alexander stopped before them, staring daggers at his so-called family and friends.

Alexander pointed at Lilian. "I have no words to describe your deception, Lilian or Lilith, whoever you are. You will pay. Did your lapdog kill my mother so you could insinuate yourself into my father's life, into my life? All for what, so you could locate the Trinian Globe? You will never find it, and you will never free the Dark One." Alexander's mouth hooked up in a bitter smile. "Oh, you thought you had me fooled. In the beginning, yes, but no more. I've warned the brotherhood, they know who you are and soon everyone here will, too."

"Do you think I fear the Custodians of Rahul, Alexander, or these village idiots?" Lilian rose from her seat and shook her fist in the air. "I fear no man, especially not the sons and daughters of Adam. They are pathetic worms."

Alexander's smile broadened as he concentrated on their true forms. He held his hands close to his body and wiggled his fingers ever so slightly so as not to bring down the wrath of the villagers for being more than he pretended to be. His brow furrowed as he used magic to strip away their disguise. Layer by layer their appearance changed; fluctuating in and out of focus as their demonic faces slowly appeared. Vasili's son, Nikolai, who now masqueraded as Beltizare, wasn't unmasked. "Villagers of Corfe Castle, behold the deceivers, the monsters who would destroy the Golden One. The Devil's handmaiden, Lilith, walks among you!" Alexander yelled, his voice echoing in the empty silence. The villagers turned towards Lilian, shocked screams of horror soon filling the ebbing silence as Lilian and her lackeys' true faces were revealed.

Zack was the only one whose appearance remained the same. Six vampires stood staring out across the crowd, their fangs extended, their faces grotesque and distorted. Lilith was a horrific sight – her lips stretched tightly over a mouth brimming with sharp fangs. Black pulsing veins surrounded her black eyes, her red irises glowing unnaturally.

Lilith and her companions looked at one another, their faces registering disbelief as the villagers hurled rotten food and rocks at them. Mothers gathered their children, herding them away from the demons standing on the stage. One soldier threw a spear; it struck the Grand Inquisitor's chest with a hollow thunk that resounded in Alexander's ears. The Inquisitor grasped the foreign object protruding from his torso and fell to his knees as his hand slid down the length of the spear, leaving a bright blood trail. The soldier's aim had been true, piercing the vampire's heart with deadly accuracy. The crowd stopped, curiosity getting the better. The Inquisitor slumped forward, his body disintegrating as his corpse hit the decking. Fiery red ash replaced his flesh as an explosion of hot cinders rained down over those standing closest to the podium. Villagers brushed the new ash from their dirty clothes, stepping back in revulsion.

Lilith eyeballed Alexander, an ugly sneer sullying her face, her teeth dripping venom. "Mark my words, Alexander, you will rue the day you set your sights on ousting me. I will destroy you and the bitch you call wife." She stabbed her finger in the air pointing at him.

"Nay, Lilith. It shall be you who rues the day! You cannot manipulate me like the weaklings you surround yourself with. I am the conqueror of all miseries, the protector, and Keeper of the Key. Do you hear me? The Keeper of the Key; the key you have been searching for all these centuries is not an object, 'tis the Golden One, you fool. The woman you were so bent on destroying is the Key of divinity and now she is lost, lost, do you hear me? *Lost*."

Alexander jerked his hand to the side, and the podium shook violently, causing those standing upon it to lose their balance. He turned as a loud crash resonated throughout the courtyard. The villagers closed in on Lilith and her disciples, he heard the townspeople cry, *'kill the demons, kill the demons'* as he walked away.

The ringing of swords and screaming was lost on Alexander as he walked towards his warhorse deep in thought. Would he see Makayla again after she saved him in the future? Would he be the same? He stopped in front of his stallion and glanced over his shoulder at the rioting crowd. Zack stood beyond the horde staring after him. Alexander turned away; ignoring the remorse on his adoptive son's face and mounted his horse. He would find his Makayla, the Makayla of this time, and protect her until it was time to reveal himself to her.

CHAPTER 1.

Zobiana and Abigail watched the dark cloud swirl about the room until it formed a column of grainy smoke. It drifted towards the dungeon wall where Alexander's unconscious body was chained. His head jolted back and hit the wall with a meaty thump. Abigail smiled at her mother before focusing her attention back on Alexander. Alexander's eyes sprang open, his piercing scream echoing as the black cloud funnelled down his throat. His body convulsed – pulling against the chains as the Dark One possessed him.

Zobiana relaxed, her shoulders loosening. She was finally free from the Dark One's tyrannical rule. She inhaled deeply, relishing the freedom she had gained through Alexander's possession.

"Should we unshackle him, Mother?" Abigail asked, glancing at her mother before staring back at Alexander's sagging form.

"No, leave him there!" Zobiana straightened, folding her arms across her chest and raising her chin in defiance.

"But—"

"No buts; the Dark One is in for a shock. Alexander won't relinquish control of his body easily."

"I siphoned his power. Weakened him so the Dark One could possess his body, he will have complete control over Alexander. I'm sure of it, my idea was sound."

"No, the Dark One won't have complete control. The moment Alexander drinks the Golden One's blood and gains strength, the Dark One will be imprisoned again. Only this time he'll not escape his prison or take gaseous or corporeal form again. The death of the vessel is the only way to free the Dark One, and the Chosen One will never kill Alexander. The Dark One will be trapped forever." Zobiana's laughter rang through the dungeon's lower levels.

"What are you saying, Mother?"

"I couldn't have come up with a more brilliant idea, Abigail. I've been trying to think of a way to be free of the Dark One for millennia, I thought finding the Trinian Globe was the answer, but it was lost and then you came to me with the notion of weakening Alexander's power so the Dark One could possess his body. I thank you. You have freed me from servitude, you have freed us all. Now I can carry out my plans to control the Earth and its gateways. Finally, we can return to Evron stronger than ever before. There's nothing stopping us now."

Zobiana smiled at her daughter. "It's time the Dark One learned the true meaning of servitude." Zobiana swept her hair over her shoulder and looked across at Alexander once more before stalking out of his cell. Abigail smirked at Alexander and chuckled before trailing after her mother.

Makayla and Lazarus materialised in a dark, empty passageway, the smell of rock, mould and wet decay surrounding them. Makayla shivered, there was no one about, no guards at all – she had a terrible feeling.

Lazarus glanced over his shoulder. "Where's Salomae?" he whispered.

"I don't know." Makayla shrugged. "It's probably best she's not here, she may have brought down the entire castle with her huge bulk, she's close by, though."

"Do you think we're in the right place? I mean, we could be anywhere."

"I think so, why would the Trinian Globe have sent me back in time if it wasn't to find Alexander?"

"Maybe it was because the next gem to be found was the Gem of Past Times and that's all it was."

Makayla looked across at Lazarus. "Why are you being such a buzz-kill?"

"I don't know, this place is creeping me out, it's strange." Lazarus shuddered.

"I think we are where we're meant to be – look around, looks like a dungeon passageway to me, so I'm guessing we're in the right place."

"How did you know your blood would activate the gem?"

"It reacted with my blood when I removed it from Lilith's neck, I figured if there was more of my blood, um, well hell . . . I don't know, it felt right. Call it a hunch."

"Do you sense Alexander nearby?" Lazarus asked, glancing over his shoulder again.

"Yes and no, he must be unconscious, it's strange though – even if he were unconscious I would sense him, unless he's at death's door. Lazarus, we need to find him now."

"Maybe we should separate; we'd cover more ground," Lazarus said, brushing the pyre ash from his shoulders that had showered him before their departure and readjusting the strap to the bag of weapons he was carrying. "Do you think Vasili's wife is with Alexander?"

"I don't know, but I think you're right, we should separate, we don't have time to waste. You go that way." Makayla pointed to a passageway on their left. "I'll keep going this way, I think Alexander may be further down, maybe deeper on another level of the dungeon. Oh, and give me the bag of weapons before you go."

Lazarus handed Makayla the bag, *"Okay, let me know when you find him,"* Lazarus said telepathically and headed off down the dark passageway.

"Likewise," Makayla said, unsheathing her sword from its scabbard and jogging off in the direction they'd been heading. "Alexander. . ." she called quietly. "Alexander, where are you?"

"Help . . . help me," someone called from a dungeon cell to her right. Makayla stopped and eyed the door. "Please . . . I implore you . . . don't leave me here, *please.*" Makayla scratched her head and looked towards the end of the passage; she didn't have time to help the man calling out, but she couldn't leave him either. Maybe he could help her locate Alexander.

She moved towards the dungeon door – there was something about the man's voice, she felt sure she'd heard it before. Makayla peered through the small, barred window in the door. The prisoner was curled up in a darkened corner towards the back of his cell and she couldn't see his face. She held her hand over the lock securing the door and manifested a flame, heating the lock until it glowed orange. She grasped it in her fist and twisted, breaking it easily. She tore it free and threw it to the ground where it hissed as the hot metal hit wet rushes, then she opened the door.

It screeched open on rusted hinges as if it hadn't opened in an age. "Why should I help you, old man?" Makayla pointed her sword at him.

"Because I will be forever indebted to you." The elderly man stood, using the moss-covered wall to pull himself up from his position on the floor. Makayla manifested a fireball and tossed it towards an unlit torch in the wall sconce, then gasped when she saw the man's haggard face.

Lazarus squinted as he followed the twisting tunnel, peering into cells when he came to them, but they were mostly empty. Those that weren't had nothing living in them but rats and skeletal human remains hanging from corroded manacles chained to moss-covered walls. This was evidence enough that if they didn't find Alexander soon, all would be lost, and he feared for Makayla and her sanity. If Zobiana got her hands on her as well there would be nothing in the Multiverse that could save them – not even the Zoldarni could stop the cataclysmic events that would follow.

Lazarus stopped as he heard the jangle of chains and footsteps coming his way. He tried to render himself invisible, but nothing happened. *Shit,* he thought, looking around for somewhere to hide. *Shit, shit, shit!* He grimaced and backed up against the passage wall. It was no surprise his powers weren't working, especially in the Rivulous Dimension. Just when he thought his cover was blown, he noticed a deep crevice in the passage wall. He sucked in a breath and squashed himself into the crevice moments before a giant of a man ambled towards his position, mumbling something unintelligible. Lazarus watched as the guard, still mumbling, stopped near a cell door and looked through the small barred window.

"Your Druid is no more," he said to the prisoner.

"No . . . you bastard!" a woman screamed. "You will die; the Golden One will end you."

"Not before I end you." The guard chuckled as he unlocked the woman's dungeon door. "Your time has come, wench. The High Priestess no longer requires your services; your usefulness has run out," the guard said, kicking the door open.

The screeching of the door masked the sound of Lazarus unsheathing his long-sword; he hunched over as he crept up behind the guard and followed him into the woman's cell. The man's great bulk filled the doorway; Lazarus watched him toss the chains he held to the ground and pull a dagger from the scabbard strapped at his waist.

"I've been waiting a long time for this," the guard taunted the prisoner, waving the dagger from side to side.

Without preamble, Lazarus angled his sword and took aim; he thrust the sword up, twisting the blade as he forced it through the guard's shoulder blade to pierce his heart. The guard gasped as he toppled forward, landing hard on his stomach in front of the woman cowering on the floor with her hands stretched out before her. Lazarus placed his foot on the guard's back and tugged his sword free, then looked up and smiled at the woman as he wiped the blood on the guard's tunic before sheathing his sword and bowing gallantly.

"It gives a whole new meaning to being stabbed in the

back, doesn't it?" Lazarus said, looking down at the guard and chuckling. "My lady, my name is Lazarus Talyian and I'm hoping you are Vasili's wife, Marianna Constantinos?"

"'Tis with great pleasure I make your acquaintance, Lord Lazarus," said the woman, who appeared to be in her early to mid-sixties. "I am indeed Marianna Constantinos."

Lazarus's smile broadened and he bowed once more before holding out his arm. "Shall we depart this godforsaken place, my lady?"

"Why yes," Marianna said, taking Lazarus's arm. "Have you found Alexander yet?"

"Not yet, Makayla's searching for him as we speak, do you know where he's being kept prisoner?"

"He is on the lower levels of the dungeon, but I fear it may be too late, the guard said he is no more."

"He's still alive, Makayla said as much, but we need to find him. Can you show me where he is?"

"'Tis this way, follow me." Marianna pointed to an ancient stairwell to the right of her cell door.

"Makayla, I've found Marianna," Lazarus told Makayla telepathically. *"She's leading me to Alexander – he's on the lower levels of the dungeon."*

"What . . . how are you here?" Makayla demanded.

"How does anybody find themselves locked up in a dungeon cell? Especially one of Zobiana's," the old man replied.

"Do you know who I am?" she asked, angling her head and scanning his face, searching for something, deceit, recognition – anything. How could he not recognise her? It hadn't been that long since she'd stood before him.

"I'm afraid not, my lady, this is the first time I've seen you. Should I know you?" the man asked, hobbling towards her. "You know who I am, but I'm sorry I'm at a loss. Tell me who you think I am, maybe you have mistaken me for another."

"Why, you're Chancellor Augustus Lagorias of the Vampire Council from the planet Evron."

The chancellor stopped in front of Makayla, squinting as he eyed her up and down.

"You seriously don't remember me? Five months ago you summoned me to a Vampire Council meeting."

"I'm sorry, no; I've been held prisoner here for a long time."

"How long have you been here?" Makayla asked, slipping her weapon back into its sheath and dropping the bag she carried to the ground.

"They abducted me in 1987."

"Son of a bitch, that's not good, you've been here thirty or so years." Makayla swiped her forehead with the back of her hand. "So . . . were you the one who planted the vault key on your son's keychain?"

"Vault key, no, why do you ask?"

Makayla gulped, swallowing the sour taste that had formed in her mouth. "There's no easy way to tell you this." Makayla cleared her throat and tried to swallow again, but her mouth had gone dry. "Um . . . God, this is so awful."

"What is it, my child?" Augustus asked, shuffling closer to her.

"Um . . . it's just, it's just . . . I hate to be the bearer of bad news, but . . . but your son . . . your son was murdered in 1987, and the key to your vault was stolen. They were after the Trinian Globe, I'm guessing this all happened after your abduction, I'm so, so sorry for your loss, Lord Augustus."

Augustus swayed on his feet, losing his balance. Makayla flung her hands out and caught him as he pitched forward; he weighed nothing and seemed so frail. Tears streamed down his cheeks as he looked up into Makayla's face. "She has stolen everything from me. . . everything—"

"I'm sorry, my Lord, I wish I could take away your pain and give back your son and stolen years. I know all seems lost right now and life doesn't hold much hope, but please don't give up, don't let your son's death be for nothing. We live in a harsh, unforgiving world controlled by Zobiana. She must pay for her atrocities and we must make her pay. Yes, she has taken your son from you, but she hasn't stolen everything, she hasn't stolen your wrath. You must find the strength to continue and take your rightful place on the council. Evron needs you, the Multiverse needs you, Earth needs you; we must unmask the imposter who fills your shoes for if we don't all will be lost." Makayla sighed, the man before her appeared older than the imposter she'd met at the council meeting. She should have trusted Vasili's word regarding the chancellor's character. "A lot has happened since your abduction, my lord. Earth is close to an apocalypse and humanity is on the brink of annihilation. Zobiana has released two viruses – one is V5, a designer drug that transforms humans into vampires that we call Newbloods. That's how she has amassed her armies. The second is the Blakspor virus, which is decimating the remaining human population, making it easier for her Newblood vampires to round people up. She's farming humans for their blood." Makayla hoisted Augustus up, helping him find his feet again. "So we really do need you."

He looked at her. His face was gaunt and the expression he wore was troubling. "I'm sorry, Chancellor, it must be a shock hearing my news, but there is no easy way to tell you what's been going on, I need you to fight, my lord. We all do."

Augustus nodded. "You were right to tell me."

"How long has it been since you last fed?" Makayla asked.

"I can't remember."

"Then you must feed, my lord." Makayla let go of Augustus, making sure he wouldn't topple over before she removed her hands and unsheathed one of her daggers. She sliced it across her wrist and held her arm out towards him.

Augustus looked at her wrist and shook his head. "I really shouldn't." His eyes betrayed his hunger as he licked his lips.

"You will feed, you need your strength, I can't be carrying you if we're to escape this place. Now, before my wound heals." Makayla shook her arm.

The chancellor moved closer to her and grasped her wrist timidly, he looked up into her face once more, she nodded, and he lowered his mouth to her wrist and drank – slow at first, but as he regained his vigour he fed deeper. Makayla felt his grip tighten as his strength returned. She was beginning to think he'd never stop when he disengaged his mouth from her wrist, flung his head back and gasped. His face filled out and his hair lost its brittle appearance, the sallowness of his skin and eyes disappeared, his spine straightened from its hunch.

"Thank you . . . I needed that, your blood is very different, my lady, unlike anything I've ever tasted."

"So I've been told," Makayla said, smiling and re-sheathing her dagger.

"May I ask your name, my lady?"

"My name is Makayla Zahirah Uriel. You know – the Golden One, the Chosen One, the first of my kind, the prophesied seraphympire queen who will save Evron and the Multiverse yadda . . . yadda . . . yadda, I could go on, but hey, time's a-wasting."

Augustus's face paled. "Are you here to kill me?"

"God . . . no, I wouldn't have offered you my blood if that was my intention, I'm here to find a prisoner named Alexander Drake, I was hoping you could help me find him."

"There was a prisoner who was brought to the dungeons

recently; he must be the one you speak of," Augustus murmured

"Makayla, I've found Marianna, she's leading me to Alexander; he's on the lower levels of the dungeon," Lazarus's voice echoed in Makayla's head.

CHAPTER 2.

Makayla followed Augustus as he led her down another dim stairwell to the lower level cells. She gritted her teeth – would she ever escape the chill that settled in her soul whenever she found herself somewhere like this? She'd thought she had overcome her hatred of dungeons when she was held prisoner briefly in the 14th century – she had remained calm then. But it seemed her fear was still intact. Maybe it hadn't bothered her in the past because it was a different era.

"Makayla dear, you will always hate and fear dungeons because you're weak," her nemesis taunted.

Makayla's step faltered. *"Forgive me, I forgot there for a minute it was you who I hate the most. Obviously you don't hate me as much as I do you,"* Makayla replied internally.

Her nemesis's tone changed abruptly. *"Hurry ... Alexander's fading, he needs your blood, hurry now ..."*

Makayla's step faltered again before she picked up her pace. "Chancellor Lagorias, are we nearly there? Alexander's not doing too well." The one thing she could always depend upon was the urgency of her nemesis's voice, although she often wondered why her nemesis even cared what happened to her or Alexander.

"When will you realise if either one of you die, then I die too, call it self-preservation . . . huuuurrrrrryy—"

"Yes, we're nearly there, it's just around the bend," Augustus said, pointing to the end of the passageway.

Makayla grabbed his arm. "I think it would be best if you got behind me, Chancellor."

"As you wish, Lady Uriel," Augustus said, stepping behind her. They continued along the passage until they came to the bend, Makayla set down the bag of weapons and nodded at him before unsheathing her sword and manifesting a protective shield about them. She signalled for Augustus to wait while she snuck a look around the corner. There was another stairwell leading up opposite a dungeon door; she assumed Alexander was being held prisoner there. She could barely sense his life force and was about to rush towards the cell when she heard footsteps coming down the stairs. Instead, she crossed the passageway and planted her back against the wall near the stairwell and readied her sword. She swung it up just as Lazarus and Marianna stepped into the passage from the stairs. Marianna gasped, her eyes bulging when she felt Makayla's blade at her throat. Makayla withdrew her weapon the moment she realised who stood before her.

"Sorry . . . I didn't mean to startle you; I heard footsteps and thought . . . well, you know what I thought." Makayla sheathed her sword. "You can come out now, Chancellor," she called over her shoulder.

Lazarus looked past Makayla as she dashed towards Alexander's cell door and peered through the barred window, his jaw dropping when he saw Augustus. "Chancellor Lagorias, what the devil are you doing here? I thought you were on Evron."

"No, Lazarus. From what Lady Uriel tells me, I've been trapped in Zobiana's dungeon for the last thirty or so years."

Lazarus looked from Augustus to Makayla. "So, who's impersonating him on Evron?"

"Don't know . . . we'll worry about it later, Laz . . . Alexander needs me right now." Makayla nodded at Marianna before looking through the cell window again. She scanned the dark room, but couldn't see Alexander straight away. She gasped when she noticed his beaten body chained to the back wall; he was covered in dirt and blood. *"Hold on, Xander, I'm here now,"* Makayla said to him telepathically. She heard him groan. It was enough – he was still alive.

"Give Chancellor Lagorias and Marianna a weapon, Lazarus, and watch the passageway for Zobiana's people." Makayla pointed to the bag of weapons just beyond the chancellor's feet, then stepped back from the door. "Move back everyone," she said, swirling her hands.

Everyone watched as blue-fire manifested about her fingertips. She focused on the door and thrust her hands towards the iron barrier; blue flames burst forward, immersing the door in shimmering light and disintegrating the iron into fragments.

Makayla raced into the dungeon towards Alexander. She grabbed hold of the chains embedded in the rock wall and tugged. Chunks of stone crumbled to the rushes as she caught Alexander in her arms and slumped to the ground. Makayla unsheathed one of her daggers and sliced her wrist for the second time. She held her arm up to Alexander's mouth, but there was no response.

"Feed Xander, *please feed.*" Makayla laid his head in her lap, brushing the hair from his forehead. Tears streaked down her face as she swallowed the lump in her throat. Alexander's cheeks were hollow and his appearance sickly, he was gaunt and malnourished. *"My husband, please feed, you will surely die if you do not, I'm here, returned from the past, please . . . drink."* Makayla held her wrist above his mouth and dripped blood onto his lips, and he began to cough as he licked them. It was a dry, hacking cough that made his body shudder violently. She watched him open his eyes and was shocked to see flames within their depths.

"Makayla," he murmured weakly before closing his eyes again. She forced her wrist to his mouth and heard another low groan as his lips began to move. Makayla sighed when he finally began to feed, then hissed when he bit down – his fangs sinking deep into her skin, his hands grasping her arm as he began to feed in earnest. She kissed his forehead and he opened his eyes and stared up at her. The flames were no longer present in their depths, but his irises were black and fathomless. There was something different about him. She brushed off the uneasy feeling, knowing a vampire's eyes were black when they were close to death and hadn't fed.

Makayla was suddenly bombarded with a vision. She saw Alexander whipped and tortured endlessly; she saw Abigail siphoning all his strength until he was too weak to fight back; and then she saw a black cloud hovering over him, but couldn't for the life of her figure out what it meant.

Makayla shook her head and the vision ended; she positioned her hand over his heart, lowered her palm to his chest and was overcome with an all-consuming love. She thought about all the intimate moments they'd shared in the 14th and the 21st centuries, she thought about the vows they'd made to one another when they were married; she let the love envelop her, every single part of her. Gold light surrounded her hand and moved up her body until she was glowing, and in every sense, the Golden One. Her skin tingled as the muscles in her back tightened and her shoulder blades began to itch, she felt her hair float up about her as if she'd been touched by electricity, and then her wings exploded from her back in a flash of flaming light. She unfurled them, stretching them out and flexing the feathers until they filled all the free space in the cell.

Alexander's pallor began to improve – his eyes weren't so sunken, his body not so malnourished; the veins just under his skin became more visible and the main artery in his neck was pumping faster now. She would give her all to bring him back from the brink of death. Alexander looked up again, his eyes no longer black, but gold-speckled amber. She smiled down at him as he disengaged his mouth from the wound at her wrist and licked it, healing it with his saliva.

"You're really here, I thought I was dreaming."

Makayla nodded and kissed his hand.

"You found me." Alexander's eyes widened when he saw the necklace she wore. He lifted his hand and touched the ruby Trinian gem hanging from her throat, then grabbed her hand and touched the eagle ring on her wedding ring finger. "It has finally happened. We're married."

Makayla nodded, the tears streaming down her face as she looked into his unwavering, amber eyes. "Alexander, I've pledged my love to you, I've promised to honour and cherish you above all others and have vowed to love you fiercely in all your forms today and beyond every tomorrow, through this life and into the next until time's end. No force shall undo what we are to each other, be they evil or good. Not Zobiana, not Abigail, nor Tyrone or the Dark One; absolutely no one will come between us or undo our bond. My husband, you are mine and I am yours forever more."

"You have no idea how long I've waited to hear you say those words again." Alexander lifted his hand and an angel wedding ring appeared magically on his ring finger. He smiled and touched her cheek, threading his fingertips into her hair as he snaked a hand behind her neck and gently pulled her face towards his to kiss her. Makayla closed her wings, cocooning their bodies in feathers as the kiss deepened, a searing heat traversing her body and rousing the fine hairs on her spine. Alexander explored her mouth with his tongue, her skin shivering as he nibbled and sucked, teasing her mouth with gentle caresses until she found herself wanting more. She broke the kiss on a sigh.

"As much as I'd love to keep kissing you, husband mine, we really need to be leaving this godawful dungeon."

"I love hearing you call me husband, I've waited centuries, but you're right. We need to find Marianna and get out of here."

"I'm here, Alexander," Marianna said from behind them.

Makayla's wings disappeared into her body as she stood and helped Alexander to his feet. He looked towards the door where Marianna, Lazarus and Chancellor Lagorias stood in the entranceway.

"Alexander, my friend, you look a bit the worse for wear," Lazarus said.

Alexander nodded. "I can only imagine," he said, stepping forward to hug Marianna and then to shake Lazarus's hand. "It's good to see you, Lazarus."

"It's good to see you too, Alexander, but damn if you don't smell like a latrine, ol' boy." Lazarus pinched his nose.

Alexander looked down at his dirt-caked torso and shredded trousers. "I'm in need of a shower and a shave, I'm afraid." Alexander swiped a hand over his jaw.

Makayla clenched her fists into tight balls, her nails digging into her palms when she noticed the tangle of scars marking his back.

"Chancellor Lagorias, I'm surprised to see a member of the Vampire Council here."

Chancellor Lagorias's mouth dropped open, startled momentarily by Alexander's familiarity. "No more than I am at being here, son, but I'll certainly be glad to leave this awful place."

"Makayla, do you think you'll be able to teleport us all out of here?" Alexander asked.

"I doubt it, not after all the blood I gave you and the chancellor. But I can try, and if I can't, I can always ask Salomae for help."

"Where is Salomae, anyway?" Alexander stopped near the entrance and looked over his shoulder at Makayla.

Makayla angled her head. "I don't know exactly, but she's close, I sense her presence nearby."

"When did you bond with her? I've been wondering for centuries now."

"It happened just after you were taken captive. Do you remember the dragon Guardians you told me about when we first arrived in the Congo?"

"Yes," Alexander said, facing her.

"Well, you know when we cut our hands to unlock the temple door?"

"Uh-huh…"

"I rested my bleeding palm against one of the Terrin statues nearby and . . . Um . . . well, my blood . . . kind of brought her to life."

Alexander chuckled. "Those Sons of Anak are pretty crafty."

"Yeah, sneaky buggers," Makayla said, pushing him towards the door and ushering everyone out into the passageway. "We should leave now, before Zobiana and Abigail return."

Makayla crouched and unzipped the bag on the ground, removing a sheathed sword and tossing it to Alexander. He caught it and winked at her. God, she'd missed him, she needed to get him, everyone, out of there safely. She eyed Alexander thoughtfully, what did the vision mean? What was the black cloud that had hovered above him? Was it symbolic of what was ahead of them – darkness, or was there more to it?

"Is everything okay, Makayla?" Alexander whispered, moving closer.

Makayla nodded, zipped up the bag and stood. "It's . . . it's been a rough few days . . . months . . . is all. I won't be able to relax until we're out of here. I have a bad feeling this is just the beginning of Zobiana's devious plans." Makayla gathered up the bag of weapons from the floor and tossed it to Lazarus. "Could you hang onto the bag, Laz? We're going to need the weapons before this day's end." Makayla noticed Alexander's expression change. "I'm sorry, Xander, that was insensitive of me. If anyone's had a rough few days and months it's you."

Alexander fastened the sword Makayla had given him to his waist and looked at her. "It's been rough, but nothing I couldn't handle, you are, we are . . . worth it."

Makayla wanted to drag Alexander into her arms and never let him go, but rubbed her forehead and cast her eyes about instead. "Okay . . . so, I'm going to try to teleport us out of here." She looked down at her feet and took a deep breath. "If you could all keep quiet so I can concentrate..." She looked up again and nodded. "Okay . . . here goes." Makayla closed her eyes and slowed her breathing; her heart began to speed up as she focused on teleporting everyone to the entertainment room back at the underground compound. Her skin began to tingle and itch. There was a low hum in her ears as her senses coalesced. Gooseflesh spiked all over her body as a cool wind whipped about them. The wind strengthened as she exerted the power to transport the group. The wind died as Makayla opened her eyes. They were still in the dungeon passageway. "Son of a bitch," she hissed, closing her eyes again. *"Salomae, if you're about, I kind of need your help."* There was no response from Salomae. "Shit!" Makayla's shoulders slumped.

Alexander placed his hands on her shoulders as she opened her eyes. "It's okay, we'll get out of here another way." She looked at his hands on her armour – the very same armour he shouldn't be able to touch. Their blood-bond was strong.

Makayla covered his fingertips with hers and sighed.

"Sorry, everyone, it looks like we're going to have to take the long way, I can't contact Salomae. So, who knows the way out?" She glanced about the group. "I'm guessing nobody . . . right?" They shook their heads.

"I tried to memorise the way when I was first brought here," Alexander said, lowering his arms to his sides. "But I'm afraid with everything that's happened I've forgotten. We do need to get to the upper levels, though, and pass through a wall. . ."

"Pass through a wall?" Makayla eyed Alexander. "Did I hear you correctly?"

Alexander nodded. "The guard traced a rune in the air over the wall before we passed through it. I remember the rune he traced, if it helps." Alexander grinned, his dimples hidden beneath his facial hair.

"What a relief," Makayla uttered, wanting to kiss her husband all over again. She shook her head to dislodge her wayward thoughts knowing they weren't out of danger and needed to get out of there.

"There'll be plenty of time for debauchery later," Her nemesis teased.

Makayla grimaced, ignoring her. "I can get us to the wall; Laz, can you give me the leather canister from the bag?"

"Sure," Lazarus said, unzipping the bag and digging through its contents. He tossed Makayla the canister. She caught it and immediately opened it and removed the map.

Alexander smiled when he saw the map. "I can't believe

you actually brought the map with you."

"What are you implying, Alexander . . . that I don't listen? You did tell me the map would help, and so it has. I was set on finding you no matter the cost!" Makayla pinned Alexander with her eyes.

Alexander grasped her face in the palms of his hands, "I'm not implying anything, I'm just happy you listened."

"If you two are quite finished, I think it prudent we left this cold abyss before the High Priestess decides to sacrifice us all," Lazarus said, clapping Alexander on the back.

Alexander released Makayla's face and stepped aside to give her space.

Makayla cleared her throat and scanned the map, trying to pinpoint their position. "It's this way." She pointed back the way she and the chancellor had come. "Lazarus, you bring up the rear." Makayla unsheathed her sword. "Aunt Marianna, if you could walk between the chancellor and Alexander you'll be more protected, Vasili and Nikolai will have my head if anything happens to you.

CHAPTER 3

They'd been walking through twisting tunnels thick with moss for what felt like hours, though it had been mere minutes. Time seemed to warp in the Rivulous Dimension. Goosebumps covered Alexander's body and he clenched his jaw trying to stem the sound of his chattering teeth; the chill was beginning to needle under his skin.

He cocked his head and listened to the sounds of the tunnel; his hearing was acute to the point of annoyance – he could hear the smallest of sounds. Dripping water, scurrying rats, scuttling insects moving in wall crevices, the crackling flames in wall sconces, Marianna's laboured breaths and the most distracting of all: Makayla's strong pounding heartbeat. Their hearts beat in time now, synchronised. He wondered if she was aware – she had to be.

Alexander peered down at his hand and wiggled his

fingers; his wedding ring glinted in the quivering firelight illuminating the passageways. It had happened; they were married. Makayla was now the woman he'd first met in the 14th century, the woman he'd first fallen in love with. Not even when she'd Soul-melded had she been quite the same as she'd been the first time he'd laid eyes on her in the past.

Alexander remembered the night she'd saved him from his cousin Tyrone's killing blow, the same night they'd made love and she'd discovered him lounging on the sofa listening to music and staring at their wedding rings. He'd been melancholy about their past, a history he couldn't divulge to her – a time she hadn't yet experienced. How could he not compare the past and future Makayla? He'd wanted his wife, a woman Makayla had been jealous of. He hadn't been able to explain to her at the time that she'd been jealous of herself, someone she'd yet to become.

Now he understood what she'd been talking about when they'd made love in the 14th century; he'd been different, they'd been different together. Would the next time they made love be different again? Would it finally be right? Would they be in sync?

He studied his wife's silhouette, her fiery, copper-gold hair hung below her well-shaped, combat-pant-clad hips. Alexander gulped down the lump forming in his throat – how could he be thinking about making love to his wife when he'd been on death's door only moments ago? He shook his head and refocused, but his mind kept returning to his wife. He imagined touching her naked form and his fangs lengthened. He swallowed the venom pooling in his mouth – it felt strange to be responding to her with such an animalistic urge. He cleared his throat and shook his head again as she led them along the dungeon corridors.

Alexander glanced about as they snuck along the dark passageways, searching for Zobiana's men. Where were her people? Why weren't they about? He had a terrible burning feeling in the pit of his stomach. At first he'd thought it was his hunger, but it hadn't receded after he fed. Something was wrong. Had the Dark One succeeded in inhabiting his body? He couldn't sense its evil presence.

Makayla held up her hand and they stopped while she referred to the map again. "It's this way," she said, pointing towards another twisting passageway off to their right. Makayla looked over her shoulder at him before continuing down the passage once more; her expression changing when she glanced at his mouth. Alexander held his breath when he saw her bite the corner of her lip and then dart her eyes back towards the passage. He recognised the hunger in her eyes, she needed to feed.

They walked along until they came to the wall Alexander had spoken about.

"Is this the wall, Xander?" Makayla re-rolled the map, slid it back into the leather canister and shouldered it before placing her hand on the barrier and looked over her shoulder at him again.

Alexander nodded and moved towards the rock wall, he stopped next to Makayla and covered her hand with his, his fingers curling over hers. Makayla looked up into his face and he sensed her worry. "It'll be okay."

"Something's not right, Xander. Tell me you feel it too?"

Alexander looked from Makayla to Lazarus before taking a deep breath. "I feel it, but what can we do? It's the only way out, unless you can teleport us out of here."

"I've been trying to, I need to drink your blood, Xander, and you're not strong enough yet."

"You could drink mine," Lazarus volunteered.

"No, Lazarus, I need you strong too." Makayla squeezed Alexander's fingertips before taking her hand from the wall. "If we're going to do this we need to do it now."

Alexander watched Makayla remove something from the pocket of her combat pants, there was a sparkle of silver and then he saw the Nomadian device Zack had gifted her the night they'd made out by the pond, the same night her brother, Darrius, had delivered the letter from her father, Sebastian. He'd been so jealous of the unknown vampire at the time; it seemed so trivial now compared to what they'd been through in recent months.

"No, you can't give me the Nomadian it's yours," he protested, shaking his head as she undid the chain clasp and draped it about his neck and re-clasped it.

"Don't shake your head, it will protect you, Marianna and the chancellor if anything happens to Lazarus and I when we go through the wall, and if something goes wrong, at least you'll be able to form a shield and teleport yourselves away."

Alexander looked down at the Nomadian. "We should use it now, it may work."

"I tried using it while the chancellor and I were looking for you, it didn't work, but it will once you pass through the wall."

"I'm okay now, really, I can fight." Alexander grabbed Makayla's arms, her armour tingling his fingertips as he stared into her eyes, shaking his head again. "I can't let you do this alone, it's too dangerous."

"You're not strong enough yet, Xander and neither are Aunt Marianna or chancellor Lagorias, it's why I gave you the Nomadian. It will protect and aid you in your escape. If things get dicey Lazarus and I will stay back until you get to safety and follow shortly after."

"I am strong enough. I can't let you do this alone."

"She's not alone, Xander. I'm here in case you didn't notice," Lazarus said, coming to stand beside him. "Makayla's right, you need to get Marianna and the chancellor out of here as quickly as possible, we'll be right behind you."

Alexander glanced at Lazarus and then across at Marianna and the chancellor before releasing Makayla's arms. "Okay, but like I said before, I have a terrible feeling about all this."

"Ditto," Makayla said, frowning. "Remember, the green button activates the Nomadian, the purple button forms a protective shield about you, and the yellow button opens a wormhole to any destination you wish to go. To shield others you need to touch them. I suggest you switch it on the moment we pass through the barrier, Marianna and the chancellor will have to hold on to your elbows as you go just in case, okay?"

"Okay," Alexander replied, watching her unsheathe her swords and step back to make room for him to trace the runes on the wall. He smiled at her, and she frowned again.

"What are you smiling at?" she muttered.

"I was thinking about the first time you said the word okay to me all those years ago, I thought you were addled in the head at the time." He chuckled. "Hearing you say okay still makes me smile.

Makayla grinned. "Hey, it was only six days ago for me remember."

Alexander's stomach did a flip, six days for her and seven hundred years for him. With every passing decade, his love had grown fiercer, stronger; he feared he'd lose his soul if anything were to happen to her. He cringed and bent over, grasping his middle, the burning in his stomach amplified by the hollow emptiness.

"Xander, are you okay?"

"I'm fine." Alexander straightened, shaking his head and ignoring her concerned look. "I'm fine," he said again.

"Xander, are you sure you're okay?"

"Let's get this over with." He closed his eyes brushing off her concern and pictured the runes in his mind before opening his eyes again. "Okay, let's party." He winked at Makayla trying to make light of their precarious situation.

Lazarus chuckled; Makayla frowned at him, shaking her head as she lifted her swords preparing for the worst. Alexander's stomach lurched again; he gritted his teeth, ignoring the gut-wrenching pain.

Makayla watched Alexander close his eyes again and place his right hand in the centre of the wall, his fingers widespread, his brow furrowing as his eyes scrunched tight in concentration. The wall wavered and shimmered; one moment it was solid rock and the next its solid form liquefied, forming a wall of molten silver that rippled like water.

Alexander withdrew his hand from the wall and opened his eyes. "I can't believe that worked."

Makayla snapped her mouth shut when he glanced in her direction and encouraged him to continue with a wave of her sword, he nodded and faced the wall again. He raised his hand once more and dipped his forefinger into the liquid wall, his fingernail disappearing as he traced rune-like symbols onto its surface. The liquid silver barrier glittered brightly before disappearing altogether, there was a loud hiss, and then a dim corridor materialised.

Makayla studied the passageway, searching for guards, but there were none that she could see. She glanced at Lazarus and jerked her head, indicating for him to go through the opening. The moment Lazarus passed through, she moved in front of Alexander, Marianna and the chancellor, and encouraged the trio to follow her across the invisible threshold.

Alexander pressed the yellow button on the Nomadian and there was a flash of brilliant gold light; Marianna went to grab hold of Alexander's elbow but Makayla whipped her hand out and stopped her.

"Sorry, Aunt Marianna, he must touch you first or else you could be rendered unconscious. As the one wearing the Nomadian only he can break the field."

Marianna covered her mouth with her hands in embarrassment, but Alexander simply took her hand and placed it on his elbow and then did the same with the chancellor. "We need to follow this corridor for about two hundred steps and then we turn left and walk another three hundred steps."

"I thought you couldn't remember the way, Xander?" Lazarus queried.

"I remember getting to the secret wall, I just couldn't remember the dungeon corridors, I'd begun transitioning into a vampire by then and the pain in my gut had become unbearable. Sorry, I was flogged not long after and anything I'd memorised was lost."

"You should leave with Marianna and the chancellor while you can, Xander," Makayla said.

"Come with us." Alexander said.

"No, the Nomadian may not work, there's too many of us, and I'm not willing to risk your lives."

"How will you find your way out?"

"Don't worry about Lazarus and me, we'll be fine; I can communicate with Salomae now, she's close."

"I'm not leaving; I'll lead you out first."

"NO ... you won't. Our powers will return once we distance ourselves from the Rivulous Dimension doorway."

"YES ... I will, this is not a debate, Makayla, let's go. The sooner I show you the way out, the sooner you'll be rid of me and we'll be out of your hair."

Makayla cringed. Being rid of him was the last thing she wanted; she didn't bother arguing with him – she was too shocked by his words and the flames burning within the depths of his eyes to rebuff him. She inhaled deeply and watched him stride down the corridor, Marianna and the chancellor in tow.

Makayla glanced at Lazarus, whose mouth was ajar. He closed it and shrugged when he noticed Makayla's concerned look. "He'll be fine, he's been through a lot, Makayla. Come on, let's go before we lose them." He took off after Alexander.

A deep feeling of foreboding seized hold of Makayla as she realised the opening they'd just passed through wasn't closing, but she followed Lazarus and the others. Was she letting her anxiety get the better of her and just not used to seeing the vampire side of her husband? She'd never sired anyone before and Alexander wasn't a typical vampire. What *did* a Druid become when he was sired by a seraphympire? What was Alexander now? Druid, seraphympire, vampire; she hadn't a clue, and that's what worried her the most. She could manipulate fire, was that why she could see fire in the depths of his eyes? Or was there something else? Had Zobiana and Abigail done something more despicable than whipping him?

CHAPTER 4.

Zobiana stepped out from an alcove hidden in the passage wall and looked over her shoulder. The doorway into the Rivulous Dimension would remain open until she closed it – and she wouldn't close it until Alexander was back in his cell.

The moment Makayla rounded the bend, Zobiana nodded. Newbloods flooded the passageways. She signalled her men to follow and trailed after them. She was in no hurry as she progressed down the shadowed corridor, knowing she'd find the Golden One and her entourage subdued by her guards and in Tyrone's capable hands. Abigail was another matter altogether though. Her daughter had grown unpredictable and her anger raged like the fires of hell. Abigail's jealousy of her half-sister was a festering wound that grew with every passing day.

Zobiana had taken the long way back to her quarters after

leaving Alexander's cell. She'd had a lot on her mind. Freedom from the Dark One was something she'd not contemplated, but now the prospect was a reality her thoughts were more focused on returning to Evron than ever. She'd walked the upper levels of the dungeon for nigh on thirty minutes thinking of ways she could accomplish all her goals when she'd heard voices coming from Chancellor Lagorias's cell. It had been a surprise to see Sebastian's progeny offering the vampire her arm to feed upon. The moment she'd caught sight of the Golden One she'd known she was there for Alexander; she'd been expecting her. She'd had an insane moment of clarity and knew she would let Makayla rescue him. The Dark One would be her problem then. It wasn't in her nature to just let them escape, though, not without putting up a fight and discovering the Trinian Globe's location first.

Makayla rounded the corner to see Alexander had Abigail pinned to the wall by the throat. His clenched fist was white with exertion. Flames billowed about his body in a display of power he shouldn't even have possessed in his weakened state. Chancellor Lagorias and Marianna stood outside the Nomadian's protective shield surrounded by Newbloods. Lazarus was fending off the encroaching vampires, his swords drawn. Tyrone was relaxed against a nearby wall, his feet crossed, watching. Why wasn't he helping Abigail? It seemed out of character. Makayla sensed Salomae in the vicinity and drew power from her to form a protective shield about

Marianna, the chancellor and Lazarus.

Abigail turned her head towards Makayla and sneered. "See what he has become? He is no longer the man you knew; he is more, much more," she choked out between gasps, cackling and gagging as Alexander applied more pressure.

"You're dead, I will kill you and your mother for your betrayal," Alexander growled in an unrecognisable voice. "You will burn in the pits of hell for your deception."

Flames spun in a raging inferno about his body, contained within the Nomadian's protective shield. Black ash floated outside the shield, spinning above his head in a halo of soot. The biting flames leapt and chewed at Abigail's clothing and flesh. The charred odour of her skin was overpowering, smelling of singed hair. Makayla didn't care about Abigail or her mother, and would sooner see them dead – what bothered her was how different Alexander seemed.

Makayla lifted her sword and pointed it at Tyrone as more Newbloods rounded the corner, followed by Zobiana. The smug smile disappeared from Zobiana's face the moment she took in the scene. Her eyes darted towards Alexander and her daughter, and her hands became ensconced in a searing white, electric light almost immediately. She hurled the lightning ball towards Alexander. The shield surrounding him and Abigail simply absorbed the intense energy.

Zobiana was about to take a step in Alexander's direction but stopped dead in her tracks, the colour draining from her face, when she noticed the ruby gem hanging about Makayla's neck.

Makayla smiled when she realised what had caught Zobiana's attention. "I guess you've been wondering where I've been hiding the Gem of Past Times all these years," Makayla said, caressing the ruby gem. "Funnily enough, I've only just recently acquired it."

Zobiana held out her hand and took a step towards Makayla. "Give it to me now; it belongs to me."

"Not anymore it doesn't. It's mine now. As I was saying, it was only an hour ago I removed this gaudy piece of jewellery from your pasty, white neck. It felt good punching you in the face, Lilian. How's the nose by the way?"

Zobiana's eyes bulged as she gaped at Makayla.

"That's right; an hour ago I was burning at the stake for witchcraft. I thought you were smarter – how could you not know I was fireproof?" Makayla chuckled again. "You've been busy since then haven't you, Lilith?"

"*Argghhhh*, give me the gem. It's mine!"

Alexander cocked his head towards Zobiana when he heard her scream and released Abigail. Abigail dropped to the rock floor with a loud thud. She lay groaning in a smouldering heap at his bare feet.

Alexander pivoted and focused on Zobiana. Makayla gasped and stepped back when she saw his face. It was as though he had no eyes at all, just black empty sockets filled with flames.

She glanced towards Lazarus. "*Get Marianna and the*

chancellor out of here now!" she said telepathically.

"What about, Xander?"

"I'll take care of Xander; just get your arses back to the compound before all hell breaks loose here. GO . . . NOW!"

Lazarus nodded and stepped between the chancellor and Marianna, the air changed, wavering and crackling about the trio as they disappeared.

Makayla exhaled in relief and turned to Tyrone. He hadn't moved from his position against the wall. The smile on his face hadn't disappeared with Zobiana's arrival either. If anything, it had broadened; what was his deal? He wasn't fighting, he wasn't helping, and he hadn't stopped Lazarus from escaping with Marianna and the chancellor.

The hairs on Makayla's neck spiked. She dropped her mind-shields and probed the minds of everyone standing in the vicinity. The Newbloods seemed to be waiting for Zobiana's command but they clearly feared Alexander.

Makayla stared down at Abigail's broken body lying on the floor. Smoke tendrils rose from her incinerated form. She glanced back towards her husband. Raw emotions had taken over – rage in its purest form controlled him; his hatred palpable. Who was this man? He wasn't the man she'd fallen in love with, and he certainly wasn't the man she'd married. She didn't recognise him at all.

For the first time in her life, she didn't know what to do. Should she try to get his attention, and if she succeeded, would she be the subject of his wrath? How long before his strength waned, and he too was lying unconscious on the floor? Makayla sheathed her sword and was about to grab Alexander's arm when Zobiana dropped to her knees and bowed, placing her forehead on the ground before Alexander's feet. As if he were a God.

"My lord," Zobiana grovelled.

Makayla's jaw dropped. "My lord? What the fuck is this shit? You held him prisoner, tortured him for months, and now you're calling him your lord? Xander, let's kill these fuckers and get the hell out of here. NOW."

Tyrone laughed.

Makayla leapt forward and smashed Tyrone's head against the rock wall. He didn't defend himself, didn't even fight back. "What the fuck is the matter with you?" Makayla yelled, throwing him like a bowling ball towards the Newbloods standing behind Zobiana. They toppled over like pins – *strike* – a tangled mass of arms and legs. Zobiana didn't move from her position on the floor. She was oblivious to the riot Tyrone and her Newbloods made behind her. Squabbling as they untangled themselves.

Alexander stepped towards Zobiana, a malevolent smile forming on his face. He seemed just as oblivious to the commotion as Zobiana. It was as if Makayla wasn't there.

"XANDER . . . let's get out of here!" He didn't respond. "XANDER—" still no response. *"ALEXANDER!"* Makayla screamed at the top of her voice.

He didn't hear her. Instead, he seized Zobiana by the throat and lifted her into the air. The Nomadian shield grew larger, encompassing both their bodies. The raging inferno within the shield immediately engulfed Zobiana – scorching her clothing and body as it had her daughter. The shield pulsated as if it had a heartbeat. An electrical charge gathered about its exterior. Expanding strands of electricity sparked out from its ever-swelling mass until finally the Nomadian shield failed with a sizzling sputter. Flames flared, overwhelming the space surrounding Alexander. He was a flaming beacon of light in the once-dark passageway. The Newbloods standing behind Zobiana scrambled back, trying to escape the inferno that was Alexander.

Makayla looked from Alexander to Zobiana. Why wasn't she retaliating? Wasn't she supposed to be the one in charge? Instead she cowered away from Alexander. He should have been the one cowering, considering what they'd put him through. Alexander angled his head, apparently hypnotised by the flames scorching the flesh on Zobiana's face. He flinched, his shoulders jerking as he grimaced in pain. Makayla experienced his pain as if it was her own. A coiling burn rose from her stomach, searing her oesophagus in the same manner as a severe case of indigestion.

Makayla stepped closer to Alexander, wanting to touch him, but not daring. He seemed larger than life, at least three feet taller than his usual six feet five. Had his vampire transition altered him so much? The thought had circled in her mind on a continuous loop since she'd first entered his dungeon cell. What had she done to him? Or rather, what had Zobiana done?

Alexander's black, empty eye sockets returned to their normal amber shade. The flames surrounding him fizzled out, hissing as if someone had doused him with water. He gasped, his mouth opening and closing as he took in his unfamiliar surroundings. His height reverted to normal and his grip on Zobiana's throat relaxed. Zobiana's head lolled to the side. He flung her away, repulsed, and she bounced off a nearby wall to land on the floor with a sickening crunch.

Alexander looked down at his hands and flexed his fingers. Flaking black ash lifted into the air. He glanced at Makayla, his face white with shock. He extended his hand towards her and took a step in her direction, but faltered. His eyes rolled back in his skull and he collapsed. Makayla dashed forward and caught him in her arms, dropping to her knees from the momentum of his falling body. He was half the size he'd been in the past, but still heavy. She swept the hair from his forehead, noticing his trembling body was deathly cold. Makayla heard someone unsheathe a sword and looked up. Tyrone towered over them, leering down at her as Newbloods gathered behind him.

"Well, this has been entertaining, but it's back to the dungeons with you both."

"What, now you react? What the fuck's with you, Tyrone?"

"Nothing now; take them to the dungeons," he ordered the Newbloods.

"Touch a single hair on either of our heads and you will end up looking like them," Makayla said, pointing at Zobiana and Abigail.

"You haven't any powers, you're weak, if you did, you'd have a shield about you."

"SALOMAE," Makayla called telepathically, a smile creasing her face as she looked up at Tyrone.

The walls shuddered with a rumbling groan, pebbles showered down from an opening crack above their heads. Tyrone looked at the ceiling and the Newbloods retreated further down the passageway.

Smart, Makayla thought, looking at Alexander once more. She kissed his forehead and drew power from Salomae to form a shield about their bodies just as the ceiling fractured and collapsed in a crumbling shower of debris. Rocks bounced off the wavering shield she'd manifested. Abigail and Zobiana lay silent, buried in rock debris.

Salomae materialised, her huge bulk smashing through solid rock, turning it to shrapnel and spraying the space in rock projectiles. A thick mantle of swirling dust shrouded everything. The ground shook as she stomped her feet, spread her wings and lobbed her tail in Tyrone's direction. It connected with his body and hurled him further down the passageway, taking out the huddling Newbloods for a second time that day. The Terrin let out an ear-splitting roar as she sprayed the tunnel in dragonfire; flames blackened the walls and desiccated the Newbloods trying to regain their footing.

Tyrone lay unconscious in a shimmering heap in the rubble, unaffected by the flames.

Salomae bent her head towards Alexander, nudging him with her snout and sniffing him.

"He'll be okay, I think . . . I hope," Makayla said, looking about. Abigail and Zobiana were buried, covered in a thick layer of rubble. "Get us out of here, Salomae."

CHAPTER 5.

Vasili paced the chiselled, underground passageways. They now lived permanently in bunkers kilometres beneath London's streets. It was the safest place on the planet. The Blakspor virus had spread like wildfire throughout the world.

Ever since he'd heard Makayla had the Trinian Globe, Vasili had known it was only a matter of time before his visions came true. What he feared most were the visions of everyone dying – his wife in particular. Would Makayla find her and Alexander? Would he see his beloved again? He'd worried over it for centuries and dreaded yet craved to know the outcome.

When Makayla had followed Alexander to the Custodians' meeting all those years ago, it had surprised him to see her, even though his visions had alerted him to the possibility.

There were always ripple effects, especially when someone found themselves in another time – particularly if the person had arrived from a future time, like Makayla had. The ripple effects, although small and inconsequential in the past, could have tsunami-like effects in the future, sometimes wiping out whole family lines and creating others not meant to exist. Possibly even unravelling time itself.

Outcomes were always volatile because choices balanced on a knife's edge. It was the reason he'd kept the information from Makayla regarding her prophecy.

Even in his waking hours his visions haunted him because the outcomes were never clear. They'd grown confusing of late – with far more death and mayhem than usual; it kept him awake at night. Sometimes there were two, three even four outcomes when more people were involved.

Vasili stopped mid-thought when a newly graduated Shadow Seeker ran past. He watched the recruit until he turned the corner. When another two recruits ran past Vasili shrugged and continued on his path.

Seconds later, Gabriel barrelled around the corner and came to an abrupt halt when he saw Vasili. "Vasili we've been looking for you everywhere."

"I've been wandering the lower levels of the Compound. I needed to think, although it has done little good. I can't seem to focus on anything."

"I figured as much. I tried to contact you, but you were shielding. You need to come with me right now."

"Does it have anything to do with the new recruits who just ran past?" Vasili asked, trying to read Gabriel.

"Ah, no, no it doesn't." Gabriel looked past Vasili and then back the way he'd come. "I'd rather not discuss it here, the walls have ears."

Vasili's eyebrow rose. "As you wish; lead the way."

Gabriel about turned and took off at a brisk pace; Vasili followed, all the while wondering what had Gabriel in such a state. He couldn't read his mind – which was unusual, because Gabriel usually withheld nothing from him. Neither one of them spoke as they marched along deserted passageways towards an uninhabited part of the underground compound. Dripping water and the hollow sound of their footsteps had an unnerving, eerie quality. The stale air grew stronger as they trekked deeper underground. The longer they walked, the darker the passageways became and the more edgy Vasili became – Gabriel's clandestine behaviour was out of character.

Gabriel stopped in front of an ancient door and looked back the way they'd come, then glanced towards Vasili and placed his forefinger to his lips. They stood in complete darkness for a moment longer, making sure no one had followed. When Gabriel was sure they were alone, he turned the doorknob and pushed the door open with shaking hands. The screeching door hinges set Vasili's nerves further on edge, prickling his spine with goose bumps. Gabriel nodded; Vasili crossed the threshold and held his breath while the door screeched shut.

They were in a sparsely furnished room, a single lamp sat on a bench by the door, bathing the area in golden light.

"What's with all the cloak and dagger, Gabe?"

"It's still not safe to speak, Vasili we have to go down to a secret part of the catacombs, this way, if you please." Gabriel picked up the lamp and strode across the room; he waved his hand over the wall and another door appeared magically. Before Vasili had time to respond, Gabriel was off again. They stopped when they came to a narrow rock stairway leading down into the catacombs. Vasili shivered as they descended the spiralling stairs. The stale air began to get the better of him as they progressed deeper. He took note of the cobwebs and the caked dirt gathering in the corners of each disused step. When they came to an ancient door at the bottom of the stairwell, Gabriel unlocked it with a giant brass key. There was a ripple of light and a mechanical whir as an invisible barrier broke. The clank of rattling bolts moving within the door sounded loud as it unlatched. Vasili waited for the telltale sound of unoiled hinges to break the unsettling silence, but was surprised when the door swung open on silent hinges. The door appeared older than the one they'd just come through.

The moment they crossed the threshold Gabriel locked the door again and sagged against it as he pocketed the keys once more. Vasili heard his loud exhale and noticed his shoulders relax.

"What's wrong, Gabe, has something happened?"

"Yes, sorry for being so cryptic, but we have spies within the compound and I couldn't risk them finding out."

"Finding out what? Vasili queried, trying to read Gabriel's

thoughts again, but still getting nothing from his mind.

"You'll see, come on," Gabriel said, before lifting the lamp once more and turning towards yet another dark passageway. "It's this way, we're almost there." He motioned Vasili forward with his free hand.

When Gabriel came to an abrupt stop, Vasili nearly crashed into his back. They were in a large cavern. Vasili could see movement off in the distance, but it was so dark, even his vampire sight couldn't penetrate the murky space. Three figures walked towards them – Vasili finally recognised Lazarus, but he was blocking the view of the other two people behind him. When Lazarus stepped aside Vasili almost choked.

"Augustus, what, what happened? What are you doing here?" Vasili asked, his voice catching when he took in Augustus' haggard appearance.

"Zobiana happened, my old friend." Vasili was about to ask what Zobiana had done when a hooded figure stepped out from behind Augustus. Vasili angled his head as the person lowered the hood of their cape. His eyes bulged when he saw his wife's smiling face staring back at him.

He swept her into his arms and crushed her to him, tears streaming down his face as he hugged her. He leaned back to look at her; she was as striking as she'd been the last time he'd set eyes on her even though many years had passed. Framing her face with his hands, he kissed her and then hugged her once more. "Marianna, my beautiful Marianna, I thought I'd never see you again." Vasili looked about. "Where are Makayla and

Alexander?"

"About that," Lazarus cut in. "There's been a complication."

"A complication?"

"Alexander's acting a little strange; hell, the whole situation was just plain weird."

"Strange? How do you mean?" Vasili asked.

"Alexander was on fire; as if something had control of him. No matter how many times Makayla called his name, he didn't respond, he didn't recognise her. I don't know what happened afterwards because Makayla told me to get the chancellor and Marianna out of there before everything went awry, but she should have been here by now." Lazarus shook his head looking from Vasili to Gabriel.

"Makayla has never sired anyone before. The changes Alexander is undergoing could well be the result of his transition. No one knows what he will become and how it will affect him because he was a Druid. He's a hybrid now; it's anyone's guess." Vasili said.

"I was thinking the same thing." Lazarus said.

Vasili glanced towards Augustus. "What were you doing there, Augustus? I thought you were on Evron?"

"I was locked up in one of Zobiana's cells."

Vasili's face drained of colour. "I beg your pardon?" Makayla's words crashed through his mind. She'd said something about Augustus being compromised when the Trinian Globe had first gone missing; it seemed so long ago now. She'd been right all along, but not in the way he could have ever imagined. "When were you taken, Augustus?"

"The morning of the 25th of March 1987," Augustus replied, his voice trembling. "Makayla told me my son was murdered the same day."

Vasili gasped, how had he not foreseen it? "Who has been impersonating you all this time?" he asked.

"That's the million dollar question," Lazarus said, resting his hands on the hilts of his swords hanging at his hips.

"I thought you seemed different, but assumed it was the grief of losing your son."

The chancellor swept his hand over his eyes and brushed away the gathering tears. "Makayla told me everything when she saved me. The strange thing is I don't remember being taken. All I remember is going to bed and waking in the dungeon the next day. I'd invited guests over the previous night, and we had one or two drinks. Nothing dramatic, but I excused myself and went to bed because I didn't feel well."

"Do you remember who your guests were? Maybe they spiked your drink?" Gabriel asked.

"It was my father," Lazarus said.

Augustus's eyes fell on Lazarus. "Why yes, how did you know?"

"I've learned a few things recently and realised just how manipulative and deceitful my father truly is. Quite frankly, the signs were there all along, I just needed to connect the dots."

"What are you saying, Lazarus?" Marianna asked,

speaking for the first time since they'd returned.

"I'm not sure if you're aware, but when Makayla placed the Gem of Sorrows and the Gem of Souls into the Trinian Globe it opened up a wormhole and shot her back seven hundred years into the past to the fourteenth century. Vasili, I'm sure you know of what I speak."

Vasili nodded. "Yes, I remember; the visions also indicated as much, but I couldn't reveal what I knew. I knew if I ignored my better judgement and told Alexander and Makayla what was ahead of them the world wouldn't survive, it still mightn't. I also had other personal reasons for not telling them." Vasili glanced at his wife and took her hand in his.

Lazarus glanced about the group. "The moment Makayla put the golden armour over her head and survived I knew the Oracle's predictions were at hand. I've tracked her for centuries; it was my duty to help her. The night she placed the gems into the globe and I saw the fire-moon I knew I had to follow her through the wormhole. It was there I discovered how deep my father's treachery went. All those years of not knowing why he'd left and where he'd disappeared to left my family wondering what had become of him. He was always a forceful, sadistic man. We assumed he'd met with a violent end. When I discovered him masquerading as the cardinal in the 14th century, it shocked and disgusted me. He'd fooled us. He'd aligned himself with Lilith. So it's with a heavy heart I say this: I believe my father is now masquerading as the chancellor and he was the one who had your son killed, Lord

Augustus. I am ashamed of his actions, and on my word of honour you will have justice. My father will die for what he has done."

CHAPTER 6.

Sparks and ash spun about Salomae, Alexander and Makayla as they appeared in an underground cavern. Makayla glanced about as the light dissipated. Shadows moved down the lengths of the walls in oscillating peaks and settled in the dark rock crevices. She formed a fireball in her hand and held it aloft to get a better view of their surroundings. There was a wall sconce with a torch not too far from their position. Makayla hurled the fireball towards the ancient torch and watched as it caught fire.

"Where are we, Salomae?" Makayla asked, stretching back to look at the high ceilings. Echoing drips of water emphasised just how massive the cavern was, but otherwise it was eerily quiet. The air was cool and smelled of rock and earth. At least it was fresh, even if it was a little chill. "What do you mean we're below the compound? I don't recognise this place."

Alexander groaned, drawing Makayla's attention towards her lap where his head rested. She placed the back of her hand on his forehead; he was hot to the touch and shivering, his teeth chattering. She bit her wrist and held it to his face. He didn't respond. Blood dripped onto his bottom lip, trickling into his mouth, and his tongue swept the droplets from his lips. Makayla touched her open wound to his mouth, and he fed. Alexander's fingers curled about her wrist, digging into her skin as he latched on with his fangs. She grimaced, her body jolting as Alexander bit even deeper, his fangs grating on the bones in her wrist. The slurping sound he made grew louder with every mouthful he took.

Salomae nudged Makayla with her snout. "I'll give him as much as he needs." Makayla frowned at the Terrin. Salomae nudged her again, trying to dislodge Alexander's mouth from her wrist. Alexander opened his eyes and snarled. Makayla gasped, his eyes were black again. She looked closer and noticed flames once more within their depths.

"Alexander, you need to stop feeding now," she murmured – but there was no response. "Alexander, you will kill me if you continue feeding." Alexander blinked his eyes rapidly. Makayla swept his hair back from his face in a soothing motion. "Xander ... STOP ... NOW ... *Please!*" Alexander paused and blinked again, his eyes returning to normal as he focused on Makayla's face. Makayla wriggled her wrist free of his mouth, noticing how chewed up it appeared. Alexander struggled to sit upright, but collapsed with the effort. Makayla grasped his elbow and helped him get up.

"*Sorr. . . rry*," he slurred, then groaned as he grasped his head. "I'm still getting used to these things." He pointed at his fangs and winced again. "Where . . . where are we?"

"We're in the catacombs beneath the compound. I don't know where, though, I've never been here before."

"Where are Marianna, the chancellor and Lazarus?"

"I imagine they're here somewhere, but I haven't seen them yet as we only just got back ourselves," Makayla said, staring at the scars on Alexander's back.

"What happened?" Alexander asked, swiping hair out of his eyes.

"What do you remember?"

"The last thing I recall was running down the passageway with Marianna and the chancellor."

"That's all? You don't remember the altercation you had with Abigail and Zobiana?"

Alexander shook his head. "No, why . . . what happened?"

Makayla frowned. "You were, um . . . you were different is all."

"Different . . . what do you mean different?"

"It was like you were someone els— it's nothing, it doesn't matter, it's over now, you're all right, forget about it."

"Makayla, what . . . what happened, what did I do?"

"It's not what you did so much, it's what you became."

"What I became? What are you talking about?"

"It doesn't matter, we need to—"

"It matters, Makayla, what happened?"

"I'll tell you later, we need to get you to the infirmary." Makayla felt his forehead again; he was still hot to the touch, even after feeding from her. "You've got a fever I'm beginning to worry about."

"Tell me what I did, I need to know!"

"It doesn't matter, you're okay now."

"Tell me, tell me now!"

Makayla's skin crawled at the prospect of telling Alexander what she'd seen him do, voicing it made it real; she didn't want it to be real. She shivered and glanced down at her clenched hands before looking back up into his eyes. "Xander, you grew an extra three feet IN HEIGHT – you were huge; your eyes were hollow, black pits – it was like looking into the pits of hell... and you were on fire. The worst thing of all was what Zobiana did, what she called you."

Alexander's face paled, his mouth working open and closed. "What . . . what did she do?" he stuttered.

"She got down on her knees and called you 'my lord'. You terrified them. And do you know what was worse? You didn't recognise me, Alexander. What the bloody hell did they do to you?"

Alexander cleared his throat and swallowed. "I was tortured and whipped. Beyond that I don't remember much, I was in and out of consciousness most of the time. I hallucinated a lot, but I couldn't tell you what was real or imagined."

"It's okay, Xander, it will be okay. I'm sorry it took me so long to find you, but right now your temperature worries me, you need to see Ava and get cleaned up.

Alexander sighed. "I feel fine, really I do," he said, scratching his jaw. "Ugh." He grimaced when his fingertips tangled in his scruffy beard. "I must look a sight." He sniffed his armpit and choked. "God, I smell terrible too, how can you stand it?" he said, waving his hands about to disperse the shock of body odour wafting off him.

Makayla shrugged. "I don't care what you look or smell like, Xander, I'm just glad to have you back."

Alexander grinned. His smile hidden by the scraggly overhang of his moustache.

Makayla returned his smile. "All you need now is a shave, a shower and food, and you'll be as good as new." She traced a finger down one of the healing lacerations on his chest. Her smile withered as she took in the devastation his body had undergone. He covered her hand.

"It's not your fault, Makayla," he said in a more serious tone.

Makayla glanced up into his face, tears gathered in her eyes and cascaded down her cheeks as she tried to blink them away. She shook her head. "You're wrong, it's all my fault. Everything that's happened to you, the humans of Earth, it's all my fault. The Earth's in turmoil because of me."

"No, it's not your fault, you can't control Zobiana and what she does, no one can."

"See, that's where you're wrong. There wouldn't be the

Blakspor virus if it weren't for me."

"Wait, what, what's the Blakspor virus?"

Makayla chuckled sardonically. "Something Zobiana concocted. Why? So she could farm humans for their blood and control Earth's gateways. My blood was the platform used to concoct the virus. Now the people of Earth have succumbed to its devastating effects. Ava and Tess can't find a cure. Drinking mine and Tristan's blood seems to be the only cure," she sobbed, covering her face with her hands.

"All you do is cry. Some warrior you've turned out to be – you're pathetic." Her nemesis mocked. Makayla didn't respond to the hated voice in her head. Her nemesis was right. All she did was cry these days. What the bloody hell was wrong with her? She felt so out of her depth, so emotionally out of control.

Alexander drew her hands away, cupped her face in his palms and lifted her chin. "Like I said, it's not your fault, even Salomae agrees with me."

Makayla looked up at Salomae before looking back at Alexander. "I should have stayed with you in the past. We might have been able to change this future we now find ourselves in."

"You were right to leave. For a long time, I wished you'd stayed, but I came to realise if you had, time itself would have become unstable. You couldn't inhabit two spaces in one time because the space-time continuum would unravel."

"I'm so sorry I left you, Alexander, I let you down."

"You could never let me down. Time was always going to

be the space between you and me, Makayla." Alexander smiled, then lowered his face to hers. The prickle of his beard tickled her cheeks and lips as he kissed her. She felt the tip of his tongue touch the seam of her lips and opened to him. He dipped his tongue into her mouth, the subtle metallic flavour of her blood filled her mouth as he deepened the kiss further.

Makayla shivered, overcome with warmth and an inescapable yearning to be one with him. It was overpowering. Desire rose to the surface, almost combustible in its purity. It warmed her skin with a simmering heat – an unquenchable burn that needed more than kisses. Alexander was the sole person in her life to elicit such a response. She'd missed him – missed the feel of his arms – missed his mouth doing delicious things to her body. She'd missed him with her entire being.

"I want you," he murmured between kisses. "I need to be in you . . . now."

"I seem to recall you saying something like that to me before, many times before, in fact," she mumbled against his lips. "But, sadly, I must decline. You really do reek. I don't know about you, but I could use a shower right now."

"Sounds good. My room or yours?" Alexander asked, nibbling her throat.

Makayla angled her head to the side and wiggled her shoulders. A wave of goose bumps rolled over her skin as Alexander's whiskers tickled her throat. She giggled as his mouth followed a path up to her ear.

"Do you think you can stand?"

"We don't need to stand to do what I have in mind."

"Really, what happened to taking a shower first?" She pushed him back gently and stood, holding out her hand to him. "Before we do anything, let's go to the infirmary and get you a bill of good health."

"I'm fine, really," he said, grabbing her hand and pulling himself up from the ground. Makayla watched him stretch all the kinks from his body as he straightened to his full height. He was different to the person she'd left behind in the past, and half his normal size. After the incident with Zobiana and Abigail, he'd reverted back to the malnourished state she'd first found him in. She looked down to stop from staring at his gauntness.

"God you're a sight for sore eyes," he said, shuffling closer.

"Ditto," she murmured.

Salomae snorted, reminding them of her presence. "Yes, I know, Salomae, we'll go now."

"Come on, the sooner you see Ava the sooner we can have that shower."

"Promise?" Alexander smiled.

"Yes, that's a promise."

"Thank you, for coming . . . for savi—" Alexander's face paled, he grimaced and bent over, clutching his stomach.

"Xander, what's wrong?" Makayla asked, grabbing his arm.

"I don't feel so good, *arghhhh...*" he gasped, and looked

up into Makayla's face. His bloodshot eyes rolled up into the back of his head as he collapsed unconscious.

Makayla drew strength from Salomae and lifted him into her arms. "What's wrong with him, Salomae?"

Salomae snorted and lowered her head to sniff Alexander, she snorted again, flapped her wings and whined.

"What do you mean the darkness has him?"

CHAPTER 7.

Debris lay in broken, jagged chunks, entombing Zobiana in a thick layer of rock. A sharp piece of rubble pressed against her ribcage, hampering her breathing. She groaned, gasped in a shallow breath and coughed. Her nose twitched when she smelled the sour odour of sweat and charred flesh. Dust particles stuck to the inside of her throat as her swollen tongue suctioned the roof of her mouth. She dry-swallowed and wheezed and coughed again, choking on the musty air as she struggled to move. A sharp pain shock-waved up her side and anchored in her head with a piercing shudder. Crushing weight pinned her to the castle floor, sandwiching her between the two rock surfaces like a flower press. She fluttered her eyelids to blink away the sweat stinging her eyes and tried to focus on dematerialising from beneath the claustrophobic rubble, but sagged in defeat when nothing happened. Her encounter with

Alexander had left her weaker than expected.

Zobiana pushed her trembling hands up against a flat section of rock. The abrasive surface scratched her palms as she pushed. She gritted her teeth and twisted her body to reposition her shoulder against the barrier barring her way. The flat sound of her charred, silk dress snagging and tearing was a hollow echo in her ears. If she could move the rock blocking her way a little, maybe she could free herself. She pushed – nothing happened.

"Tyrone, where the hell are you?" she screamed in frustration. There was no response. "Hello . . . is anyone out there?" She cocked her head, listening for a response – still nothing.

She gasped in another breath, tasting the dirt on her tongue. Gathering strength, she hissed and pushed on the barrier again. Pressure built and popped in her ears as the obstacle shifted a little, showering her in pebbles. Zobiana brushed the grit from her eyes encouraged by the slight movement. She drew energy into her palms and slammed them against the obstruction.

There was a loud crack as the rock split in two. An avalanche of debris slipped through the gap, filling the space around her body. It crushed the air from her lungs, burying her further. Her life flashed before her eyes. Zobiana envisioned the devious things she'd done and all the innocents she'd killed. *Is this it?* She thought to herself. *Is this how my long life will end?* She refused to accept dying in such a pathetic way and expected to go down in a blaze of glory. Fighting, not crushed to death by rocks. She knew she had to change to gain redemption. Spending an eternity burning in hell with the Dark One was not an option for contemplation. Freedom was what she craved, it always had been. Freedom from the rocks restraining her, freedom from the Dark One, freedom from the guilt and the terrible atrocities she'd committed. She longed for freedom, liberty and independence – instead she'd become the Dark One's lap dog. If she died, here and now, she'd die the lap dog she so despised and would never be free of him. If she couldn't escape the rocks imprisoning her, her plans, her destiny, would never be realised.

There was only one solution to her current dilemma. Blood. The only blood she had access to was her own. The power she gained from drinking her own blood would be brief. If she took too much, she could end up killing herself. She was as good as dead anyway if she didn't at least try. She groaned in despair, *so be it*, she thought in resignation and bit down on her wrist to feed. The buzzing in her ears subsided and her breathing evened out. She sighed in delight as the coppery liquid flowed over her tongue and down her throat. It hit her cramping stomach and filled her body with sizzling energy. When her fingertips began to tingle, she knew the effect wouldn't last long. She needed more than just blood to access her powers. To escape her rock tomb, she needed to look deep within herself and feel every emotion she'd ever felt in her long life to muster the strength.

With that in mind, Zobiana gathered her pent-up emotions

and drew power from them: anger, hate, loathing, vengeance, fear, guilt and the vague memory of love. Taking shallow breaths, she focused and centred her breathing. The deep well of hatred within her was infinite. Searing light manifested in the palms of her hands and lit the darkness with an ambient glow. She would not die, not this day, not from the crushing rock pressing down on her. Everyone had a role to play, a destiny to fulfil, a payment to make, and hers was owing. Her destiny was fixed on a destructive course. The ball had been set in motion millennia ago. She would make it right, even if it cost her, her life. Someone would die, of that she was sure. If not her, the Dark One, Alexander or the Chosen One, but someone would perish. No matter the end, she would be free and that was all she desired, it was her ultimate goal. All she had to do was bring the firestorm.

The glowing energy encompassing her hands gathered strength. Zobiana's circling thoughts amplified the power bubbling within her. Her skin crackled as a shiver of goose bumps traversed her body. Her hair floated about her face weightless – electrified. A roaring scream burst from her mouth as she thrust her hands against the pillar of stone and shot a blinding pulse of light into it. The rock slab disintegrated the moment the pulse hit.

Zobiana exhaled and stretched out on the debris-laden floor. She pulled herself into a sitting position and uncurled her limbs. Straightening the kinks from her body, she pushed up to kneel, then stood. A wave of nausea and dizziness hit her and she flung out her hands and balanced against the broken wall waiting for the dizziness to subside. Hazy dust particles circled about her in a flurried cloud as she recuperated. She sighed and glanced upward. There was a gaping hole in the roof revealing gathering storm clouds and letting in a chill. Shivering, Zobiana rubbed her arms and checked her surroundings – the castle corridor resembled the twisted aftermath of a bombing – mounds of rubble everywhere.

A rock fell from the top of an unstable mound to her left, followed by a shower of loose pebbles. Zobiana's eyes tracked the path of pebbles and saw Abigail's limp hand protruding from beneath the rubble.

Tess lowered her eyes to the microscope eyepiece and adjusted the focus dial to study the latest antidote specimen. It looked perfect. Exhaling, Tess leant back in her chair and swiped hair from her eyes.

"Why won't it work?" she mumbled to herself.

"Still no luck with the vaccine, then?" Bryce asked from the laboratory doorway.

Tess shook her head. "I don't understand why it's not working. It should. The composition is perfect in every way."

Bryce leaned against the door frame, crossed his feet and folded his arms over his chest. "It can be as perfect a copy as you like, but it's still just a copy and not the real thing. Makayla is the Chosen One, she's special you know." Bryce shrugged. "The healing properties in her blood may have everything to do with that aspect alone. She is one of a kind. You may have to accept her blood might be impossible to duplicate."

"I refuse to believe that. There has to be a way to replicate her blood and find a cure for the Blakspor virus. If we don't, it will be the end of humanity and many Off Worlders too. It's just—" Tess removed the slide from under the microscope lens and replaced it with another slide containing a sample of the Blakspor virus.

"It's just what?" Bryce encouraged.

Tess looked up at Bryce. "The virus doesn't behave like a normal virus." She scratched her head, her forehead creasing as she tried to make sense of it all.

"That's because it isn't a normal virus, Tess, it was created from the blood of a supernatural being, how could it possibly be normal?" Bryce responded.

"Why, then, are some Off Worlders affected by the virus and others, like yourself, unaffected? Shouldn't it affect everyone to some degree, humans and Off Worlders alike?"

"I don't know," Bryce said, looking over his shoulder into the other room where Freya lay comatose in the infirmary.

"I mean, you and Freya were both exposed to the Blakspor virus."

Bryce shook his head and glanced back at Tess. "Why does being exposed to radiation cause cancer, yet it is also used to treat some cancers? There is a scientific explanation to why it works, I know, but still, it seems illogical. Why does cancer affect entire families and skip others? We could go round and round and question everything for hours and still come up short. There is no logical answer; what works for some doesn't for others. I witnessed it myself every day when I worked in the children's oncology ward. I believe our individual genetic makeup, our DNA, holds the key." Bryce's mouth sagged, his eyes sad and unfocused. "Yet, how is it possible for a child no older than a month to be struck down with aggressive brain tumours or leukaemia and its identical twin be left unscathed? There is no logic to it, yet it happens. You may never discover a cure or replicate Makayla's blood, it is just the way life is – cruel and unpredictable."

Tess sighed, thinking of how cruel life had been for her and her husband before lowering her eyes to the eyepiece again. "I can't give up, Bryce. It's like you giving up on Freya ever waking up – can you do that?"

"No, I can't. I know she'll wake up," Bryce said, looking back towards Freya.

"Just like I know I'll find a cure. I'm close, I can feel it. I'm missing something, but for the life of me, I can't seem to figure out what the missing element is. In theory, it should work." Tess sighed again and rolled her head and shoulders, trying to relieve the stiffness in her neck and spine. She looked towards Bryce again. Pain marred his handsome features. "You love her, don't you?"

Bryce nodded. "Yes, but not in the way you think. She's

like my little sister, or the sister I wish I had."

Tess leant back in her chair, eyeing Bryce thoughtfully.

"Maybe what you're missing is the woman herself?" Bryce said, giving her his full attention again.

"What do you mean?"

"Makayla. Maybe you need more than her blood."

Tess smiled. "You're right. If she were here I'd be studying her bone marrow right now, but she's not here, is she?"

"That's not what I meant, granted it may help, but I doubt it – you need her magic."

"What do you mean 'magic'? I didn't know she was magical?"

"Well, technically it's not what you would call traditional magic; it's the essence of who she is. Makayla inherited mystical powers from her parents. She is, after all, the first female born of two ancient races, vampires and seraphim; she may need to give your sample life."

"Give the sample life? Now I'm confused."

Bryce unfolded his arms and held his hands out towards Tess, wiggling his fingers. "You know, zap your sample with her healing powers." Bryce raised his right eyebrow and wiggled his fingers again until Tess understood his meaning.

BANG.

There was a bright flash of light and the clatter of objects hitting the floor in the infirmary. "Someone help me," a frantic voice yelled.

Tess recognised Makayla's voice at once and kicked her chair over in a rush to get to the other room.

"Makayla, what happened?" Bryce jumped to action and helped her lift Alexander up onto an empty cot next to Freya's bed.

"Where's Ava? I need Ava, something is terribly wrong with Alexander."

"I'll go find her; she just went to her quarters to have a small rest. I'll be right back," Tess said, taking in Alexander's deteriorated state.

"No, you stay and help, it will be faster if I go," Bryce said, disappearing in a cloudy haze.

Tess nodded, scooping up a stethoscope from a nearby table and striding towards Alexander. "What's wrong with him?"

"If I knew what was wrong with him, I wouldn't be here," Makayla replied.

"Sorry, that's a really stupid question," Tess said, placing the stethoscope ear-pieces in her ears and checking Alexander's heartbeat. It was unusually fast. "Quick, get me the sphygmomanometer."

"What the bloody hell is that? Speak English, woman." Makayla asked, her face scrunching up in confusion.

"I need to check his vitals and take his blood pressure, it's the machine over there." Tess pointed to a machine in the corner of the room.

"Oh." Makayla rushed to do her bidding, bumping into a

hospital trolley in her haste. She shoved the trolley out of the way and pushed the blood pressure device to Alexander's bedside. Tess removed the stethoscope from her ears and let it hang around her neck as she secured the blood pressure arm cuff to Alexander's left bicep and pegged a heart and oxygen monitor on his right forefinger. She pressed a button on the machine and there was a mechanical hum as the machine measured Alexander's vitals.

The temperature in the room plunged and there was a loud buzzing as the pressure dropped and a mini tornado manifested. Paper towels, suturing paraphernalia and other small objects were caught in its windy trajectory and fell to the floor the moment Bryce and Ava appeared. Ava rushed towards Alexander's bedside, Makayla stepped out of the way to make room for her.

Makayla watched Ava place the back of her hand to Alexander's forehead. *"How long has he been like this, Makayla?"* Ava asked telepathically, pulling the hospital trolley closer. She washed her hands at a nearby sink and slipped on a pair of latex gloves before moving back to Alexander.

"Um, I couldn't tell you, but this is the second time he's lost consciousness in the time it has taken me to save him from the dungeon and get him back here to the compound. I gave him my blood, twice, but it hasn't helped. From the moment I found him, he has had a temperature. I don't know if it has to do with his transitioning into a vampire or if it is something else. I'm worried, Ava, my blood should have helped, but he needs more than I was able to give him. I'm too weak to feed him properly. I think he's anaemic and needs a transfusion. I can give him blood, but I need to feed to gather my strength."

"We have a full stock of Alexander's blood if he needs a transfusion," Tess said.

"It won't work. The moment Alexander and I blood-bonded and he became a vampire his blood changed; it won't be the same as it was before he transitioned.

"We still have a little of your blood in stock, but not enough for a transfusion, we've been using it to cure the infected and trying to come up with a viable vaccine. Our stores are low," Tess said, looking at Makayla before glancing back at Alexander.

"If you have a full stock of Alexander's blood that's all I need – his blood is the only blood I can feed on that gives me strength. And while I feed we can transfuse my blood into Alexander directly."

Ava nodded and glanced towards the monitor displaying Alexander's vital signs. Makayla watched Ava turn back towards Alexander and lower her forehead to his. She closed her eyes and used her elemental powers to assess his condition.

"Well, he's anaemic. That also explains why he has an elevated heart rate. If we don't transfuse him, he could have a heart attack. He doesn't have enough haemoglobin in his body to carry oxygen to his brain, vital organs and extremities –

hence his cold hands," Ava said, touching Alexander's hands. *"It's why he keeps losing consciousness. Fatigue, dizziness, shortness of breath, headaches, coldness in your hands and feet, pale skin and chest pain are all symptoms of anaemia. It's his elevated blood pressure that has me worried, though, because it means his kidneys may be failing. It doesn't explain why he has a temperature. A temperature would indicate some sort of infection. So for now we need to perform a direct transfusion like Makayla suggested. Makayla, you need to feed, but we need to get your blood into Alexander immediately or he may die."*

"I noted a little arrhythmia when I listened to his heartbeat earlier," Tess said, removing the blood pressure cuff and the heart and oxygen monitor peg.

Ava nodded. *"It confirms everything I've been saying. Let's hook Alexander up to an EKG heart and blood pressure monitor and prepare him for the transfusion. We need to take some blood samples as well and find out what's causing his high temperatures because I can't seem to sense what's wrong. Bryce, can you retrieve all of Alexander's blood bags from the refrigerator for Makayla? Tess, if you could prepare the necessary equipment and get the kit we need to perform a direct blood transfusion. Makayla, could you get the EKG monitor over by the wall?"* Makayla watched as Bryce and Tess proceeded to fulfil Ava's requests. *"Makayla, did you hear me? Could you get me the EKG monitor so we can keep an eye on Alexander's vitals?*

"Ah, yeah, sure," Makayla said, wheeling the machine over to Alexander's bedside. She watched Ava attach sticky patches on Alexander's chest and another heart and oxygen monitor peg to his index finger and turn on the machine. The monitor screen instantly lit up with Alexander's vitals.

Makayla stared at the monitor, watching the jagged line bouncing up and down and listening to the beeping that represented Alexander's heart. She glanced back at her husband, the sound of the heart monitor fading until she could hear her own heart. Its racing beat keeping time and sync with Alexander's heartbeat. It was a fast, steady throb that pounded throughout her body. A resounding *BA-boom* that seemed to have settled in her ears to eclipse all other sounds. *BA-boom, BA-boom, BA-boom, BA-boom*. Would she lose him? *BA-boom*. After everything they'd been through, would this be how it all ended for them? *BA-boom*. A tear slid down her cheek as the pounding in her head escalated.

"You're pathetic," BA-boom. *"A fucking disappointment!"* BA-boom. *"He will die because of you!"* BA-boom. *"You're to blame!"* BA-boom. *"It's . . . all . . . your . . . fault!"* Her nemesis's voice cut through the pounding in her skull with precision.

Her nemesis was right, it was her fault.

CHAPTER 8.

Heatwaves billowed and danced along the ground in wavering slivers. Alexander squinted and looked about. His nose crinkled and his lips peeled back from his teeth when the stench of sulphur overwhelmed his senses. Once he grew accustomed to the reek of rotten egg gas, he continued surveying the area. Fire surrounded him in a hypnotic, undulating spectre of orange and gold. He closed his eyes to the glare and swallowed, his dry throat chafing. His tongue stuck to the inside of his cheeks, thick from lack of saliva. If not for the rotten stench the place would have been pleasant, beautiful even.

Alexander lifted his hands away from his body and spread his fingers. He stood naked within the fire, but felt no discomfort, the heat soothing his cold skin as if he were being caressed with tender fiery fingertips and wrapped in the *warmth of a loving embrace.*

He looked up again, there was only black space lit by fire. If it was night-time he couldn't see the stars, and if it was daytime, the sun didn't spill its light across the terrain. Where was he? Underground? Alexander circled on the spot, taking in the empty black void. He was alone in a cavern of sorts, but not the one he and Makayla were in only moments ago. Where had she disappeared to?

"What is this place?" he murmured to himself.

"Your destiny," a forbidding voice replied.

Alexander shivered, searching for the owner of the voice. "This fire pit is not my destiny, I have one destiny and her name is Makayla Uriel!"

The ground trembled. "Wrong, I am your destiny," the voice said with rumbling malice.

"If this place is my destiny, how can you be my destiny too?" Alexander taunted.

"I am your destiny!" the voice growled.

"As I said before, I have one destiny and her name is Makayla Uriel!"

"She will be mine too."

"Not likely." Alexander stepped from one foot to the other, folding his arms across his chest as he pivoted and craned his neck, looking about. "Who are you – really?"

"I am the end and the beginning."

"In that order?" Alexander asked, smiling.

"I am the end and the beginning," the voice repeated.

"Yeah, right." Alexander laughed. "You're hilarious."

"Do not mock me, Druid."

He laughed again. "Mock you? You're the end and the beginning, seriously, who says shit like that?" Alexander's laughter echoed throughout the underground chamber. "And I am more than a Druid now."

"I AM YOUR MASTER AND DEMAND OBEDIENCE!"

"Hang on, I thought you said you were my destiny? No, wait, the end and the beginning? Sorry, my mistake, master, you're not confused much are you?"

"YOU WILL OBEY ME OR SUFFER MY WRATH!"

"Hey . . . Fuck you, whoever the fuck you are, I am the master of my destiny and most importantly, my life, not some fucked-up entity that's just a figment of my imagination and too scared to show his ugly face!"

"ARGHHHHHHHHHHHHH . . ." came a diabolical scream.

Alexander heard a loud crack and almost lost his balance as the ground trembled under his bare feet. He flung his arms out to steady himself and looked down. The rock floor shuddered; the rumbling grew louder fighting for supremacy over the ear-splitting roar of the escalating fires within the cavern. The sound of tearing rock grew with intensity as the ground fractured further. Alexander watched a nearby fissure grow wider before it split off in a diagonal chequer board effect across the rocky floor; he continued watching the growing hole until it disappeared off into the gloom.

Small rocks fell from above, showering red hot debris over him. Alexander looked at the ceiling – a ceiling he hadn't been able to see previously. It too was covered in a zigzag of cracks and crevices, fire leaped from the gaps forming above him until the flames licked and spat from the openings in a heated frenzy.

A bubbling sound had him re-directing his eyes back down to the ground where lava boiled up through the ever-expanding chasm in the floor to form a river of molten rock. Alexander grimaced as he balanced on the remains of what was once the ground, but was now one of many floating chunks of rock in a river of magma. He stood within a volcanic epicentre that was about to explode. He knew where he was now.

Makayla looked up when she heard a crash near the infirmary doorway. Zack came to a sliding halt after banging into the open door and almost falling over in his haste. He cast an eye over her face, a trembling smile hovering upon his lips as he regarded her. His smile disappeared the moment his eyes fell on Alexander's withered form. He acknowledged Ava, Tess and Bryce as he stepped through the doorway.

The steady beep of the machine measuring Alexander's heartbeat had blended with all the other mechanical sounds in the room. All Makayla could hear was a whirring, humming sound in her ears and the voice of her ever-present nemesis. She'd grown accustomed to her nemesis, but the nagging and ridiculing was taking its toll on her shattered nerves. If only she could punch the bitch, maybe she'd shut up. Usually Alexander's blood silenced her annoying monologue. Makayla had to wonder why his blood wasn't working as fast as it normally did. Was it because he was no longer just a mere Druid, but something else entirely different now?

Makayla didn't say a word to Zack as he moved to Alexander's bedside, she watched him brush her husband's matted hair back with his fingertips and bend to kiss his forehead.

"I'm so sorry, Xander," he whispered.

Makayla was too numb to react to Zack's show of affection. She just picked up another bag of Alexander's blood and bit through the plastic. Her head dropped back, her eyes rolling in their sockets as the blood sluiced down her throat and hit her belly. She moaned as warmth spread through her body and bled out into her extremities. A surge of goose bumps covered the surface of her skin. The buzzing in her ears and her nemesis's voice began to recede.

Ava and Tess bustled about her and Alexander, making sure there were no problems with the blood transfusion connection. Bryce stood off to their left near Freya's bedside, keeping out of their way. Makayla glanced at the tubes linking her to Alexander, hoping he would recover quickly and gain enough strength to wake from his comatose state. They'd been hooked up together for only a short while, yet it felt like she'd been sitting beside him for hours.

Makayla tossed the empty blood bag in a biohazard bin nearby and scooped up another from a trolley sitting by her. She stabbed her fangs into the bag and siphoned the blood from it until it too was empty. She exhaled and sagged in her chair, the fatigue having caught up with her. Makayla had two more bags of Alexander's blood left and needed to pace herself or she'd run out before they finished the transfusion. Alexander needed her blood more than she needed his at the moment. Makayla's eyes fell on her Druidoynan armour sitting on the floor in the right corner of the room, she'd removed it in a flurry to take care of Alexander's needs. The last thing she wanted was to render someone unconscious if they came into contact with the metal. She glanced at the tube siphoning blood from her left arm and then at her trembling hands lying in her lap.

Zack knelt before her, cupping her face in his large hands and lifted her chin until she looked into the depths of his vibrant gold-flecked blue eyes.

"Are you okay, my sweet Makayla?"

Tears pooled in her eyes and flooded down her cheeks, she shook her head quickly and began to cry. "No . . ." She sobbed covering her face with her free hand. "It's all . . ." She hiccupped. "It's all my fault."

Zack pulled her into his arms and hugged her to his body, taking care not to disconnect the transfusion lines. "My beautiful Makayla, it's not your fault."

"I'm so sorry, Zack, you were right to hate me," Makayla

uttered, looking down at her feet as her tears renewed.

"I could never hate you, you are everything to me; you always have been."

"You hated me when you handed me over to the inquisition."

Zack gasped aloud and lifted her face to look in her eyes. "So it has happened, the past has met the future?" He brushed hair from her eyes.

Makayla noticed him staring at the red ruby glistening at her throat. He swallowed before looking down at the wedding ring adorning her ring finger.

"Ma . . . Makayla, please forgive me for my dishonourable actions in the past." He stuttered.

"There's nothing to forgive, Zack, it's as I told you back then."

"I was jealous of you, Makayla. Alexander was all I had. I'll never be able to atone for my actions." Zack looked over his shoulder at Alexander before looking back at her. "You should both hate me for my intolerable actions."

"I have one destiny and her name is Makayla Uriel," Alexander's voice boomed.

Everyone in the room jumped and eyeballed Alexander in surprise. No one was more surprised by Alexander's outburst than Makayla, he spoke with such conviction.

Zack and Makayla stared at one another.

"Not likely," Alexander said.

Makayla looked back towards her husband. *Who was he*

talking to? She thought, watching him. Zack stood and faced his bedside.

"Yeah, right." Alexander laughed. *"You're hilarious."*

"Xander," Zack said, stretching his hand out towards Alexander.

"Hey . . . Fuck you . . . I am the master of my fate!"

Makayla inhaled a shocked breath and was about to stand when Zack placed a firm hand on her shoulder. "Careful, you'll tear the tubes from your arm." Makayla looked up at Zack, the colour had drained from his face. "He's delirious, Zack, he wasn't talking to you, you know that, don't you?"

Zack nodded vigorously. "Um, yep," he said, gulping and dragging his hand through his unruly hair.

Makayla looked down at the tubing connected to her arm. She tried to move her chair closer to Alexander's side, taking care not to yank the tubes from her arm. "Xander, come back to me." She brushed the hair from his forehead.

Alexander sounded like a broken record as he mumbled. *"I'm the master of my fate."* Over and over again.

CHAPTER 9

Augustus glanced about his surroundings, feeling displaced and confused. He held a glass tumbler filled with a generous helping of port. The burgundy liquid rippled as he lifted his trembling hand and took a lengthy draught. Alcohol sluiced down his parched throat and warmed his empty belly. The pleasing aroma of ash tree logs burning in the nearby hearth was soothing. Weak with lethargy and hunger he closed his eyes and relaxed into the padded velvet chair. Warmth cocooned him, heating his old bones; it was a warmth he'd not known in a long while. He heard the rustle of fabric as someone moved, but didn't open his eyes – the pull to sleep was strong. There was a shift in fragrance, Augustus sighed as the scent of cedar and burning sage enveloped him in a pleasant cloud.

The voice of an angel began singing an old folk song. He'd heard the familiar tune echoing throughout the dungeons on many occasions. Usually when he was about to give up and allow death to massage the life from his withering body. A simple melody from his past had kept him from death's lingering embrace, saving him countless times over the drawn-out years.

He opened his eyes and saw Marianna kneeling before the hearth plucking leaves from a dried sage cutting. He could hear a faint rustle and swish as she twisted and crushed the leaves between her fingertips before tossing them into the fire. The fire would flare momentarily with each pass of her slender hand. Vasili stood nearby, regarding her with an adoring, soft smile, his elbow resting on the fireplace mantel. The luminance of Marianna's skin identified her seraphim heritage. He hadn't noticed it until they were in a better lit area. There was much he'd not known about his old friend Vasili. Marianna was his best kept secret.

Augustus sighed. "Your singing was my saving grace, Lady Marianna. Many times I'd given up, but then I'd hear your exquisite voice drifting along the dungeon corridors. The melodies were like floating memories, echoes of a lost life I thought I'd never see again. For a short lapse in time the music masked my surroundings and breathed life back into this aged body."

Marianna brushed the sage particles from her hands and stood, turning towards him. "I know, Lord Augustus, 'tis why I sang. I sensed your hopelessness."

Augustus's jaw dropped. "How . . . how did you know?"

A gentle smile curved Marianna's mouth, lighting up her face and creasing the corners of her eyes. "Not all my powers were rendered useless in the Rivulous Dimension, my lord. My intuition, for one, never left me. I sensed your desolation at your lowest times, perhaps because I too struggled with a similar bleakness. It was different with Alexander. He was complicated because he was transitioning into a vampire."

"I felt the pressing need to end my existence." Augustus sighed. "Many times I wanted to die. Thank you for serenading me away from death's tragic door."

"You are most welcome, your grace, 'twas my duty to help."

Augustus nodded and finished the remainder of his beverage before placing the empty glass on a nearby table. He sank once more into the welcoming comfort of his chair and glanced about the spacious room. Wine-red velvet drapes hid windows that stretched towards lofty rock ceilings. An enormous Persian carpet in tones of burgundy, navy, beige and brown covered the floor. A brown antique oak coffee table from the Renaissance period graced the centre of the room. The apron and legs of the table were intricately carved with curling Fleur-de-Lis scroll-work.

A matching dining setting sat towards the back of the room, the grand table was nearly the same width as the room and was surrounded in robust yet delicate carved chairs. Exposed wooden beams adorned the high ceilings, adding to the room's magnificent homey appearance. Wavering gold light illuminated the chamber, hundreds of lit candles adorning an immense chandelier that hung from a sturdy central beam. The opulence reminded Augustus of what he'd been lacking during his incarceration in the abysmal, dank dungeon. He'd missed the comfort of a home filled with warmth and elegance – a grandeur he'd not seen since his abduction. The room was so handsome and architecturally divine he'd almost forgotten what it was like to look upon such majesty.

Augustus's eyes halted on his fellow councilman Sebastian, who stood off to the right, deep in conversation with Gabriel and Lazarus. Sebastian was the firstborn, and rightful heir to the vampire throne. The next in line to be king and chancellor of the Vampire Council by royal edict. Sebastian had wanted none of it and abdicated both entitlements after his father's mysterious death, insisting Augustus take his place on the council as chancellor. Augustus had accepted the position with one stipulation: that Sebastian became a member of the council, but in a lower level capacity. At the time he couldn't fathom why Sebastian hadn't chosen his younger brother, Malachi for the position, but after everything that had transpired the reasons were becoming all too clear. Augustus sensed there was more to the story than what was being presented to the masses. Had Malachi been involved in their father's death? Had Zobiana woven her web and ensnared Malachi in her twisted scheme to overthrow the royal rulers of Evron? Was there more to Sebastian and Zobiana's falling out than just a lovers' tiff? Had she been involved in King Eridan's

RENEE SPYROU

demise? So many questions.

The duties of the royal family were complicated at best. Much had changed in the aftermath of the king's death. The eve before Sebastian's coronation was to take place, Sebastian met with the seraph king, Uriel Chevez, and had discussed a truce between the two ruling factions of Evron. To this day, no one knew what was discussed, but nothing was the same afterwards. The laws were changed and the Seraph and Vampire Councils ruled Evron together in reasonable harmony. The squabbles and skirmishes of the past that had often pitted vampire and seraphim against one another in bitter battles over borders and territories had dwindled. Now the borders and territories were controlled equally by both factions – likewise Evron's gateways to Earth and other Offworlds.

Technically leadership hadn't changed; it had just been redefined and reallocated. Both royal families continued to rule Evron, but through the scope of the vampire and seraph senates. Bickering was confined to the council chambers rather than spilling out onto the battlefields as it had in the past. A time of peace and prosperity had prevailed. Animosity towards one another had reduced to a slow burn instead of an inferno of hatred and bitterness. An amicable truce had been reached as a result of King Eridan's untimely death.

Augustus was in charge of the vampire senate, or to be more precise, he had been in charge until he was imprisoned and his identity stolen. Truthfully, he hadn't wanted the position of chancellor, but Sebastian had left him with no choice. Who else could have led the vampire people without prejudice? He and Sebastian were like-minded in their views, so as far as Sebastian was concerned, Augustus had been the only choice. Having royal blood had also been a deciding factor. Augustus hadn't the political power Sebastian and his family had, but his family were royal nobles nonetheless. So Sebastian had handed over control of Evron, not totally absconding from his legacy and royal duty, but taking a back seat until he felt the time was right for him to take his rightful place upon the throne.

Sebastian cracked his neck, rolled his shoulders and clasped his hands behind his back. He glanced from Lazarus to Gabriel, all the while wondering if Makayla and Alexander were okay.

"So what you're saying is you went back in time to the year 1307. How is that remotely possible?" Gabriel asked.

"I don't know, all I can tell you is that's where we ended up," Lazarus said. "It happened so fast. The Oracle said the fire-moon and the dragon were the precursor to it all; the circle's beginning and the circle's end. If I was to fulfil my destiny, it was my duty to watch over the Chosen One and wait for the signs to reveal themselves.

"I followed Makayla to Corfe Castle, and it was there that I finally saw the signs I'd been waiting for centuries – the fire-moon, the Terrin and the explosion of light coming from Makayla's window. I'm guessing the gems integrating into the Trinian Globe was what caused the light show. There was another burst of light, almost like a solar flare before Makayla disappeared."

"How can you be sure the Trinian Globe was the cause?"

"I can't, but there was a hovering orb pulsing in the centre of the room. What else could it have been?"

"It was the Trinian Globe, Gabriel, there's no doubt." Sebastian sighed. "I've read enough ancient scrolls about the Globe to know it couldn't have been anything else. I just can't understand why it would transport you back seven hundred years into the past."

"Hang on a minute; did you say gems, plural?" Gabriel questioned.

"Yes. There were two distinct flashes of coloured light. So I'm guessing there were two gems, yellow and purple." Lazarus held up his forefinger. "Actually, there were three flashes of coloured light, yellow, purple and red. At the time I assumed the red light had something to do with the fire-moon. Now that I come to think of it, it makes perfect sense."

"What makes perfect sense?" Sebastian asked.

"The next Trinian gem colour was red. Zobiana had a ruby gem in her possession. The Gem of Past Times, I think that's what she called it. I'm of the opinion it was the next gem to be located by the Globe. That must have been the reason we were transported back to the 14th Century."

Sebastian's mouth suddenly went dry and the room closed in about him. He felt faint and clammy as he recalled the gaudy, gold-encrusted ruby necklace Zobiana had worn centuries ago. She'd never been without it. He'd asked her about it once, but she'd laughed, coyly avoiding his question. He'd been young, gullible and easily distracted in his youth – it wasn't until much later that he'd found out who had given it to her.

"Where's the gem now?" Sebastian asked, pinching the bridge of his nose and massaging his forehead, trying to ease the growing ache throbbing behind his temples.

"Makayla has it. I don't know how she figured it out, but her blood was the catalyst to our escape. The Inquisition was about to burn her at the stake for heresy and being a witch."

"I beg your pardon?" Gabe shuffled closer.

"That's not the worst of it. I found my father."

"Malachi," Sebastian croaked.

Lazarus cleared his throat. "He was masquerading as the Cardinal and in league with Zobiana. I don't know what their connection is, but it can't be good."

A commotion and booming voices drew everyone's attention to the closed doorway. Vasili glanced towards Sebastian, his eyebrows rising. Sebastian stayed Vasili with a slight movement of his hand before glancing towards Augustus.

"Step aside, Tristan."

"No, Nickolai, don't go in ther—"

"Remove yourself from my path or I'll smash through you and the door barring my way!"

BANG.

The door crashed open, hitting the wall and vibrating the door hinges. Two men stood before their small group. Judging by their similar appearance, they were both seraphim if Augustus was to guess their genealogy. The seraph who forced the door open was the first to enter, but stopped abruptly when Marianna stepped out from behind Vasili.

"Nikolai." Marianna's face broke into a radiant smile, her eyes filling with tears when she saw the man standing before them. She held out her arms towards him.

"Mother." Nikolai ran to her and lifted her off her feet, hugging her in a tight embrace. "You're truly here, I cannot believe it. I've been searching centuries for you," Nikolai said, lowering his mother to the floor.

"All thanks to Makayla and Lazarus," Marianna replied, brushing hair from her son's eyes.

"Come now, it was all Makayla's doing," Lazarus said, moving closer to them accompanied by Gabriel and Sebastian.

Marianna's face crinkled. "Nay, Lord Lazarus, you saved my life too."

"Where's Makayla? And what of Xand—?" Tristan stopped mid-speech when he spotted Augustus reclined in a chair near the hearth watching him.

He glanced across at Sebastian. "Father, I'm sorry. When you asked not to be disturbed I had no idea the chancellor was here too."

Sebastian glanced towards Augustus. "It's all right, Tristan. Augustus was being held captive by Zobiana as well."

Nikolai bowed. "My most humble apologies, Lord Chancellor. In my eagerness to be reunited with my mother, my good judgement was overruled. Please forgive me for the interruption and my deplorable behaviour.

"Truly, there's nothing to forgive, I understand completely." Augustus looked from Vasili to Sebastian. "I'd stand to greet you properly, young man, but under the circumstances, I find I'm quite fatigued."

"Lord Augustus, I'd like to introduce you to, Nikolai, Vasili's son." Sebastian indicated Nikolai with a regal flutter of his hand. "And this is, Tristan, one of my sons. I'm afraid we owe you an apology for our omissions concerning our marital and family status. As you can imagine, we couldn't divulge such volatile information regarding our unlawful unions. It's against the law for vampires and seraphs to marry one another, and as you're well aware, punishable by death.

Augustus looked from Vasili to Sebastian and then to their sons and smiled. "My lord, you are the vampire king of Evron and owe me no explanations. The heart wants what it wants. Laws can be changed. They should be changed." Augustus's smile widened. The heavy tension in the room immediately dissipated. "I understand now, Sebastian. Makayla is your daughter, isn't she? The prophesied one, the firstborn of the two royal houses, vampire and seraph. How did I not see it? You could have come to me, Sebastian. I would have kept your secret; yours too, Vasili."

"We couldn't risk it, Augustus. Vasili and I discussed the

notion at length, but we couldn't put you or your family in danger, or jeopardise your position as chancellor in the vampire senate."

"'Tis why you abdicated?" Augustus asked, attempting to rise from his seat. Sebastian placed a gentle hand on his shoulder. "Don't tire yourself on our account, my lord; relax, you need to rest and gather your strength."

"Does Uriel know?" Augustus sank back into his chair, shifting position until he was comfortable.

"Yes." Sebastian nodded, brushing a hand through his hair and exhaling. "It was his daughter Ambrosia whom I married."

"I see, so the truce between the seraph and vampires is largely because of your relationship with his daughter?"

"Partly, but not entirely. There were many other factors, but I'm unable to disclose the nature of the truce or the terms of the agreement. What happened to my father is likely to happen again if I divulge such information. Suffice to say, the persons responsible for his death are still at large and the risk is too great."

Augustus nodded and bowed his head. "As you wish, your highness."

"Please, don't call me that, I'm not the king."

"Be that as it may, Sire, you will always be the heir to the throne. Regardless of your choices, no one can take your place. No one but the firstborn of your progeny can do that. Not even your brother can become king. You may have abdicated, but that won't stand forever, there must be a royal ruler of the vampire nation. One day you will take your rightful place. If not you, then your daughter, Makayla."

CHAPTER 10.

The repetitive *clip, tap, clip, tap, clip, tap* of Zobiana's pacing, stiletto heels smacking the rock floor, resonated throughout the dim chamber. The unending clatter bounced off the cracked walls and kept time with the swinging pendulum of the great grandfather clock by the doorway. Every time the clock chimed Zobiana would stop pacing, curse to herself and glance towards the doorway.

"Has anyone heard from Beltizare?"

"No, my lady, you did send him on a wild goose chase, remember." Tyrone rolled his eyes. "I fear the Trinian Globe is long gone."

"What about Malachi? Have they located him yet?" Zobiana paced again.

"Not that we know of," Tyrone offered with a shrug.

"Well, what the bloody hell do you know, Tyrone?

Anything?"

"I'm in the dark as much as you are, my lady."

"Surely it's only a matter of time before the senate finds out."

"Finds out what?"

Zobiana stopped in front of Tyrone and placed her hands on her hips. "Seriously, haven't you been paying attention? Were you not present when everything went to shit? They found Augustus in our dungeon, dammit; they found the one person who could ruin everything. Honestly, one would think you were off gallivanting with the fairies."

"They found three people, my lady." Tyrone smirked.

Zobiana fixed him with a mutinous glare, the whites of her eyes turned black; her irises infusing red and her teeth lengthening to sharp points. "Something's been bothering me, Tyrone." She angled her head and stalked closer to him. "Why didn't you stop them from escaping, or at least try?" She pushed her face into his. "Why didn't you help us when Alexander attacked us? You just stood there like a fool with a stupid grin on your face. WHY?"

"Obviously, it wasn't Alexander. How was I going to go up against the Dark One, Lilith? With my bare hands?"

"Don't call me Lilith," she screeched, stomping her foot. "I HATE IT, it's not my name, it's a label he gave me."

Tyrone smirked again. "I have powers, but nothing compared to the King of Hell,"

"I don't understand; the Dark One shouldn't have had so

much power, not when he's only just possessed Alexander's body," Zobiana mumbled to herself.

Tyrone continued, ignoring her childish outburst and clasping his hands together. "Tell me how I could have helped? I would have died, I nearly did. If it hadn't been for all the Newbloods standing in front of me, the dragonfire would have killed me for sure. We were lucky."

"Lucky, huh? Abigail's barely alive; she's been hooked up to an IV unit for hours and still hasn't awakened. She looks like the scorched remains of Freddie Krueger's handmaiden. You call that luck?"

"She's alive, isn't she? You should be grateful."

Zobiana chuckled, her laughter turned hysterical, until the chamber echoed with the screams of her frustration. Her chest heaved as she gasped. "I never took you for a fool, Tyrone, in all the years I've known you you've never been a fool. I guess it was bound to happen. Do you think the real Augustus Lagorias is going to hide in the shadows? The first thing he'll do is assemble the Vampire and Seraph Senates and inform them of Malachi's deception. We should have killed him while we had the chance."

"Maybe, maybe not. Augustus is a broken man. He'll need time to recover from his incarceration and regroup, and remember, he will only just have learned of his son's death; he'll be grieving. We cannot predict what his next move will be. He may play it safe – and let's face it, nobody knows what Malachi's next move will be either. He has only ever had one agenda: becoming king."

There was a sharp knock and they glanced towards the door. The knock came again. Zobiana's face relaxed, reverting back to normal as she smoothed her hair, straightened her clothing and faced the door. "Come in," she said calmly. She clasped her hands together, squeezing and twisting them until all the sensation drained from her fingertips and all she felt was tingling pins and needles.

The door opened revealing her manservant, who bowed graciously. "You have a visitor, my lady." He bowed once more and extended his arm for the messenger to enter.

Zobiana knew the messenger was a pureblood vampire the moment he entered the room, she could smell him. "That will be all," she said to her manservant and waited for him to close the door.

Zobiana's eyes narrowed as she watched the hooded stranger stride into the room. He was dressed from head to toe in black and stood a foot taller than Tyrone's six feet six. His three-quarter length jacket brushed the backs of his legs as he came to a halt not two metres from them. With a stiff posture he bowed from the waist. Zobiana eyed him, noting the decorative swirls of silver filigree on the hilts of the swords strapped to his back. Her gaze wandered down the length of his body and stopped at his clenching and unclenching gloved hands at his sides.

Zobiana sidled up to him; the itch to touch was compelling. *Why not?* She lifted her slender fingertips to his body. He was rock-hard, all chiselled muscle, what she wouldn't give to see him naked – he felt divine. His body tensed, stiffening as she trailed her hands over his broad chest. Intrigued by his response, she leaned in close and inhaled. His scent was intoxicating. It tickled the back of her nose with a woodsy, resinous scent – rich and earthy. The smell of amber – mysterious, exotic and familiar. She'd often seen him walking the great castle hallways of the vampire senate on Evron, but never without his hood.

She stared into the shadowy depths of his hood, all the while feeling an erotic, simmering burn within her body. Something she'd not felt in centuries. What did he look like? Was he as enticing in appearance as his scent? Zobiana angled her head, trying to see past the shadows. She understood his need for anonymity, but she would see his face if it was the last thing she did. Tyrone cleared his throat, snapping Zobiana from her outright appraisal of the vampire. She looked over her shoulder at Tyrone before stepping back beside him, a toothy grin spreading across her face.

"Remove your hood," she ordered. "I like to look people in the eyes when I speak to them.

"NO."

"I beg your pardon." Zobiana grinned, his refusal a blatant invitation. Now she wanted, needed to see his face more than ever. "Why so insolent, my youthful vampire?"

"I cannot, my lady. If you were to see my face I would have to kill you."

Zobiana chuckled. "Really? I've heard that before. Well, what does one call you, or is your name as ambiguous as your appearance?"

"They call me Kraegan."

"And what news do you have for me, Kraegan?"

"The chancellor has disappeared; no one knows his location, not even the senate."

"Curious. I've heard the chancellor is a busy man, meticulous when it comes to planning his timetable. Wouldn't he inform his council if he were leaving? Schedules need to be adhered to – updated?" Zobiana scratched her head, playing dumb. "It's protocol."

"I wouldn't know about council protocol, I'm just a messenger," Kraegan said, folding his arms behind his back.

"Yeah, right," Tyrone said. "Messengers don't have weapons like those strapped to their backs." He crossed his arms, indicating Kraegan's weapons with a nod of his head.

"What about Malachi? There are whispers he has returned to claim the vampire throne."

"There are always whispers, Mistress, but whispers are just that, whispers." Kraegan shifted from foot to foot and crossed his arms over his chest, mimicking Tyrone.

Zobiana's eyes fluttered closed when Kraegan's scent enveloped her, she circled her head back, her lustrous hair brushing her hips in soft, shimmering waves. A serene smile stole across her features. Kraegan's voice was like liquid gold, smooth, accented, masculine. The hairs on the nape of her neck sprang to life as if the man himself had leaned in close and whispered the words into her ear, a tickling seduction meant for her ears alone.

"Will that be all, my lady?" Kraegan enquired.

"No," Zobiana snapped, opening her eyes. "I have more to discuss with you, Kraegan. Alone." She looked at Tyrone and winked. "That will be all, Tyrone." She dismissed him with a quick nod of her head.

Zobiana's smile increased when Tyrone's mouth dropped and his eyes widened. He masked his shock and nodded. "As you wish, my lady." He bowed and stalked out of the room in a huff.

Zobiana waved her hand and the locks engaged the moment the door slammed. She focused her attention on Kraegan and beamed. "I thought you'd never get here. Now remove that damn hood and tell me where your father is."

Broken furniture littered the rooftop bar of The Devil's Pit. Smashed porcelain plates lay scattered about the floor. A kaleidoscope of brilliant colour reflected off shards of shattered glass, sparkling in the fading light as the winter sun farewelled another chilly day. The bar was no more, damaged beyond repair. Not that it bothered Makayla; she was happy for the solitude, having spent five worrisome days by Alexander's bedside. He still hadn't woken. Nor had she heard from her cousin Lazarus either, not since he'd whisked Marianna and Chancellor Lagorias away from the dungeons. The only communication she'd had was from her father; they were recovering well and lying low in her parents' castle for the time being. It was too dangerous for them to be at the compound. Especially the chancellor. If they wanted to catch the imposter, Augustus had to be kept hidden. Makayla had to wonder, though, who had infiltrated the compound? Zobiana or the phony chancellor's people? Were Zobiana and the chancellor's imposter working together?

The tinkling of glass fragments distracted her from her musings. Makayla shaded her eyes and looked up as fighter jets zoomed by. The crack and boom of the engines sent warm air down to whip her hair about and disturb the rubbish on the ground. The whistle of bombs falling from the sky could be heard off in the distance as the jets dropped their lethal cargo. The building shuddered as the ground was struck by an unyielding destruction. Multiple plumes of black smoke appeared, twisting up into the mottled sky.

Makayla sighed and shook her head. "Humans, always flexing the wrong muscles." The disdain in her voice was unmistakable. She shook her head again.

"Which muscles would you prefer them to flex, Makayla, the ones between their legs?" Her nemesis mocked.

"Hey, maybe if they pulled em' out and shook them about a little, the dick-measuring contest could be satisfied and a clear winner chosen."

"You're hilarious!"

"I know, right?"

"No, not really. Men aren't that easily satisfied."

"And you'd be an expert on satisfying men?"

"You'd be surprised by my expertise."

"You're delusional. Correction, I'm delusional. You're a figment of my imagination."

"If you say so, but, consider this: maybe I'm not a figment of your imagination."

"In what universe could you possibly be real?" Makayla grumbled. "Look at them, just look at them," she said, extending her arm and indicating the planes with an angry shake of her fist. "Stupid sons of bitches!" Makayla shook her head a third time when the jets circled again, preparing to drop more bombs. "Bloody fools! There'll be nothing left if they keep bombing the shit out of everything. Well, nothing worth salvaging. Maybe a dick-measuring contest is the go."

"They're dying and are being rounded up like sheep, what else would you have them do? What do you expect them to do? Lay down and die without a fight. Why do you care what the humans do? You haven't before?"

Makayla grimaced as she lowered her hand and glanced about the rooftop. "Is there a reason you're here? If not, go away!"

Makayla stepped over the crumbling remains of a chimney stack that had fallen from a nearby building and landed on the rooftop. She navigated around upturned circular bar tables and stools. There were upended tables and chairs everywhere, a few still covered in faded red tablecloths. A number of tablecloths were hooked on building wreckage and fluttered like wild creatures ensnared in traps, whipping and snapping as the gusts of wind grew stronger. Rubbish and paper flyers twirled about in embellished air funnels. Makayla likened the bar to a child's toy box; messy, mixed up, with many broken toys and their missing parts, a result of animated play.

Ashy clouds billowed about Makayla's feet, dusting her boots in black soot as she trudged towards the roof edge. She ignored the crunch of broken glass underfoot as she made her way through the debris. The moment she reached the rusted railing she looked out towards the city. The cityscape had changed somewhat since the last time she'd gazed upon it.

Twisted steel building girders thrust heavenwards like metal skeletons with warped fingertips, straining for God's absolution. Fragmented remains of buildings, towers and skyscrapers stretched across the entire skyline like broken teeth in varying states of decay. The London Eye lay tilted at an impossible angle, the carriages dislodged and hanging by bolts and hinges. The Big Ben clock tower had plumes of smoke billowing from it, one of the clock faces covered in a huge, shredded tarpaulin with a gigantic black Biohazard symbol painted on it. The last rays of sunlight highlighted the symbol as if Big Ben was an actor on a stage taking his final bow for an applauding audience.

Makayla shoved her hand in her jacket pocket and pulled

out her Zippo and cigarettes. She tapped the bottom of the packet and removed a cigarette with her lips before shoving the crumpled packet back into her pocket. Cupping her hand around her mouth, she lit the cigarette, inhaled deeply, holding the smoke in her lungs before exhaling smoke rings. Makayla looked down at her feet and pinched the bridge of her nose. She kicked the dilapidated railing over the edge of the building and cleared a space on the roof ledge with the toe of her boot before sitting. She swung her legs over the side of the building and sagged against a steel pole, resting her head against the cool metal as she took another drag on her cigarette.

The thumping *doof, doof, doof,* beat coming from the club below was a stark reminder that life went on. The Devil's Pit was no exception to the rule. Fully operational no matter what. Day or night – there was no deviation, it was open twenty-four hours a day. Even when the world was on the brink of destruction. The club gathered its fair share of patrons and seemed busier than usual with its regular clientele of Off Worlders who had a funny habit of enjoying themselves no matter the circumstances. They'd become quite blasé about the events affecting humanity and were used to Earth's increasing chaos over the centuries. Humans had an uncanny knack for destroying themselves, even when they hadn't caused the events directly. Humanity was a bothersome irritant, more often than not, aggravating the situation rather than finding a solution to the problem.

Makayla had become desensitised to the troubles and

turmoils of humans over the years, and from what she could ascertain by London's horizon, things had got worse than they'd been before she'd travelled back in time. Earth's occupants were always at war or in a dire situation in some capacity, why should it be any different now?

Only it was different, very different.

"I thought I'd find you up here," Darrius said, appearing out of thin air beside her.

Makayla took another drag on her cigarette. "Am I that predictable?" She exhaled and rested her hand on her knee, watching the smoke-plume spiral from the glowing tip of her cigarette.

"No, far from it, I come here when I need silence to think too." Darrius made a space next to her and sat. He swung his arm around her shoulders and hugged her tight. "It's not your fault, stop blaming yourself."

Makayla stubbed out her cigarette and flicked it over the building's ledge. "You really should stop reading my mind, Darrius."

"Who said I was reading your mind? Give me some credit. I know my place and respect your privacy." Darrius squeezed her shoulder again before releasing her and leaning back on his arms.

"So, why do you think I blame myself for all this?" Makayla swept her arm out indicating the city scape.

"Oh, I don't know, because that's what you seem to do. It's what you've done from the beginning. Your eagerness to blame yourself is the only predictable thing about you."

Makayla looked towards an adjoining building and saw Salomae's silhouette on the rooftop; she'd been unusually quiet. She ran her fingertips over the scar on her wrist, all was black – the Terrin was sleeping.

"She's magnificent, your dragon," Darrius said, admiring the creature.

Makayla smiled. "That she is, she's taken up the responsibility of being my protector and overbearing conscience. The little angel on my shoulder if you will." Makayla chuckled. "She's saved my life more times than I can count."

Darrius's forehead furrowed. "Where have you been, Makayla? You've been missing for months?"

"What are you talking about? I've only been gone six days."

Darrius shook his head. "You've been gone longer than six days, Makayla. This shit doesn't just happen overnight, and certainly not in six days." Darrius indicated the city with a nod. "Where have you been?" he asked again.

"Hmm, that's a tough question; I've been to hell and back."

"I hope you don't mean that literally."

"No, of course not. I've been in the 14th century."

Darrius sat up straight and stuck his face in Makayla's. "You're serious."

"Damn bloody straight I'm serious. I travelled back in time

to the year thirteen hundred and seven. The Inquisition even put me on trial for being a witch – if you call their bullying a trial. They tried burning me at the stake, too. The stupid fucks didn't know I was fireproof, lucky for me. It was quite the spectacle."

Darrius swept his hand through his hair. "Fuck me."

"Yeah, no thanks, I'll pass." Makayla chuckled. "You missed out, Darrius, Lazarus was there with me."

"Lazarus has been telling me for centuries something like this would happen. I didn't trust him and ignored his warnings. He always said there was more to your prophecy than the oracle had revealed. I thought he was trying to stir up trouble and believed he was going to out our family to the vampire senate." Darrius folded his hands in his lap.

"It's funny you should say such a thing, 'cause he's family. He's your brother, or fake brother – our cousin. What would he have to gain by outing us? He would have done it already if that was his intent."

"So you know then." Darrius looked out towards the horizon.

Makayla searched his face. "Why would he help me? He has saved my life more times than I can count."

"Oh, that's what he does," Darrius said with bitterness, rolling his shoulders in discomfort. "He'd have everything to gain, Makayla, everything."

"What do you mean by everything, Darrius? What's between you two? I know there's something you're not telling me."

"It's not important. Not anymore."

"Clearly," Makayla replied. "What did he do to you, Darrius?"

Darrius glanced back at her and the look on his face was enough to send shivers down her back. "It wasn't so much what he did, Makayla, it was the lack thereof."

"What does that even mean?"

Darrius swallowed and rubbed the top of his shoulder blade with his hand. "Can we not talk about this? It's ancient history. Let's leave it in the past, all right? Just be on your guard around him, he's cut from the same cloth as his brother."

"He's nothing like his brother."

"And how would you know?"

"I killed his brother, remember? Or did you forget? Now he was a psycho bastard. Don't put Lazarus in the same category just because he's related. Lazarus is nothing like Kraegan; you're too blinded by what happened to see him for who he is."

Darrius clenched his jaw, his face flushing with heat. "Blinded? I think I see him far clearer than you, Makayla. Take off the blinders, maybe then you'd see just like I do."

Makayla held her hands up in submission. "Sorry, I didn't mean to hit a nerve." She wasn't going to hound her brother any further, he'd tell her what was between him and Lazarus, eventually. Or someone else would.

"What else do you know?" Darrius asked.

Makayla eyed her brother and noticed his shoulders relax

when she didn't pursue her questioning. "I know where our missing uncle disappeared to…"

"Which uncle are you referring to? We have many."

"You know which uncle; Lazarus's father, the father you're pretending to be the son of."

"Malachi. No one knows where he is."

"I know where he is, or was."

"How could you possibly know? You don't even know what he looks like."

Makayla crossed her arms. "He looks a lot like our father, a bit shorter and pudgier, not as good looking, but completely recognisable if you know what to look for."

"The suspense is killing me. Where has he been hiding all these years? Do tell."

"He was the Cardinal who tried to burn me at the stake in the past. Our family is seriously fucked up, Darrius."

Darrius grimaced. "You have no idea just how fucked up our family is, Makayla, but I think you're beginning to understand."

"That's not the best of all, though; our uncle was very chummy with Zobiana, who, by the way, just happened to be Alexander's stepmother. I found out a lot of weird shit while I was in the past. You could say things are clearer now."

"I don't understand. How the hell did you wind up in the 14th century?"

"The Trinian Globe shot me there, the only conclusion I can come to is this." Makayla unclasped Zobiana's gaudy ruby necklace from her throat and passed it to Darrius.

Darrius took it from her hand and held it up in front of his eyes. The oval gem spun on the gold chain. A glistening prism of red light caught and reflected the last rays of sunshine as the gem oscillated. Darrius's eyebrow raised, and he glanced at her with a questioning look. "What's so special about this gem? Aside from it being, what I'm assuming is a Trinian Globe gem?"

"It's the Gem of Past Times."

Darrius whistled. "No shit." He frowned. "*No. . . Shit*," he repeated in whispered awe. "It was the next gem in line, wasn't it? Holy crap, it transported you back in time, that's some weird-arse shit right there. How come I've never heard of this gem? Where'd you find it?"

"Hanging around Zobiana's neck; hence the gaudy gold chain. It's the ugliest piece of jewellery I've had the misfortune of seeing. The bitch wasn't too pleased when I punched her in the face and ripped it from her throat," Makayla chuckled.

"I don't understand, how did you find your way back to the present, and more to the point, how did you find Alexander? Was he in another dimension like I said?"

"That's the million-dollar question, isn't it? I have no idea. I went with my gut. The gem seemed to react to my blood. I don't know why – I'm guessing it's because of who I am, you know, the Chosen One, yadda, yadda, yadda. Truthfully, I'm at a loss. I have so many questions to ask Alexander. I think he may know why, but he's unconscious, and something is really wrong with him. Some very strange things happened when Lazarus and I were trying to save him, Marianna and Augustus from Zobiana's dungeons. Oh, and yes, they were in another dimension like you said."

"Hang on a minute, slow down. Augustus, you don't mean Augustus Lagorias the Chancellor of the Vampire Council do you?"

"The one and the same."

"So who's been impersonating the chancellor, and for how long?"

"We don't know, but Augustus hadn't a clue about his son's death so we're assuming whoever abducted him did it the same day they killed his son."

The colour washed from Darrius's face. He stood abruptly and paced along the roof edge, mumbling to himself.

Makayla pulled herself up using the pole she'd been leaning against. "What's wrong, Darrius?"

Darrius stopped and frowned. "Do you know what this means?" Makayla shook her head. "It means Zobiana has been in control of the vampire senate all these years, manipulating everything from behind the scenes. Why would she want you to have the Golden One's armour and weapons? What's she up to? Why would she give you the power to destroy her?"

"Who's to say she's been the one in control? She wasn't in the past, not really. I think she's being manipulated, too. By whoever's masquerading as the chancellor? What we need to be asking ourselves is who has the most to gain and who is the imposter?"

Darrius glanced down towards the street. "What the—"

Makayla sidled up to her brother and trained her eyes on the street below. What she saw froze the blood in her veins.

CHAPTER 11

The monstrous gateway loomed, overshadowing and obstructing the sky. Vasili looked about his surroundings, making sure no one followed; he couldn't sense anyone's presence, but not sensing someone didn't mean they weren't there. He noticed a stand of trees to his left and stared into the murky depths with his vampire vision. There was no one there. It didn't lighten his apprehension, though. *You're being paranoid, Vasili,* he thought to himself before refocusing his attention on the task at hand.

He craned his neck back to look at the Zoldarni gateway. It was by far the largest of all the hidden gateways on Earth, and the most exquisite. The gateway stood several metres high, five metres wide and three metres deep, with three distinctive layers. There were three pointed arches, each decreasing in size within the other. Each curving arch comprised of slender stones in varying sizes. Every arch point was held in place by a large, triangular keystone. The most defining features were the swirling mosaics built into the outer arch.

The arches were separated by steps measuring one metre in depth. Iridescent velvety moss grew within the joins, outlining each stone. Rose-coloured flower buds and blooming, winter jasmine carpeted the gateway exterior walls with petite star-shaped flowers. Vasili lifted his nose and breathed in the pleasing scents of his surroundings. The fragrance of jasmine didn't overpower or mask the musky scent of soil, or the earthy smell of fallen leaves and grass.

Nature enveloped him. Birds chirped, crickets buzzed, trees rustled in the wind, the sound of a babbling brook could also be heard off in the distance. The loud crunch of his shoes disturbed the natural order as he trekked along the overgrown rocky path leading towards the gateway. As he climbed the stairs, he looked through the gateway to the other side. The descending sun hid behind pink-, purple- and orange-tinted clouds. Shards of light beamed down on a far-reaching field, highlighting the long blades of winter grass with gold sunlight, as if someone had traced the outer edges with a fluorescent yellow marker. A smile hovered on his lips as he absorbed the natural beauty surrounding him. He hadn't appreciated the simple pleasures of life in a long time, not since his wife's abduction.

A light breeze caught the hem of his cape, the fabric billowing out like boat sails as he climbed the stairs towards the gateway. The smile fell from his lips as the gravity of Earth's dire situation hit him. His brow furrowed as the abhorrent acts of Zobiana and Malachi filled his troubled thoughts again. The task ahead was sobering. He leaned the shillelagh he was using as a walking stick against the wall and removed the Zoldarni gateway key from an interior pocket in his jacket. Like the gateway in front of him, it too was unusual and unlike any other key in existence. It was larger than an ordinary gateway key, made from Uraninite, a highly radioactive black metal lethal to humans. The central gem was a black seraphinite, named for the swirls of iridescent silver within the crystal that bared a striking resemblance to the feathery wings of the six-winged seraphim. Off Worlders called it the stone of enlightenment. The gem was also known as the angel crystal because of its powerful healing properties and its ability to align elements with nonphysical bodies.

The irony was not lost on Vasili. The gem colour changed often, usually when in proximity to the gateway. Vasili held the key up to eye level and watched as a red fluttering cloud appeared within the centre of the gem. Colour bled outwards like coloured dye in water. Vasili traced his fingertip over the cool surface as the colour changed from red to orange and then to yellow.

Vasili rarely travelled through the Zoldarni gateway, and never without invitation. It was high treason to do so, but he had no choice – things had become desperate. The Earth was falling into ruin, and if Zobiana and Malachi had their way, it would fall further into anarchy. Before the end, Zobiana would have complete control of all the gateways on Earth. The Zoldarni would lose the governing power of the Multiverse planets if he didn't inform them. Zobiana would systematically destroy and take control of every planet caught within her trajectory. The only ones standing in her way were the Zoldarni.

He stepped closer to the wall and brushed dirt residue from a circular indentation. The key heated within his fingertips as he placed it into position with a snap and a click. The gem palpitated as if it were a living being with a beating heart. It doubled in size, bulging outwards from the device. Everything froze and silence ensued. Birds stopped chirping. The wind stopped blowing. The sun stilled its descending path. The flowers and foliage were no longer fragrant. The immediate area was a vacuum of sorts, blocking and nullifying everything.

Vasili looked up, falling leaves and birds were unmoving above him, he flicked a leaf and nothing happened. The air felt solid, a pressing, heavy weight. The only noise he could hear was a humming, static buzz coming from the gateway itself. The gem flared bright; he shaded his eyes, pressed the gem into the body of the key and turned it. There was a loud *thunk* as it clicked into its final position. Vasili grabbed his shillelagh, clenching it tightly, and stepped back. There was an ear-splitting bang that evolved into a howling scream of wind, a rushing blast of air pushing against him, almost toppling him to the base of the stairs. He leant into the air, trying to find purchase. A funnel formed in the centre of the gateway, opening as the wind changed direction, reversing on itself. Leaves, twigs, pebbles and larger debris lifted off the ground and were sucked into the maelstrom. Vasili's cape whipped about his legs as he lost his balance and was pulled towards the gateway.

Vasili noticed white electrical currents flashing in front of him as he lifted off the ground and into the air. In a brilliant flash of light, he was drawn into the funnelling vortex. The hair on his head stood on end and his skin prickled. He was jettisoned through a spiralling wormhole. Somersaulting in midair, he spun and twisted as he was conveyed along. There was an additional flash of light as he was thrust through another gateway opening. His shillelagh clattered to the ground as he landed on his stomach. The air knocked from his lungs as he hit the hard rock surface. He lay on the ground spluttering and coughing for oxygen, tears streaming from his eyes and blurring his vision. The cold tip of a lethal sword was thrust beneath his bearded chin. Large hands grabbed his arms. He hissed when stabbing fingertips dug and pinched the tender skin under his arms as he was hauled to his feet and his bones popped from the force. A cloth was thrust into his mouth and a hood was shoved over his head, his arms were wrenched behind his back and his wrists shackled.

Vasili felt many hands upon his body as he was dragged along the ground. Someone smacked the back of his head with an open palm; the blow forcing his head forward with a snap.

He groaned as a sharp pain reverberated down his spine and lodged in his lower back. He tried to speak, mumbling incoherently. When that didn't work he tried to communicate telepathically, but he was in between worlds, in another dimension – not a planet, but a bubble within time and space. A place of neutrality where abilities were rendered useless. Each person only as strong as their physical body. Vasili was powerless and in the hands of Aurylian guards. He wasn't expected, and they knew it, hence the harsh treatment. He was pushed, prodded and dragged along for a short while. They stopped a moment as the guards spoke to someone and then they were off again. A door opened, they passed through, and there was more talking before the door closed. Vasili didn't hear much, his ears still ringing from the smack he'd received to the back of his skull. The guards slapped him a few more times after the hood was pulled over his head. His hearing was returning by the time they arrived at their intended destination.

There was a jingle of keys and the clunk of a key turning in a lock. Vasili heard the screech of another door opening and banging against a wall before he was airborne. He hit the floor with a crunch, his shoulder dislocating as he struck the hard surface, a muffled scream caught in his throat as a choking coughing fit overpowered him.

"The Zoldarni do not tolerate disobedience, Vasili. You come to Cwonoth by invitation only!"

Malachi rested against a tree with his booted heels crossed and his arms folded over his chest. He didn't baulk or hide when Vasili glanced his way, Vasili couldn't see him, not in his invisible state.

Malachi smiled and licked the tips of his fangs. His smile widened further when he sensed Vasili's apprehension. He'd waited at the Zoldarni gateway all week expecting Vasili to show. He'd known it would only be a matter of time before the leader of the Shadow Seekers appeared. Zobiana's activities on Earth wouldn't go unnoticed for long. He was surprised Vasili hadn't requested a meeting with the Zoldarni first though. Such blatant disrespect of the Zoldarni laws was unheard of. No one broke the chain of command and went through the gateway without an invitation. Malachi was certain Vasili hadn't an invitation because the Zoldarni guards were known for waiting at Earth's gateway for the person afforded a scheduled meeting.

The moment Vasili retrieved the gateway key from his jacket pocket, Malachi uncrossed his feet and leaned forward, placing his hands on his knees. He wouldn't miss the opportunity again, never again. This time he'd have the distraction he needed. The Aurylian guards would be focused on Vasili when he arrived through the gateway, enabling Malachi to go through unnoticed. He was taking an enormous risk by going through the gateway in his invisible state, His powers could be rendered useless, but he trusted his ability – he'd honed his powers for centuries.

Masquerading as someone else indefinitely wasn't easy, yet he'd achieved it without difficulty. Taking Augustus's form had acquired immeasurable power, and accomplishing such an undertaking was unheard of. Not many had perfected the art of transmogrification. As far as Malachi knew, he was the only one capable of withstanding the pressures and damage shape-shifting bore on the body for years on end. It took enormous amounts of energy to maintain an unnatural state of being. Malachi believed it was because of his royal pedigree and genetics.

The gem in the gateway key sparkled in the last rays of light as the sun descended on the horizon. Malachi licked his lips in anticipation and angled farther forward as if he were on the starting line of a foot race, waiting for the echoing crack of the starter gun. The moment the gateway key was placed into position and the central gem pushed, Malachi took off running towards the gateway. He knew it would be difficult to get to the gateway because time slowed just before the gateway opened. Malachi felt the pressure building around his body as time froze, halting his forward momentum. He had a moment of fear before his vampire speed kicked in and his body gathered velocity. A vortex formed at the gateway opening. He gritted his teeth, fighting against the winds preventing him from getting to his goal. There was an ear-splitting bang. The wind changed direction and sucked everything into the spiralling whirlwind at the gateway's epicentre. Malachi watched Vasili lift into the air and there was a brilliant flash of light before he was sucked into the maelstrom and disappeared. If Malachi didn't hurry, the gateway would close before he got there.

He raced up the stairs and leaped off the top step, diving for the gateway opening. He felt the sucking force take hold of his body as it wrenched him through the gateway. There was a high-pitched whistling behind him as the gateway closed. Malachi sighed as he was jettisoned through the wormhole to Cwonoth.

White electrical currents spiked about his body, disrupting his focus. He closed his eyes, trying to find a calm place, and concentrated on keeping invisible while in the wormhole. When he'd attained focus again, he opened his eyes and saw Vasili ahead of him. There was another flash of light and Vasili disappeared from sight. Malachi focused on the gateway exit preparing for the unexpected. There was another flash of light as he too passed through the opening. He hoped the Aurylian guards wouldn't notice. He landed behind Vasili to the far right of his position, near his walking stick. Luckily the guards were nowhere near Malachi. He checked his hand – his invisibility had held. All his research regarding the Zoldarni and their world had been correct. He exhaled in relief and watched as four guards hauled Vasili away. Malachi chuckled, but quickly covered his mouth with his hand, trying to stifle the sound.

One of the Aurylian guards looked back towards Malachi, his eyes narrowed as he eyeballed the space where he sat. Malachi held his breath. The guard left Vasili's side and came to a stop just in front of Malachi, looking towards the gateway.

"Ecktar, what are you doing? Let's go."

"I thought I heard something," Ecktar replied.

"There's nothing there, come on."

Ecktar nodded and moved back towards Vasili and the other guards.

Malachi watched them drag Vasili away in silence. When there were about twenty metres between him and the guards, he stood and picked up Vasili's shillelagh. It disappeared the moment he touched it. He smiled again and followed the guards – they were his only way into the fortress.

CHAPTER 12

"What the bloody hell?" Makayla gasped.

"Don't tell me that's Alexander?"

Makayla glanced sideways at Darrius. "Okay, I won't tell you." She looked back towards the rubbish-congested street. Alexander wove a trail through building debris, garbage and rusted, burned-out vehicles without a care in the world. The blue hospital gown he wore left nothing to the imagination as it flapped in the wind, revealing his bare arse. He walked with purpose, on a set path towards something – to what, Makayla hadn't a clue. His posture was straight, his head held high, his shoulders back and unyielding; he commanded attention.

"This whole scene would be funny if things weren't so screwed up," Darrius said, pointing to Alexander's left. Newbloods crept alongside him, they didn't attack or try to overpower him, they simply watched him pass. Makayla's fangs lengthened and her wings jettisoned out of her back in a flash of sparkling light. She unfurled them and was about to jump off the building when Darrius grabbed her arm and shook his head. "Wait, let's just watch; he's not in danger, the Newbloods don't seem to want to harm him. Let it play out, I'm curious."

"But—"

Darrius released her arm and held a forefinger to his mouth before shaking his head. "Shhh. Look, Makayla, just stop and look." Darrius glanced down towards the street again. "We may learn something. Aren't you a little curious? I know I am."

"You know what they say about curiosity, right? It killed the cat."

Darrius raised an eyebrow. "Are you really going to resort to using tired old clichés?"

"Damn straight I am!" Makayla swept a hand through her hair and groaned, but conceded. She pleated her wings behind her and crossed her arms over her chest, her foot tapping erratically. "If anything happens to him, Darrius, I'll be playing ping-pong with your balls!"

"You're nasty." Darrius grimaced and covered his crotch with his hands. "Just watch." Darrius pointed at the street. "Look at them, look how they bow down. It's as if they're worshipping a god."

Darrius was right, it wasn't one or two Newbloods, there was a horde. They lined the road, and no longer hid within the gloomy shadows, but gathered in great numbers – something

Newbloods never did unless Zobiana was around. As the sun descended further on the horizon more Newbloods filtered out from alleyways and dim buildings. They worshipped Alexander, bowing their heads in reverence as he passed. Some were even on their knees with their hands clasped together in prayer while others trailed behind him, following him like faithful disciples. Alexander seemed oblivious, barely registering their presence.

"Do you know what Zobiana did to him?" Darrius asked.

"I haven't a clue, all I know is the bitch tortured him. We didn't get much of a chance to talk before he lost consciousness."

"I see. That's too bad."

"I've had enough, Darrius, let's follow him now, maybe we'll find out what the hell's wrong with him."

"Okay," Darrius replied.

Makayla gazed towards Salomae. *"Wake up, Salomae, Alexander needs us."*

Makayla looked at Darrius as two huge black wings flashed from his back; he stretched, twisted and fluttered his feathers. Their blue-black colour glistened like shot silk as he flapped them. Cool air whooshed into her face as he lifted into the air. Her brother had finesse, more than she did. She dived off the five-storey building and plummeted towards the ground like a skydiver. Just as she was about to hit the ground, she extended her wings and the updraft snapped her up like a parachute. She looked back over her shoulder and saw Salomae lift off the building, her giant wings masking the rooftop. Makayla slowed as she caught up with Alexander and hovered fifty metres above him. She didn't want to distract him from his path, not that she believed he would be by the blank expression on his face. His expression was similar to the one he'd worn before she'd saved him from the dungeons. It was as if he was no longer present in his body. Darrius pulled alongside her and they followed until the sun disappeared and night bloomed.

"Where do you think he's heading?" Darrius asked telepathically.

Makayla gritted her teeth, her hands scrunching into fists, the anger beginning to consume her. Worry curled around her heart.

"Makayla?"

"Fucked if I know, Darrius," Makayla hissed, biting down on her bottom lip and drawing blood. The coppery, metallic liquid pooled in her mouth, she swallowed it down, sucking on her lip to satisfy the growing hunger in her stomach. Even though it was her own blood, it still soothed her shattered nerves.

Makayla saw Alexander stop and look down at a cast-iron manhole cover that was brown with age. He squatted by it and plunged his fingers into the decorative holes of the old lid then lifted it out of position. He didn't grunt or sweat with exertion, but tossed it over his shoulder casually as if it weighed no less than a ball. Several Newbloods cried out as the solid disc bowled them over. Makayla smiled, at least he didn't give a shit about the Newbloods. Alexander straightened to his full height and jumped down into the hole. Hundreds of Newbloods crowded around the opening, pushing and shoving one another as they fought over who would be next to follow. Makayla smiled again, she couldn't let the opportunity pass by without dispensing some of Zobiana's army. She dematerialised midair and reappeared on the outer edge of the vampire horde, pleating her wings behind her just as Darrius appeared beside her. She looked at him, a wicked smile creasing her face and she wiggled her eyebrows.

"This will be interesting," she said, rolling her shoulders and angling her head from side to side to loosen the kinks from her body, before shaking her arms and cracking her knuckles.

"Hmm, I don't know about being interesting, but it may be entertaining," Darrius replied. "What do you have in mind?"

"Oh, I'm in the mood for barbecued fledglings, what about you?" Makayla chuckled when the grin disappeared from Darrius's face.

"That's no fun at all. Can't we play a little?"

"We don't have the luxury of time; if we don't follow Alexander now we risk losing him in the tunnels."

"You're a bloody killjoy, Makayla."

"I know, little brother, but aren't all sisters?" Makayla chuckled again and looked back towards the horde of Newbloods. "Hey, Newblood scum, mind getting out of the way?" Makayla hollered. No one turned.

"I said HEY, get out of my way."

Newbloods turned towards her voice. "Who are you calling scum, Princess?" growled a beefy Newblood with a yellow-tipped bright green Mohawk and a handlebar moustache.

"Ain't he a piece of work?" Darrius mumbled. "I wouldn't call her princess if I were you, not if you want to live to talk about it."

"I'll call her whatever I like, pretty boy."

"Hear that? He thinks I'm pretty." Darrius elbowed Makayla.

"Yeah, I heard, you are pretty, compared to him." Makayla winked.

There was a murmuring in the crowd as more Newbloods turned towards them. They hissed and yelled abuse at Makayla. The Newblood with the green Mohawk walked towards them smacking his clenched fist in the palm of his hand.

"Take a look at Mr Green Lantern, he's so scary."

"The only thing scary about him is the colour of his hair and let's not forget the matching moustache."

"Hmm, what about the T-shirt he's sporting?"

"Hey, don't diss Batista, he rocks." Makayla glanced sideways at Darrius and then back at the horde of Newbloods. "We don't have time for this bullshit. Salomae, light these fuckers up," Makayla yelled.

Salomae swooped down and a gust of air rained over them, disturbing the litter and rubble covering the roadway as she landed behind them. The ground trembled as she set down. They could hear a loud ripping and cracking sound as she stomped her feet. Makayla could have fought the Newbloods off, even thrown a few fireballs, but the look on her adversaries' faces when they saw Salomae was priceless. The Mohawk Newblood stopped his fist slapping, his jaw dropped and his shoulders slumped as if he were withering in on himself. He stared up at the dragon standing metres behind them and backpedalled with the rest of the Newbloods.

Salomae snorted, exhaling warm air as a low growl rumbled in the back of her throat. She swung her tail, and it connected with the broken remains of a shop front. The sound of shattering glass and the clatter of brick walls crumbling and toppling in an avalanche of glass, mortar and stone resonated with an eerie quality. She swung her tail again, and it connected with the rusted shell of a black cab and jettisoned it into the air. There was a piercing scream and the metallic crunch of twisted metal as it landed on some Newbloods in front of them.

Transparent blue shields lit up about Makayla and Darrius as they chased after the Newbloods heading towards the manhole. Salomae stomped her feet, drool dripping as her mouth snapped open and closed. Smoke plumes spiralled from her nostrils as she let loose a wall of dragonfire. Fire blasted past Makayla and Darrius, bouncing off their shields as they ran into the throng of screaming vampires. Makayla clenched her jaw; she couldn't think of a more horrifying way to die. She gulped, trying to shut out the pain masking the fledgling vampire faces, but she couldn't shut out the sound of their sizzling skin. She cringed as the skin peeled off their burning bodies and turned to ash. The sickening odour of scorched flesh assaulted them as they reached the manhole.

Makayla looked about, smoke and the curling remnants of burned litter floated in the air, the edges forged in smouldering orange. There was nothing left of the Newbloods but ash. Black soot covered the street and the remains of burned vehicles. The wind tossed cinders about, spinning them on the ground in twisting wind funnels as if the breeze were playing with the remains.

"After you," Darrius said, extending his hand in the direction of the manhole.

Makayla looked at Darrius before looking back towards Salomae. She watched as the Terrin flapped her wings and lifted into the air. A clear patch of ground appeared as gusts of wind fanned down over the street. The darkness didn't hinder Makayla's vision, yet she rubbed her eyes from the stinging smoke drifting into the night in apathetic plumes. She scanned the outlying buildings for Newbloods; there were none about. All she could see were heatwaves radiating off burned automobile skeletons and warping the air as buffeting ash suffocated crackling spot fires.

"Makayla, we should go."

"Yeah, okay." Makayla nodded, her wings disappeared into her back as she jumped through the manhole, Darrius followed.

CHAPTER 13.

Zobiana watched Kraegan lower his hood; he hadn't changed, not that she'd expected him to. Dark wavy hair hung in his equally dark eyes. Zobiana licked her lips as she considered his mouth and angular, stubbled jaw. His lips curled upward as a smile arced across his face. He was still as handsome as ever. The last time she'd seen him alive he'd been standing on the fringe of a crowd, watching the proceedings of her murder trial. Far too long in her books. The only other time she'd seen him after that was centuries later, on the day of his death.

She'd got off lightly, so they'd said. She considered exile from Evron a harsh punishment – harsher than when she'd left the Garden of Eden. Although for a time she'd found unlikely happiness in the arms of the guard they'd sent back with her to Earth. They'd hated each other for millennia, until hate had turned to love. Zobiana shook her head and shut down any thoughts of love. Love always ended in death where she was concerned. That was why she and Kraegan fit so well together; they understood one another and had shared a connection long before she'd been exiled. Zobiana had spent the better half of her long life trying to figure out a way to return to Evron; it appeared to be within her grasp now the Dark One could no longer dominate her.

"It would seem you still have a penchant for theatrics, Zobiana."

Zobiana chuckled. "I've missed you, Kraegan, why have you stayed away so long?"

"Why indeed?" Kraegan crossed his arms and leaned against the wall. "You know why, my lady, I'm supposed to be dead, remember?"

"How she got the better of you still mystifies me to this day."

"You're not alone in that opinion; it mystifies everyone, me included."

"Where have you been all this time? I've searched for you over the centuries."

"You sound like you care, Zobiana."

"I'm no longer bound to the Dark One."

Kraegan's eyebrow arched. "Impossible, you're bound to him for eternity, there's no escaping a life sentence with the Dark One."

Zobiana's cheeks warmed as she smiled again. "There is

when he possesses a person so powerful it renders him weak."

"No such being exists," he said in a sardonic tone.

"There is one, newly created."

Kraegan stepped away from the wall and stopped in front of Zobiana.

She looked up into his tense features and noticed his jaw clench, she licked her lips again, itching to touch. The repercussions of such an action would make her appear weak. Zobiana angled her head and glanced up at him through her eyelashes and bit the corner of her lip. She'd got away with touching him earlier because of Tyrone's presence, but Kraegan wouldn't tolerate her touch a second time, not unless he made the first move. The muscles flexed along his jawbone as he gritted his teeth, the tension creasing his forehead and furrowing his eyebrows as he glared at her.

"You jest."

"I never jest." Zobiana lifted her hand and Kraegan caught it, crushing her fingertips in his grasp.

"How?" he demanded, his grip tightening.

Zobiana's shoulders stiffened, she refused to make a noise, to let him know he was hurting her. She held her head high. "Don't you mean who?" Zobiana said, as the delicate bones in her hand cracked.

"Who, how, whatever. Just tell me."

Sweat gathered on the back of her neck and trickled down between her shoulder blades. "Are you quite done flexing your muscles, Kraegan?"

Kraegan looked at their joined hands before releasing her. She swallowed down a sigh of relief and wiggled her fingers to straighten the broken bones before they knitted and healed. "Was that necessary? Why do you have to be such an arse? I guess I shouldn't be surprised, you were raised by a Neanderthal." Zobiana pinned him with her lethal red gaze, her eyes shimmering black. "I expect more from you."

Kraegan lifted his arm to backhand Zobiana across the face. She raised an eyebrow and his hand froze in place. "If you think you have power over me, Kraegan, you're sorely mistaken." Zobiana stalked around him, prodding him with her uninjured hand and came to a stop before him. She glared up into his face, a sneer twisting her features as her fangs lengthened. "Who do you think you're dealing with, one of your whores? I tolerated abuse from the Dark One because I had no choice, but I will not tolerate it from the likes of you! You forget your place. Have you forgotten what I did for you all those years ago?"

"For fuck's sake, woman, just tell me who sired such a being and be done with the charades, I have enough fakery in my life as it is."

Zobiana smiled again. "The one person you could not best, Kraegan. The one who killed you has sired a powerful Druid. A hybrid of unspeakable power."

Kraegan's jaw went slack and dropped; his pallor paled as he lowered his hand and stepped back. He bowed his head and took a knee. "Forgive me for my insolence, Zobiana, I meant no disrespect."

Zobiana's smile broadened, she placed a palm on his head, twining her fingertips into his thick, lustrous hair. She grabbed a handful and yanked his head back; he looked up into her face with a lost look in his eyes. His Adam's apple bobbed up and down in his throat as he swallowed. Zobiana's eyes narrowed in on his bulging jugular.

"Tell me where your father is; tell me what he's planning."

"I do not know, my lady."

"How can you not know his whereabouts or his plans? You're his right-hand man."

"I haven't heard from him in over a week and my father never tells me his plans until the moment is upon us."

"Hmm, curious. He trusts no one, not even his own offspring. If you won't tell me where your father is, your blood will." Zobiana dropped to her knees and lunged, driving her fangs into Kraegan's neck. His skin popped deliciously around her teeth as she latched onto his jugular. Blood gushed into her mouth as she siphoned the knowledge from him. He was telling her the truth. Zobiana's eyes flew open in surprise. She'd almost forgotten what the truth sounded like when someone was honest with her.

An erotic groan vibrated out of his mouth as she continued feeding from his throat. The frenzy for information abated and turned into desire – greedy, hot, yearning desire. She was enveloped in Kraegan's lust, a lust she'd almost forgotten at the hands of the Dark One's twisted perverseness.

Zobiana sensed Kraegan's intent to feed from her. *"Before I allow you to feed from me, Kraegan, I have something more to ask of you. A task I entrust only to you,"* she spoke into his mind, savouring the flow of blood into her mouth as she fed from his vein.

"Anything, I'm yours to command," he responded, eyeing her throat.

"When the time is right, I will call upon you to undertake this task without question, do I have your word of honour, your oath you will do whatever I ask of you?"

"Yes, I swear on my life, the life you re-gifted me. I'm your man, I always have been."

"Good. You may feed, my love." Zobiana smiled against his throat, everything was falling into place.

She felt Kraegan's fangs pierce her throat as he latched onto her neck to feed. In all the millennia, Kraegan was the only person she'd ever allowed to feed directly from her. Over the long, drawn-out years she'd sired vampires, but had never allowed her fledglings to feed from her; she preferred them to drink her blood from drinking vessels. With Kraegan she'd made an exception; after all, she was the one who'd brought him back to life after he'd been killed by the Chosen One.

The mechanical *clackety clack* and whir of suspended rectrabeds circling above on laundromat-style conveyor belts was deafening. The grim warehouse was as welcoming as a graveyard and its silent occupants were nothing more than ghosts of their former selves. Zack looked towards the office doorway where Nikolai stood leaning up against a wall watching for guards. Anna, Reece and Jackson were in various parts of the facility also keeping watch. They'd been conducting surveillance of the farm for nigh on two weeks, gauging the level of activity and the comings and goings of the guards. The reason they'd chosen the facility was because of its size, it was the smallest of all the facilities they'd identified with the least security.

"Are you nearly done, Zack? We've already wasted fifteen minutes here," Nikolai said, checking his timepiece for the hundredth time.

Zack looked up from the computer he was trying to hack. "Hey, they have some major firewalls in place, I need time to crack the codes; it's not just simple mathematics you know."

"We don't have time," Nikolai whispered. "The guards' shift will end soon, and then we'll be in a right, fine pickle."

"It would help if I knew what I was looking for," Zack said, glancing back at the computer monitor, the glow of the screen highlighting the dips and hollows of his face.

"I told you what to look for; we need the codes to shut down the rectrabeds without harming the people housed within them. If we don't disable the lethal injections before we try to free everyone imprisoned here, every single person in this farm and every other farm, will die." Nikolai rubbed his eyes, his features creased with fatigue as he glanced over his shoulder at Zack.

Nikolai hadn't slept properly since Makayla's disappearance, neither had Zack for that matter. They'd shared many late nights mapping farm locations across the UK and discussing ways to shut them down without harming the human captives. All of which, so far, had amounted to nothing. There was no solution, yet.

Zack had tried to access the farms' computers from his computer back at the compound, but all to no avail – the farms were set up on their own server, with additional protection from superior Off Worlder technology. Now they were on site, though, he had access to their computers.

"*Yes*," Zack smiled, rubbing his hands together. "I cracked it, finally."

"Well hurry up and locate the codes."

Zack searched the files as quickly as possible, nothing stood out to him and he sighed. This was their first attempt at obtaining the codes and no matter what he searched for he kept coming up empty. There was nothing on the computer that indicated a way to disable the lethal dose of cyanide. He feared they were looking in the wrong place.

"This isn't going to work, Nikolai, it's bogus."

"What do you mean it's bogus?" Nikolai scrutinised Zack's face in frustration, his forehead creasing and his mouth becoming a hard line. "There has to be something, tell me you have something?"

Zack scanned the data on the screen and shook his head. "Nope, there's nothing. From what I'm seeing here it appears all the farms' computers are controlled by one mainframe operating system, and I'm guessing it controls the entire farming operation, the rectrabeds, the conveyor belt system, and blood retrieval, everything."

"What do you mean?"

"It means there is one big computer somewhere, in control of all the rectrabed systems of all the farms." Zack scratched his head. "There might be a way to override and infiltrate the system from this computer, but it's a long shot."

"Well, try it, and try it fast." Nikolai looked at his timepiece again. "You have five minutes. After that we've got to get the hell out of here."

"Okay." Zack laced his fingers together and cracked his knuckles. "Here goes nothing. Prepare to run just in case this backfires." Zack looked at the computer screen and lowered his hands to the keyboard. His fingertips struck the keys in a frenzy until he finally stopped typing and looked up at Nikolai. All he had to do now was press the enter key. "Are you ready?"

Nikolai nodded. "Just let me warn the others."

Zack waited for Nikolai to communicate telepathically with the rest of their group.

"Okay, they're ready."

Zack lifted his forefinger in the air and slammed it down on the enter key. The computer screen went black momentarily and then spewed out data, code filling the screen like something from *The Matrix*, and then stopping. The cursor blinked twice before the screen turned red. A skull and crossbones began flashing on the screen as ear-piercing warning bells began to sound out.

"Shit." Zack stood up in a rush, kicking the chair out from beneath him and covering his ears as he dashed towards Nikolai by the door. The alarm was so loud Zack wouldn't have been surprised if it woke up the catatonic people in the rectrabeds. Jackson, Reece and Anna came to a sliding halt by the door, crashing into each other.

"What the bloody hell did you do, Zack?" Jackson asked, looking over his shoulder.

"Shit, we've got to get the hell out of here, before they catch up with us," Reece said, pointing back the way they'd come and grabbing Anna's hand. "And now."

There was the sound of running feet as guards came around the corner after them. A bullet struck the top of the door frame just as Reece huddled everyone together and teleported them out.

CHAPTER 14

Methane gas was a stench Makayla could do without. She didn't like her chances of tolerating it for long, not without throwing up the contents of her stomach, which would no doubt eventuate the longer they were underground. She held her breath and tilted her head back to stare about. The two hundred-year-old dank, bricked sewer tunnel she and Darrius found themselves in was in surprisingly good condition for its age. It was three metres wide and arched four metres over their heads and connected to a network of other tunnels leading out into various parts of the city.

The persistent dripping and sloshing of stagnant water hitting the slime-coated walls as they waded through the frothing liquid heightened the putrid stench of ammonia and faecal matter. Makayla exhaled and gulped in her next breath and almost choked. She shivered and held her breath as she attempted to settle her roiling stomach.

She sensed Alexander further ahead, but had yet to see him in the flesh. Darrius waded through the murky water two metres in front of her; she watched the cold water ripple around his legs and form small waves as he continued forward. The water was getting deeper as they headed further in. When they'd first jumped through the manhole and landed with a splash, it was ankle-deep, now it was just below their knees and rising steadily. There were no walkways in the section of tunnel they progressed along so they had to grin and bear the freezing muck.

Darrius looked over his shoulder and shook his head at her obvious disgust, a smile tickling the corners of his mouth. "Would you hurry up, we're going to lose Alexander if you don't stop acting like a sissy girl."

"Sissy girl, you're kidding me, look at it, it's following me like a lost puppy," she said, pointing at a brown object floating near her.

Darrius's grin widened. "Talk about close encounters of the turd kind." He sighed as she continued her complaints. "Sorry, I don't have any air freshener available to ease your discomfort, would you just get over it already? It doesn't smell that bad." Darrius lifted the wooden torch he'd found when they'd entered the sewers, the flame wavering with the movement.

Makayla's eyebrow arched. "Not that bad, are you serious,

I haven't smelled anything this bad in centuries." She crinkled her nose. "I'm surprised we haven't blown ourselves to kingdom come with the flame of that torch you're holding. And tell me, why don't we ever use battery operated torches? We're not living in the dark ages for crying out loud."

"Says the one who still uses swords. And it would be impossible to blow ourselves up with all the gas vent pipes removing the methane gas build up down here. Fear not, we're quite safe." Darrius smirked when he noticed Makayla's glazed expression.

Makayla snapped her mouth shut and grimaced as she swallowed. "I don't give a shit, Darrius, if I wanted to know the workings of the sewers I would have asked. I can taste the stench of this place on my tongue, and tell me, how the hell am I going to get rid of this stink from my clothes? I'll have to burn them."

Darrius placed his free hand on his hip and faced Makayla. "Are you done bitching? You never whinge, what the bloody hell has got into you? You're acting like a spoiled little rich girl who just cracked a fingernail." Darrius angled his head and studied her. "You're awfully hormonal, Makayla, are you okay?"

"WHAT? Did you just call me hormonal? What the fuck, Darrius, never call a woman hormonal, NEVER! Not if you want to live to see a new day!"

"He's right, you seem out of sorts, Makayla dear, what ails you? As if I didn't know," her nemesis goaded, chuckling.

"What would you know?" Makayla defended herself, knowing full well her nemesis and Darrius were right about her unusual behaviour, something wasn't right. She never bitched about trivial things.

"I know more than you do. Stop deluding yourself, dear, surely you sense it? You're awfully moody of late, it's as if you're going through puberty all over again." Her nemesis's laughter echoed in her head.

"Piss off!" Makayla shook her head, trying to shake free of her nemesis's words. She looked Darrius in the eyes. "I'm fucked if I know what's wrong with me. I've been feeling weird ever since I got back from the past. One minute I'm laughing the next I'm crying and then I'm as angry as a viper with no fangs. I don't even give a shit about this sort of stuff usually, especially my clothes. My sense of smell is sensitive and seems to be overactive. It's not like I haven't been down in the sewers before. The smell never irritated me like this. I feel like I'm going to empty the contents of my stomach at any given minute. And I'm hungrier than usual, I mean, I've always had a healthy appetite, but it's getting ridiculous. I feed and I'm hungry ten minutes later. I usually feed once a week, what's worse, nothing satisfies me these days, nothing, but Alexander's blood, and I drank the last five bags we had in stock yesterday. I'm screwed because Alexander isn't in any state to give me blood, I can't risk weakening him."

"Maybe you should get Ava to run some tests; you may have an infection or something."

"Ha ha, that's funny, Darrius, I never get sick. Look, don't worry about me, I'll be fine, it's probably just a reaction to time travelling." She shrugged. "We're wasting time, let's go find Alexander before he disappears altogether."

"You're the one holding us up, Makayla. Just saying."

Makayla gave a derisive laugh as she waded past Darrius. "Ever the comedian, aren't you? Close encounters of a turd kind, where d'you dig that one up from? As if I didn't know. I'm going to have a harsh word with Reece. Come on, Captain Ridiculous, before we lose ourselves in this floating turd pile."

They journeyed through twisting tunnels until they came to a junction with four different routes. Makayla closed her eyes, lifted her head and reached out to Alexander with her mind. She was met with an impenetrable mental block, but instinctively knew it was him because it was the same darkness she'd encountered when she'd saved him from Zobiana's dungeons. Something was terribly wrong with him.

"He's this way," she said, pointing towards a tunnel on their right. Darrius nodded and followed her lead. Makayla trusted her intuition and the blood-bond connection she had with Alexander to navigate the winding passageways, but had to wonder what they'd find when they finally located him.

They continued to travel deeper into the sewers until they came upon a one metre barrier preventing the sewer water from cascading down a stairwell that led deeper underground.

Makayla glanced towards her brother, frowning in puzzlement. "What is this?"

Darrius shrugged. "I have no idea. Have you noticed the smell isn't as bad as it was when we first entered the sewers?"

"Yeah, I have actually, and the water is a great deal clearer now too. I have a really bad feeling about this, Darrius. I mean, look at this place; the walls are ancient compared to the rest of the tunnels we've passed through, it's like something from the Roman era. Don't you think?"

"It's a lot older than a mere two hundred years, that's for sure," Darrius said, dragging his hand through his mussed hair. "I know London was built over ancient Roman ruins." He shuffled closer to the stairs and held the torch out to see further into the depths of the stairwell. "But stairs in a sewer, that makes no sense."

"Could this be a relic from the past? It has to be at least two thousand years old."

"Definitely, but why is it here? Do you sense Alexander down there?"

Makayla nodded. "That's the thing, I do, but he's also not quite himself either, it's strange. There's something else down there with him too, I don't know what, but whatever it is, it's pure evil."

"Beware; darkness lurks in the deepest depths," her nemesis whispered.

Makayla shivered, she knew her nemesis's prophetic words to be true because she sensed the darkness herself. *"What darkness do you speak of?"* she questioned her tormenter turned protector.

"Beware, he lurks, waiting to be released. BEWARE!"

Her nemesis's words of premonition and disaster wouldn't go unheeded. Makayla glanced down the stairs again and shivered. Goose bumps crawled along her spine prickling her skin. She unsheathed her seraph swords, consternation warring with her need to flee and her need to find Alexander.

"Shall we?" Darrius asked.

Makayla looked at her brother and nodded. She cleared her throat and stepped over the barrier holding back the water, then stood on the top step for a few minutes staring down into the twisting gloom. Trepidation swallowed her resolve. She remembered many other stairways where she'd reacted the same way. She always felt the same impending doom. This stairway was different, though, it wasn't just impending doom she felt so much, but an innate knowledge of what lay ahead. What lay beyond the stairs would change everything. Whatever it turned out to be she knew it would be cataclysmic and the catalyst for all the unfolding events. This pivotal point in time would determine how things played out in the end. It would be a world-destroyer. She felt it, knew it, within the deepest, darkest part of herself. The end of days was upon them.

Makayla stared at her feet; moisture gathered where the wall and stairs merged, bleeding out and framing the edges with a dark, wet layer of mud and moss. She inhaled deeply, no longer smelling the sewer but the heady damp, musky scent of closed underground spaces similar to cave dwellings. She shivered as the cold stroked her skin with icy fingertips, a frosty harbinger of death; a rigor-mortis for the senses rather than the body. It unsettled her more than she cared to admit.

"Makayla, why do you delay? Are you okay?"

"Uh-huh." She rolled her shoulders and lifted her seraph swords before descending the ancient stairs. Makayla heard the ring of steel echo in the closed space as Darrius unsheathed his own sword. Light from the billowing torch flame he held rippled on the walls beside them, it flared briefly before hissing and sputtering out. Makayla shivered again and recited an incantation. Her swords began to glow with incandescent blue seraph light, illuminating the stairs. Makayla watched Darrius set the extinguished torch in a wall sconce.

He grasped her shoulder and squeezed, nodding with encouragement. "Come, sister-mine, let's find your man."

Makayla's back stiffened at her brother's firm grip; she glanced about the gloomy underground surroundings. Were the walls closing in on her? She shook her head and gasped in a deep breath, swallowing down the rising panic simmering just below the surface and tasting the stale air on her tongue. She licked her lips and grimaced, *you're so pathetic*, she chided herself. Why couldn't she recover from the time she'd spent rotting in a dungeon? She was a warrior for goodness sake. What was she missing? Why couldn't she let it go?

Makayla's step faltered when she heard the unmistakable voice of her nemesis again. She tried to ignore her, but there was only so much pretending she could do before Darrius became even more suspicious of her weird behaviour. Their sibling bond grew stronger with every passing minute they spent together; he was quite attuned to her mood swings.

"A warrior does not let fear control them, Makayla. Your time in the dungeon brought us together. You may think of me as your nemesis, but I am more, much more, and before the end is realised, you will understand just how much strength you gain by my presence. I am not a curse. I was a gift to you from one who is cursed. You're a being of light and dark – seraph and vampire. Your dual nature makes you whole. Darkness will always surround you; it has for millennia and will continue to for millennia. You must embrace it, and overcome your fear, harness it, because darkness is the only way you will defeat the Dark One. The Dark One is always watching, always waiting. When you face him, and you will, do not show fear or he will conquer you. You must draw from the strength growing within you, 'tis what amplifies your power. Heed my words: to defeat the Dark One you must kill him first – you must give up that which you love most."

"Who must I give up, and who must I kill first?"

Her nemesis was silent.

"Tell me!"

No response.

What did it mean? Her nemesis had never spoken to her with such prophetic depth, never with guidance and never at such length. She always had a ready insult at hand, and certainly never spoke with encouragement or caring. Just who was her nemesis? Makayla had always believed her nemesis to be a figment of her imagination. Was she haunted by the remnants of an actual person? What was she missing?

Her nemesis was right, though, she had to stop letting fear control her emotions and right now fear wouldn't help her, not when Alexander's life hung in the balance. Tormented thoughts circled in her head as they continued their downward journey. Makayla raised her hand abruptly, halting their movement when she noticed an orange glow illuminating a doorway at the base of the stairs. She lifted a forefinger to her mouth, Darrius nodded in understanding as they crept forward. The orange glow grew brighter as they drew closer to the bottom of the stairs. An ever-expanding tightness swelled within Makayla's chest constricting further with every anticipated step she took. What would they find?

They emerged in a huge rectangular subterranean cavern with an arched ceiling. Darrius and Makayla stood gaping at an ancient temple carved into the back wall, similar to the magnificent temple Al-Khazneh, the Treasury, of Petra in Jordan. Standing some twenty-five metres tall and eighteen metres wide, the structure loomed over them. Corinthian columns lined the left and right sides of the walls all the way down to the temple. Seraph statues topped each of the columns with six huge, gold gilded wings arching over their bowing heads as they prayed. Flaming fire-pits built into the floor, all the way down to the temple, illuminated the room, reflecting and refracting ambient orange light off the golden statues. The temple was totally Roman in appearance.

They advanced further into the rectangular room, all the while turning about to take in the hidden beauty. The vast space surrounding them absorbed their footsteps and soft gasps as they trod across the cobblestone floor. It was as though they'd stepped three thousand years back in time. The ancient temple was perfectly preserved. The cool temperatures and the cave itself having served as a time capsule.

Four stairs led up from the cobbled floor to a square platform within the temple. The temple itself had two levels, each level with two separate architraves. There were chained statues within the architraves of cruel, screaming demonic entities with twisted features and sharp canines. The demons appeared lifelike as if they'd been turned to stone by the cursed sight of Medusa's glare. The architraves were held up by smooth Corinthian columns, four columns in front and four columns in back on both levels. Two columns were positioned closer together on both left and right sides, leaving an entrance space in the middle that led into the depths of a square stone gazebo-style structure.

On the top level, behind the second architrave, there was a smaller four-column structure with a dome roof. A statue of a muscular, winged, manlike beast squatted atop the dome roof, his bat-like wings outstretched as if he were about to launch himself from the rooftop. His face looked downwards, his eyes taking in his surroundings.

"Nothing disturbing about the statues in this place," Makayla said, looking up at the architraves on the temple before focusing her gaze on one of the angel statues.

"Yeah, nothing out of the ordinary, a lot of temples have these sorts of statues," Darrius said, coming to a stop next to Makayla.

Makayla stared up at the angel statue they'd stopped in front of, its gaze looked away from her, towards the temple itself. In fact, all the statues appeared to be looking towards one singular point. A point hidden in shadow. Makayla squinted, trying to see into the black depths of the inner temple, but even her vampire sight couldn't penetrate the darkness.

"What is it, Makayla?"

"It's just, I mean, it's kind of creepy."

"What's creepy?"

"Have you noticed, every single angel statue is looking towards a point in the temple."

"What's so creepy about that?" Darrius angled his head towards the temple before looking back at Makayla.

"Well, when we came in, all the statues had their heads bowed in prayer, now they're looking towards the temple at a point within those four columns holding up the architrave. Don't you find it a little creepy?"

"Are you sure? Maybe you imagined them praying."

Makayla scowled at her brother. "I'm not blind, Darrius, a bit moody, maybe, but not blind, I didn't imagine it." Makayla glanced back towards the statue she'd been staring at and gasped. The statue's eyes were focused on Makayla now, and glowing orange. The angel no longer clasped her hands in prayer, but pointed towards the temple.

"What's the matter now? Ohhhh…" Darrius stuttered when he noticed the statue staring at Makayla.

The detail spent crafting the statue's face was impressive. The only reason someone would assume the statue wasn't alive was the stark white nature of the marble it was fashioned from. But clearly the statue *was* alive to some degree, judging by its movement.

"It's Baslian," Darrius said in a hushed voice.

"What's Baslian?"

"Baslian is living stone. In all my years I've never encountered such a thing, but I've heard of its existence."

"What do you mean? What's living stone?" Makayla asked.

"Living stone can move, but minimally. It can't walk from place to place, but it can move in place if it calls for it. Baslian is used when great evil needs to be contained. There is no other sacred stone strong enough to imprison immense evil."

"So what you're saying is we've happened upon a prison from ancient times."

"Not necessarily. Yes, this place is old, and without a doubt holy, but what's imprisoned here may only have been here for a short while. There are ancient places like this all over the world, used through the centuries to imprison undesirables."

"Great, that makes me feel all fluffy inside. If I wasn't on edge before, I certainly am now!" Makayla held up her finger. "Hang on a minute, what would cause living stone to move?"

Darrius glanced in the direction the angels were pointing. "They move to warn the living of danger."

"Wonderful," Makayla said, rolling her shoulders and shaking her arms before lifting her swords again.

"Do you sense Alexander?"

Makayla pointed towards the temple with one of her swords. "He's somewhere inside the temple. Come on, let's go, before whatever's imprisoned becomes a problem."

They edged towards the temple, scanning the inner recesses as they climbed each step. The forbidding black depths were enlivened with malevolent swirling tendrils of smoke-like entities. Makayla's hackles rose, her anxiety elevating further as she moved into the obscure shadows. Her ears pricked when she heard muffled chanting – an ancient language she didn't recognise. The shadows thinned as they continued into the depths. A silhouette took form towards the back wall, it was Alexander. His hands were spread wide and planted high above his head; he was the one chanting. His voice sounded different, deeper, darker, more animal than human.

Makayla stopped two metres from him and regarded the wall where his glowing hands rested. There were six circles decreasing in size carved into the wall. Each circle consisted of different hieroglyphic writings. Makayla couldn't make sense of them, but assumed they were dead languages. The writings on the outer circle were lit with shimmering yellow light that pulsed in time with the rise and fall of Alexander's voice. The second row of writing fluctuated with red light. Each circle of writing decreased in size and colour. The colours interchanging in a checker board effect of red and yellow sequences. The circles rotated in anticlockwise and clockwise directions. All yellow writing moved in a clockwise direction and all red writing moved in an anticlockwise direction. The grinding movement of the wall and lights was dizzying. How they hadn't seen the flashing light from outside of the temple mystified Makayla.

The room looked like something out of the twilight zone, as if the circus had arrived in town or an alien spaceship was lifting off. Alexander's voice began to rise to a shout. Wind whipped Makayla's hair about her face; she swept it out of her mouth and looked across at her brother. His face was an unreadable mask.

"Darrius what is this?" she asked him telepathically.

He glanced her way and shrugged. *"I have no idea what we've walked in on, Makayla, but I do know Alexander's speaking Aramaic and Akkadian. If we don't stop him, something awful will happen to all of us,"* Darrius said, looking up at the ceiling and pointing.

Makayla followed the line of his hand, the ceiling was beginning to crack, pebbles and dust sprinkling from the expanding fissures. The floor began to tremble and roll under their feet.

"Xander, what are you doing?" Makayla yelled, raising her hand to shade her eyes from the falling debris. He didn't respond. "Xander, stop!" she screamed, still no response.

Makayla's mouth dropped open when his hands caught fire.

"Do something, Makayla, before he brings this place down on our heads." Darrius resheathed his sword and flung his hands up to form an invisible protective shield above them.

"What the bloody hell do you want me to do, Darrius?" she said, sheathing her swords and placing her hands on her hips.

"I don't know, think of something. Kiss him, he's a man for crying out loud, he'll respond. Hurry up though, 'cause I can't hold the ceiling up forever," Darrius said, the strain evident even in his telepathic voice.

"Yeah, um, I'm not in the mood for kissing right now," Makayla said, moving towards Alexander. His hospital gown disintegrated as the flames circling his hands exploded and enveloped him in a raging fire.

"XANDER, STOP!" Makayla yelled again. He was in a trance. She lifted her hand and touched his shoulder; he was ice-cold even though he was ensconced in an inferno of flames. She leant in close, ignoring the blaze and whispered in his ear. "I love you, Xander, come back, please come back to me, baby."

Alexander stopped chanting, angled his head and glanced her way. His face was expressionless – no recognition for her whatsoever. Makayla gasped when she saw his eyes, they were totally black except for the billowing flames within their depths. Makayla gulped and licked her lips. Maybe Darrius was right. She looked at Alexander's mouth – his lips were chapped but he was still as handsome as ever even with his gaunt face covered in facial hair. She stood on the tips of her toes and leaned in to kiss him on the lips. The prickle of his whiskers tickled her mouth as she touched her lips to his. He didn't respond at first, but began to kiss her back little by little. He stopped kissing her abruptly, removed his hands from the wall, grabbed her by the throat and pushed her up against the side wall, wedging her between his body and the rock. Her teeth chomped from the sudden force and her skull smashed against the temple wall. Darrius made to help her, but she held up her hand and shook her head.

"I'm fine, Darrius, you did say to kiss him, remember."

Makayla looked back at Alexander, his forehead wrinkled as a frown formed on his face and his grip on her throat eased. He lowered his mouth to hers again, grinding his hips against her and trapping her body in place. He pushed his tongue into her mouth, a deep growl reverberating from the back of his throat. Makayla moaned, desire building within her, she missed his touch; even in the state he was in, she still wanted him. The kiss changed and Alexander's grip tightened again. Makayla swallowed down the burning sensation as he lifted her up by the throat. She didn't fight for freedom, but raised her hands and covered his. He swivelled his body and threw her through the air. She landed at Darrius's feet with a thump and a crunch. She whimpered as a sharp pain travelled up her leg and settled in her hip joint with a dull throbbing. She bit her lip and suppressed the pain, tears streamed down her cheeks as she pushed up from the ground. She watched Alexander place his hands back on the wall. He uttered three words and the ancient writings stopped moving and darkness enveloped them. A flash of searing light ignited the room. The wall shimmered and became translucent, Alexander lowered his arms to his sides and stepped through the wall. The wall expanded and shrouded him in a reflective bubble as he passed through the once-solid barrier. It clung to him momentarily, dipping and stretching before releasing and closing behind him as he disappeared into a room beyond the wall.

CHAPTER 15

Icy water smacked Vasili in the face, rousing him with a shuddering jolt.

"Wake up. Overlord Avinash and the voiceless convocation will see you now."

Vasili grimaced as he sat up shivering, his dislocated shoulder throbbing with a bone-grinding ache. It was the second time the guards had come to his cell since his arrival – the first time they'd unshackled his hands so he could eat. Vasili retrieved a handkerchief from his jacket pocket and mopped the dripping liquid from his face before squeezing out the excess water and returning the damp object to his pocket. Vasili hadn't a clue how long they had detained him, he'd been in and out of consciousness since his arrival. Judging by the stiffness in his neck and the ache in his back and shoulder, he'd been incarcerated for some time. He pushed up from the floor using the wall and his uninjured arm for balance, stumbling as he stood. His legs were heavy, numb from inactivity; it was as though he wore leaden boots. The guard seized his injured arm and tugged; Vasili screamed as a sharp pain shot up his limb and settled in his shoulder socket. His dislocated shoulder popped back into position with a hollow *thunk* and the pain subsided leaving a dull throbbing in its wake. He staggered forward and almost fell, but was hauled up by the armpit before he toppled to the ground. It had been millennia since he'd been mistreated in such a manner, but it wasn't unexpected given the circumstance of his arrival on Cwonoth.

Vasili was escorted down a high-ceilinged corridor by an Aurylian guard. Humans thought Aurylia was a hypothetical planet they had made up, but in fact it really existed. Aurylia was an Earth-sized planet that orbited a red dwarf star. Its gravitational orbit locked to the red dwarf star in a similar way to the Earth and its moon. It had a harsh environment, with one side of the planet shrouded in perpetual darkness and the other in scorching daylight frequently plagued with intense ultraviolet radiation solar flares. Like Earth, seventy percent of it was covered in water, but the similarities stopped there. The atmospheric composition of Aurylia was seventy-eight percent Nitrogen, twenty-one percent Oxygen and one percent other.

Most Aurylian cities were underground and under the oceans due to the harsh nature of the planet's environment; extreme cold and extreme heat. Life and vegetation still thrived on the daylight side, though. It wasn't exactly an unliveable atmosphere so much, but the Aurylians considered it safer underground.

All Zoldarni guards were Aurylian and were feared among their peers. They were chosen for this task because they were regimented, incorruptible, respected, and the toughest warriors in all the Multiverse. They had to be tough to survive the unsympathetic nature of their home world. Above all else, they were honourable beings, praiseworthy of the highest order. You couldn't bribe an Aurylian; their word was their bond, and once given they'd die to keep it. They believed in equality for all the planets and beings in the Multiverse, and protected and upheld the laws governing all Off Worlds. God help anyone who went against the Aurylians because they upheld the Zoldarni laws and their edicts with a ferocity that rivalled none. Vasili could be put to death because he'd broken the law by showing up unannounced. There were protocols to be followed even in the most dire of situations.

It was another reason Vasili couldn't believe Zobiana had the audacity to go up against the Zoldarni and carry out the atrocities she'd committed on Earth. Her brazen activities should have had the Zoldarni up in arms, yet they were doing nothing. Did they even know? All things considered, the Zoldarni feared no one and weren't threatened by Zobiana. Why were they ignoring her acts of terror and the annihilation of Earth's people? She was a threat to the Multiverse. She was a threat full stop, and soon she'd have complete control of Earth's gateways, if she didn't already. Whoever controlled the gateways controlled the Multiverse, so, why weren't the Zoldarni doing more?

Vasili glanced sideways at his Aurylian guard as they walked along. He was dressed in the attire all Aurylians wore: a blue-black metallic armour. It was made of Zoydanin – an impenetrable lightweight, flexible metallic ore mined on Aurylia that moulded and moved with the body. The metal was unlike any ore on Earth, or anywhere else in the Multiverse. It was highly sought after, but very hard to mine because it was found on the dark side of the planet. The Aurylians guarded the Zoydanin mines voraciously. It was their main source of income. Vasili sighed and inhaled deeply as he observed his companion.

The Aurylians were tall, slender beings standing eight feet high with delicate scaled, pale purple skin similar to an Earth shark. They had long necks and abnormally long arms that hung well below their hips and reached their knees. Their hands were similarly long with an opposable thumb and three four-jointed fingers that tapered to sharp points. Their bodies were lean and covered in well-defined muscle. Four large bulging eyes sat high on their elongated skulls, surrounded by fine, dark purple veins. Their eyes were silver and intricately patterned and flecked with bronze metallic hues. Their pupils were vertical slits and dilated like snake eyes. They had no outer eyelids. What made their eyes so special were the transparent scales that protected their eyeballs. When they blinked, the transparent scales shuttered closed vertically, preventing their eyes from drying out.

They had severe angular jaws, and a small slash for a mouth with no visible lips. Their noses were flat, X-shaped slits in the middle of their faces that opened and closed when they breathed and looked similar to the blow holes of whales and dolphins when closed. They could also breathe any planet's atmosphere and were adaptable; their noses filtered out the impurities their bodies didn't use, making them ideal warriors. Their hearing was beyond exceptional, but they had no visible ears, just small round cavities on the sides of their heads. Their muscular legs were triple jointed and had two sets of ankles, one lower on the leg and the second about fifty centimetres above the first, making it appear as though their knees bent backwards. Their knees sat higher on their legs and folded down on top of their ankles in a similar manner to an accordion, giving their legs a zigzag appearance.

In a relaxed state Aurylians stood at six feet and walked with their ankles and knees bent close to the ground. When under threat they uncurled and straightened their legs and stood at their full height of eight feet to intimidate their adversaries. They wore no shoes because their meaty three-toed emu-like feet made it impossible. It also gave them an advantage over their adversaries because they were undetectable – their predatory silence when they walked was their greatest asset.

When they arrived, the Aurylian guard released Vasili's arm and nodded at the two armed guards standing either side of a massive dark green double door.

"Ecktar, Overlord Avinash and the silent convocation requested you accompany Lord Constantinos to the meeting." Ecktar nodded and held his arm out for Vasili to precede him.

Vasili straightened his stance as the doors were opened by each of the guards. He visibly gulped and swallowed down any misgivings he felt at his mistreatment, knowing full well his life hung in the balance. The Silent Convocation would have no qualms in ending his life if they saw fit. Would he see his wife again? He hoped so; he'd only just been reunited with her.

Vasili glanced at his escort and noticed him staring back the way they'd just come. He watched the guard's pupils dilate while he scanned the gloomy corridor. The Aurylian frowned, his forehead creasing as he concentrated on a spot where the corridor divided. He glanced back at Vasili.

"YOU . . . Wait here," he commanded gruffly. He unsheathed one of the two swords strapped to his back and stalked towards the corridor junction, glancing around the corner and then back in the opposite direction. He resheathed his sword and scratched his head with a mystified look on his face. He lifted his nose high in the air, sniffing the surroundings. Vasili watched Ecktar's nose crinkle, opening and closing as he surveyed the corridor. Could he smell something – someone hidden? The Aurylian guard returned to Vasili's side.

"If you sense something, Lord Ecktar, trust your instincts. I've lived long enough to know when something doesn't seem right, it usually isn't," Vasili said, looking back towards the empty corridor.

"Humph . . . Let's go, Overlord Avinash doesn't tolerate tardiness." Ecktar extended his arm, indicating the doors for the second time.

"As you wish," Vasili murmured and passed through the entryway. Ecktar looked over his shoulder once more before following him.

Vasili was enveloped in darkness as he was guided into a room with no walls. Technically, it wasn't even a room he was entering; it was just black space. There was no light, no chatter, no smell; there was nothing but the silence of space, because that's where he was − in a lost dimension. A dimension unknown by the confines of physics, it was a place that defied all logic. It was a space that separated him from his loved ones. A space that had no time − he could be trapped there forever and time wouldn't elapse. The Overlord could leave him in there indefinitely, or he could be transported to the outer regions of Cwonoth where the Voiceless Convocation lived and deliberated on Multiverse politics.

The only light visible in the room with no walls was the light coming from the open door behind him. It disappeared the moment Ecktar passed the threshold and the Aurylian guards closed the door.

A circular beam of light appeared twenty metres from their position, like a spotlight on a stage. Vasili and Ecktar made their way towards it; the echoing tap of Vasili's feet breaking the silence as they crossed the floor.

They came to an abrupt halt when they reached the circle of light. Vasili glanced down at the floor and watched the circle expand enough to accommodate them. The beam of light had glowing orbs the size of fireflies floating within it like dust particles floating in a room of sunshine. Vasili passed his hand through the shaft of light and the orbs electrolysed, vibrating like bees. Ecktar encouraged Vasili to step into the beam with the sweep of his arm and a nod of his head. Ecktar followed Vasili the moment he moved into the shaft of light.

The glowing orbs began to move, reacting to their intrusion, pulsating with a heartbeat-like vibration and illuminating and fading repetitively. The flashing vibration gathered momentum. Orbs circled, spinning about their bodies until their feet lifted off the ground and they were buoyant. Vasili glanced towards the ground and noticed the circle of light expand further as if another person had stepped in with them. Ecktar's forehead creased, his eyes narrowing as he scanned the area. Vasili had the weirdest sensation they weren't alone.

Vasili's ears buzzed, he opened his mouth and his eardrums popped. Orbs whizzed about them, his stomach cramped, his skin grew hypersensitive and he became light-headed. He had to close his eyes because watching the dizzying orbs was a nauseating blur. He couldn't breathe as the pressure built and squeezed his body; it was as though he were trapped in the suffocating coils of a python. Vasili opened his eyes again when the buzz in his ears evolved into a high-pitched squeal. He couldn't see the individual orbs now; they were no longer singular entities, but a body of swirling solid light. The squeal intensified, growing louder with each rotation the orbs took. Vasili lifted his hands until they were in line with his eyes. He wiggled his fingertips, mesmerised by the transparency of his hands. He glanced upwards, the beam of light seemed to go on forever; he looked towards his companion. Ecktar watched him, his chin elevated at a slight angle, his gaze contemplative as his eyes roved over Vasili's countenance. The corner of his mouth curled upwards just before everything coalesced and they were shot up through the beam of light. One moment they were in the dark room with no walls and the next they were standing in another dim room surrounded by unusual hovering faces that blurred in and out of focus.

"Ah, Lord Constantinos, I see you have arrived," a rasping voice echoed about them.

"Yes, yes I have," Vasili stammered, looking about for the speaker.

"You realise you are in direct violation of Zoldarni laws by travelling through the Earth's gateway to Cwonoth without an invitation."

"I'm aware of my misdemeanour, Overlord Avinash, and I apologise for the infraction. I would not have breached the Zoldarni mandates had I any other choice. The Earth balances on the edge of Apocalypse. I fear, if the Zoldarni do not intervene, Earth and its people will come to an abrupt end that will affect all the worlds within the Multiverse." Vasili got down on his knees and bowed his head. "I implore you, Lord Avinash, *please*, please forgive my intrusion and grant me an audience."

"If we ignore your blatant disregard of our laws and let you go unpunished, then others may take it upon themselves and ignore our laws and follow suit. The Zoldarni govern all worlds and if we become lax in our duty to maintain Multiverse directives, what does it say about us? It says we're weak and cannot govern the Multiverse. Our position could well be compromised, and others may challenge our leadership."

"I understand, Overlord Avinash, and I'm prepared to take the punishment you administer, but please, I beg you, hear me out first."

Vasili looked up at Ecktar from his position on the floor; he seemed preoccupied, his eyes probing the hidden spaces within the obscure space. What was he searching for? A multitude of nonconforming faces from countless worlds flickered in and out of obscurity. Their voices echoed in Vasili's head as the Voiceless Convocation debated with one another. They spoke telepathically, never aloud; Overlord Avinash was the only one who spoke aloud when called for.

There was silence and Vasili waited for Overlord Avinash's response.

"We will grant you an audience this once, Lord Vasili, but if you violate our laws again, you will be executed on the spot." The Overlord lifted his arm, holding up his index finger. "But, granting you an audience does not go without punishment, you must be reprimanded, we must uphold the laws. We will deliberate your punishment after we've heard what you have to say. Now rise."

Vasili struggled to stand, the ache in his shoulder having become almost unbearable. Ecktar gently grabbed his forearm, aiding him to rise from the floor. The Aurylian's empathy surprised Vasili after his previous rough treatment. He nodded his thanks once he was upright again.

Overlord Avinash appeared out of the darkness three metres from Vasili and Ecktar. He sat upon a throne-like structure and seemed suspended in the air above Vasili's head. He appeared humanoid with some differences. He had an elongated neck, pointy elf-like ears and pastel, lime-coloured skin. Pale grey decorative markings were visible on his forehead comparable to the patterned markings on animal hides. The markings shadowed across his forehead, his cheekbones and down the length of his neck and chest, only hidden by the neckline of the robe he wore. His auburn hair glistened unusually, with an internal phosphorus ambience unlike anything Vasili had ever seen.

"Now, explain why you're here, Lord Vasili. What has happened that would necessitate such drastic measures and force you to break Zoldarni protocols?"

Vasili gulped before answering the question. He spoke of the atrocities Zobiana had committed. What was happening on Earth, the designer drug V5, and how it was turning humans into Newblood vampires. He warned them of the widespread Blakspor epidemic plaguing the world and how the virus not only infected humans but also Off Worlders. He informed the Convocation of how Blakspor-infected humans were being rounded up like cattle by the Newbloods and transported to farms for the harvesting of their blood. He spoke of Malachi's deception and the Trinian Globe. He emphasised that if nothing were done the gateways and access to the Multiverse worlds would come under the control of Zobiana. He told them of Makayla and her prophecy and how it was coming to fruition. More than half an hour passed before he finally finished speaking.

Vasili glanced across at Ecktar, who looked stunned.

"Why are we just hearing of these matters now? Why haven't you approached our Zoldarni emissaries on Earth?"

"I tried contacting your emissaries, Lord Avinash, over six months ago, on many occasions. Your emissaries have yet to respond. 'Tis why I broke protocol and travelled through the gateways to speak with you and the Voiceless Convocation. I suspect my petition for an audience to speak with you was intercepted and your emissaries have been captured, or worse, are already dead," Vasili replied, bowing his head.

"Ecktar, our London ambassadors were to return to Cwonoth last week. Have Idgar, Tahlia, Nyshtar and Ensor returned?"

"No, my lord, we were preparing an Aurylian envoy to travel through the Earth's gateway and determine what was prolonging their arrival."

"I see." There was a murmuring of voices in Vasili's head as the Silent Convocation and the Overlord discussed the events that had led Vasili to disregard Zoldarni law.

"Vasili, under the Zoldarni laws, section thirty-four, paragraph two, citation seven, we'll overlook your infraction this time. In accordance with citation seven you haven't broken Zoldarni law. Due to the nature of your visit, we concur with your reasoning for travelling through the Earth's gateway to Cwonoth. Ecktar, I want you and thirty of your most trusted men ready to travel within the hour. You will accompany Vasili back to Earth and discover what has become of our London emissaries. Contact our other emissaries on Earth and make sure they haven't met with foul play. We need to know if Earth's gateways have been compromised. And Ecktar . . . You have my complete authority to aide Vasili and the Shadow Seekers in any way. The Earth cannot be taken; do what you must to prevent this, by any means necessary."

Ecktar bowed his head. "Yes, Sire, and if the gateways have been compromised and our emissaries harmed, what then?"

"Notify me immediately."

"As you command, Sire."

"You are both dismissed," Overlord Avinash murmured.

"Many thanks, Overlord Avinash," Vasili said, bowing.

Light flared as Vasili and Ecktar departed. Malachi examined his surroundings as the council chambers were temporarily bathed in light. The room was of medium size with high ceilings and a platform structure towards the back of the area. A sizeable black throne-like chair graced the middle of the platform where Overlord Avinash sat. There were no other furnishings in the room other than the huge chair on the stage. Malachi scrutinised the leader of the Zoldarni as he rubbed his forehead and swept a hand through his hair. Malachi had originally wanted to oust the Zoldarni from their governing power over the Multiverse, but he'd realised such an endeavour was foolhardy. He didn't have the manpower to usurp such a great power, so he figured he'd do the next best thing: infiltrate and seize control by impersonating the leader. It had worked many times in the past before, so why not now?

The Zoldarni were a powerful force, why oust them when he could take control of them? Malachi grinned and followed Overlord Avinash as he turned to leave. He would study the Overlord's mannerisms, how he spoke, how he interacted with people, how he ticked. Malachi would learn every conceivable thing there was to know about Lord Avinash, even if it took him years; he had nothing but time on his side. When the time was right, he'd take his place and become the leader of the Zoldarni and the Multiverse. His plans of becoming king of Evron was a thing of the past; Zobiana could have Evron with his blessing. He had set his sights higher.

CHAPTER 16.

The room trembled and pebbles showered from the ceiling as Makayla hurled another fireball at the wall separating her from Alexander. Flames licked the barrier and sputtered out with a sizzling hiss. The room flared with light as she launched four more fireballs and she screamed in frustration when she was met with the same outcome. Makayla rushed towards the wall and hammered her fists against it, trying, but failing, to make a dent.

"You can throw fireballs and strike the wall as much as you like, Makayla, but it won't work, you won't get through."

"We have to get in there, Darrius."

"I know we do, but only the gatekeeper of this vault can pass."

"Alexander can't be the gatekeeper."

"No, he shouldn't have been able to pass through the wall

at all, even if he can read the hieroglyphs. Please don't take this the wrong way, but I don't think it was Alexander who passed through that wall," Darrius said, pointing at the wall. "Whoever it was, was in control of Xander's body. There's something seriously wrong with Xander, Makayla."

"I know, I'm worried about him, Darrius."

"Xander's mind is strong, whatever's controlling him won't be for long. At the moment he's weak from his transition and the time he spent in the dungeons. Once he drinks more of your blood, he'll be his usual self again, he'll be stronger and not so malnourished, you'll see."

"That's the thing, Darrius, how much of my blood does he need to drink? He has already drunk from me twice and he has had blood transfusions." Makayla swiped hair from her eyes. "Do you . . . Do you think he's possessed?"

"It's quite possible. I don't know how Zobiana could have pulled off something like possession. The thing is, no one knows what she's capable of. There is one person you could ask, though."

"Who?"

"Aunt Marianna. Wasn't she there? I mean you did save her along with Augustus and Alexander."

Makayla slapped the side of her head. "You're right, it never occurred to me to ask. I'm an idiot. I'm afraid I may have been a little rude to her. I didn't really acknowledge her when we met in the dungeon, I was too concerned with saving Alexander. She probably thinks I'm ill-mannered."

"I think she'd understand, given the circumstances. You should ask her. She's recuperating at Wigmore Castle with our parents along with Augustus."

Makayla glanced back at the wall she'd hammered with fireballs. "Do you think it's possible though?"

"What?" Darrius asked, focusing on the wall Makayla was staring at. "Alexander being possessed?"

Makayla nodded. "With everything that's happening with Xander at the moment it's the only thing that seems logical. Unless his transition isn't complete. God, what if the vampire he's becoming is this, this entity we're seeing right now? I've never sired anyone before. I mean, we're not even vampires, are we? We're seraphympires, what the bloody hell would he even become?"

"I'm at as much a loss as you, Makayla. The only person I ever came close to changing was my wife, and the only reason I didn't go through with it was because it was against her wishes. She feared losing the babe. Instead, I lost them both."

Makayla looked across at her brother, he was pushing a pebble around on the ground with the toe of his boot. He glanced up when he noticed her watching him.

"I'm sorry for your loss, Darrius. I've never told you because I've never known how to bring it up without hurting you. I can't imagine the loss you must feel, but I'm beginning to understand."

"How do you know about my wife's death?"

"I've been in your head Darrius, I sensed your loss."

"Oh, it is what it is. It's been a little over a thousand years now, the pain isn't as raw, but there will always be an ache in my heart for what could have been. I miss her, mostly at night when I'm alone. You never stop missing them."

Makayla nodded. "There is one thing I'm curious about though."

Darrius slanted his head and smiled. "Didn't I say something about curiosity earlier in the tunnels?"

"Actually, that was me, you said something about using tired old clichés."

Darrius's smile widened. "I stand corrected. So, you were paying attention. What's got you curious?"

"You and Morgan."

"What about us?" Darrius crossed his arms over his chest.

"You know."

"No, I don't."

"Something's going on, I was just wondering what?"

"Nothing's going on, not really. She has problems of her own, Makayla. We talked, nothing more." Darrius shrugged again and looked away. "We need to leave here now. We're not helping Xander by remaining here."

Makayla glanced back towards the wall blocking their way. If Xander was in the other room, she no longer felt his presence. "Okay," she said, nodding again. "Let's go back to the compound, maybe someone will know something about this place." Makayla indicated the underground room with the wave of her hand. "And then I will go speak with Aunt Marianna –

hopefully she won't be too disgruntled by my poor behaviour."

Darrius chuckled. "You've changed, Makayla, you've never given a shit about anyone's feelings before. You're evolving, sister-mine. I guess it had to happen eventually."

Makayla smiled. "You may be right. Whether it's a good thing, though, is debatable."

Sebastian turned from the window and faced Augustus. "Do you think it wise to return to Evron?"

"What else can I do? My impersonator hasn't been heard from in a week. I think it's safe to say he's left and won't be returning. The sooner I go back and take my place as chancellor of the Vampire Council, the safer everyone will be."

"What if the council notices the changes in you? You're not the same, my lord, in appearance or character."

"Maybe I can help, Sebastian," Ambrosia said as she entered the room. "Sorry for my interruption, I was coming back from settling Aunt Marianna in her room when I overheard your conversation."

Sebastian kissed Ambrosia's cheek as she came to a stop beside them. "How would you help?" Sebastian questioned.

"Why, Augustus could drink my blood. It would restore him to good health and he'll be stronger too. I am, after all, the daughter of Uriel, the heavenly fire, the flame of God himself. My blood is potent."

"Absolutely not," Sebastian said.

Ambrosia moved closer to her husband and placed a gentle hand on his forearm. "Sebastian, it's my decision, and you know it's the only thing we can do. The world we know has changed. We need someone we can trust in the Vampire Council on Evron and Augustus is the man. You were the one, after all, who appointed him this position. My father has control of the Seraph Council and has always accepted you and your mandates. You are a son to him, no matter your vampire heritage, but the Vampire Council is, as we've recently found out, compromised. Until you take your rightful place on the throne as king, this is our only avenue. Augustus must return and resume his position as the head of the Vampire Council. It's the only way."

Sebastian covered Ambrosia's hand with his. "You know why I abdicated, Ambrosia. It was so I could be with you and bring peace to Evron. You remember the skirmishes and discord there was between the vampire and seraph nations before the truce. Even with the truce in place there are still squabbles."

"I know, my love, but 'tis time you took back the throne – you are the heir. My father would agree. Especially now. Look at what Lilith has done here on Earth. It's only a matter of time before she takes her vendetta to Evron if she hasn't already. The laws that bound her from returning to Evron are no more. She has gained too much power– look at the army she has amassed, how can we ever hope to stop her? She wants war and she shall have it one way or another. After everything that has happened between the three of us, surely you must know this. She's always had her sights set on you and controlling Evron. She was meant to be your queen, not me. She's bitter and angry. Hell hath no fury like a woman scorned, and she is unlike any other woman in the Multiverse. She will not stop . . . ever. Not unless you discard me and take your rightful place on the throne with her at your side as queen."

"I will never abandon you, Ambrosia, my death or yours, is the only thing that would separate us, and even then I'd find a way to be with you. Lilith and I were friends, nothing more; she wanted power, and I was the means of achieving it – her goal was something she set long before I was born. I just happened to be a stepping stone to her final reward – dominion.

"Lady Ambrosia is right about the High Priestess, your highness. Lilith is dangerous, believe me, I discovered this the hard way and against my will. But, I'm afraid I cannot drink your blood, my lady, not without Lord Sebastian's consent. I am his servant and am bound to his word and must honour his decision because you are his blood-bonded mate."

"No, Augustus, Ambrosia's right. You'll need all your strength and drinking my wife's blood will give you an edge no other vampire on Evron has. You'll be stronger and able to see things no ordinary vampire can see. You'll know the truth when you hear it, especially when someone lies to you. I have no idea how I missed the telltale signs of my brother masquerading as you. He has always had the gift of impersonating others. Yes, you must drink Ambrosia's blood, but I have one condition; you'll not drink directly from my wife's vein. As her husband that right is mine alone."

Augustus bowed. "I am honoured by your offering, my lord, my lady."

Ambrosia removed a golden dagger accentuated with silver filigree from a hidden pocket in her gown. She spun the glistening blade on her palm and between her fingertips, twisting and flipping it with the expertise of a warrior. Sebastian smiled as he retrieved an empty glass tumbler from a nearby table, remembering the first time he'd seen her do the same trick. She'd been wearing the gold-silver armour of the Seraph Guard. Her six wings were fully extended with twin seraph swords strapped between her shoulder blades. The wild look on her face had shocked him, he'd never seen such beautiful animosity on a seraph's face. Hell, he'd never seen a female Seraph Guard before, either. She'd had him pinned against a wall ready to slit his throat from ear to ear. At the time he hadn't worried about dying, she'd fascinated him. He'd wondered why he'd never seen her before.

Ambrosia angled her head and flipped the dagger in the air once more before catching it on its spiralling descent. She sliced the honed steel across her wrist with a quick flick of her hand. Sebastian held the tumbler under her arm and watched her blood fill the glass. His eyes dilated as the enticing scent of her blood weaved an invisible path to his nostrils. He gritted his teeth and suppressed a predatory growl of ownership, then held out the full glass to Augustus with a stiff, unyielding arm. All he wanted to do was drink the glistening gold liquid himself. Augustus lifted his trembling hand to take the glass from his tight grip. Sebastian sensed his fear at once. Another male drinking a bonded vampire mate's blood wasn't tolerated, a dangerous risk at best. Sebastian glanced back at his wife and lifted her wrist to his mouth, licking the wound on her arm and healing it with his saliva. His eyes rolled back in his head the moment he tasted her blood.

Augustus stepped back from Sebastian the moment the glass was safely in his grasp and waited for his king to give a nod of approval before drinking.

"Take a seat, Augustus. Ambrosia's blood has quite a kick and you may be temporarily incapacitated. Makayla's blood is very strong, which you know already, but not as strong as her mother's. Drinking the blood of a royal pureblood seraph will knock your socks off, believe me, I know from experience. Oh, and I must warn you, seraph blood is very addictive if you're not bonded to the seraph. 'Tis why the laws against vampires and seraphs consorting exist. Make this a one-time thing, Augustus, because if you drink seraph blood again you'll lose your mind, your soul – you'll give up everything for another taste, be warned."

Augustus's mouth dried as the scent of Ambrosia's blood reached his nostrils. It was intoxicating, the sweetest thing he'd had the pleasure of smelling, and unlike anything he'd smelled before. It was a mixture of blooming flowers and herbs, but no flower or herb he could identify. The exhilarating bouquet of her blood was much like Makayla's, but definitely stronger.

Augustus glanced at Sebastian whose jaw had tensed as he flexed and ground his teeth together. Only a fool would drink the blood of the king's wife, but he had no other choice, not if he wanted to return to Evron and resume his position as chancellor of the vampire senate. Sebastian's warning terrified him, but living in a world controlled by Lilith scared him more.

Ambrosia smiled and nodded her encouragement. Augustus looked down at the rippling gold liquid glistening in the glass he held and licked his dry lips. He tried to swallow again, but his mouth was too dry to ease his apprehension. He closed his eyes and took a calming breath to settle his trembling mind and hand. *You can do this, you have to do this,* he thought to himself before opening his eyes and sitting down in the nearest chair.

Augustus sank back into the comfortable chair with a bone-creaking lethargy. He looked at his hosts once more before lifting the glass tumbler to his lips. Four gulps and the glass was empty. He groaned in pleasure and closed his eyes again as the blood flowed down his throat. Ambrosia's blood was like all the finest wines in the world rolled into one. Augustus gasped and opened his eyes. His ears buzzed, much like the rest of his body. His senses became hyperactive – he was a mass of live-wires. Colours seemed brighter, smells stronger, sounds louder, everything was enhanced. Warmth ballooned within him, bleeding from the centre of his chest into his extremities until his entire body was a reservoir of tingling sensation. He lowered the glass onto a nearby table and raised his hands to his eyes. His cracked fingernails and the dry, sagging skin on his arms and the tops of his hands transformed in the blink of an eye. Wrinkles filled out, fingernails became smoother, the sallow colour became vibrant and healthy. Gone was the ache in his lower back, gone was the lethargy – replaced with an energy he'd not known since his youth. His mouth was no longer dry, but pooling with saliva; he ran his tongue over the points of his fangs, they seemed sharper. He licked his lips and looked up at Ambrosia, his natural urge was to take more of her blood. Sebastian was right, addiction would be a happy respite for him. His skin bristled with awareness and anticipation; he was about to stand when Sebastian stepped in front of Ambrosia, blocking Augustus's view of her, Augustus tried to look past him.

"Augustus, snap out of it. One glass is all you get. It's all you need, don't be a fool, man."

Augustus blinked and focused on Sebastian and exhaled slowly. The buzzing in his ears subsided and he slumped back into the lounge chair. He shook his head and tried to swallow the river of saliva pooling in his mouth. He brushed a hand across his forehead and covered his face, taking deep breaths as he got control.

"I'm sorry, my lord, I don't know what came over me.

Please, forgive me, Lady Ambrosia."

"There's nothing to forgive, Lord Augustus, I understand."

"Here, drink this," Sebastian said, thrusting a glass of brandy into Augustus's hand.

Augustus guzzled the alcoholic beverage down, lifted the glass for a refill and drank the second glass moments after it was replenished. "Thank you," he gasped placing the empty glass alongside the glass tumbler that had held Ambrosia's blood. He cleared his throat and pushed up from the chair to stand. He cracked his neck and back, a wide grin spreading across his face. "When you said seraph blood had a kick, I had no idea just how much of a kick you were referring to. My goodness, I've never experienced such a thing in my life."

Sebastian clapped him on the back and smiled. "I warned you, old boy."

"Yes, that you did. Well, I must return to Evron, I imagine a lot has changed. You have my deepest gratitude. Thank you both so very much." Augustus bowed his head. "And when you see your daughter, please extend my thanks to her as well."

"You're welcome, Lord Augustus," Ambrosia replied.

Augustus turned to leave.

"Augustus."

Augustus stopped mid-stride and looked over his shoulder at Sebastian. "Yes, my lord?"

"Take the hidden gateway to Evron, you know the one I speak of; the other gateways may not be safe."

"Yes, my lord." Augustus bowed once more.

"Oh, and Augustus, safe journey."

"Thank you, my lord. Once I am positioned as chancellor again, I'll send word."

"Here, use this so I know for sure it's from you." Sebastian removed a ring from his pinkie finger and handed it to Augustus.

Augustus took the ring. His mouth dropped when he saw what he held. "I cannot take this ring, it's above my station."

"Not any more, Augustus. When I take my throne you will be at my side, my trusted friend and confidant. You will be the hand of the king as you were always meant to be."

CHAPTER 17.

A light breeze swept the hair from Zobiana's face as she stared out Abigail's window. She sighed and contemplated the Carpathian Mountains while waiting for news from Nathaniel regarding Earth's gateways. Nathaniel was loyal and the only one who wanted nothing from her, nothing that she knew of anyhow. Oh, he was ambitious, of that she had no doubt, but his loyalty was his most redeeming quality, that and his far-seeing ability. She'd yet to learn his machinations and wondered why he followed her. Zobiana figured blind ambition and fear were great motivators. She'd feared the Dark One for millennia; it had kept her alert over the extended years. She would always fear the Dark One, she feared him now, even when he was stuck in Alexander's body. Zobiana knew it was temporary and only a matter of time before the Dark One was free again. By the time he gained his freedom, though, she would have gained hers also.

Everything hinged on Earth's gateways. If she controlled them, she controlled the Multiverse. Not that the Multiverse was her main goal. She just wanted Evron, but if controlling the Multiverse meant she controlled Evron, then she would take control however it came to her. The Earth and its gateways were practically hers. Her people were already in place all over the world. While the Shadow Seekers scrambled to save humanity from her farms and the Blakspor virus, her people were in position, securing Earth's gateways one by one. Implementing a gateway takeover had always been her plan, and the Shadow Seekers playing right into her hands was just the icing on the proverbial cake.

The only thing standing in her way now was the Zoldarni. The Shadow Seekers were like irritable little insects, easily manipulated. No matter what they did now, they couldn't stop the prophecy from playing out. The moment she'd set eyes on the Gem of Past Times hanging around the Golden One's neck, she knew there was no going back. Zobiana chuckled at the pun, *no going back*. Makayla's trip back into the past had set the ball rolling. Not even she could stop its momentum now.

"Mother, is that you?"

Zobiana turned and made her way towards her daughter's bedside. "Yes, Abigail, 'tis I." She brushed the hair from her daughter's forehead. "I'm glad you're awake, dear, because we have work to do." Zobiana smirked at the prospect of what lay ahead. She lifted her hand and uncurled her fingers, the fingernail on her index finger elongated and she slashed her wrist with the sharp tip. Blood spurted out of the open vein, threading snail-like trails down the length of her arm. She lowered her wrist to Abigail's mouth. "Here, drink, quickly now, you'll feel much better once you do."

Abigail grasped her mother's arm and covered her mouth over the open wound, slurping and licking until she gathered more strength. Zobiana gasped and clenched her teeth together when Abigail's grip tightened and her fangs chomped down harder. "That's enough now." Abigail's eyes turned black, her grip strengthening further. "ABIGAIL. . . ENOUGH!"

Abigail gasped and released her mother. "Sorry, it feels like I haven't fed in an age, and I've never fed from your vein before, why . . . why did you allow me to feed from you? It's not like you."

Zobiana shrugged. "I need you at the top of your game, and right now you're the only one I can trust."

"Trust . . .? What about Tyrone? He has never let you down."

"Humph . . . Tyrone's not himself . . . watch what you say to him."

"But—"

"No buts, Abigail, trust me. Tyrone's behaviour is perplexing; he's hatching a scheme, I know it. His blatant disregard for our situation when Alexander attacked us has set me on edge. I can't look past his argumentative attitude either; he challenges my authority at every turn. Something's not right."

"Mother . . . Tyrone would never cross you, he has always been by your side, why would he turn on you now after centuries of faithfulness? It doesn't make sense."

"That's what worries me. Now, tell me . . . how do you feel?"

"I feel fine, why?"

"Because you've been unconscious for almost a week."

"WHAT?" Abigail sat up and kicked the bed sheets off her legs. "Why didn't you wake me sooner?"

"We tried but you were badly burned. We thought it better to let you heal before trying to wake you again."

"So, they got away?" Abigail said, ripping the I.V from her hand and swinging her feet over the edge of her bed.

"Yes. A lot has happened while you slept. Earth's gateways are all but ours. Malachi has disappeared – we haven't a clue where he is, but I have my suspicions. There's a lot you don't know, Abigail, dear. Now get cleaned up, we have work to do."

Makayla and Darrius appeared just outside the entertainment room. They lingered in the doorway where they could hear a heated conversation was in full swing at the bar. Zack and Reece were arguing about something. Darrius and Makayla looked at one another.

"Curious right?" Darrius grinned, wiggling his eyebrows.

"Don't." Makayla held up her finger. "Just don't . . . if you bring up curiosity and the cat one more time I fear I may strangle you and the next cat I see, and that would just piss me off, 'cause I like cats."

Darrius chuckled. "So, you like cats . . . huh?"

"Darrius—" Makayla made to punch his arm.

Darrius raised his hands in surrender. "Okay . . . okay, all right, I'll stop. What do you think's got them up in arms? I'm not getting much from their minds."

Makayla opened her mind to those in the room and was hit with a barrage of images. She couldn't get a clear idea of what the argument was over either, except for the fleeting impression of hundreds of humans frozen in weird bed-like contraptions hanging from a ceiling in circulating rows, and a room filled with computer consoles.

"I'm guessing it's something to do with the human farms," Makayla said.

"Come on, let's settle down the children before they resort to throwing each other around or worse."

"What were you thinking, Zack? You could have got us all killed."

"Stop being so melodramatic, Reece. It was a long shot, it could have worked, and at least we know now," Zack said, pouring himself a shot of whiskey.

All the Shadow Seekers were there except Thomas, Freya, Gabriel and Ava. Makayla noticed Lazarus and Nikolai deep in conversation further down the bar away from the main group, oblivious to the commotion surrounding them.

"Know what?" Makayla asked, as she and Darrius came to a stop near the group.

Everyone turned towards them. Makayla noticed the shared look between Morgan and her brother, but didn't comment. Zack lifted his shot glass in a toast to her, sculled it down and refilled it afterwards.

"Reece is bitching like a whiny kid," Zack said, saluting her before upending his second shot.

"You used to be more fun, Reece, why so serious all of a sudden?" Morgan said, taking her eyes from Darrius and refocusing on Reece.

"You weren't there, Morgan. So your opinion doesn't count," Reece snapped.

"And what, your opinion does? Oh, that's right, I forgot, Reece, you were the favourite child, weren't you? Your opinion always mattered to our parents!" Bryce said, folding his arms across his chest and death-staring his brother until he looked away. "Morgan's right, you used to be more fun."

Makayla smirked and looked from Bryce to Reece before focusing on Morgan. She had to agree with Bryce; Morgan was right, but Makayla wasn't going to tell them that. Makayla knew why Reece was so uptight and felt sorry for him. She glanced towards Anna, who was looking up at the ceiling, pretending she didn't give a damn, but Makayla knew Anna was pissed, she'd glimpsed it the moment she'd opened her mind up to the group.

Makayla dematerialised and reappeared behind the bar next to Zack; she grabbed two empty glasses and a bottle of Southern Comfort from a shelf on the wall and filled the glasses with ice and alcohol. She handed one to her brother, who'd seated himself on a bar stool next to Morgan, and clinked her glass with his before raising it to her mouth. She guzzled down the alcohol, her mind never straying far from thoughts of Alexander even when she was with others.

Where was he? Would she be able to help him? What had Zobiana done to him? Would he be another casualty on the long list of people who'd died because of her? Would there always be unforeseen forces tearing them apart? Was their love destined to destroy them? Would she end up losing him too? These were the questions circling in her mind.

She shook her head and focused on the bottle of Southern Comfort sitting on the bar in front of her. She scooped it up and refilled her glass for a third time before gulping down the amber liquid; the growing warmth in her stomach having already settled her nerves.

"So, you didn't answer my question, Zack, what happened?" she asked again, leaning an elbow on the bar and setting her empty glass down.

Zack met Makayla's penetrating stare and exhaled. "I fucked up."

"Thank you," Reece said in exasperation. "It's good you realise your mistake."

"Reece, you're not helping," Makayla reprimanded. Reece

opened his mouth to speak, but thought better when Makayla raised her hand for him to be quiet.

"We've been running surveillance on one of the Newbloods small human farms for two weeks now," explained Zack. "Nikolai and I have spent a lot of late nights mapping farm locations across the UK and discussing ways to shut them down without harming the human captives. We thought if we could access the computers and find the codes to disable the injection modulators on the rectrabeds then maybe, just maybe, we could free the captives.

"The reason we chose the smallest of the farms was because there were fewer guards patrolling the premises and minimal danger. The probability of being caught while trying to free the humans was lower. Less risk all round."

"Humph, less risk; there's always risk," Reece grumbled.

Makayla frowned, the throbbing in her temple was expanding across her frontal lobe. "Reece, if you don't shut up and let him finish I'll make you!" Makayla indicated Zack with a nod.

Zack glanced between Reece and Makayla before continuing to speak. "Um, yeah, Nikolai and I figured if we could work out a way to shut down a farm from the inside, we'd be able to do the same with the remaining farms. But the computer system was booby-trapped. It wasn't a total loss, though. I may have blown our cover, but we found one thing out for certain. All the farms are controlled by one mainframe, a supercomputer located at the largest of all the farms. 'THE' farm. If we can get in and hack the mainframe, we could deactivate the injection modulators in all the farms simultaneously. But because it is the location of the mainframe for all the farms they'd have even more security and safeguards and potential traps in place. Another problem would be rescuing thousands of people at the same time, but if we could disable the injection modulators, we'd have more time to rally our people and the Vampire and Seraph Guard and coordinate a synchronised rescue and save every captive."

Zack swept his hand through his dishevelled hair and shrugged. "I've tried to access the farms' computers from an outside terminal and failed. 'THE' farm has its own private server and no matter how hard I try I can't gain access. So that's why we went to the smallest farm – to see if I could access the mainframe from inside. I couldn't. It was a long shot, I know, but worth a try. I may have fucked up—" Zack looked at Reece "—but now we know for sure that we have to infiltrate 'THE' farm and hack the mainframe from inside."

Makayla scratched her forehead. "You found a farm?"

Zack nodded. "Shit, yeah, sorry, Makayla, I forgot, you don't know about the farms at all, do you?" Zack asked.

Makayla shook her head watching as Nikolai and Lazarus rose from their seats and made their way towards the group. "I had no idea."

"We haven't located them all, but I figure once I've hacked the mainframe I'll be able to discover the locations of the other farms."

Bryce saw Makayla was still confused and quickly jumped in to explain what he and Freya had found.

Makayla was dumbfounded. "Zobiana must have been planning this for years."

"She has, but there was never a way for me to warn my father, not without compromising my cover," said Nikolai. "I think Zobiana suspected me as a spy because she excluded me from important meetings."

"I don't know how you were able to withstand being undercover for so long, Nikolai, it's unfathomable," Ashley murmured.

"It wasn't without its trials, but I had a purpose for being there. It was incentive enough," Nikolai said, glancing at Makayla.

Makayla lowered her eyes and stared at her empty glass. She had an innate understanding of why Nikolai had sacrificed so much to infiltrate Zobiana's people. She hadn't in the beginning, but with everything she'd been through with Alexander, she had a better comprehension for his reasons. She looked up again and noticed the grim look on Lazarus's face. "Is everything all right, Laz?" Makayla asked.

Lazarus shook his head, his eyebrow raising as he looked around the room. He pulled her in for a hug and buried his face in her hair. "A lot has happened since we last saw one another."

Makayla frowned, looking between Lazarus and Nikolai. "Is everything okay with Aun—"

Lazarus squeezed her so tightly the embrace became

uncomfortable. She stopped talking as he released her and placed his fingertip to her lips, stopping her from speaking. *"Don't mention your Aunt Marianna or Augustus out loud, the compound has been compromised. Is there somewhere safe we can meet? We need to talk,"* Lazarus communicated to her silently.

Makayla nodded, understanding lighting her features. *"My Greek island is isolated and safe."* She visualised her home and showed Lazarus how to get there.

"I have things to do first, but I'll meet you there in a few hours."

Makayla nodded again. *"Okay."*

"I best be leaving," Lazarus said, eyeing her and then nodding at Darrius before he left the room. Everyone watched him leave.

"I have to leave too." Nikolai smiled, and grasped her shoulder. "It's good to see you again, Makayla." He winked. *"I will see you later at your parents' house?"* he added telepathically. *"Come before you meet with Lazarus, I, too, wish to speak with you."* His eyebrow lifted in question, she nodded and watched him leave. She couldn't help wondering what Nikolai and Lazarus had been discussing when she and Darrius had arrived. Their behaviour was most unusual.

"Hey, where's Xander?" Jackson asked, looking about. "I went to the infirmary earlier to say hi and he wasn't there, I figured he was with you, Makayla?" Jackson grabbed a handful of potato crisps from a bowl on the bar and shovelled them into his mouth.

Makayla focused her eyes on Darrius; Darrius nodded and looked at Jackson.

Makayla cleared her throat. "Darrius and I followed him down into the sewers. He was in some kind of weird trance, it was sort of like he was sleepwalking."

"That's odd, do you think he's infected with the Blakspor virus?" Ashley asked.

"No, it would be impossible for him to have contracted the Blakspor virus. He has drunk an awful lot of my blood recently."

"Why would he have drunk your blood, Makayla?" Morgan asked.

"Because I sired him."

"Sired? What do you mean? Are you saying he's a vampire now?" Morgan gasped.

"Well, I don't know what he is, I'm not exactly a vampire myself. I'm considered more of an abomination than a vampire. He's a seraphympire hybrid if that's what you're asking. I'm buggered if I know what to call him, though, considering he's a Druid as well."

"Holy shit, what did you do, Makayla?"

"What did I do? Weren't you bloody listening, Morgan? I changed my husband into a seraphympire hybrid, or whatever the bloody hell you want to call him. That's right, you heard me, HUSBAND. Please, just stop with the questions all right, because I've had a rough few weeks. I mean I was teleported seven hundred years into the past for crying out loud. Where I discovered Lilith, you know the one, Adam's first wife. As it turns out Eve wasn't Adam's first wife, Lilith was. Yeah, correct, Adam from the garden of Eden was married to Lilith first, who in actuality is Zobiana, which is seriously fucked up if you ask me. Oh, and guess what, Lilith, A.K.A Zobiana, just happens to be Alexander's stepmother, go figure, and if that wasn't bad enough, I was put on trial by the Inquisition for being a witch and worshipping the devil. Like that's even a remote possibility, but hey, everything's possible when you're in the 14th century, archaic times call for archaic measures. Not only was I put on trial for being a witch I was convicted and thrown into another dungeon and later burned at the stake. Bloody fools didn't know I was fireproof. And did I mention I found the Trinian Globe, or I should say, it found me because I was in possession of the first gem, wait it gets better. Not only did I find the Trinian globe, but I also found the third Trinian gem, you're probably wondering what happened to the second gem right? I had the Gem of Souls all along, hanging around my neck. That's right the amethyst gem given to me at birth was a Trinian gem, until recently I didn't know it was called the Gem of Souls, which is kind of ironic considering I had two souls not too long ago, yay for me. And if that's not enough, Zobiana used the third gem, the Gem of Past Times, this gem." Makayla indicated the ruby gem hanging around her throat. "To travel back in time and destroy my village, the one I lived in when I was a teenager. Admittedly, she was trying to kill me, it seems to be her life's obsession, you know, destroying me and my family. Alexander saved my teenage self while Zobiana was killing every single person who meant something to me. So the next time someone says I've had a lovely little break away, think again, the only good thing that happened to me while I was in the past was Alexander, whom I married just before Zack here," Makayla pointed at Zack. "Dobbed me into the Inquisition for being a witch, don't blame Zack though, I don't, I've forgiven him, he had every right to feel the way he did, after all, I led the army that wiped out his entire village and killed his father. So before you go asking what I did, and why I did it, think twice and just shut-the-fuck-up and don't go there. OKAY!"

Makayla poured herself another glass of Southern comfort and gulped it down before slamming the empty vessel on the bar again. She looked about the group, they stared at her with shocked, wide eyed, open mouthed expressions. Zack's face held nothing, but shame, his shoulders slumped and he stared at the glass he held in his hands with a lost look in his eyes. She shook her head, she'd done it now. If she wanted to ostracise herself more, she'd succeeded swimmingly. Makayla wrapped her arm around Zack's shoulder and pulled him into a hug, he didn't hug her back, he stood rigid in her arms.

"I'm sorry Zack, I'm so sorry, everything that has happened is because of my actions and I take full responsibility for them. Please don't blame yourself. Never blame yourself."

Zack looked into her eyes and finally relaxed in her arms.

"Makayla . . . I didn't mean . . . I mean I didn't, I didn't—
" Morgan stuttered.

"Makayla, I don't think Morgan meant to insult you," Darrius said cutting Morgan off.

Makayla released Zack from her embrace and glanced at her brother. "It doesn't matter, Darrius, really it doesn't. I'm sorry for my outburst, I get it, I do, I'm tired and worried about Xander, and what we just saw defies all logic!"

"What defies logic?" Anna asked.

"Alexander and what we saw him do."

"What did Zobiana do to him?" Anna asked, giving Makayla her full attention. Makayla knew Anna was attempting to defuse the tension.

"I have no idea what Zobiana did to him besides whip the crap out of him. He was nearly dead when Lazarus and I found him, lucky we found him in time. I'm afraid I didn't get a chance to speak to him much before he lost consciousness. Your guess is as good as mine, but it can't have been good."

"Where did Alexander lead you when you were down in the sewers, Makayla, and what did he do that defies all logic?" Reece asked, scratching his eyebrow.

Makayla re-counted the unfolding events she and Darrius had experienced in the sewers. When she'd finished speaking, she exhaled and looked about the group; they stared at her with mouth-gaping expressions. Makayla studied Reece, he'd grown quiet, introspective, absorbed in thought. "Reece, are you okay?" Makayla asked. He didn't answer. "Reece?"

"Huh . . . ah, yeah, sorry . . . I've got to go, I . . . I have to be somewhere," Reece said, dematerialising.

Makayla shared a look with her brother. "Was it something I said?" Makayla murmured.

Darrius shrugged. "You did have quite a bit to say," he chuckled.

"Well, this has been fun, remind me to do it again, NOT," Jackson said, finishing his beer and shovelling another handful of potato crisps in his mouth before turning on his heel and heading towards the door. "Who's coming?"

Makayla watched the remaining Shadow Seekers follow Jackson out the door one by one, each nodding at her as they departed. Zack didn't move, he stood staring at the bar top, tracing his finger in the condensation pooling on the counter under Makayla's empty glass.

"Is it just me or was that the strangest response you've ever experienced?" Makayla glanced at her brother. "Do you think they know something and are too scared to say?"

"You did just tell them to shut the fuck up if they had nothing to say?"

"Don't you think they'd be a little more interested in the Roman ruins and Xander's disappearance, though?"

"I don't know, Makayla; personally I think you just scared the shit out of everyone, but you know them better than I do."

"I'm guessing I don't know them as well as I thought," Makayla said, groaning when she noticed Morgan hovering by the door, waiting for her brother.

Morgan's eyebrow raised in expectation as she stared at Darrius. He smiled and she uncharacteristically returned it. "Sorry, Makayla, gotta go." Darrius smirked when Makayla rolled her eyes. *"I'll see you at home when you drop in to see Aunt Marianna,"* he said.

"What, you heard my conversation with Lazarus and Nikolai?" Makayla responded.

"There's not much I miss, sister-mine." Darrius winked. "Ta-Ta, for now," he said aloud, walking towards Morgan.

"I think I'm going to be sick," Makayla said, shrugging and glancing back towards Zack.

CHAPTER 18.

Ecktar peered over his shoulder as the remaining Aurylian guards arrived through the gateway. The moment the last man stepped through, light flared and faded and the gateway closed. Vasili shivered, rubbing his hands up and down the lengths of his arms as he looked beyond the gateway towards the dark horizon; all he could see were the black jagged mountain silhouettes in the distance. He clenched and unclenched his fists, turning on the spot and looking for his shillelagh. He remembered leaning it up against the gateway before travelling to Cwonoth, but couldn't recall picking it up afterwards. It was gone now.

He wondered how much time had lapsed since he'd first travelled through the gateway. It was night-time now, but whether it was closer to dawn or midnight, he hadn't a clue. His inner clock was all messed up from his time on Cwonoth. He shuddered, the hairs on his body prickling with unease as he contemplated his surroundings. Silence was prevalent, the eeriness malevolent. A vast difference from the last time he was there. The area was empty of life, not a single bird chirped, the crickets and frogs and other sounds common to forested areas were eerily quiet. It unnerved him more than he would have liked to admit. There was no sound at all, no whistling wind rustling the leaves, nor was there even the fragrant smell of flowers covering the gateway or the scents of fallen leaves and the soil underfoot. Even when they walked, the sound of crackling leaves underfoot was absent. The area was no longer vibrant with life, but something closer to a deathly void.

Vasili didn't comment on the inhospitable surroundings to the Zoldarni; they wouldn't understand or care either way. They were there to discover what had happened to their emissaries and secure Earth's gateways. Yes, Overlord Avinash had given Ecktar complete authority to aide Vasili and the Shadow Seekers in any way and by any means necessary, but Vasili still needed to be cautious around the Aurylians, especially after the harsh treatment he'd been subjected to while being held captive.

Vasili waited for the guards to move away from the gateway before climbing the stairs to retrieve the key he'd placed there the day he'd travelled to Cwonoth. He rubbed a thumb over the central gem and felt an electric tingle zap his fingertip. Vasili removed his handkerchief from his pocket, dusted the key off and wrapped it in the cloth before pocketing the lot. He'd feel better when it was safely hidden away and planned to give it to Makayla as soon as possible. She was the only one it would be safe with and he had a terrible premonition she'd need it to travel to Cwonoth. Why, he hadn't a clue, but he never ignored his intuition.

The Zoldarni guard formed a circle around Ecktar as he gave them their orders; there was much discussion within the group before silence prevailed.

Ecktar turned towards Vasili. "Lord Vasili, when was the last time you were in direct contact with our emissaries?"

Vasili scratched his head. "I would say it was at least seven, possibly eight, months ago that I spoke with Idgar, Tahlia, Nyshtar and Ensor directly. I stopped receiving correspondence from them not long after."

Ecktar frowned. Vasili watched Ecktar's face crease and then smooth out; he'd seen countless other Off World species over his lifetime, but the Aurylians mystified him, especially Ecktar. Ecktar was the only Aurylian he'd met who showed emotion. His face was unusually expressive. Aurylians usually gave away nothing; their usual unemotional state of being was why they were so effective as the Zoldarni guards. It was also one of the reasons their race had been tasked with upholding Zoldarni mandates and protecting the Multiverse.

Ecktar divided his thirty men into fifteen groups of two. "Illiyaird, I want you and Targul to stay here and guard the gateway. Under no circumstances, I repeat, under *no* circumstances will you allow anyone to travel through the gateway to Cwonoth. As of this moment all travel to Cwonoth is suspended under direct orders of Overlord Avinash. If you are met with violence, you are to consider it an act of war and terminate the offenders post haste."

Illiyaird and Targul nodded their heads and climbed the stairs to take up guard in front of the gateway.

Ecktar gave the rest of his men their directives. Vasili watched as the Aurylian guards punched buttons on silver apparatuses attached to their wrists. Multiple portals appeared and the Aurylians disappeared in their respective pairs until there were only two guards remaining with Ecktar. Ecktar spoke to them momentarily and they nodded their heads in understanding. He then turned towards Vasili and acknowledged him with a brief nod of his head. "Take me to your compound, Lord Vasili, I wish to speak with the Chosen One."

Vasili's mouth opened and closed. "I'm not sure if she's at the compound, Ecktar."

"She's there, take us now before she leaves, I need confirmation."

"Confirmation of what?" Vasili angled his head.

"Confirmation she is the one of prophecy."

"What about your two remaining guards?"

"After they fulfil my request, they will await my return."

"As you wish," Vasili agreed.

Saliva drooled from Alexander's mouth in a steady stream to the cobbled ground. He groaned and rolled to his back the scarring on his body causing him discomfort. He hissed as loose pebbles scraped and dug into his naked flesh. Alexander opened his eyes and was met with pitch blackness. Blinking, he rubbed his eyelids and tried to make out familiar shapes, but the darkness was absolute. How long he'd been lying on the floor naked was anyone's guess. Judging by how dry his mouth was, it had to have been a while. It felt as though he'd consumed a bucket of sand.

Alexander rolled to his side then pushed into a sitting position and regretted it immediately. Piercing pain shot around his body, making him curl his toes as the pain tap-danced down his spine, circled his rib cage and settled in his lower back, throbbing in perfect time with his heartbeat. He waited until the pain subsided before moving again. Hindered by his stiff movements, he bit down on his bottom lip, drawing blood as he got his bearings. His bones popped as he stretched the stiffness from his body. Where was he and why was it so dark? Was he still in the cave, and if he was, where was Makayla?

His nostrils flared and his lip curled as the odour of his surroundings hit him full-force. "What is that God-awful stench?" He lifted his arm and sniffed his armpit. "Thank goodness it's not me," he murmured, scratching his whiskered jaw.

Someone chuckled. "I believe that is the odious smell of

hell."

Alexander stopped moving. "Who's there?"

"No one of consequence, old chap. Many thanks for freeing me from my entombment."

"Freeing you? What are you talking about? I don't remember freeing anyone."

"Oh dear, we are in a pickle then, aren't we?" The man chuckled again.

Alexander shivered; whoever he was speaking with gave him the creeps. His voice held an otherworldly tone; an inherent evilness lurked beneath his comments, as if he wasn't a man at all, but another entity altogether.

"A pickle; that's an understatement if ever I heard one," Alexander said, finding his feet and standing. He puffed out his chest and removed the kinks from his body with a swift stretch.

There was a rush of air near Alexander. "What would you call this situation we now find ourselves in, then?" the voice said close to his ear. Alexander jumped and stepped back in surprise, feeling sharp stones dig into the soles of his feet. He couldn't see a thing, but he had the distinct feeling his companion wasn't so hindered by the darkness – something Alexander would soon rectify. He cracked his knuckles and shook his hands before swirling them in front of his body in an ever-expanding loop. His hands caught fire, and the room was bathed in light. Alexander noticed torches in wall sconces spaced around the room. One more flourish of his hands and the torches lit with a hissing, flamboyant burst of flames.

"Bravo . . . Bravo," his companion said, clapping his hands with the enthusiasm of a theatre audience. "I haven't had this much fun in a long while. Begging your pardon, sir, but what century is it, if you don't mind my asking?" A gentleman said from where he lent against a vacant patch of wall near what appeared to be a sarcophagus.

The sarcophagus appeared Egyptian with ancient writings scrawled on its exterior in a deep maroon. From what Alexander could surmise, the sarcophagus appeared to be made of jet stone. It stood upright against the wall near where the man stood observing Alexander in the middle of the room. Alexander glanced about again, there were many other sarcophagi lining the room's circular wall.

"Well then, are you going to answer my question, lad? Come, come, what century is it?"

Alexander looked at the man across from him, whose appearance contradicted how he'd imagined him to appear. Had he been mistaken? Had the shadows got the better of him? No, he doubted it, his intuition was screaming to get away from this person who had clearly once been a part of the aristocracy. A rich man, no doubt, by the looks of the outdated attire he wore.

"Ahem," the man cleared his throat, his eyebrows rising in question as he looked at Alexander expectantly.

Alexander opened and closed his mouth as if he were gasping for oxygen. "Um, sorry, it's the 21st century," he stuttered, looking about again before focusing on the gentleman sporting a somewhat threadbare top hat.

"Well, well, it seems I've been incarcerated for quite some time then." Alexander's companion looked him up and down with a raised eyebrow, smirking at his state of undress. "Not to fear, though, I'll have plenty of time to catch up." The gentleman twirled the corners of his black moustache, wiggled his eyebrows and straightened his crumpled woollen vest. He opened the sarcophagus door and retrieved a jacket, which he shimmied into and buttoned with hasty fingers. "I'd offer you some clothes, but I rather need mine right now, sorry, old chap, you understand how it is," he said, removing an Ulster Overcoat and dancing into it with the enthusiastic vigour of a much younger man.

Alexander looked down at himself; he'd forgotten he was naked. His state of undress seemed to have become a regular occurrence. He crossed his arms over his chest as clothes magically appeared on his person.

"What a clever trick; is that what they're wearing these days? I prefer my moth-eaten duds over yours any day. You look like you're about to attend a funeral, is black the new trend?"

Alexander sighed, shook his head and watched the man retrieve a walking stick from the black sarcophagus. The eccentric man tipped his top hat, clicked his boot heels together and spun his cane in a Charlie Chaplin manner. "Well then, once again you have my gratitude. Tally-ho, I'm off to wreak havoc on an unsuspecting world, there's still much fun to be had I'm sure. Au revoir, old chap." The gentleman spun on the spot towards the wall and snapped his fingers, the wall shimmered red then became translucent.

"Wait, you didn't answer my question, who are you?" Alexander said, in a last-ditch to find out the man's identity.

The gentleman looked over his shoulder and pinned Alexander with a wicked glare and chuckled again. His laughter turned malicious. The kind of laughter that sent chills down your spine. A laughter so malignant that it evoked pure, evil dread.

"If I told you who I was, young Alexander, then I'd have to kill you." The man's eyes turned crimson as he tipped his hat once more and stepped through the shimmering wall.

CHAPTER 19.

Reece materialised in the shadowy, underground Roman Chamber Makayla and Darrius had mentioned. It hadn't changed in over a century and looked the same as the last time he'd been there, but it felt different now. He sniffed the air and pinched his nose, scrunching his face up in distaste. Appearances weren't always absolute; darkness hid many unappealing things until light seared the truth from the ambiguous crevices.

The chamber held the usual underground aromas: the unique smell of moss; wet dirt; musty dampness; stale air and a closed musky, earthy scent. There was also a rank, sulphurous odour sullying the air; it was strong, still fresh. It smelled as though the bowels of hell had spewed up the contents of its stomach, and maybe in a sense it had.

Reece moved towards the first seraph statue to his left. He

removed a dagger from a sheath attached to a belt on his thigh and sliced the palm of his hand. He resheathed the dagger and watched as blood pooled in his palm. He dipped his index finger into the blood and spread it over the entire surface of his palm, mumbling an incantation as he made sure the underside of his hand and fingers were coated in blood. Once finished, he stared up at the seraph statue until she looked down at him. Her eyes glowed and an indent in the shape of a hand formed at the base of her skirt. Reece placed his hand into the indent, making sure every part connected with the Baslian stone. There was a slight pressure as his hand was suctioned to the living stone. Reece closed his eyes and focused on finding calm, then said another incantation. His palm was instantly released. He lifted his hand and stared at it; small threads of glowing gold light twirled on the surface of his palm and it tingled with electricity. If someone were to touch him they'd be rendered unconscious from the taser-like electric jolt, they'd receive. His body squirmed with sensation as though he were covered in crawling insects and he had a mad urge to brush them off, even though he knew it wasn't real. The fine hairs along his spine bristled, brushing against the fabric of his shirt, tender to the slightest touch. Reece shivered, curled his shoulders and hunched his back until the strange feelings subsided. He shook his head and took a deep breath before turning towards the temple at the back of the room. The demon statues had changed position. Their stone wings were now spread, their heads low, their mouths gaping and snarling, and their eyes watchful. They looked as though they were about to leap off and devour him. He angled his body, stepped forward with his right foot and raised his glowing hand above his head towards them, his palm open and fingers spread wide. A shaft of light burst forward, lighting up the shadows and surrounding them in a flash of shimmering light. The demonic statues reverted to their former unthreatening states.

Reece exhaled and lowered his arm, flexing his fingers. His hand still glowed with circling threads of light. He faced the temple with a deep sense of foreboding. Had the demon he'd entombed there over a century ago been set free? God help them if it had. He feared for Anna the most because the demon would come for her first.

For an instant the room expanded and lengthened as he strode towards the temple. He was bombarded with horror movie scenarios where victims experienced similar phenomena – creepy how they'd got that little insight right, he thought. He shook off the eerie feeling, ignoring the moving angel statues as he passed them. He paused at the bottom of the stairs before ascending to the temple alcove. His unease intensified as he scanned his surroundings. He opened his hand to illuminate the darkness with the light orbiting his palm. The wall was intact, with no obvious cracks signifying a break, but that didn't mean it hadn't been breached. From what Makayla and Darrius had said, Alexander had passed through the wall into the crypt beyond. Reece gulped and moved closer, studying the wall for less obvious signs. The hieroglyphs weren't aligned; they were mixed about, indicating something unnatural had passed through.

Reece's heart fell into the pit of his stomach. His worst fears were about to be realised.

He placed his glowing palm in the centre of the smallest circle of hieroglyphs. The rough surface scratched his already tingling hand. Gold light bled from his palm into the rock, highlighting the centre caricature carved into the wall. Reece stepped back and massaged his palm before lowering his hand to his side. He watched the light snake from letter to letter until all the hieroglyphs were highlighted with a shining luminescence. There was a burst of energy as an EMP ripple passed through the room. Reece splayed his arms out to get his balance when the floor shifted beneath his feet. Pebbles showered his head and there was a grinding of rock as the wall split in two, sliding open like a doorway.

Reece waited for the dust to settle before passing through into the crypt beyond. His eyes were drawn to the back wall where there stood the one sarcophagus he'd hoped would still be intact. It wasn't. The lid was a yawning reminder that some things weren't meant to see the light of day.

"Well fuck," he said, swiping his hand through his hair.

"I'd say that's the understatement of the year," Alexander said.

Reece turned around. Alexander sat on the floor with his feet crossed and his back propped against the wall.

"Xander."

"The one and the same," Alexander said, waving his hand in greeting.

"What the fuck have you done?"

"I have no bloody idea, but when I awoke there was a gentleman here who thanked me profusely for setting him free. He was a tad moth-eaten, but in rather good spirits, understandable given his circumstances. He was seriously creepy, though," Alexander said, standing and walking to Reece's side.

"He was an upper level demon, you bloody fool."

"A what?"

"That's right, one of the Dark One's right-hand men; not a man really, but a psycho butcher with a twisted perversity for mutilating women's genitalia."

"Holy shit!"

"Holy shit doesn't describe the shit-storm coming our way. Come on, let's get the hell out of here before Makayla destroys London looking for you," Reece grumbled.

Makayla poured herself another shot of Southern Comfort and sat on a nearby barstool. Zack twirled a drink coaster between his fingers.

"So, do you hate me like you used to?" she asked, tossing back the alcohol and refilling her glass.

Zack sighed, and sat on a stool beside her. "Nope. I

deserved far worse."

"Hey, don't be so hard on yourself, I'm just sorry I brought it up, I'm still trying to wrap my head around everything that's happened. I mean seriously, a week ago I was in the 14th century. That kind of shit just messes with your head." Makayla tapped the side of her forehead with her index finger. "I have no tact whatsoever and I'm sorry for my outburst."

"It's okay, Makayla, really it is, but can we put it behind us now? I hate what I did to you and you hate what you did to me. Let's leave it in the past and accept what we did and move forward. Do you think that's possible?"

Makayla nodded. "Sure. Um . . . Zack, I've been thinking. If you have your powers back and you're a telepathic technopath, theoretically you should be able to access the human farms' computer mainframe with your mind, right?"

"Huh, Shit . . . you're right. I never even considered it. It's plausible, but I'd still have to be where the mainframe is located to access the computers. Thanks, Makayla, I can't believe I never thought of it myself."

Makayla smiled and took a sip of her drink. "Zack?"

"Mmm-hmm?" Zack stopped twirling the drink coaster and looked across at her.

"I'm worried about Xander. Something's off with him and it scares me, I mean it really, really scares me. There's darkness in him now that wasn't there before. God, I wish I knew what Zobiana did to him, apart from the obvious."

"Give him time, Makayla. Do you remember how you

were after being in the dungeon? You were withdrawn and uncommunicative for over three years, perhaps longer. You're still traumatised by it even now. It will take time for him to heal, and if anyone can help, it's you. He needs you now more than ever. You understand better than anyone what he experienced. He'll be okay because he has you."

"Maybe, I don't know how much help I'll be if I can't find him." Makayla sighed and brushed her hands over her face. "I'm so tired, I feel like I could sleep for a month."

"Have you slept at all?"

"No, I've been with Xander in the infirmary for the last five days."

"You should have a hot bath and catch some Zs. Oh, and burn your clothes – they stink to high heaven." Zack pinched his nose. "Peeehew, did you go swimming in the sewers or what?"

Makayla crinkled her nose. "It smells like it, doesn't it? I don't have time to soak in a hot bath, as good as it sounds; I have to get back out there, so a quick shower will have to do. I'll talk to you later, Zack." Makayla stood and pecked him on the cheek.

Zack nodded. "Be careful out there."

"I will, don't I always. . .? Shhhh, don't say a word." She lifted a finger to her lips. "Okay, not always." Makayla smiled at him, but couldn't help notice the sad smile he returned that didn't reach his eyes. She sighed inwardly; all she ever did was hurt the people she loved. She squeezed his shoulder before striding towards the door. She had a little time to get cleaned up before heading to her parents' to talk to Nikolai and meeting up with Lazarus.

Alexander and Reece materialised back at the compound shortly after they'd left the underground chamber. Xander looked around; they were in a room he didn't recognise.

"We're in the catacombs beneath the compound," Reece answered his questioning look.

"Thanks, Reece. I was relieved when you turned up. I'd tried everything I could think of to get out of that chamber, but nothing I did worked," Alexander said, brushing a hand over his jaw and grimacing as he felt his shaggy beard. He needed a shower and a shave.

"That's because it's a prison. No one gets out, not even you."

"Then how—"

"How did the upper level demon get out?"

"Yeah."

"Because of who he is; he's powerful, that's why he was in the spelled sarcophagus. Only someone with knowledge of dead languages, someone like you, could have set him free."

"But, Reece, I don't remember anything, least of all setting the man, sorry, demon, free. The last thing I remember was being with Makayla in a cave below the compound after she rescued me and then I blacked out."

"How do you feel now?"

"I feel fine; actually, I feel better than fine."

"What did Zobiana do to you, Xander?"

"It wasn't so much what Zobiana did, but what Abigail did that worries me. She's a succubus, did you know?"

"No, I didn't, but it makes sense. Her mother's a succubus, so it only stands to reason she would be too. What does her being a succubus have to do with you, though?"

"The bitch tried to siphon my power, nearly killed herself in the process, I think."

"Why would she do something like that?"

"She said something about weakening me so I could be used as a vessel to house the Dark One."

"I beg your pardon?" Reece shook his head. "No, that would be physically impossible. The Dark One can't possess Off Worlders, least of all you, you're too powerful," Reece said, running his finger over his eyebrow in contemplation.

"I thought the same thing, but with everything that's happening do you think it's even possible?"

"Do you sense him inside you?" Reece asked.

"Not at all, and that's what worries me. Would I even know if I was possessed?"

"Believe me, you'd know if you were possessed; you'd hear his voice in your head all the time. He'd wear down your defences. The Dark One, from what I've heard tell, would drive you insane until you surrendered complete control of your body to him."

"Well then why am I blacking out?"

"It could be your vampire transition. Makayla has never sired anyone before and given what she is, no one knows for sure what you would experience during your transition."

"How did you know I was transitioning?"

"Makayla had a meltdown earlier, she mentioned that and more. That's how I knew where to find you. She and Darrius tracked you through the sewers where you led them to the underground chamber I found you in."

"How would you know where it was unless—"

"Unless what?" Reece angled his head.

"Reece, are you the gatekeeper of that underground vault?"

"Yes, or I was. I thought I'd never have to go back there again. How wrong I've been."

"Why would you be a gatekeeper? Has this got something to do with the brotherhood, the Custodians of Rahul? If it has, how come I don't know about it?"

"It was a private mission I'd been working on back in 1888; no one knows about the mission details but Vasili and I. Look, Alexander, I've got to find Anna, I think she's with Jackson. Will you be all right to find your way back up to the compound? It may take you about half an hour to get back to the main area. Sorry, this was the safest place to return. Be on your guard, there are spies among us." Reece moved towards the door, Alexander followed. "Just take the stairs beyond there," Reece said, pointing towards a poorly lit doorway.

"Sure, go find Anna, I'll find my way back to my quarters."

Reece dematerialised before Alexander had the chance to thank him again.

Alexander looked about when he heard laughter; he shivered and the skin on his neck bristled with unease – no one was there. He shrugged off his discomfort and headed towards the stairs to make his way back up towards the compound. He needed to talk to Vasili.

CHAPTER 20.

Jackson had high-tailed it out of the compound as if the hounds of hell were gnawing on his ankles. He couldn't be in Makayla's presence longer than ten minutes without feeling the tiger squirming beneath his skin. Ever since he'd tasted her blood to combat the effects of the Blakspor virus a hunger had grown, one so lethal he feared he'd succumb to the beast and attack her. He knew Makayla could defend herself, but he didn't hold much hope of surviving a confrontation with her. Her blood was unlike anything he'd ever tasted. Sure, Tristan had cured him first with his blood, but they'd given him an extra dose of Makayla's blood to be sure he was cured. Her blood was nothing like Tristan's. It had awoken something primal within him, something he'd feared for centuries – something he barely had control of at the best of times. It was why he'd taken V5 to begin with, to control his baser instincts.

He'd never been in control after that first incident, but there had been a time when he and his tiger lived in harmony and then the murders began. He'd killed his best friend, someone he considered a brother. It'd been an accident, but death was death and he'd been the instigator. That first taste of human flesh had been the spur to a killing spree that had taken years to come back from. His addiction to V5 was the lesser of two evils.

"Hey, Jackson, hold up," Ashley called out.

Jackson stopped and looked over his shoulder at Ashley as she jogged to his side. Anna lagged fifty metres behind them, kicking debris as she ambled along. Reece appeared out of nowhere and grabbed her arm, forcing her to stop. He said something Jackson couldn't hear, but suspected it irritated Anna by the way she reacted. Jackson crossed his arms and waited for Ashley to catch up. Anna was shaking her finger in Reece's face before prodding his chest. Reece was shaking his head and waving his arms in the air.

Ashley glanced towards the arguing pair and sighed. "She's really pissed at him."

"I don't know why, he was doing what he was ordered to do," Jackson said.

"I wish they'd work it out, there's so little joy left in this world."

"There's no joy left in this world, Ashley. None whatsoever."

"There's love," Ashley said, taking her eyes off the arguing pair and focusing her attention back on Jackson. "They've loved each other for so long and wasted so much time already."

"Love . . . Humph, love will get them killed. Just look at Makayla and Alexander, what has it brought them? Nothing but trouble." *You're one to talk, Jack, when you loved Sienna you were the happiest you've ever been in your life,* he thought to himself.

"How can you say that, Jack? You're right about this world, but we still have our friends, we have each other. When it comes down to it, what is life without love?"

"If you say so," Jackson said, turning to leave.

Ashley grabbed his elbow, and he stopped. "Are you okay, Jack? You don't seem yourself. Do you struggle in Makayla's presence too?"

"Why would you ask me such a thing?"

"It's just a look you get on your face when she's in the same space as us. I struggle, I figured you did too."

Jackson faced Ashley again. "How do you struggle, Ashley?"

"Do you really have to ask? I'm a vampire, her blood scent makes my mouth water, it's like nothing I've ever tasted. I just want to rip her throat out and satisfy the hunger."

"You're kidding, I thought I was the only one."

Ashley shrugged. "We were the only two infected, remember. I doubt Freya will feel the same hunger – we are predators."

Jackson glanced back towards Reece and Anna. "For fucks

sake, would you two bloody well stop ear-bashing each other and settle your problems and get on with the make-up sex!" Jackson yelled. "Before we end up kickin' the bucket waitin'!"

Reece and Anna stopped arguing and angled their heads in Jackson's direction. The death stares they threw his way would have stopped him in his tracks had they the ability to kill with their eyes.

"Or not," he murmured to himself with a grimace.

"Well, that helped exacerbate the entire situation, Jack," Ashley said.

"You know what, let's just get the hell off this street. We're asking for trouble being out in the open."

"What about Reece and Anna?" Ashley asked.

"They're grown-ups, they're so pissed off with one another I doubt anyone in their right minds would get in the middle of that, not even a Newblood. They'll be fine. Besides, I think they need to figure their shit out first." Jackson took off down the street.

"Did you have a destination in mind?" Ashley asked, keeping pace with him. She looked back at Anna and Reece once more. They still argued. She didn't bother calling after them.

"I've heard some strange things in the shifter community about the gateways; Ava mentioned hearing things too. We spoke to Gabriel about our concerns – he's apprehensive and asked me to check out the rumours."

Anna watched Jackson and Ashley head off down the road. The emptiness she felt inside was ever-expanding. Why couldn't Reece accept her rejection and leave her alone? It wasn't like he loved her, because if he loved her he would have acted on his feelings, not pushed her away every chance he got.

"What do you want, Reece?"

"You, I want you, I've always wanted you!"

"You have a funny way of showing it."

"I was bloody well protecting you, Anna, I've told you time and time again, I was undercover. What if they'd found out about you, about my feelings for you? Do you think you'd be alive today? No, you'd be DEAD."

Anna chuckled bitterly. "What you don't realise is that I'm already dead inside. You killed what was left of me, what I gave to you freely. My love wasn't good enough, was it? I was just a lowly whore in your eyes. Never good enough for the likes of your pure blue blood. Do you know what's sad? I wasn't on the streets selling my body, Reece. I would never lower or debase myself to where I couldn't respect myself afterward. When my husband died, if you could call that piece of shit, drunkard, wife-beating bastard a husband, I worked in the wash-houses. The only reason I was on the streets that night was because I needed to buy medicine for my children. My babies were sick. I was on my way back, but because of that butcher psycho, and you, they're dead now, aren't they? They didn't have a chance in hell, though, not with the influenza wreaking havoc on their tiny bodies. And now I'll never have children again because I'm a fucking vampire." She stabbed her finger into his chest. "I hate you, I hate you for making me like this." Reece went to embrace her. "Don't touch me, don't fucking touch me, leave me alone, Reece, just leave me the fuck alone."

"Anna . . . I, I went back to give them the medicine, but I was too late, they, they were—"

"I know . . . They were already dead, I know. Goddammit, I know!" she sobbed, the tears pooling in her eyes and streaking down her face. She scrubbed the tears away with the heels of her palms. "Why couldn't you just let me die? I'd be with them now if you had just let me die. I have nothing, do you hear me? Nothing."

"You have me. You've always had me."

"No, you're wrong, I never had you, Reece. Just a desire to have you. A desire that wasn't reciprocated."

"You know that's not true. I've always wanted to be with you; I was protecting you by keeping you at a distance?" Reece pulled her into his arms, she tried to push him away, but he was much stronger. She beat against his chest, struggling to free herself.

Reece took her punishment and held her tight. "I will not let you go, Anna, you can hate me for the rest of your life, but I will love you forever and I'll never let you go again."

"Why, why can't you just let me go?" Anna hiccupped, "It

hurts too much, Reece, I can't live with this pain any longer, it's killing me inside. I miss my babies," Anna sobbed again.

"I'm sorry Anna, I'm so, so sorry, but I will not let you go, ever," Reece said. "I can't give you up, I can't give up on us, and I won't deny my feelings for you any longer. I love you too damned much. I'm just sorry I took so long to act on my feelings and tell you. It took losing you to wake me up." Reece placed his finger under her chin and lifted her face until she looked up into his eyes. He smoothed her hair back from her forehead and brushed the tears from her cheeks. Anna gulped in a breath and hiccupped again, noticing his red-rimmed glistening eyes.

"I'm your sire, Anna, how could you think you were alone? You've never been alone; I feel your pain and your emptiness. Every emotion you've ever felt since your transition has been mine as well. All the nights you cried yourself to sleep in the darkness, I stood in the shadows wanting to comfort you. You were never alone because I was there beside you. Your pain has always been mine. I share your burden because your burden became mine the moment I made you a vampire."

"Why have you said nothing until now?"

"I couldn't. I didn't want to burden you with such knowledge; you could barely handle your own pain, let alone mine. If you'd known it would have been unbearable. I tried to dampen your anguish and you seemed to respond, but I ruined it. I should have told you how I felt. I should have told you what I was about to do, but I feared you'd get caught up in my tangled mess and I didn't want another butcher trying to kill you. All I have ever wanted to do was protect you. Please understand, my intent was never to hurt you, but it's what I ended up doing. Everything has backfired horribly." Reece looked heavenward and sighed. He brushed his hand through his hair before looking back down at her.

"But . . . how come I've never felt your pain? You're my maker, I should have."

Reece smiled softly. "I've shielded my mind from yours because you are young, Anna. If you felt my pain, the pain of millennia would cripple you. I'm old – not as old as Makayla, but older than you by two and half millennia."

"If you love me, truly love me, Reece, you would let me in, you would open your heart and mind and let me in. I can handle it, I know I can." Anna's chest constricted, would he finally let her see all of him?"

"How can you say that when you were ready to give up just now? Didn't you just say it hurts too much? There's a lot you don't know about me, Anna. My life hasn't been easy, sure, I come from money, but life was never easy growing up with parents who were tyrants."

"I want to know everything, Reece. It's the only way we can move forward." Anna touched his cheek, wanting, hoping he would let her in and hoping above all that she hadn't sealed her own fate to the same depths of despair she'd spent a lifetime trying to overcome.

Reece looked about, checking the roadway and their

surroundings, before glancing down at her again. "It's not safe here, but I know somewhere we could go that has been a haven for me over the years. But there's something you need to know before we go, it's important."

"What?" Anna asked, as she felt Reece's body tense. "Reece, what's wrong, has something happened?"

"He's free."

"Who's free?"

"The psycho who almost ended your life."

CHAPTER 21.

L ight flared and receded as the gateway closed behind
Augustus. He looked left and right, making sure he was
alone. The abandoned cavern where he'd arrived was on the
outskirts of Sebastian's palatial grounds. It was a circular
chamber with alternating layers of multi-coloured sandstone in
varying hues of yellow, orange, pink and rich earthy reds. Its
high ceiling made it appear larger than it was, yet it could house
thousands of men if needed. He took a moment to admire his
surroundings. The Golden One's prophecy was carved into the
circling walls, every space covered in hieroglyphic script.
Augustus's eyes travelled the length of the wall. The writing
was a confusing jumble of indecipherable squiggles. No one
understood the prophetic writings, only the great oracle who
had written them and those of the royal bloodline. The
hieroglyphs spoke of the past and future events to come. The

gateway was as ambiguous as its location. A location surrounded by a forest shrouded in a thick veil of mist. Its myth was far-reaching. A myth of a haunted forest filled with horrifying, soul-eating spirits. A myth Sebastian had spent centuries nurturing, a mythical enigma in which to safeguard the cavern and gateway's existence. A myth so terrifying people spoke of it in hushed whispers. Many had searched for the hidden cavern and failed. Those who had found the forest and dared to go beyond its borders never returned.

Augustus stepped down from the gateway dais and strode across the cavern. He stopped when he reached the passage leading into the castle. The moment he stepped into the passageway, stale air and the damp, musty odour of closed spaces assaulted him. He swept aside thick cobwebs weighed down with dust particles and shook off the sticky fibres clinging to his fingertips. He hunched over to dodge more cobwebs as he travelled along the dim, narrow passageway.

His passage disturbed the dust and he pinched his nose to hold back the building sneeze. All he needed was for someone to hear him. He lightened his step to lessen the kick up of dust – an impossible task. A thick cloud ballooned about him like bothersome flies and cobwebs bandaged him like an Egyptian mummy. There were decades of sediment and cobwebs covering the walls and floors – avoiding them was impossible. Augustus smiled; at least this was a clear sign no one had used the passageway.

He came to a masked doorway that opened into a secret

compartment in his closet. Only he and Sebastian knew of its existence. Not even Malachi knew. Those who'd built it had died long ago, taking the knowledge to the grave with them. He opened the door and stepped through. Everything appeared to be the same, but even after his thirty Earth years of imprisonment, much could have changed. Not long in Evronian time, but long enough for changes to occur.

Augustus placed his ear to the walk-in closet door and listened before opening it a crack. He peeked through the gap. When he was certain no one was there, he edged out from the safety of the closet and rushed towards the chamber door. He engaged the lock, sagged against the door and lent his head back. He glanced towards the bathroom and then looked down at the rags he'd worn for the last thirty years, his lip curled in distaste. Augustus stripped off his mangy clothes, threw them onto a grate in the fireplace and set them alight. The threadbare fabric caught fire the moment the flames engulfed them.

He strode towards the bathroom with the focus of a much younger man, all thanks to Ambrosia's blood. He formed a list in his head of all the things he needed to do. First: clean himself up; he could only imagine what he looked like. Second: speak with Uriel. Uriel needed to know about Malachi and Zobiana's treachery and Augustus's own kidnapping and imprisonment. Third: go over the council transcripts for the period of his incarceration, ignorance was unacceptable. If the Vampire Council discovered an imposter had infiltrated his position, he'd no longer have a place on the council. Malachi didn't do things by half measures; there was no telling what new laws he'd implemented. Fourth: find out who on the Vampire Council was collaborating with Zobiana and Malachi.

The alcohol burned Tyrone's throat as he threw back another tequila shot. He was sick of waiting for things to happen. How many years, decades, and centuries did he have to wait for his promised retribution? He was still waiting. "Not long" was Zobiana's comeback for everything. *"Not long now, Tyrone, we have them where we want them."* It was always the same, he'd finish one directive and soon after she'd give him another. There was always something else to do. He didn't mind doing things for her, that wasn't his grievance. It was the wasted time taken to carry out the task. Eight hundred years was a long time to wait to set things right.

"Not long now my arse!" Tyrone picked up the bottle of tequila and drank. They were on the cusp of controlling Earth's gateways. He wanted his share of the glory and had waited an eternity. Now, when the finish line was so close, it looked like he was about to get shafted. *Over my dead body*, he thought to himself. He'd invested too much time and wouldn't be set aside. He'd prove his worth if it killed him.

Yes, he'd got sloppy and made a mistake when Alexander attacked Abigail and Zobiana. There was nothing he could have done, though. There was no stopping the Dark One, not even in his current state. The Dark One at a third of his strength was still lethal. Tyrone wasn't a fool. Although he'd often played one.

Tyrone had been sitting in an alcove by Abigail's bedroom door when he'd overheard Zobiana speaking to her daughter. He'd protected Abigail and Zobiana for longer than he could remember. There was no room for doubt, but Zobiana doubted him now. He couldn't allow her doubt to fester or he'd be a dead man. After the incident with Alexander, he'd nursed both Abigail and Zobiana back to health. Not that Zobiana had known – she'd been unconscious.

He was sick of being overlooked; overshadowed by others. He'd had enough of it as a boy. His father had always praised Alexander's achievements. There was no escaping Alexander's brilliance, not when you were the sickly runt of the family. Tyrone had had to fight, scratch and crawl out from under Alexander's shadow his entire life. He was still trying to step out from his shadow. There was no pleasing his father, so he'd stopped bothering. It was one reason he'd joined Zobiana's ranks and not looked back. She'd seen his potential and encouraged him, offering him something he couldn't refuse. He'd stand by her even if she thought him a traitor.

"Hey, Tyrone, mind if I sit?" Abigail asked, coming to a stop beside him.

She was as beautiful as ever, her exotic, dark, almond-shaped eyes had always entranced him. "Are you sure you want to associate with the traitor?"

"You're no traitor," Abigail said, pulling a dining chair out and sitting beside him. She held her hand out for the bottle of tequila; he handed it to her and watched her lift it to her lips.

"Humph, not what your mother implied earlier."

"You heard then?" Abigail handed the bottle back to him; he took it from her and gulped down two mouthfuls before placing the bottle on the tabletop and folding his hands.

"I did. Nothing gets by me, Abigail." Tyrone glanced towards the bottle of Monte Alban Mezcal Tequila. The bottle was almost empty. He stared at it in remembrance; the plump grub at the bottom brought back memories of a life he'd chosen to leave behind. The last time he'd eaten grub larvae was the night before becoming a vampire. Tequila wasn't produced until the sixteen hundreds, but there'd been similar spirits to Tequila with similar grub larvae in the bottom of the bottles. He'd been so hungover and sick from all the alcohol he'd drunk and had spent most of the next day vomiting in a ditch. He glanced back at Abigail. "Do you think I'd betray you or your mother?"

"No, never. Mother's just paranoid. Your behaviour was a little strange, though."

"I hate him, Abby, I hate him so much. I was smiling because he'd got what he deserved. You more than anyone should understand my hatred, you hate him as much as I do."

"I would have been smiling as well, had I not been cooking like pork crackling."

Tyrone chuckled.

"What's so funny?" Abigail asked.

"I was just thinking of something your mother said about you when you were unconscious."

"What did she say?"

"Oh, just that you looked like the scorched remains of Freddie Krueger's handmaiden."

Abigail smiled. "Ever complimentary, isn't she? She's never been one to mince words."

"How can I make amends to her, Abby? How can I make her understand why I reacted the way I did?"

"We need to draw Makayla out," Abigail said, scratching her forehead.

"How do we do that?

"We take something that means the world to her."

"We did that already, with Emily, but your mother exchanged her for Alexander."

"Yes, we did, but I think it will work again if we try a different tactic to bring Makayla down a peg; you know we need to hobble the confident bitch. I say we go back and destroy them all, and the one way we can achieve that is by giving my mother what she has always wanted."

"And what has she always wanted?"

"My father."

"What do you propose we do?"

"We eliminate the one person standing in the way. Ambrosia." Abigail pushed the chair with the backs of her legs and stood up. "Come on, let's get out of here. Mother wants us to check how the gateway takeovers are progressing. Afterward, we should broach the subject we were discussing with her. You should explain to her why you acted the way you did, she'll understand. Alexander has been the bane of her existence ever since Makayla came onto the scene. I'm sure she'd forgive you."

"Sounds like a plan." Tyrone stood, picked up the tequila bottle and downed the remaining liquor. The grub slipped into his mouth and he chomped his teeth together. The pop of soft flesh in his mouth brought a smile to his face. The grub disintegrated in his mouth like a piece of fine chocolate. When he'd finished eating, he licked his lips and opened his eyes again.

Abigail smiled. "Hey, we may get lucky and find more Zoldarni emissaries to torture. The last one I sucked the life out of gave me a buzz that lasted a week. Come on, let's round up the Newbloods and be on our way."

Tyrone nodded and followed Abigail to the door.

CHAPTER 22.

Shattered glass covered the kitchen floor; Makayla tightened the bath towel around her chest and stared down at the mess. Water dripped from the strands of her wet hair and trailed a path down the bridge of her nose, collecting in the corners of her mouth. She licked the residue from her lips. The buzzing in her ears was getting louder and the white fuzz collecting at the edges of her peripheral vision was expanding. Makayla closed her eyes, took a deep breath and exhaled before opening her eyes again. She flexed her fingers, opening and closing her trembling hands until the blood circulated. She should have known better, you don't pick up a glass with wet hands.

"Distracted much, Makayla?" she said to herself. It always started in her hands. The tingling and numbness was a sensation she'd got used to over the centuries. She needed to feed. She dragged a chair to her side and slumped onto it. The burning in her gut was overpowering her other senses, making her clumsy. She shouldn't be hungry; it hadn't been that long since she'd last fed. Her stomach rumbled anyway. Makayla opened the refrigerator and grabbed a bag of synthetic blood. One of the benefits of her poky little kitchen was that everything was within reach. She uncorked the blood bag and guzzled its contents.

"Ugh, that's so bad." She grimaced and retrieved, then drank, another two bags, her face scrunching up in distaste.

"Synthetic blood won't work. You need Alexander's blood. Find him," her nemesis commented.

"What, no snide remarks?" Makayla said, tossing the empty bags in the bin and standing. The blood had taken the edge off her hunger, but it wouldn't last. She scooped up the mess on the floor with a dustpan and brush, threw the rubbish in the bin and eyed Alexander's door. He wasn't in his room and she didn't sense him nearby. Had he even returned?

Makayla ripped the towel from her body and slung it over the chair. She stalked to her cupboard across the room and rummaged through its contents until she found something to wear. She dressed quickly, braided her hair, put on her boots and armed herself.

BANG. . .BANG. . .BANG.

Makayla removed a dagger from her thigh holster and tiptoed towards the door.

BANG. . .BANG. . .BANG.

She sidled up to the door, put her back to the wall and

waited.

"Makayla, are you in there? It's me, Thomas, I need to speak with you."

Makayla sagged against the wall and holstered her dagger before easing the door open and tugging Thomas into her room. She poked her head out through the opening and checked the corridor to make sure no one had followed him. She closed the door and engaged the lock before facing Thomas. He stood fidgeting in front of her, shuffling his feet, and clasping and twisting his hands together.

"Was it necessary for you to make so much bloody noise? I was ready to slit your throat. I would have, had you not spoken. The way you were hammering on my door, a person would think you were trying to break it down."

"Sorry, I'm still getting used to my vampire strength."

"Is something wrong? You look like you've seen a ghost."

"I don't know what I saw, but whatever, whoever it was, he scared the bejeezus out of me. Freakiest thing I've ever seen, he was huge."

"And you're telling me this why?"

Thomas shrugged. "I don't know."

"Why are you here, Thomas? What do you want?"

"Oh, right, yeah, Vasili asked me to come and get you. He needs to speak with you."

"Why would he ask you to get me when he can speak to me with his mind? You know what, don't answer that, I'll ask him myself. Is that all?"

Thomas nodded, if he shook it any faster Makayla swore it would fly off his shoulders and lodge somewhere in the ceiling.

"You can go now, Thomas, I'll be along shortly." Makayla opened the door for Thomas to leave.

"Oh, okay, sure." Thomas twisted and fiddled with his shirt collar before slipping past Makayla into the corridor. Makayla sensed the Newblood's apprehension; he was acting like a frightened child scared of the boogie man hiding in the closet.

"Thomas, everything will be okay, you know."

"Will it? I don't know. Have you been outside? It's terrible." Thomas looked up into her face, his dark eyes almost eclipsing his pale face, they seemed so large. He was a good head shorter than she was. Makayla could smell his hunger and he appeared undernourished. Hungry Newblood vampires had a sickly smell, like their bodies were deteriorating; the odour of dying flesh was unmistakable.

"Thomas, have you fed?"

Thomas shook his head. "Ah, no, not since I first came to the compound."

"That was months ago. Feed, if you don't, you'll die, or worse, you'll kill an innocent, and believe me, you don't want that on your conscience. Wait there." Makayla retrieved two bags of synthetic blood from her refrigerator and handed them to him. "You need to feed. It's synthetic blood and tastes like shit, but it will sustain and nourish you."

Thomas took her offering. "Tha-thank you, Makayla, thank you for everything."

"You're welcome, kid." Makayla tousled his hair. "Now get your arse to your quarters and feed or, so help me, God, I will pinch your nose and pour it down your throat myself."

Thomas nodded a third time and scrambled down the passageway. Makayla watched him until he turned the bend.

Something wasn't right. Vasili always contacted her telepathically if he needed to speak with her.

Makayla closed the door, but before she had a chance to return to her closet and retrieve more weapons, her Druidoynan armour lifted into the air, it hovered for the briefest moment and then the intricate gold filigree highlighting the eagle on the breastplate shimmered. Small orbs of light sparkled into existence as if the light had leaped off the armour. The firefly-like orbs began to vibrate and buzz. The sound escalated in volume as the glowing orbs brightened further. There was a flash of brilliant light. Seconds later her armour crystallised and disappeared altogether before reappearing on her body. The metal was no longer black, but white with intense heat, although Makayla wasn't affected by the heat or the magical properties emanating from the metal. There was a fizzling sound and then the armour returned to its former black appearance. Makayla could hear a low-frequency hum and feel the metal vibrating against her body. The last time the armour had done something similar, she'd awakened seven hundred years in the past. She shivered, the hairs prickling on her body. If ever there was a warning system in place, her armour was it. And Vasili sending Thomas confirmed the warning.

Vasili sat behind his desk waiting for Makayla's arrival. He hadn't seen her since her return from the 1400s. From what Marianna had told him there'd been quite a confrontation when Lazarus and Makayla had shown up and saved them. Vasili regarded Ecktar, the Aurylian guard stood by the door surveying the room. He was paying particular attention to the vibrantly coloured Monet painting on the wall above Vasili's head. Vasili wondered how Ecktar planned to prove Makayla was the Chosen One. How many times would she be subjected to the countless trials to demonstrate her authenticity as the Chosen One? Vasili hoped his test wouldn't get Ecktar killed. Makayla's temper rivalled none; she wasn't a lightweight by any means, not anymore.

There were three brief knocks, then two heavier successive knocks on his door. Vasili relaxed in his seat, crossing his legs and folding his hands on the desktop in front of him. She'd understood his warning. Vasili and the Shadow Seekers had come up with a sequence of knocks to communicate with one another. Much like the secretive gestures used by baseball pitchers and catchers.

"Enter," he said in a calm, authoritative voice. Ecktar moved away from the door to the opposite side of the room. He crossed his arms over his chest and waited for Makayla to enter.

The door eased open and Makayla crossed the threshold into his office and closed the door. Her rigid posture belied her calm appearance. She was a warrior through and through, armed and battle-ready. Her Druidoynan armour had become a part of her everyday attire. Vasili said a silent thanks to Alexander for asking Zack to make it for her.

Makayla's face gave away nothing as she entered his office. When she noticed Ecktar standing on the opposite side of the room, she nodded a respectful greeting and then focused her full attention on Vasili. Not giving an inch. Vasili couldn't help but feel impressed by how well she was holding it together. She'd changed a lot.

"You wanted to speak with me, Vasili?" Makayla stood with her hands resting on the hilts of her swords, relaxed and waiting for him to respond.

"Yes, we have important matters to discuss with you. I'd like to introduce you to Ecktar, the commanding officer of the Zoldarni Guard from Cwonoth. Ecktar, this is Makayla Uriel, the young lady I spoke of with Overlord Avinash."

The Aurylian guard bowed his head and extended his lengthy arms away from his body. "'Tis an honour to make your acquaintance, Lady Uriel."

Makayla chuckled. "Believe me, I'm no lady, not the kind you're used to, anyhow, although . . ." Makayla shook her head and chuckled again. "Sorry, I don't mean to be disrespectful, and I know I'm being rude, but I'm trying to picture the female of your species and am failing dismally. You'll get used to me and realise your mistake; I'm not a lady."

"Nevertheless, 'tis an honour."

"Why are you here, Commander Ecktar?"

Vasili coughed, and cleared his throat, Makayla glanced towards him. "What, aren't I allowed to ask?"

Vasili was about to speak when the Aurylian guard raised his finger to silence him.

Makayla eyeballed the weird-looking humanoid creature. Who was she kidding? He didn't look human at all. He was the strangest compilation of weird body parts she'd ever seen put together. Whoever had created his species, be it God, aliens, whoever, must have had one helluva warped sense of humour. Let's give this guy an extra set of eyes, oh, and we mustn't forget the protruding forehead and a jaw like the cornerstone of a house. He'll look so cool. Makayla's mouth hooked up in a stupid grin. What planet did he come from? He looked like a child's drawing, all out of proportion. Mr purple-people-eater. He had no nose just an X to mark the spot, like a pirate's treasure map leading to gold. Makayla was pretty sure his X didn't lead to Gold though. And what had happened to his ears? No, let's not give this poor guy ears, he doesn't need them, two holes will do.

Ecktar observed Makayla with a growing smile. His head tipped back, and he laughed out loud. "You're very humorous, Lady Uriel. I don't have ears because I hear with my mind, ears are unnecessary for Aurylians like myself. They come in handy, however, when I need to hear conversations from a great distance."

"Son of a bitch," Makayla said, eyeing Vasili and then glancing back at Ecktar. Now she understood why Vasili hadn't contacted her. She'd been shielding her mind, but not like she did with Off Worlders. She reinforced her thoughts, throwing up barriers no otherworldly being could break.

"Now, for the reason I'm here," Ecktar said, observing her with a thoughtful glint in his eyes.

Makayla watched Ecktar uncurl to his full eight feet and almost wished he'd hit his head – no such luck. He spread his arms and stretched out his neck, his head and hands almost touching the ceiling and walls on either side of him. Seven lines appeared on each side of his throat similar to fish gills, but the similarities ended there. Makayla glimpsed dark purple, feather-like filters between each slit. They swelled out, expanding like balloons. The feather-like barbs and veins separated, oscillating back and forth as they quivered. Makayla heard Vasili's guttural gasp and glanced towards him. He was hunched over his desk, and his blood coated hands were covering his bleeding ears. That's when Makayla heard a chorus of people screaming in pain throughout the underground compound. Vasili's eyes were bulging, as if they were about to pop out of his skull. Whatever Ecktar was doing didn't affect Makayla. She couldn't hear a thing, but she felt the air pressure vibrating around her.

She swung her arm up and twisted her hand. Ecktar lifted off his feet and hit the ceiling; there was a loud crunch as his skull connected with the rock. The screaming throughout the underground bunker stopped the moment his head struck the ceiling, and he fell to the ground in a crumpled heap. Makayla stepped forward and grabbed him by the throat, she squeezed as she lifted him above her, his hands limp at his sides. The gill-like slits were no longer visible. Ecktar came to with a jolt and stared down into her upturned face. A jagged smile formed on his features.

"As I said, earlier, 'Tis an honour to meet you, Chosen One of Prophecy," he spoke into her mind.

"What the fuck, Ecktar? What the hell are you trying to prove?" Makayla threw him across the room towards the couch against the wall opposite Vasili's desk.

Ecktar coughed, rubbing his throat, and struggled to stand.

"Don't, just don't, all right. I swear if you stand up, I will end you, Zoldarni guard or not. I don't give a shit who you are. If you go all man-from-Atlantis on me again, I will rip your gills out and stuff them down your throat just for the fun of it!" Makayla moved towards Vasili and helped him back into his seat. He'd slipped from his chair and had fallen to the ground. "Are you okay, Vasili?"

He nodded. "Yes, I'm all right," he choked, spluttering as he captured his breath.

"I needed proof," Ecktar said.

"Proof, proof of what? God, not you too? Don't tell me, you needed proof I am the Chosen One. How many times do you people need to do this? Seriously, there has to be a better way, you could have asked me to do something only I, the

Chosen One, could do."

"I did. You didn't react to the shalzing did you?"

"Is that what you call what you did?"

Ecktar nodded.

"Well, if you do that again, I shall incinerate you, you got it?"

Ecktar nodded, smiling at her again,. "I never thought I'd meet you in my lifetime, Lady Uriel. I beg your pardon, your highness." He slipped off the couch and knelt before her, bowing his head and touching his forehead to the ground.

"Please, get up off your knees, and don't call me highness. I'm nobody's highness, and I'm not a lady, call me Makayla, or Kayla if you'd prefer, just don't call me your highness. Call me anything, but that." Makayla helped Ecktar back onto the couch and turned towards Vasili. He was wiping blood from his beard and ears. "Where have you been, Vasili?"

"I've just returned from Cwonoth where I spoke to, Overlord Avinash, the leader of the Zoldarni. We discussed the disturbing atrocities committed by Zobiana and what has been happening here on Earth. Commander Ecktar here accompanied me back with thirty of the Zoldarni guard to secure the gateways and find out what happened to the Zoldarni emissaries here on Earth. They've disappeared. We fear they may have met with foul play."

"If you haven't been able to contact them, then it's more than likely they have. I've much to tell you Vasili, but not now, not here." Makayla eyed Ecktar, who was listening intently.

"Did you tell them everything?" Makayla indicated Ecktar with a shake of her head.

Vasili nodded. "Yes."

"Did you know what he was going to do? What was it you called it, Ecktar, shalzing?"

Ecktar nodded. "Correct."

"Did you know, Vasili?"

"Sorry, no, just that he needed to prove you were the Chosen One."

"Fair enough," she said, looking over her shoulder at Ecktar. "Well, I have to go to my parents' house and speak with my aunt." Makayla raised her eyebrow at Vasili in warning. "When I get back, we need to discuss the matter of my partner; he's gone AWOL."

Vasili kept his face neutral, shielding his thoughts from Ecktar as best he could. "All right, Makayla, give my regards to your family. I have to go with Ecktar and locate the emissaries. Oh, before I forget, I have something for you." Vasili removed a small box from his desk drawer and handed it to her with a nod.

Makayla took it, hiding her curiosity and turned to leave.

"Makayla?"

"Hmm?"

"Be careful. We live in dangerous times." Vasili pointed to the ruby gem at her throat. "She'll be coming for it. You need to find the other gems before she does. It's the only way we can defeat her and stop any of this. If we have all the gems and the globe in our possession, we have a chance at setting things right again."

"I know, I'll try, but without Alexander to help me crack the codes, I don't know if I'll have much success in finding them. Although something strange happened when the gems I had in my possession came into contact with the Trinian Globe. I was instantly transported to the next gem without even having to translate the codes on the artefact. I was expecting it to be harder to locate the gems."

"It's usually the first gem that's the hardest to locate. Things will fall into place and end how they're meant to, have faith and everything will work out," Vasili said, standing and moving in front of his desk.

"I hope so, Vasili, but nothing ever goes to plan for me, ever," Makayla said, dematerialising.

Vasili looked across at Ecktar. "Did she pass your test?"

Ecktar stood and clapped Vasili on the back and smiled his enigmatic smile. "Yes, in all my years no one has ever bested me. She did it with the wiggle of her fingers. She is the Chosen One of prophecy. She has yet to come into her full power, though, it's just beyond her reach. Once she possesses all the gems and controls the Trinian Globe, she will be unstoppable."

CHAPTER 23.

Steam billowed about Alexander as he wrapped a towel around his waist and wiped a hand down the bathroom mirror to remove the condensation. He couldn't remember the high-pitched squeaking noise of cleaning glass ever having sounded so loud. His heightened hearing was overwhelming. He looked like he felt: ragged and weary. At least he didn't have the hillbilly appearance anymore; sure his hair was longer, but minus the scraggly beard he almost looked human again … not that he was human. Alexander ran a hand over his clean-shaven jaw; he'd changed, not only from his vampire transition but from his time in the dungeon. He was much thinner, but wasn't as bad as he'd been when he'd first arrived back at the compound. From what Reece had told him he'd looked like a prisoner of war.

Alexander leaned in closer to the mirror. His eyes were intense. The usual amber colour now had flecks of gold in them. He blinked; there was also an unusual iridescence as if a fluorescent light shone from within them. No doubt from becoming a vampire and being sired by Makayla. He opened his mouth and looked at his eye teeth; they were longer, not fully extended, but longer than he was accustomed. He touched the tip of one fang and snatched his hand back when he pricked his finger. A bead of blood pooled on the tip of his finger and the coppery metallic smell of blood surrounded him. He gulped down the saliva pooling in his mouth and licked his fangs as they extended. Alexander looked back into the mirror. His eye colour was no longer amber, but instead red with gold flecks. He watched his face change as he stuck his finger in his mouth and sucked the blood from its tip.

"Hmm," he groaned in pleasure. His eyes turned a deeper shade of red. Black veins formed in the skin surrounding his eyes, pulsating in time with his heartbeat. He slipped his finger from his mouth, moving his head from side to side, mesmerised by the changes in his appearance. The length of his fangs had doubled in size and his eyes ... his eyes were just plain creepy. "You're really rocking the new look, Alexander," he said to himself. He shook his head and took a deep, calming breath before exhaling, repeating the breathing exercise until his face returned to normal. He heard laughter but there was no one there. "You're losing it, Xander," he mumbled to himself, "talking to yourself and hearing voices in your head are clear signs of just how far you've fallen." Laughter again. Alexander shook his head a second time, trying to dislodge the gathering disquiet growing within him. He didn't know if it was part of being a vampire; or if it was a consequence of Makayla siring him. She had similar problems to contend with; voices in her head. Had he inherited the same condition? Or was it something more sinister?

He traced a fingertip along one of the thin scars marring his chest, and could only imagine how bad his back was as it had received more attention. He didn't look, it was best he didn't know. Whip scars covered his body, all thanks to Abigail and the salt she'd rubbed into his wounds. He remembered his uncle telling him as a teenager to avoid swimming in salt water when wounded because salt prevented the body from returning to its former appearance after injury. Abigail had made sure he'd remember her brutality by leaving a reminder. Not that he'd ever forget.

Alexander turned away from the mirror and switched off the light before exiting the bathroom. He made his way into his room and sat on the edge of his bed. The room hadn't changed. His stomach growled, reminding him of his hunger, his appetite was unquenchable. It was the weirdest sensation. Becoming a vampire wasn't what he'd expected and understanding the signs his body was giving was a contradiction. He'd never fully understood Makayla's hunger, until now. It was a hunger that overshadowed and consumed everything.

Alexander swallowed the saliva pooling in his mouth then swept his hand through his wet hair and stood. He removed the towel from his waist, tossed it into the air and snapped his fingers. The towel vanished at the same time his clothes and weapons appeared on his body. He was glad his magic was still intact. Alexander wondered where Makayla was. He'd sensed her presence when he'd got closer to the upper levels of the compound, but then she'd disappeared. He knew where he had to go, but would Makayla find him? Would she think to look? He had to trust she would because he needed to go and check the object was still where he'd hidden it long ago. But he needed to speak with Vasili before he left.

Alexander stepped into the corridor, closing his door behind him. There was no time to walk, so he jogged. The compound was empty; not a soul was about. He supposed everyone was out patrolling London's streets or sleeping in their quarters. He reached Vasili's door and could hear Vasili talking about Makayla with someone inside. He knocked on the door and waited.

"Come in, Xander, I've been waiting for you," Vasili said.

Alexander edged the door open and was surprised to see a Zoldarni guard standing in Vasili's office. "Sorry, I didn't mean to intrude."

"It's no intrusion, come in," Vasili invited.

Alexander closed the door behind him. As he entered, the Zoldarni guard turned towards him. When Alexander realised who the guard was, he smiled. "Ecktar, it's been a long time;

it's good to see you again."

Ecktar returned his smile. "Yes, it has been way too long, old friend. *I was* sorry to hear about your capture. How are you faring?"

"A little better now I'm back; better than I was when I arrived at the compound, that's for sure."

Vasili watched Ecktar and Alexander as they shook hands and clapped each other on the back. Alexander chuckled when he noticed Vasili's confusion. "I was unaware you knew one another," said Vasili.

Xander nodded. "We've known each other for aeons. I met Ecktar when I was a lad of fourteen. Ecktar was part of an envoy patrolling our region of the Multiverse. We'd been having problems. I can't recall the specifics, but once the Zoldarni showed up the problems stopped. Ecktar was one of the young officers invited to a banquet held at my parents' home on Avalon. He'd only just finished his training, but had already made a name for himself." Alexander turned to Ecktar. "Things must be bad if you're here on Earth."

Ecktar's smile disappeared as he nodded. "Yes, things are very bad."

"What happened during my incarceration? Do I even want to know?" Alexander looked from Vasili to Ecktar and back again. "What's Zobiana done now?"

Twenty Newbloods surrounded the gateway, and more were spread out throughout the forest. It was the seventh gateway Ashley and Jackson had come upon with Newbloods guarding it.

Ashley shook her head. "We can't take them on alone, Jack, there's too many of them."

"I know, but my tiger could."

"I thought you lost control when you shape-shifted?"

"I don't lose total control, well, not around Newbloods anyhow. Their blood stinks, so we should be okay – just don't go cutting yourself."

"Is that supposed to ease my mind?"

Jackson shrugged and smiled sheepishly.

"Do you want to be captured again? I don't. We can't take the risk, we're only meant to be checking the gateways, let's get out of here before it's too late."

"Well, well, well, what have we here? A lovers' tryst?"

"Shit." Jackson tensed when he felt the ice-cold blade of a sword touch his throat and heard Ashley's squeak of surprise. Ashley was hauled up by the armpits and pulled against the body of a lanky Newblood. The Newblood leered at her and licked his lips before licking the length of her throat.

Ashley cringed and squeezed her eyes shut. Her mouth turned down in disgust as her shoulder came up to dislodge his mouth from her neck.

"I'll be 'aven a fine time with your wench now, matey," the Newblood said, squeezing Ashley's breast. Ashley elbowed him in the stomach and Jackson watched her right hand inch down her leg towards the dagger she had strapped to her thigh.

The Newblood chuckled. "That's right, girlie, I like it when my bitches struggle, the fight makes it more fun."

A low guttural growl vibrated from Jackson's throat as he watched the Newblood groping Ashley. Jackson was dragged from the long grass where they'd been crouching forty metres away from the gateway. He glanced back towards the gateway to see if the other Newbloods guarding it had noticed. Thankfully they were oblivious to the commotion and had their backs turned away. He focused his attention on the two guards detaining them and winked at Ashley. Ashley understood his signal and dropped, becoming limp in her captor's arms. The sudden shift in weight caused the Newblood to lose his balance. Ashley retrieved her dagger with lightning reflexes and spun to face the Newblood as they toppled to the ground. She smashed her free hand into the Newblood's throat, incapacitating and silencing him. He was choking for air when she stabbed him in the heart. Blood spurted in her face as she pulled the dagger free from his corpse and rolled away.

Jackson shifted the moment Ashley brought down her opponent. His prickling skin was hypersensitive with the change his body was undergoing. He ignored the pain and gritted his teeth. The sound of tearing fabric and the crunch of his breaking bones reforming echoed in his ears. He rolled his head as his clothes tore from his body. His nose became a snout and his canine teeth lengthened to lethal points. Fur rippled down his spine, muscle and cartilage re-knitting within his body as he morphed into a white tiger.

The Newblood trying to detain Jackson barely had time to register his transformation. Jackson struck, swiping his clawed paws up and out in a circular motion. One paw knocked the sword from the Newblood's hand and the other clawed its throat, severing his jugular before he alerted the others in his group. Blood spurted in gushing maroon arcs, splattering the grass and Jackson's fur.

"We've got to leave, Jack, before they realise what we've done," Ashley whispered. She squatted beside the dead Newblood and wiped her bloody dagger along his trouser leg, then holstered her weapon.

Jackson rubbed his body against her in a comforting feline gesture. *"Come on, jump on my back and let's get back to the compound. We need to let Vasili and Gabe know what's going on,"* Jackson said to her telepathically. Ashley nodded and vaulted onto his back, grabbing a fistful of his neck fur for balance. Jackson took off, weaving a path away from the gateway. He kept well away from the patrolling Newbloods in the forest, scenting their presence and avoiding them as they left.

CHAPTER 24.

Tristan glanced from the fire in the hearth towards his mother. "Is Aunt Marianna okay?"

"Yes, she's resting, she needs to recuperate. I've helped as much as possible, if Makayla were here she'd be able to help with her healing touch."

"She looks so old, Mother, it's unusual for a seraph to age; will she recover?"

"She's been isolated a long time, Tristan. It happens when seraphs go for too long without contact with our own kind."

"I had no idea. Is it the same for Vasili? He also appears much older than he should."

"That's because Vasili is Aunt Marianna's blood-bonded mate, but it will reverse when they're together. I fear he hasn't fed properly since her abduction either. Seven hundred years is a long time to be separated from one's soul mate, but it was made worse by their bond."

"I've always wondered why Vasili looked so much older than the rest of us," Makayla said from the lounge room doorway.

Tristan and Ambrosia turned towards her. Makayla couldn't help smiling when her mother opened her arms for a welcoming embrace. Makayla dematerialised and reappeared in front of her, and her mother folded her within her arms and squeezed. When she released Makayla, she held her by the forearms and looked into her face with a wide grin. Her mother lifted her hand and swept the hair out of Makayla's eyes.

"My turn," Tristan said, dragging Makayla into his arms and hugging her too. He clapped her on the back and ruffled her hair after releasing her.

"We've been worried sick about you, Makayla. Where have you been and what took you so long to come home?" Her mother asked.

"I travelled seven hundred years back in time to the past; I found Alexander and then lost him again. Oh, and I found the third Trinian gem. So much has happened; I'd need a whole month just to tell you about it," Makayla said, looking about the room. "Where is everyone? How are Chancellor Lagorias and Aunt Marianna doing?"

"They're well. Aunt Marianna is resting and Chancellor Lagorias returned to Evron—"

"What, so soon? Isn't that dangerous? He wasn't in any condition to return to Evron, especially with an imposter loose."

"That's the thing, Augustus's imposter is missing. It's been over a week now, and he's nowhere to be found, he just disappeared, no one knows where," Tristan said, shoving his hands in his trouser pockets.

"That's strange, but not surprising considering the real Augustus was held captive by Zobiana. Do they have any idea who the imposter was yet?"

"They have their suspicions, but no real proof. The only certainty is the imposter's connection to Zobiana," Tristan replied.

"What's Augustus going to do when he gets back to Evron?"

"Why, take his place as chancellor of the Vampire Council, of course," her mother said, sitting down in a chair near the hearth. She invited Makayla and Tristan to take a seat. They complied and sat either side of her.

"Mother, they will surely realise something's amiss with him; Chancellor Lagorias looks nothing like his usual self." Makayla rubbed her forehead; an ache was taking hold.

"He looked fine when he left because I fed him my blood."

"You did what? Seraph blood is addictive – does Father know?"

"Yes, I know," Sebastian said, striding into the room. "Seraph blood is addictive if it's consumed too many times. It can be imbibed once and only once. I'm surprised you gave Augustus your blood so freely, Makayla, because your blood is also addictive."

"Sorry, Father, but I had no choice, I had to give Augustus my blood or I wouldn't have been able to save him and the others from Zobiana's dungeon," Makayla said, standing to greet her father. He embraced her as if he'd not seen her in an age – and he hadn't. Makayla hadn't expected the hug, but it was nice nonetheless.

Her father held her at arm's length. "You did the right thing, Makayla. As did we; your mother had to give Augustus her blood too. It was the only way he could return to Evron, to his position as chancellor on the council. We need him there now more than ever. He's the only one we can trust. We don't know who on the council is faithful. Your mother's blood will give him the edge he needs to weed out Zobiana's people. He'll sense when people are lying to him. Your mother and I decided it was the right thing to do."

Makayla nodded. "Father, have you had time to speak with Lazarus? Do you know what happened to us, do you know about Malachi?"

"Yes, sweetling, Lazarus told me everything. How are you faring, are you okay? How's Alexander?"

Tears pooled in Makayla's eyes at the mention of Alexander.

"Oh, sweet girl, don't cry, everything will be okay, really it will." Her father pulled her into his arms again and stroked her hair. A lump formed in Makayla's throat, she wrapped her arms around her father's waist, feeling as if her world was ending;

she felt so misplaced. Where was Alexander and what was wrong with him? Would things be okay? She felt as though they'd never be okay again, not with the way things were spiralling down lately. So much depended on Makayla and her prophecy. The weight of the world, every world in the Multiverse, was literally on her shoulders.

"I'm not strong enough, Baba, I can't help myself, let alone the ones I love, how am I going to fulfil my prophecy? I'm letting everyone down. I can't find Xander, I've lost him again – something's seriously wrong with him. I don't know what Zobiana did to him or if what's happening to him is because I turned him. He's not the same and I'm so, so scared what I've done is killing him. I can't lose him, I can't, Baba, I'm not strong enough, I'll not survive another loss." Makayla sobbed so hard she lost her footing; her father caught her and held her upright as he lowered her to a couch and sat beside her.

"Makayla, you must hear my words, sweetling, you are stronger than you know, you have the strength of both seraph and vampire bloodlines. You are stronger than both your mother and I put together. You don't know this, but when I met your mother, she was the general of the Seraph Guard on Evron. You remind me so much of her. You are a warrior and you come from a long line of warriors – never forget it. You will succeed, you will defeat whoever stands in your way, and Alexander will be by your side. I've seen it, sweetling, I've witnessed your greatness in a vision. Have faith, all will be right in your world."

Makayla looked into her father's face and he brushed the tears from her cheeks. "How can you say that? What kind of warrior cries like a baby?"

"The best of us cry, Makayla," Tristan said, sitting down beside her.

"I've shed my fair share of tears, Makayla, and I was a warrior once," her mother said, kneeling on the floor before her. "I may not look like a warrior now, but in my heart, I will always be the warrior your father fell in love with. No matter what role I play, be it mother, wife, friend or foe, the warrior is always below the surface. It's a part of who I am. As it is a part of who you are. Even the greatest warriors cry."

Makayla glanced at her mother. "I came here to speak with Aunt Marianna and apologise to her and what am I doing? I'm blubbering on your couch. I'm so sorry for my meltdown; the last few weeks have been crazy. I'm an emotional roller coaster, and it's so out of character. I never cry, and all I've done since I've returned from the past is cry. I'm so moody all the time, one minute I'm laughing, the next I'm angry and then I'm crying like a spoilt child who hasn't got their way. I'm so out of control my mood swings are giving me whiplash. I'm all over the board."

Makayla noticed the shared look between her parents; it was so brief she wasn't sure she'd seen it.

Makayla stood abruptly, an uncomfortable feeling forming in her chest because of her foolish breakdown. "Well, if you could point me towards Aunt Marianna's room I'd be grateful."

"Her room's two doors down from Emily's room," Her mother said, standing with the aid of her father. "She's a little weak, if you're able, could you help aid in her recovery?"

"Oh good, I can drop in and say hello to Emily as well. And I will do what I can to help Aunt Marianna." Makayla kissed her parents and Tristan on their cheeks before bolting out of the room without a backwards glance.

"You're such an idiot," she mumbled to herself as she strode towards her aunt's room. She was surprised her nemesis hadn't made any snide or derogatory remarks during her meltdown, it wasn't like she hadn't had plenty of opportunities – she'd had two, in fact. Her meltdown with her parents and the meltdown with the Shadow Seekers. Makayla was winning on all fronts.

Makayla stopped at Emily's door first, was about to open it when she heard growling. Makayla smiled, Izzy was doing his job. She knocked instead. "Emily, are you in there? Can I come in?" There was a thump and the patter of running feet. The door was thrown open with such force Makayla expected the handle to embed in the wall.

"Makayla, you're here, yay!"

Makayla laughed and caught Emily as she bounded into her arms. "Goodness, you weigh a tonne, what have you been eating, rocks?"

"No silly, I eat food not rocks," Emily giggled, and wrapped her arms around Makayla's neck, flowering kisses all over her cheeks."

"Goodness, I guess you're happy to see me then?" Makayla said, kissing Emily on each cheek. There was more laughter as Makayla closed the door and carried Emily back into her room. Makayla petted Izador's head as she sat down on Emily's bed. "Looks like you're not the only one who got big, Emily, Izzy, you're huge." Izador barked twice. Makayla chuckled. "You remembered, two barks for yes, huh?" Izador barked twice again. "Good boy," Makayla scratched him behind the ears. Izador was nearly as tall as Makayla, almost up to her shoulders, and he was still a pup.

"How have you been, sweetheart?" Makayla asked.

"I'm okay," Emily said, playing with the tail of Makayla's plait.

"Only okay?"

"I miss Adrian, I wish he was here." Emily's face dropped, her eyes tearing up.

"Oh, sweetie, I miss him too, but he will always be with you. No matter where you go you will always carry his memory in your heart. I know that doesn't make you feel any better, because it would be better if he were here, but sometimes things happen that we have no control over, and it sucks, it really does. Missing the ones we love lets us know they were real and not a figment of our imagination. Adrian is with us in spirit and always will be, no matter where you are, okay, pumpkin?"

Emily nodded, she covered her mouth and yawned, her little eyes drooping. "I missed you too, Makayla."

"What a coincidence, I missed you as well. But looks like I will have to tuck you back into bed because it's late and you need your beauty sleep."

Emily giggled again. "Only grown-ups need beauty sleep, Makayla, didn't you know?"

"Actually, no, I didn't." Makayla helped Emily under the covers and handed her Adrian's teddy bear. She cuddled it to her body as Makayla pulled the covers up and tucked her in. "Goodnight, sweetheart, try to get some sleep, I love you."

"Good night, Makayla, I love you too." Makayla kissed Emily's forehead and scratched Izador's head. "Watch over her, Izzy, and don't let anyone hurt her." Izador barked yes. "Good boy." Makayla left Emily's room and walked the two doors down to her aunt's room. She knocked on the door twice.

"Come in, Makayla," her aunt called.

Makayla edged the door open and peeked through before entering. Her great aunt was sitting in a rocking chair beside a king-size four-poster bed, knitting. The clicking of her needles and the creak of her rocking chair as she rocked back and forth were unfamiliar sounds to Makayla. Marianna stopped what she was doing and smiled.

"Finally, we get to meet properly," she said, placing her knitting in a basket beside her chair. "Come, child, come sit by me," Marianna patted the bed beside the rocking chair.

"I'm surprised you want to talk to me after my deplorable behaviour at the dungeons. I was so rude. I'm so sorry, Aunt Marianna, please forgive me." Makayla crossed the room and sat on the bed beside her.

"It was a stressful time, Makayla, I understand why you acted the way you did, it was no place for introductions. Alexander was on death's door, your mind was elsewhere, it was understandable given the circumstances." Marianna patted the top of her hand.

Makayla stared at her aunt; she looked so much younger than when she'd first seen her in the dungeons. Makayla glanced down, at the soft-beige coloured carpet covering the floor. She put her hand in her pocket and clasped her Zippo lighter. There was something else in her pocket. "Oh, I almost forgot, I wanted to return this to you." Makayla slipped the golden locket Nikolai had given her out of her pocket.

Her aunt's forehead furrowed. "What would you have to return? I don't recall giving you anything."

Makayla held up the large oval locket, letting it swing by the chain. "Your locket, Nikolai gave it to me to help find you."

"My word, I haven't seen that locket in centuries." Marianna took it from Makayla's fingertips. Makayla watched her aunt run her thumbnail along the edge of the locket and pop it open, a soft smile curving her lips when she viewed its contents. She handed it back to Makayla, Makayla looked at the miniature portraits, there was one of a young couple, Vasili and Marianna in their youth, and on the other side of the locket there were two young men, Nikolai and another lad Makayla didn't recognise.

Makayla smiled, handing it back to her. "Your sons. I

recognise Nikolai, but who's the other man?"

"That was Benjamin, Nikolai's older brother; he died shortly after the miniature portrait was painted." Marianna's eyes glistened as she looked at the likeness of her sons. "We don't know what happened, we found him dead in his lodgings. It was as if he'd died in his sleep, but he was so young, we suspected foul play. To this day, we still don't know what befell him."

"I'm, sorry for your loss, Aunt Marianna. It wasn't until a few months ago I learned of your existence, I wasn't even aware Vasili had a wife, let alone sons. I thought I was the only seraphympire in existence. Imagine my surprise when I found out I wasn't the first seraphympire to be born after being told for centuries I was."

Marianna leaned forward and took Makayla's hand in hers. "You are the firstborn of both vampire and seraph royal families. Yes, technically you're the third seraphympire to be born, but you are the first female."

"If you say so. Aunt Marianna, there's a reason for my being here."

Marianna released Makayla's hand and sat back in her chair. "I know, child. You wish to know what Zobiana did to Alexander."

Makayla nodded briskly, biting her bottom lip. "Yes, I'm worried about him, he's changed, as you would expect after the torture he suffered. But I need to know if there was something done to him other than the whippings."

Marianna sighed. "Not that I know of. I dressed his wounds and helped him through his transition and fed him my blood; he would have died had I not. They were whipping him a great deal. As soon as he healed, they would whip and torture him again. From what he told me they were trying to locate the Trinian Globe and the Gem of Sorrows, he did not know their location – they disappeared the moment the phony gem was placed into the globe."

"Thank you for your honesty, Aunt Marianna." Makayla's shoulders sagged.

"Is Alexander okay?"

Makayla brushed back the hair hanging in her eyes. "I don't know, he's disappeared again, I don't know where he is."

"Do not worry, you shall find him. You are his maker and soul mate. You need only calm your thoughts and rid your mind of the negative. Meditating is good for locating your bonded mate, trust me, I know. It's how I was able to locate Vasili. Clear your mind and focus all your thoughts on him, and you shall see. You are still finding how you fit together as a couple and as his sire. It takes time."

"Mother told me you were feeling weak; I may be able to help, if you'll allow me?"

"Your mother was always perceptive. I am a little weary, but it shall pass."

"I can help, please let me help. Alexander would agree with me – it's the least I can do, especially after everything you did for him."

Marianna nodded. "How can I refuse?"

Makayla lifted her hands and placed her palms over Marianna's heart. Her hands grew warm, a soft glow radiating from her fingertips, gold sparkling iridescence spread up her arms until her body was immersed in blazing gold light. The hairs on her arms stiffened as the warmth from her hands transferred into Marianna's body. Marianna gasped, her mouth opening and closing as she trembled. Makayla saw the years dissolve from her aunt's face as time rolled backwards. The grey hair at her temples disappeared, the fine lines and dark circles and puffiness surrounding her eyes vanished. Her skin tightened and lifted and her posture straightened. The glowing light faded from Makayla's hands as she lowered them to her lap.

Makayla angled her head, taking in her aunt's altered appearance. Her dowdy clothes didn't suit her youthful appearance. Marianna looked half her age, like a woman in her early thirties, if that. "Now you look just like your miniature portrait." Makayla picked up a Victorian handheld mirror from the bedside table and handed it to her aunt.

Marianna took it from her with shaking hands and turned the mirror towards her face. She gasped, lifting her free hand to her cheek in shock. "How, how is this possible?"

Makayla shrugged. "I have no idea, it's something I can do."

"Have you tried doing it to Alexander? I think you should; it may help him recover as well."

"Huh, I never even considered it, thank you, I will."

There was a light tap on the door before it opened. "Mother, are you in here?" Nikolai asked, opening the door. Makayla stood as Nickolai entered the room. "Oh, sorry, I didn't mean to disturb you." Nikolai looked at his mother and nodded in greeting. "You wouldn't have seen my mother by chance, Makayla?"

Marianna glanced towards Makayla and then back at her son and chuckled. "I'm right here, Nikolai."

Nikolai's jaw dropped. "What, what happened to you? You're young, you're stunning!"

"My work is done." Makayla smirked in his direction.

"Makayla helped with my recovery," Marianna said, placing the mirror back on the bedside table.

"Come in, Nikolai, I'm just about to take my leave."

Nikolai closed the door and crossed the room; stopping to kiss his mother's forehead. He turned towards Makayla and pulled her into his arms, giving her a bear hug. She smiled and hugged him back. He released her and bowed his head. "Thank you for healing and returning my mother to us, Makayla. I've searched seven hundred years for her to no avail, you accomplished what I could not in mere months. I am indebted to you, your highness."

"It was my pleasure, Nikolai. We're even now; you don't owe me a thing and stop calling me your highness!"

"Nevertheless, if you ever need my blade, 'tis yours to command."

"As you wish, Nikolai. I have another matter to discuss with you though. Before you left the compound earlier this evening, you said you wanted to talk. What was it you wanted to tell me?"

"I just wanted to convey my gratitude for finding and saving my mother." Nikolai glanced towards his mother and touched her cheek before returning his attention to Makayla. "I couldn't thank you in front of everyone, not properly anyhow."

"Well, I must go; I still have to meet Lazarus before dawn. Not to mention locate Alexander."

Marianna stood and embraced her. "Thank you, Makayla, thank you for everything."

Makayla hugged her aunt. "You're welcome." She stepped back and looked down at her feet, embarrassed and uncomfortable with all the attention. "Okay, I best be leaving." She dematerialised before anyone had the chance to respond.

CHAPTER 25.

Rich, earthy soil, laced with the pleasant woodsy smell of English oak, moss, fallen leaves and the fresh musky scent of heather surrounded Anna and Reece where they stood in the forest. The moment they'd arrived, Anna felt an instant sense of calm drape over her shoulders like the comforting warmth of the sun on a winter's day. She hadn't enjoyed the sun's warmth in a long while. Not since her transition. She'd not felt altogether comfortable in the daylight. The sun wasn't her enemy; it didn't dissolve her into a pile of bubbling flesh and ash like it did Newbloods, but daylight made her vulnerable, conspicuous. People stared because she was different. Vampires were a natural lure; beautiful predators irresistible to humans. So she stayed indoors during the day because the temptation of blood was hard to resist. She had enough trouble controlling the hunger without having humans halo her like insects hovering around a lamp.

Through the clearing towards the distant horizon, dawn was approaching. Buzzing crickets and the leaves rustling in the cool breeze faded into the background as Anna turned her attention back to the great hedge in front of them. Anna's head fell back on her shoulders as she looked up, she felt so tiny, so insignificant standing by the towering barrier. The hedge extended up into the darkness, swallowed by the forest canopy. Reece watched her with a thoughtful look on his face; she'd seen that look many times since his return. He seemed oceans away from her, now more than ever. She didn't know this version of him; he was the complete opposite to the man she'd grown to love over the decades. She missed Reece the joker all the more since having met the new redefined version of him. Was he even the same person? Reece looked away from her first, a frown wrinkling his flawless features.

"Can you read my mind, Reece, do you know my thoughts?" she thought, wondering if he could hear her silent question.

He angled his head back towards her, his eye colour brightening. "Yes, I know your thoughts, Anna, especially when you focus your attention on me," Reece said aloud. *"And you can hear me too. If I let you in you'll know everything there is to know. But you're not ready to know, are you? You can't let go of the pain dragging you down, and until you are, you'll never be ready for my truths,"* he said in her mind.

Anna stumbled backwards and bit her tongue as she tripped on the remains of a log. She choked on the metallic taste of blood as it pooled in her mouth. Reece whipped his hand up before she hit the ground. Sparks of light flickered along his fingertips and time slowed. Reece was a blur of movement and before she had time to gather her bearings; she was ensconced in his arms, her palms cushioned against his torso.

Reece helped her regain her footing. "Are you okay?" he asked, picking a leaf from her clothes and sweeping hair out of her eyes.

Anna cleared her throat and nodded quickly. "U-huh, yep, I'm fine, thank you."

Reece cupped her face in his large hands. "Anna, look at me, stop avoiding my eyes."

Anna continued staring at his chest, trying to make sense of what just happened. Not only could Reece read her mind, but he could communicate with her telepathically and slow time. How, after all the time they'd spent together, could he have hidden it from her? How could she have been so blind? She shivered as she looked at the giant hedge of twisting brambles thick with spiky thorns, wondering what lay beyond its border.

"Annie, look at me," Reece said again, folding his arms about her waist and drawing her closer to him.

Anna shook her head. "I can't, I feel like I'll be swallowed up." She hated that her voice trembled.

"Swallowed up?" Reece's voice raised in pitch. "Swallowed up by me?"

Anna nodded again. "How could I have been so blind? How have you hidden your abilities from me all this time?"

"Do you really need to ask? I've told you time and time

again, it's what I'm trained to do so I can go undercov—"

"Undercover, I know," Anna cut him off. She nibbled her lip and looked up into his face. She was taken aback and almost bit her tongue again when she saw his eyes. They were a vibrant emerald green now, with shimmering flecks of blue. It was the first time she'd seen them that colour. His eyes were so ambiguous, just like the man himself, always changing with his varying moods; so dark and undefinable. She'd never seen them so bright.

"Who are you, Reece, who are you really? Please tell me."

"You're not ready—"

Anna silenced him by putting her finger to his lips. "Tell me your real name, just your real name for now, or I'll walk out of your life forever. I need to know because the deception is destroying me, you said you'd tell me in your safe place. Is this not your safe place?"

Reece looked towards the maze wall, and shook his head. "This isn't my safe place; my safe place is beyond the maze wall."

Anna didn't look over her shoulder at the wall, she didn't respond to his answer. "Who are you, Reece?"

"My name is Reece Farrington, former Earl of—" Reece shook his head and looked towards the hedge again before returning his gaze to her. "Former Earl of nothing, I renounced my titles. Reece Farrington no longer exists; it's just the name on my birth certificate. I haven't used it in a very long time. Not since my parents brutally whipped my brother in front of a gathering of guests attending a ball they were hosting," he said, simply.

"Reece Farrington," Anna repeated. "Thank you for telling me, I like it, it fits you. As much as you dislike it, I like it." She smiled up at him.

"You like it? How can you like it, it's horrible." Reece's eyebrows rose as he gaped at her.

"Just because it was your father's last name, and he was a terrible man, in no way does it represent who you are. You are not your father, Reece, you aren't the same."

"How do you know, Anna? You know nothing about me, and what you do know barely skims the surface. It's why I haven't revealed my entire history to you. I'm not the innocent man you think I am, I'm a killer, and I'm a mons—"

"We're all killers, even monsters, Reece, we're vampires. It comes with the territory." Anna swallowed the growing lump in her throat when Reece's arms tightened about her body, drawing her to him. The longer he held her in his arms, the more precarious she felt. His hard athletic build overwhelmed her senses; she could feel his heart beating against her palms and had a mad urge to place her ear against his chest so she could hear it. She looked up into his striking oval face and pondered his pale complexion. His eyes were still vibrant, no longer masked in shadow, and his shoulder length ash-blond hair fluttered freely in the light breeze. She looked down and pushed against his chest to separate herself and step out of his embrace. His arms were a vice-grip around her waist.

"No," he said.

Anna looked up into his face again, his eyes were no

longer vibrant, but dark bottomless pits.

"Yes." She pushed against his chest harder.

"No," he said again, his eyes focusing on her lips. The breath caught in her throat as he lowered his mouth to hers. She felt the smooth suppleness of his lips as they captured hers. Her skin prickled, hypersensitive, her throat tingled as sensation flooded her body. Reece groaned and deepened the kiss. Anna opened to him as his tongue plunged into her mouth. She was lost in the moment. The world disappeared, the pain, the sorrow, the devastation, the loss, the past, the Shadow Seekers, V5 and the Blakspor virus, the Newbloods, the Dark One and Zobiana. Everything faded into nothing, it was just her and Reece and their shared desire. It'd been so long since he'd kissed her, since she'd responded to him with anything other than animosity. She circled her arms about his neck as he cupped her face with his hands. He threaded his fingertips through her hair before circling them to the nape of her neck. She was a live wire of nerves as his fingertips drew circles over her skin.

"God, I've missed kissing you," he groaned, gliding his hands over her shoulders and down her body, caressing the sides of her breasts as he trailed his fingertips further down her body. "Anna, you don't know hard it's been to not touch you, to not do this to you," he said between kisses. Her knees buckled, he caught her and wrapped his arms around her waist, lifting her body to his and pinning her against a nearby tree. The bark scratched her back as he crushed his body to hers; she felt the evidence of his arousal as he ground his hips against her. The friction of their bodies elicited an unfulfilled need they'd never addressed. The cool breeze flowed over Anna's body, heightening the pleasure and sending a delicious shiver down her spine. She skimmed her hands down his chest to his waist and untucked his shirt from his trousers, then wove her hands up under his shirt. His skin was so smooth, so soft yet so hard with well-sculpted muscle. His intoxicating scent overpowered all other forest aromas. Reece's Armani cologne smelled divine but she'd always loved his own intoxicating, masculine scent. Even when he went into battle, he smelled good. It was an aphrodisiac, a natural pheromone that drew her in. Every time she was near him she battled against her baser instincts and desire to throw herself at him.

She smiled against his mouth. "You smell divine, you always have," she murmured, relishing the feel of his hard body.

"So do you," he replied, nibbling her bottom lip.
Anna felt Reece's body stiffen and he suddenly tore his mouth from hers to look over his shoulder. "Did you hear that?" he asked.

"I heard nothing," she gasped, trying to catch her breath.

Reece turned and pushed Anna behind him, his hand still grasping her waist as he searched the darkness.

"What do you hear, Reece?" Anna questioned, trying to see past his shoulder.

He held his finger up to silence her. He could hear someone laughing, and it wasn't the sound of someone enjoying a joke, no, it was sadistic. A twisted sarcastic laugh intended to intimidate and unsettle. Reece looked around for the perpetrator. No one was there, yet he felt a familiar presence he'd not sensed in decades. He knew without a doubt they needed to leave, danger surrounded them like vapour.

No sooner had that thought filled his mind than the landscape changed. A mist curled about their legs, thickening until there was a thick mantle covering their feet.

"Reece, we need to leave," Anna said with a shaky voice as she looked down at the ground.

Condescending laughter ricocheted through Reece's mind, louder this time, crude.

"Oh, don't leave on my account, ol' boy, stay; stay and play, we have so much catching up to do." Reece's back stiffened the moment he heard the haunting voice from his and Anna's past in his head.

He faced Anna; she looked so small, so fragile, her shoulders hunched and trembling. Her hands were clasped in front of her body, fear shadowing the depths of her haunted eyes. Her skin was pale and no longer flushed with the rosy glow of arousal. Reece mumbled an incantation and a transparent shield surrounded them in a protective bubble of wavering violet light. Anna's eyes widened.

Reece placed his palm under her chin and lifted her face until her eyes met his. *"Do you trust me?"* he asked telepathically.

Anna's eyes were still focused on the barrier surrounding them.

"Anna, do you trust me?" Reece repeated.

Anna cleared her throat and nodded. *"He's here, isn't he?"*

"Yes. I don't know where, but we can't lead him into the maze because if he follows us, we'll never get out alive. The ground is holy – sacred; if he enters, he'll desecrate it. If he gets in, that is. It's protected by Xander's magic. Even so I don't want to test it. If the demon breaks through the magical ward, the foliage, and every living thing within the maze will die from his demonic presence; it will become a barren wasteland. Now let's go."

Twigs snapped and the rustle of shifting leaves caught their attention. Reece spun on the spot.

"Well, well, well, it's humbling to see you again, poppet, and in such fine glowing health too. That will soon be remedied. Forgive me for being remiss; I have yet to complete my task. Fear not, I shall finish what I set out to do," a regal gentleman said, tipping his top hat and acknowledging their presence.

Reece felt Anna shudder. "Over my dead body!" Reece replied, eyeballing the man standing before them. He was wearing the same attire he'd worn a century ago when Reece had locked him in the sarcophagus, only now he looked a little the worse for wear.

"If that's what it takes, Lord Farrington, but 'tis not you I seek. 'Tis the young miss standing behind you. I am only here to wish you well and inform you the game is afoot. Set your affairs in order, my dearest Annie. When I'm ready to complete my task, you will know. Be on the lookout, lad, it will be when you least expect it, possibly even years, but it could also be on the morrow. Au revoir for now."

Reece snatched a dagger from his vest pocket and hurled it towards the demon. The dagger spun through the air, passed through the demon's body and lodged in the tree behind him. The demon smiled, the tips of his teeth lengthening into points.

"Oh please, do you think I would come here in person while I am at my weakest? Lord Farrington, you truly are daft if you think me that reckless. Ta-ta." The demon shimmered and dissolved, merging with the mist coating the forest floor. His laughter faded as he departed.

Anna dropped to a crouch and wrapped her hands about her bent legs, rocking back and forth. "Oh my God, oh my God, oh my God, what are we going to do? What are we going to do? He's going to get me, Reece and it will be far worse than the first time." Tears streamed down her cheeks.

Reece squatted next to her. "I won't let anything happen to you, Anna, I swear it. But we must get back to the compound and tell Vasili what's happened." He picked her up in his arms and dematerialised.

CHAPTER 26.

Tess adjusted the focus dial on the microscope. Why couldn't she reproduce Makayla's blood and what prevented the vaccine from working? What was she missing? How many times would they fail before they made a viable vaccine? She sagged in her seat and looked up at the ceiling, brushing her fingertips through her tangled hair.

"You should take a break," Ava said, as she washed a dirty vial in the sink nearby. *"Eat something, then lie down and have a nap. You've been at it all night, you can't work twenty-four hours straight, you're not superhuman. You need to take it easy, Tess. Go take a break."*

"We need to find a cure, and I'm not stopping until I do," Tess said.

"We'll find a cure, but you need not kill yourself in the process. When was the last time you ate or slept?"

Tess shrugged, resting her elbow on the benchtop and propping up her head, rubbing her eyes with her free hand. "I can't remember." She picked up a coffee cup and drank, grimacing when she swallowed the cold brew.

Ava glanced at the space beside her as if there was someone there speaking with her. She smiled and chuckled, nodding her head. *"Ryan says you were always like this when you worked from home."* Ava smiled and nodded, chuckling again. *"He says you'd have starved and faded away had he not been there to feed you. He says he used to tease you about it all the time."* Ava slanted her head. *"He said he used to stick celery sticks in his ears and carrot sticks in his nostrils and say 'Doc, I don't feel well', and you'd say 'maybe you're not eating the right way'."*

Tess dropped the cup in her hand; the sound of smashing porcelain hitting the ground had Ava looking towards Tess. Ava's face paled, her mouth working open and closed. *"I'm sorry, Tess, I thought you knew I could speak with the dead."*

Tess shook her head, swiping a trembling hand through her hair. "Ryan's here?"

Ava nodded. *"He's always here, he's always standing by you; he never leaves your side."*

"Why, why haven't you, why didn't you tell me sooner?" Tess stuttered.

Ava lowered her eyes to the floor and then looked to the space beside her before looking back at Tess. *"He didn't want you to know."* Ava sighed.

"So why now, why are you telling me this now?"

"Because he's worried about you; he wants to move on but can't until you let him. He wants you to stop feeling guilty. It wasn't your fault he died. He wants you to find love again; he doesn't want you to grieve for him anymore. He loves you and always will, but you need to move on because you're still alive and he's not. You have your whole life ahead of you, he's on his path to the next life. Let him go, Tess, you need to say goodbye to him."

Tears filled Tess's eyes and streamed down her cheeks as a sob caught in her throat. "How can I say goodbye to him when I can't see him? I need . . . I need to see him again, can I see him again?"

Ava held her hand out towards her. *"Take my hand."*

Tess lifted her unsteady hand and grasped Ava's fingertips then glanced towards the space. The air shimmered like billowing heatwaves over hot bitumen. The air sparkled, forming Ryan's broad silhouette. Tess looked up into her deceased husband's face. Her lips trembled. "Is it really you, Ryan?" she whispered.

He nodded. "Hi hon," Ryan said, smiling.

Tess choked on a sob, her voice catching in her throat. "I've miss. . .missed you so much," she hiccuped, swiping the tears from her eyes and cheeks. "I can't believe you're here, I thought you'd moved on." Tess lifted her hand to touch his cheek, but her hand passed through him. His face disappeared momentarily before reforming before her eyes like a holographic image. She looked at her hand – when it had passed through his face, the hairs on her skin had prickled with coolness from the slight chill of his presence.

"I've always been by your side, Tess; I haven't left it since I died. I'm worried about you, hon, you need to take better care of yourself and you haven't been. You should take Silentwind's advice. She's right. You can't focus on finding a cure if you're too tired to see what's right in front of your eyes."

Tess hung her head. "You're right, I will. I wish I could hug you one more time, Ryan."

"Me too," Ryan said, touching her cheek. She felt the icy chill of his fingertips as they caressed her skin, she'd felt it a lot since he'd died. A breath caught in her throat. He'd been comforting her in her sorrow and she hadn't realised the cool prickling sensation was caused by his gentle touch.

"I have to go now, Tess." Ryan looked over his shoulder before looking back at her. Tess saw a swirling tunnel of bright white light form behind him. "I don't belong here in this world anymore, please, let me go and live your life again. I'll always love you and be watching over you."

Tess swallowed the lump in her throat and nodded. The air caught in her throat as she gulped in another mouthful of oxygen. Her throat closed as tears flooded her eyes again and streamed down her face. "Goodbye, Ryan, I wish you could stay, but I know you can't. I love you."

"I love you too, forever. Take care, honey bee, don't be scared to love again." Ryan bent his face to hers and kissed her then turned to leave. Tess lifted her fingers to her lips; they prickled with sensation, the lingering chill left from Ryan's last kiss. She watched him walk into the tunnel of light and disappear into the distance. Tess released Ava's hand. "Thank you, Ava," she whispered, then spun on her heels and left the laboratory. She closed the door behind her and stepped into the infirmary. Bryce was sitting in a chair beside Freya's bed; he looked up when he heard the door click. A soft, sad smile curled his lips as he greeted her with a nod of his head. He looked as though he was about to say something, but remained silent. Tess was grateful; she couldn't talk even if she'd wanted to. She had no words left, just tears and a hollow heart filled with the loneliness left by Ryan's absence. Tess didn't wipe the tears from her face as she left the infirmary. She rubbed the ache between her breasts as she walked along the chiselled corridor, the tight pressure building in her chest felt as though it was about to explode. Her pace quickened to a run until she was sprinting blindly to her lodgings. Tess rushed into her room, slammed the door and leaned against it. She covered her face and slid to the floor crying, huddled against the door, her body shuddering as wrenching sobs ripped through her.

Darrius closed the library door and turned towards Morgan.

Morgan cleared her throat. "I saw a stranger coming out of the infirmary."

"What, when did this happen, can you be sure?"

"I'm sure, it happened before Alexander disappeared from the infirmary."

"Do you think it's connected to Alexander's disappearance?" Darrius scratched his head.

"Well, what else could it have been? It must be, because Alexander was unconscious before that." Morgan glanced about the library, remembering the last time she and Darrius had been there together alone. She shuffled her feet, looking down at the sheepskin rug she was standing on and shook her head to focus her wandering thoughts back to the man who'd captured all her attention.

"Maybe you were mistaken." Darrius shrugged. "Maybe it was one of the Vampire Guard looking for Vasili?"

"No, I've never seen him before and why would he go to the infirmary to look for Vasili? He'd go to his office. I think I would have noticed him among the Vampire and Seraph Guard when they arrived. Granted, there are a lot of them, but still, there was something different about this guy; he had a dark energy. You know the kind, surely you've come across entities that draw the light and positive energy out of an area and replace it with darkness and negativity? It was like he was masked in a black cloud. Not only that, his clothes set alarm bells ringing in my head. No one dresses in hooded robes anymore, not that I know of, anyway." Morgan rubbed her hands up and down her arms; the cold had worked its way under her skin. "He gave me the creeps; I haven't been able to get warm since I saw him sneaking out of the infirmary."

"Don't you think Bryce would have seen him? Not to mention Ava and Tess?"

"Ava and Tess have been holed up in the lab for weeks; finding a cure consumes all their time and the doors are always closed to keep a sterile environment. No, they wouldn't have seen him and Bryce does leave Freya's side, you know."

"Okay, okay, did you follow him?"

"I tried, but I lost him. He was no stranger to the tunnels and knew where he was going and that's what's been bothering me the most. How can anybody really know the complete layout of the compound? There are tunnels we never use. I mean we've been using the tunnels for years and still don't know where they all lead because they've never been mapped." Morgan inhaled, brushing a stray hair behind her ear.

"Where did he lead you, Morgan?"

"It was strange; I followed him deeper into the tunnels, into a part I've never been, before I had the chance to note my whereabouts he'd disappeared. He dissolved into thin air and not in the way you and Makayla dematerialise, either, it was like he just evaporated into a thick fog and disappeared into the walls. Do you think it was one of Zobiana's people?"

"It's possible and more than likely. Gabe warned me to be on the lookout for anything unusual, I think this qualifies as unusual. We've got spies among us. Gabe's worried and when Gabe's worried you pay attention. He told me to be careful and said to warn the other Shadow Seekers without alerting the

Vampire and Seraph Guards."

"Darrius, I don't feel safe here anymore, not since they arrived – especially since the Vampire Guards arrived. I know they're our kind, but how can we trust them? Vampires aren't trustworthy. It sounds terrible, I know, but I only have faith in our small circle. The Seraph Guards are on a different level. I believe we can depend on them because they're incorruptible, I mean they're angels, but vampires are a different story altogether. Vampires are power hungry and will do unspeakable things to achieve dominance over the weak, it's instinctual; we're predators."

"We're living in dangerous times, Morgan. I know you don't believe in Makayla's prophecy, but I can't deny the irony of everything that's happening. It bears remarkable similarities … no … exact matches to the hieroglyphs."

"What hieroglyphs, Darrius? I thought it was all just hearsay."

Darrius had a faraway look on his face, his eyes glazed over in memory. Morgan snapped her fingers in front of his face. "Hey, Darrius, wake up, what hieroglyphs are you speaking of?"

Darrius snapped out of it and looked into her eyes. "Sorry … Makayla's prophecy is carved into the wall of a secret cave on Evron. No one knows how old the carvings are, but they're old, I mean really, really old. My father has kept its location hidden for centuries to keep it safe. Makayla's prophecy is not some oracle's crazy prediction, it's a fact. I saw them once, the hieroglyphs I mean, I was a young man at the time, but I could understand the writings even when I didn't know the language. I asked my father why I could decipher the words and he got all mystical, something about who we were, our bloodline or something like that."

"Your bloodline? I don't understand."

Darrius checked that the door was closed, then waved his hand above his head, twisting his fingers in a swirling loop. The air shimmered with an electrical current, wavering briefly before disappearing.

"What did you just do?" Morgan asked.

"Oh, I just shielded us from eavesdroppers. I should have done it the moment we came in here, but I didn't realise you were going to tell me something. I thought you wanted to . . . never mind what I thought, it doesn't matter."

Morgan smiled, lightheaded at Darrius's words. She'd thought her feelings weren't reciprocated, but now she stared at the angular line of his lips and re-evaluated her assumption, remembering the last time they'd kissed. It'd been chaste, but it had awakened something dormant in her. Morgan looked up into his eyes, they were hooded and the violet colour of them not so vibrant. She considered what they'd been discussing. "Darrius, what's your bloodline got to do with any of this?"

"Do you know Evron's history? Our vampire history? We didn't always have a council, we had a monarchy."

"I've never cared about Evron's history, I was born here on Earth and my parents never spoke about our home world. I know royal families existed once, but I couldn't tell you their history. Vasili mentioned Makayla was a descendant of both seraph and vampire royal houses." Morgan stopped talking, her mouth dropping. "Oh wow, what a stupid thing to say." Morgan closed her mouth in embarrassment. "Sorry, if Makayla has royal blood that means you and Tristan do too." Morgan smoothed her hair back and adjusted the hair pins securing her bun.

"It's okay, Morgan, I wasn't trying to make you uncomfortable – it was just a simple question. I only asked to see what you knew of our planet's history. Back to my bloodline: only descendants of the prophesied one can make sense of the words, particularly the hieroglyphics carved in the sacred cave. My father is the Vampire King of Evron, or he should be – he abdicated his throne and formed the Vampire Council to replace the monarchy. Technically, he's still king and in control of the senate, but he refuses to take his rightful place until my mother is accepted as Queen by both the vampire and seraph nations."

"Your father is what?" Morgan said in a hushed voice.

"The King of Evron," Darrius said, folding his arms and sitting on a nearby chair. "I know, right? It's a lot to take in."

Morgan nodded, probably too quickly because she felt lightheaded. She sank onto the couch next to Darrius. "Well, that explains a lot."

"That's not the half of it; remember when you blamed Makayla for everything happening in the world?"

"Yes, not my finest moment. What can I say? Makayla knows how to push my buttons. I respect her, but sometimes she pisses me off."

Darrius chuckled. "I have a feeling she feels the same way about you. You're similar in many ways."

"I can't help it, I snap when she provokes me." Morgan sighed. "Half the time I'm not even aware I'm doing it until she reacts to my comments."

"Yeah, she has that effect on people, it's called self-preservation. I'm guilty of doing the same thing – better to push people away than form any unwanted bonds with them." Darrius rested his hand on hers and squeezed her fingers; the subtle touch making her fingertips tingle. "This war and the vendetta Zobiana has against my family isn't Makayla's fault, Morgan, it's my father's. He was betrothed to Zobiana; she was to be the queen of Evron."

"I beg your pardon, did I hear you correctly?"

Darrius looked at the ceiling. "Yep, it's so messed up, isn't it?"

"Yes. Seriously messed up. Darrius, I don't mean to change the subject, but what are we going to do about the intruder? I'm worried, I have a terrible feeling it's not the last time we'll see him."

"Leave it with me, I'll speak with Gabe and Vasili, and see what my father says too – he may be able to shed light on our unwanted guest's identity. Who knows, he may have come across someone similar."

CHAPTER 27.

Two mutilated Newblood bodies stared up at Abigail and Tyrone with vacant, soulless eyes. One with his throat ripped out, and the other stabbed in the heart. There was blood everywhere. It covered the dead bodies, the ground and coated the overgrown grass glistening in the pre-dawn light. Abigail thought it strange their bodies hadn't turned to dust but once the sun rose and bathed their corpses in light they'd be nothing more than ash. Abigail's skin bristled and anger rose with a ferocity she no longer wanted to control. She clenched her fists and gritted her teeth, wallowing in her rage as she sniffed the air. As well as the smell of the dead Newbloods, there were two more unidentified scents. She noticed a flat patch of shrubbery and a bent stalk of grass, which she snapped off and sniffed, sneering in disgust when she recognised the scent. The shifter had been there; she remembered his scent from when they'd captured him on the docks and chained him to the bomb at the nest. She recognised the female scent too, she'd been infected with the Blakspor virus as well; the underlying odour was evident.

Tyrone was silent as he stared at the bloody remains, a deep crease burdening his forehead as he frowned. Abigail elbowed him in the ribs and inclined her head towards the Newbloods loitering around the gateway. They stalked towards them and came to an abrupt stop near the main group.

"What happened here?" Abigail hissed, barely restraining her simmering anger. She directed her question to the Newblood cowering closest to her; he wouldn't look her in the eyes.

"Well?" Abigail looked from Newblood to Newblood; they wouldn't look her in the eyes either, but hung their heads in shame. "Somebody answer me," she shrieked. They jumped at the sudden change in her voice.

"Obviously, our men were ambushed when they encountered someone spying on us," another Newblood said, stepping out from behind the Newblood cowering in front of her.

"Obviously. What do you mean, obviously? If it was so obvious, someone would have heard the commotion and helped the two dead Newbloods behind us, but *obviously*," Abigail sneered, prodding his chest with her finger. "YOU . . . WEREN'T . . . DOING . . . YOUR . . . JOBS!" She pushed her face into his until their noses almost touched. "WERE YOU?"

The Newblood's eyes widened as he tried to put distance between them. Abigail leered at the other Newbloods and their faces paled as they trembled in fear. "Who's in charge here?"

"That would be me, my lady," the Newblood in front of her said, lowering his eyes.

Abigail inclined her head and returned her gaze to him. "And you are?"

"My name's Eddie."

Abigail grabbed him by the throat and squeezed. "Well, Eddie. . . you're shit out of luck." She lifted him off his feet, bringing his face to hers. "Someone here has to pay for this colossal fuck-up, and since you're responsible for this ragtag group, it looks like you're the lucky candidate."

"You're being a little over-dramatic don't you think, Abby? It wasn't that colossal of a fuck-up," Tyrone said, grinning.

Abigail chuckled. "Okay, maybe I was being a little flamboyant using the word colossal, but hey, they screwed up and someone's got to pay – it may as well be Eddie here." Abigail smirked when she noticed the horrified look on Eddie's red face. His bloodshot eyes were bulging out of their sockets, his mouth opening and closing from lack of oxygen. "Oops, sorry." She loosened her hold on his throat; he coughed and gasped.

"Any last words, Eddie? No, okay that's fine by me. My energy's ebbing, so you're just the pick-me-up I need right now." She smiled, her fangs elongating as she opened her mouth. "It's okay, this won't hurt much."

Tyrone laughed. "Don't believe her, Eddie, the pain will be excruciating."

"Why did you tell him that? Now he'll struggle. You're such a killjoy, Tyrone," she said, bringing Eddie's face closer to hers.

"Please, I can do better; I promise I'll do better," Eddie's voice trembled as he worked his fingers under her tight grasp and tried to pull her hands free from his throat.

"Too late." Abigail opened her mouth over his and siphoned the life from his body. Strands of sparkling white light floated in the gap between their mouths twisting and curling as they were sucked into her body. The light grew brighter the longer she held him in place. Eddie moved his head from side to side trying to close his mouth, but it was no use. He tried to uncurl her fingers from his throat again, but it too, was pointless. He kicked his feet and pushed his hands against her chest, trying to dislodge her fingers, but nothing he did worked. Abigail relished his struggles; his screams of terror were music to her ears and made his essence all the sweeter. The high she got from his life force would last for days. It wasn't the same high she got when she siphoned Off Worlders, there was no greater buzz, but it was the next best thing. She could sense the anxiety in the remaining Newbloods, but didn't fear their retaliation.

Eddie's body sagged in her grasp as the last silver threads of his soul drifted into her mouth. Abigail sighed and opened her eyes; light sparkled at the edges of her peripheral vision as she licked her lips. She tossed Eddie's shrivelled body at the feet of his companions, feeling her skin prickle with revitalised energy.

"Who's next?" she asked, looking at the remaining Newbloods. They cringed back in a tight huddle, avoiding eye contact. "What, no takers?" She moved towards them. "Do your jobs properly, the gateways are ours and must remain so. If there are any more fuck-ups, believe me, not only will I suck the living daylights out of you, I will make it so painful what you saw today will look like a pleasant walk in the park. If there are any more interlopers, capture and restrain them and inform me directly. Do I make myself clear?" They nodded their heads. "I didn't hear you," she said, cupping her hand around her ear.

"Yes, Mistress Abigail," they responded.

She glanced at Tyrone; he was struggling to keep a smile in check. She kicked him in the shins.

"I'm so turned on right now, Mistress Abigail," he said in a small voice.

She punched him in the arm. "Come on, let's get the hell out of here, we've other gateways to check."

Shrivelled corpses lay covered in broken furniture, shattered glass and miscellaneous objects. Ecktar shook his head and crouched beside one of the dead bodies. He removed a fragment of wood concealing the victim's face and coughed, covering his mouth and clenching his jaw as his stomach recoiled. He'd never get used to seeing dead bodies, though he'd seen too many to count. No matter how many years passed, the ache in his belly would never recede; people's brutality would always shock him and this was by far the strangest crime scene he'd witnessed. He raised his head and sniffed the air, the cottage didn't smell of death, but resembled the musty odour of a closed attic filled with old furniture and moth-eaten clothes.

Ecktar gathered and calmed his thoughts as he picked shards of glass out of the victim's hair and looked for identifying markers. He sighed when he recognised Tahlia's gold medallion clutched in her withered hand. Zoldarni emissaries were usually Fae and wore unisex uniforms; there were no male and female identifiers except the Zoldarni medallions. The medallions were given to all Zoldarni members upon graduation and displayed the individual's rank and role within the Zoldarni hierarchy.

Tahlia's remains were a sad representation of the beauty she once held. Her appearance was much like that of a four thousand year old Egyptian mummy. Her skin was dry and leathery; her eyes were collapsed hollow pits covered with the thin, sagging membrane of her ruined eyelids – bald of the once-full lashes that now scattered the hollows beneath her eyes. Her once-glossy hair was dull, matted and brittle; her voluptuous body now sinewy and skeletal.

"It looks like Abigail's handiwork," Vasili said with remorse.

Ecktar glanced about the messy room before looking up at Vasili. "Who's Abigail?"

"Zobiana's daughter," Vasili responded, eyeing the corpse. "Any idea whose remains these are?"

Ecktar chewed his lip before answering. "It's Tahlia."

"I'm sorry, Ecktar; she was an admirable woman and should not have died in such a way. I'm guessing the other three emissaries are Idgar, Nyshtar and Ensor?"

"Yes, it would appear so. You were right to travel through the gateways to Cwonoth, Vasili," Ecktar said. "Had you not we'd still be waiting for our emissaries to return. Zobiana's treachery is worrisome, as is Earth's precarious situation."

"It looks like they've been this way for a while." Vasili's eyebrows furrowed. "I tried contacting them over six months ago," he murmured.

"There's only one way to truly know what happened here," Ecktar said. "Hopefully it's not too late for me to see what transpired." Ecktar placed his hand on Tahlia's chest and closed his eyes, waiting for the death-vision to unfold. When he opened his eyes a silent holographic representation of the events shimmered into existence and the last moments of the Zoldarni emissaries' lives replayed.

He saw them lounging by the hearth, drinking wine and laughing at one of Nyshtar's jokes, their suitcases by the door.

A dark-haired woman and a tall, wild-looking man materialised behind them, along with several Newbloods. The emissaries were unaware of their presence and the imminent danger. The dark-haired woman raised her hand above her head and circled her index finger in the air. Newbloods fanned out, surrounding their unsuspecting victims. Idgar, Nyshtar, Tahlia and Ensor's faces registered surprise when the Newbloods pointed their swords at them. Nyshtar protested and made to stand, but Tahlia pressed her hand to his chest and shook her head. The dark-haired female, the wild-looking man accompanying her, circled to stand in front of their captives. Tahlia placed her wine glass on the coffee table and rose from her seat, levelling her gaze on the dark-haired woman. The other emissaries followed suit and stood beside Tahlia. Tahlia was not a trained warrior but she could still defend herself. For the most part, she relied on her companions to protect her. Ecktar could see Nyshtar, Idgar and Ensor weighing their options as their eyes tracked the Newbloods surrounding them. The dark-haired woman speaking with Tahlia had a superior air, her stiff posture and confident grin irritated Ecktar. He clenched his fists until his knuckles popped. He wanted to warn his comrades, but there was nothing he could do.

It happened fast, Nyshtar, Idgar and Ensor made their move, bringing down five Newbloods with throwing-knives. Two knives failed to meet their mark, but hovered in the air before the dark-haired woman and the intimidating man beside her. The dark-haired woman plucked one of the throwing-knives from the air, then spun it and launched it at Nyshtar. He visibly grunted in pain when it struck his right shoulder and collapsed to the floor, wounded. The two remaining Newbloods immobilised Idgar and Ensor, punching them into submission until they too flopped to the floor. The dark-haired woman yelled at Tahlia; who shook her head and refused to respond. The dark-haired woman slapped Tahlia's face, leaving a palm print on her cheek. Tahlia held her head high and smiled as she shook her head once more. Ecktar could see the frustration etched in the dark-haired woman's face. She grabbed Tahlia by the throat and pulled her close; she opened her mouth over Tahlia's and drained the life from her. Ecktar watched the soul-eater suck the life from each emissary.

Ecktar removed his hand from Tahlia's remains and rose from his position on the floor. He glanced at Vasili, who stood peering out of the window.

"What is it?"

Vasili turned his attention back to Ecktar. "I don't know, but we should leave, something's off here. When we arrived there were the usual sounds: crickets, hooting owls and other such noises, but now I don't hear a thing."

Ecktar made his way across the room, navigating around the debris on the floor. Vasili stepped aside, making room for Ecktar to look out of the window. Ecktar moved the curtain aside and peered through the crack. He wasn't hindered by the darkness but couldn't see anything suspicious or out of the ordinary. It didn't mean they weren't being watched. Vasili was right – something was off. Ecktar stepped away from the window and looked about the room.

"Did you learn anything?" Vasili asked, indicating the fallen Zoldarni.

Ecktar nodded. "Yes, I saw the ones who committed the crime, I'm unsure of their identities – maybe you can help?"

"I'll do my best."

Ecktar placed his fingers to Vasili's forehead and showed him what had transpired. Vasili's body stiffened the moment Ecktar opened his mind to him, only relaxing when the vision finished and Ecktar removed his hand.

Vasili let out a long breath of air. "It's Abigail and her companion Tyrone, they're Zobiana's people. I'm sorry for the loss of your comrades, Ecktar, but we need to leave now. I sense dark magic at play here, I noticed it when we first arrived. Something's coming."

Ecktar glanced at his fallen comrades and removed a silver tube from his belt. He twisted the top part and pressed a sequence of buttons. There was a low-frequency hum as the end of the device lit up with violet light.

"Forgive my ignorance, but what is that device?" Vasili asked.

"It's a Tylol. We use them to retrieve and move bodies to a secure location here on Earth where our people can prepare and transport them back to Cwonoth for burial," Ecktar said, holding the device away from his body and directing the violet light over Tahlia's remains. She glowed as sparkling light circled her body and dissolved into fine particles before disappearing altogether. The circling light fractured and shot into the air, then passed through the ceiling with a mechanical hiss. Ecktar did this with each of the emissaries' remains.

An animalistic roar captured their attention.

"Time to go," Ecktar said, clipping the Tylol to his belt. He looked up at the ceiling as the hanging light fixture shuddered and swung back and forth as the ceiling began to crack from the vibration. Figurines bounced on a shelf nearby, dancing along the edge until they toppled off and shattered on the ground. The thundering sound of heavy footfalls grew louder as whatever approached grew closer.

Vasili looked out of the window once more. Trees were falling over, and the ground was buckling as if an earthquake had the ground in its crushing fist. The cracking, deep popping sound of trees splitting and crashing to the rumbling earth made Ecktar's skin crawl. Ecktar sidled up beside Vasili and peered out the window, another deafening roar had them covering their ears. The only thing Ecktar could see was a dark mass approaching at breakneck speed. The sight transfixed them, as they tried to make sense of what was heading their way. It was a black, undulating mass that rippled and shivered with no distinctive shape. It looked as though it was solid, but as it advanced it lost form and reshaped again as if it were made up of smaller creatures. Every step it took its mass grew larger. Ecktar squinted all four of his eyes, trying to focus on the grainy creature and get a clear view. When he'd thought he'd got a fix on it, the creature changed form. There was a loud, insect-like humming that grew in volume as it drew closer.

"What is it? It's unlike anything I've ever seen." Vasili narrowed his eyes on the beast.

"I have no clue, best not to stick around and find out, I say." Ecktar grabbed Vasili's arm and pulled him towards the back door in the kitchen. Vasili stumbled on the remains of a broken table, but regained his footing.

"Why don't we just teleport out of here?" Vasili asked as they burst out the kitchen door and ran towards the back gate.

"Because it will draw the creature to us rather than the cottage. It may be attracted to us from the electromagnetic fields when we first teleported here," Ecktar said as the creature smashed into the cottage. The door they'd passed through only moments ago flew into the air, spinning above their heads along with shards of broken glass and chunks of the building walls and roofing.

Ecktar and Vasili stood transfixed, staring up at the monstrous swarm of thousands of creepy-crawlies, every conceivable insect and undesirable critter possible. Something clearly controlled them and they watched the mass circle the cottage in a hurricane of movement, smashing the building until there was nothing left but dust and wood pulp.

"Let's go, Vasili," Ecktar said, tapping him on the arm, "before it sets its sights on us."

The swarm grew quiet and the silence was a briefly welcome relief.

"I think it has set its sights on us," Vasili responded.

"All the more reason to get out of here before it locks onto my transporter again." Ecktar pressed some buttons on the silver apparatus on his wrist and a shield formed about them. He grabbed hold of Vasili's arm and they dematerialised.

CHAPTER 28.

The sand squeaked as Makayla sat down on the beach. She hadn't been home to her secluded Greek island since she'd dropped off the chests the Vampire and Seraph Councils had gifted her with on Evron. It felt like years had passed since then. She looked up into the heavens expecting to see her wedge-tailed eagle, but saw Salomae circling above instead. The distance seemed ever-expanding between her and Alexander. She shook her head and rubbed her chest, the ache in her heart increased every minute he was absent from her life. She'd found and lost him again in the blink of an eye.

Makayla's mind wandered as her eyes fixed on the horizon. When was the last time she'd actually sat and watched the sun rise? She couldn't remember – that had been Kayla's thing. She smiled to herself; it was now hers as well. Ever since their soul-melding she'd felt an inner peace, even in the most unexpected moments when nothing but turmoil and death surrounded her. She couldn't understand the mechanics of the soul-meld, and she didn't know why her souls had split in the first place. Her brothers hadn't experienced a split and neither had Danny from what she'd been told, so why her? Why was she so different? What made her so special, besides her prophecy?

Makayla undid the laces on her boots and tugged them off along with her socks. She stretched out, resting her elbows behind her and digging her toes into the cool sand. She shaded her eyes and looked up when she heard Salomae's loud screech. The Terrin dove, folding her wings into her body and shooting towards her at breakneck speed. Makayla watched in awe as Salomae spiralled down in a corkscrew, her body twirling in a gold blur as she drew closer. At the last minute she fanned out her giant, leathery wings, they ballooned and caught in the updraft of air. She looped and dove multiple times and Makayla tracked her movement until she was a black speck on the distant horizon.

"Show-off," Makayla said to Salomae. *"Oh, don't give me that. You are."* Makayla laughed. *"I know. . .I know, there's nothing wrong with it, I'm guilty of doing the same thing on occasion."* Makayla looked towards the horizon again, shards of brilliant light rebounding from the surface of the water and setting fire to the dark blue heavens. The water rippled with vibrant oranges and yellows as the sun fractured the sky with blinding light.

Salomae circled back towards Makayla, her wing dipping in the sea and spraying a curl of white wash into the air as she swung her body around in a tight arc. She was an exquisite sight with the sun rising behind her and reflecting off her scales and framing her body in orange and gold light. She flew low to the water, her tail cutting through the surface and creating a churning column of waves behind her. Makayla watched Salomae dip her head, arch her neck and extend her feet as she landed in the water with the grace of a swan. Waves washed ashore as she folded her wings and glided to the water's edge in front of Makayla. She smiled as Salomae lowered her head to the sand beside her.

Makayla sat forward, lowered her forehead to Salomae's and caressed her cheek. *"Stop worrying about me, I'll be fine. Xander's the one we should be worried about."* Makayla shook her head. *"No, I don't know where he is."* Salomae whimpered. *"I know, I should be able to sense him."* Makayla leaned back and rubbed her forehead with her palm. *"I don't know what to do, or where to look for him."*

Salomae snorted. *"What do you mean I do? I have no idea where he could be. NO, I DON'T!"* Salomae growled low in her throat. "Sorry, I didn't mean to raise my voice. I'm just frustrated," Makayla said aloud.

"That makes two of us," Lazarus said, plopping down beside her. "Hey, cuz, how are you?"

"Is that a trick question?" Makayla slanted her eyes to him.

"Dumb question, huh?" he said, wrapping his arm around

her shoulders and squeezing her as he looked at Salomae. "Hey, gorgeous." Salomae nudged him with her snout and he stroked under her chin.

"She's not a cat."

"She sure sounds like one, you hear that? She's purring." Salomae lifted her snout, giving him access to her throat. "She doesn't know what she's talking about, does she, girl?"

Makayla groaned. "So what was it you wanted to tell me?"

"Be careful."

"Is that it, you wanted to meet somewhere private just to tell me that?"

"No. I think my father has been masquerading as Chancellor Lagorias and was the one who killed Augustus's son." Lazarus removed his arm from Makayla's shoulder and clasped his hands in his lap.

"Can you be sure, do you have proof?" Makayla said, running her fingertips over the ruby gem necklace hanging about her throat and looked at Salomae as she lowered her head to the sand and began to snore. How she slept at any given time and so quickly still mystified Makayla.

"No, I don't have proof, it's just a gut feeling and I've always trusted my gut. After what we saw in the past with him disguised as the cardinal, I wouldn't put it past him. He's an ambitious man who has connections with Zobiana, who else could it be?"

Makayla pinched the bridge of her nose. "At this stage it could be anybody. The world we knew doesn't exist anymore.

So much changed while we were in the past and everything that's evil is coming out of the woodwork like bugs."

Lazarus chuckled. "If we were dealing with bugs at least we'd be able to spray the little buggers with bug spray and solve the problem."

Makayla smirked, shaking her head. She wiggled her toes and dug her feet deeper into the sand.

"Who are you and what have you done with the creepy vampire I met on Evron? You've changed, Laz. I don't get it, why?"

Lazarus shrugged. "I haven't changed, Makayla, you see me now, as I am, or I should say, as I let you see me. You must remember I can't be my true self on Evron or they'd eat me alive. I did that once in my youth and paid a heavy price for it." Lazarus looked down at his feet; his shoulders sagged as he brushed a hand over his face. "I get so tired of the charade sometimes; my father was a hard taskmaster and would beat me when I showed weakness. He never had to beat Kraegan. My old man was a vicious bastard, nothing like his brother. Uncle Sebastian is the most honourable man I know." Lazarus ran a finger down the scar on his cheek. "I learned my lesson well, probably too well." He looked back at Makayla with sad eyes. "I hated him, you know, my brother. I hate my father too, but I hate Kraegan more – he took so much away from me and Darrius. What he made me do, what he did to Darrius, is unforgivable." Lazarus looked towards the sunrise with his forearms resting on his knees and his hands hanging limply. He rubbed his thumb above his forefinger over and over as he spoke.

Makayla watched him; she didn't want to push for information regarding the rift between him and her brother. She sensed his anguish and she wanted to know, but couldn't bring herself to ask. It had plagued her mind ever since she'd witnessed Darrius's reaction to Lazarus when they'd arrived on Evron. Wanting to know the truth was a sour taste in her mouth that she craved to wash away with knowledge. Makayla grasped the ruby gem at her throat and pulled the necklace, it bit into her flesh before it broke. It crunched as she crushed the metal in her hand and removed the ruby from its gaudy housing. Makayla tossed the gold chain to the sand and held the ruby gem up to the sunlight. A prism of red light reflected on her arms and legs as she rotated it back and forth between her fingers.

"I'm glad you killed him, Makayla, but I have a bad feeling he's still alive. Everything that's happening reeks of him and Zobiana. And my father. He's in a despicable category all his own," Lazarus said, his eyes falling on the gem she held in her hand.

"I killed him and made sure he was dead before I got the hell out of there." Makayla eyed him as she pocketed the gem.

"Did you know he was Zobiana's apprentice before Beltizare?"

"No, that's news to me. May I ask why you think he's still alive?"

"His body was missing from the family crypt. I know he was there because my father put him there on the day of his burial. The only reason I attended his funeral was to make sure the bastard was dead. Why would his body be missing, Makayla? Who would want to steal it?"

"You've answered your own question. If he was Zobiana's apprentice; she was most likely the one to have taken his body."

"Do you think she's capable of bringing him back to life?"

"After what I've seen, yes, I think she's very capable. My mother brought Alexander back to life using the resurrection spell. He was dead, Lazarus, dead as a doornail. I don't know if it's a seraph thing and something only angels can do, but I wouldn't rule it out when Zobiana's thrown into the mix, she's capable of anything. Do you know of any vampires having brought people back from the dead?"

"You're kidding, right? Look at the Newbloods she's created; they're undead in a sense, and certainly not like the rest of the vampire race, that's for sure."

"Come on, Lazarus, you know what I mean. Do vampires have a process similar to the resurrection spell my mother performed on Xander?"

"Not that I know of, but Zobiana's not your typical vampire now, is she?"

"No, she's not. According to what my father says, she's the first vampire, the mother of our race. It must kill her to know she'll never be queen of Evron. Shit, how did I miss it? She wants to be queen."

Lazarus laughed. "She'd have one hell of a fight on her hands; the council rules Evron now, not the monarchy, it has for decades—" Lazarus stopped speaking, his face paling.

"What, what's the matter?"

"My father was masquerading as Augustus Lagorias, the High-Lord Chancellor of Evron's vampire senate. The real Augustus was confined to a cell in Zobiana's dungeon. She's planning to overthrow the council and bring back the monarchy by placing herself on the throne as the queen. Why else would she have blackmailed our grandfather into betrothing his firstborn son to her? She wanted to be queen even then. It makes perfect sense."

Makayla shook her head. "What are you talking about, Laz? What does this have to do with my father? I know he's royalty and all, but it doesn't make him king."

"You don't know, do you?"

"Know what?"

"Your father was first in line to the throne, a position my father coveted even though it wasn't his right. When our grandfather was murdered, Uncle Sebastian was to become king, but he abdicated the throne to marry your mother. No one knew of their relationship, though. My father saw this as his opportunity to go after the throne. He was the youngest, the second son and not the legal heir, but believed he had a legitimate right to the throne. Before he had a chance to make a move and take the throne for himself, your father dashed all his dreams. Your father spoke with Aunt Ambrosia's father who was the seraph king then. They came to an agreement and formed the Vampire and Seraph Councils; it brought peace to Evron. Our nations were at war for centuries before that. They formed the council as a part of the truce, but it was also to protect your parents' relationship. If the public were to learn of your parents' marriage and their love for one another, they would have been crucified, not to mention there would have been complete anarchy as a result."

"Holy shit, I had no idea, I thought no one knew about them and it was a clandestine affair. So what you're saying is the council knew of their relationship?"

"No, no one knew except the two kings."

"When you say two kings, who are you referring to?"

"Your father and Uriel Chevez, your mother's father."

"Uriel Chevez is my grandfather?"

"Yes, didn't you know?"

"No, I didn't." Makayla shook her head and looked down at her trembling hands, remembering the first time she'd seen Uriel Chevez. His reaction had surprised her, now she knew why. When he'd first set eyes on her he'd stood in the doorway with his mouth gaping; all the Seraph Guards behind him had dropped to their knees and bowed.

"It explains a lot, but how do you know all this?"

"Do you remember our first conversation, Makayla? It was just after your youngest brother died. You were in the entertainment room listening to music and drinking at the bar if

I recall."

Makayla nodded. "Yes, I remember, I was a right bitch to you, Laz, sorry."

Lazarus bumped his shoulder against hers. "Don't apologise, Makayla, you didn't know me then. I was just the creepy Vampire Guard checking you out at the council meeting, as far as you knew. I must admit though, I was very impressed the first time I set my eyes on you. What you said still makes me chuckle. Seriously, I'll never forget what you said: *'Are you going to open the door or just stand there fucking me with your eyes?'* I laughed for months afterwards. I mean, who says shit like that to a perfect stranger and a Vampire Guard no less?"

Makayla raised her hand like a student vying for the teacher's attention. "That would be me."

Lazarus smirked. "I loved your take-no-shit attitude, it was refreshing; everyone's so uptight on Evron."

"Sorry, Laz, I can be a little abrasive sometimes."

Lazarus chuckled. "Abrasive. Woman, you give the word a whole new meaning. I find it the most authentic thing about you – at least a person knows where they stand. Vampire Evronians can be deceiving and manipulative and will do most anything to get their way. My father is a perfect example."

Makayla smiled sheepishly. "What can I say; I was of two minds back then, literally. I've changed."

"Yes, yes, you have. Anyway, I digress. I knew everything about your family because I was secretly working for your father; he wanted me to keep him abreast of what the council was doing. Even though he was a member of the council, he wasn't always able to attend the monthly meetings – not to mention he wanted to know what they knew regarding your family. Funny how things play out. I was to keep a particular eye on his most trusted man, Augustus; Uncle Sebastian wanted to know if he was loyal to him. Luckily I didn't expose myself to Augustus because had I said anything, not knowing my father was masquerading as him, he would have known everything. He must have known anyway because of the way things have played out."

"Why you, Lazarus? Why did my father choose you for this job?"

Lazarus swept his hand through his hair and exhaled. "It's a long story, from long ago. My parents didn't marry for love; it was a strategic marriage of convenience and power on my father's part. My mother had no choice, she had to marry a man she despised and was dragged to the wedding against her will. Your father was her saving grace, she trusted him. They grew up together. Her brother was his best friend, and she was the little sister he'd always wanted. They had a great deal in common in those days. He was betrothed to someone he didn't want to marry, and she was married to a man she didn't love or respect. My father used to beat her. All I've ever known is a violent, hateful, jealous man, a man I, too, despised. There were times I jumped between my parents to protect my mother from another of my father's violent tirades." Lazarus looked out towards the sunrise. "I called your father after one such occasion. My mother had been badly beaten. She'd been pregnant at the time, close to full term and was haemorrhaging. My father found out the baby she was carrying wasn't his and lost his temper. She went into early labour because of the beating. I contacted your father and he helped deliver the baby – my youngest brother. I remember holding him in my arms afterwards; he was so tiny, so beautiful, so different. I was the one who named him. I called him Zarik. No one else knows his name but your father and me. He's half fae and half vampire, could you imagine the backlash my mother would have received had people known she'd birthed a Zoldarni emissary's half-breed child? There would have been a public outcry. Your father whisked him to safety in much the same way he did for you. To this day I don't know where he is, all I know is he's safe.

My mother was never the same after. She loved the baby's father, I can't recall his name now after so many years, but he was an honourable man just like your father." Lazarus glanced over at Makayla, who was speechless. "You do know the story of my long-lost missing brother, right?"

Makayla nodded. "The lost brother Darrius is pretending to be?"

"Yes, the one and the same, only people don't know my long-lost brother is a fae-vampire hybrid. So, now you know why your father chose me. We have a history, he trusts me as I do him. My mother was in the same position as he and your mother are in – an interspecies relationship. As far as I'm concerned, love is love in whatever way, shape or form it comes in."

"I had no idea, Laz. What a snake pit." It was a lot to take in. Makayla rubbed her eyes and looked at Lazarus. "Lazarus, I thought the scar on your cheek was on the right side of your face, not your left?"

Lazarus lifted his hand to his left cheek and smiled. "It's on both." His ambiguous smile made Makayla grin.

"How so?"

"I try to mask the scars on my face and body; sometimes they show through when my concentration lapses or if I'm relaxed."

"Scars? There's more than one? What happened to you, Lazarus?" Makayla raised her hands. "Sorry, you don't have to tell me, it's none of my business."

"We all have scars, Makayla, some you can see and others you can't. Your scars, for instance, are on the inside, they're not as visible as mine." Lazarus caressed her cheek. "If I show you how utterly deformed my face is, will you promise not to cringe."

Makayla gulped, she'd never seen this vulnerable side of Lazarus before and prayed she'd not disappoint him. She nodded and watched as Lazarus's face changed to its true form. She covered her mouth. Tears pooled in her eyes and streaked down her cheeks when she saw his disfigurement. He was still very handsome; the scars were more severe than she could have ever imagined, but not so terrible that they made him look ugly. They gave his face a hard, battle-worn edge that would make the toughest warriors shake in their boots. The scar on his right cheek was thicker and more raised than she'd first thought, not a faint silver line. Makayla lifted her fingertip to the top edge of the scar near his eyebrow and traced it down his cheek to the corner of his mouth where it tapered off over his chin. There was a second scar on the left side of his face, a third of the length of the one on his right cheek, but it wasn't as severe. It curved across the middle of his cheek horizontally and ended on the bridge of his nose. There were many other scars on his neck, slashing down over his collarbone and disappearing beneath his clothing. Makayla cupped his face in her hands and looked into his eyes. "You're still handsome, Lazarus, these scars enhance your masculine appearance, they become you. You look the part of a warrior, but I can heal them for you, if you like," Makayla said, kissing each scar on his face one by one.

Lazarus shook his head. "No, they can't be healed, salt was rubbed into the wounds for my disloyalty, and even if I could remove them, I wouldn't. They serve as a reminder of what I should never have let happen."

"Did Kraegan give you those scars?" Makayla asked.

"Yes, but what he did to Darrius was far worse."

Makayla raised her face to the heavens. "I don't think it's my right to ask what happened, and you can shut me down if you don't want to answer. Does the rift between you and

Darrius have something to do with what Kraegan did to you both?"

"Yes." Lazarus lowered his gaze to his feet and wrung his hands.

"I've asked Darrius many times what's between you; he refuses to answer and always changes the subject. Will you tell me?"

"I can't tell you exactly what happened, Darrius obviously isn't ready for you to know and I respect him too much to divulge all the information. It's his story not mine. He will tell you when he's ready one day, but when he does, please don't think less of me. I was as much a victim as Darrius was. My brother was not an honourable man, he threatened the life of my wife, and now she's dead because of him. He retaliated when I fought back and saved Darrius's life and it cost me my wife."

"Oh, Lazarus, I'm so sorry for your loss, I didn't know you were married." Makayla glanced down at her hands before looking back up into his face. If sorrow had a face, it would have been Lazarus's at that moment; his eyes were red-rimmed and glassy, his throat was blotchy, a vein twitched in his temple and his jaw clenched and unclenched as he bit down, grinding his teeth. Makayla could no longer fight the pull to ask. "Can you tell me anything?"

"I can't, Makayla, I've already said too much, but I will ask you a question instead. Have you ever wondered why Darrius has only two wings when he should have six?"

CHAPTER 29.

The room was empty except for the portrait of Makayla above the fireplace. Alexander took in his surroundings, thinking about Vasili's words and everything Zobiana had done in his absence. He scratched his head and tried to remember when he'd last been home to Corfe Castle. There was a light tap on the door and he walked over and eased it open. Agatha stood twisting the hem of her apron in her hands. He smiled at his long-time friend and housekeeper.

"Hi Aggie," he said, his face warming with embarrassment. "Sorry it's taken me so long to come home. I didn't have the heart to stay. Well, you know all too well what happened." He gestured behind him. "I seem to remember there being more furniture in my room before I left, though."

Agatha pulled him into her arms and hugged him in a tight embrace. "I've missed you, laddie." She brushed hair out of his eyes. "After the package arrived with your note and the bottle of your blood, I was scared I'd never see you again in this lifetime. It does me good to see you again; it's been too long. You look like you've been through hell and need a good meal to fatten you up. Come, let's go to the kitchen and I'll fix you something to eat."

Before Alexander could respond, Agatha was dragging him by the elbow out into the corridor. He smiled to himself. There was no fighting Agatha. Food was her remedy for every ailment. He accompanied her down the stairs and she continued chattering until they reached the warmth of the kitchen – her domain.

"You were right about Makayla, she was different from the first time I met her. She's quite special, your lady. I promise I didn't mention having met her before in the past, although she may have suspected something was amiss. I can see why you love her, though."

"Yes, she's very special. I've missed you, Aggie. I really have," he said, sitting in the chair Agatha pulled out for him. "But I don't think food will do the trick."

"Oh, hush, I know food won't do the trick, especially now you're a vampire. I'm not daft, Xander. Makayla has thought of everything, just like you did. She told me about how she'd sired you, and said if you ever returned you'd need her blood. She made me promise not to let anyone know about you being a vampire. When she saw you in a vision chained to a whipping pole in a dungeon, she thought it was the end for you. She was terrified Lilith would kill you – only she didn't call her Lilith she called her . . ." Agatha stopped and scratched her head in thought. "Z. . . it started with Z, oh bother, for the life of me, I can't remember."

"Zobiana," Alexander supplied. "So I wasn't hallucinating. I told her to go home; I didn't know if she'd understand my meaning."

"That's the one. No, you weren't hallucinating; she was desperate to find you. She feared Zobiana would send her people here in search of her because of the connection she made with you, but they never came. The night she disappeared was the night all your furniture disappeared too."

Alexander thought for a moment, rubbing his jaw with his fingertips. After Makayla arrived in the past, some of his bedroom furniture had suddenly appeared in his secret cave – albeit it had appeared much older. He'd dismissed it at the time, he'd been shocked enough to find Makayla standing in his secret cave and had paid little attention to the furniture; even then she'd captivated him. Time and time again he'd returned to his cave, because of the memories they'd made there together, he'd felt closer to her somehow, but he'd never returned to Corfe Castle. He'd made sure the tenants in his care were protected and tended to, but after what had happened in the village square he hadn't the heart to stay. She'd obviously been in his bedroom when the Trinian Globe transported her back to the past; it all made sense now.

"Sorry," said Aggie, unaware of the turn his thoughts had

taken. "I don't know where your furniture disappeared to, but I figured when you returned you'd remedy the problem." She wiggled her fingers in his face and chuckled as she bustled about the kitchen. "You being a Druid and all."

Alexander smiled, he'd missed sitting in the warmth of Agatha's kitchen surrounded in the pleasant aromas of cinnamon and basil and spices. There was always a mouth-watering scent of food wafting down the hallways whenever she was in the swing of cooking. He particularly liked when the kitchen smelled of her chocolate chip cookies.

The microwave dinged and Agatha removed a tall, wide glass filled with blood and placed it in front of him. "Here you go, laddie, there's more in the refrigerator if you're still hungry afterwards." Alexander's fangs descended the moment he scented Makayla's blood. He lifted the glass to his mouth and gulped down the contents in a rush, licking his lips and savouring the metallic taste of Makayla's unusual blood. Then he handed Agatha the glass for another. She refilled the glass and placed it in the microwave to heat before handing it to him again. Alexander drank it down with gusto, feeling revived and sated.

"Thank you, Aggie, I needed that. I was famished; I'm hungry all the time. It's the strangest sensation, my gums burn, my eye teeth ache, my mouth dries out and my vision blurs when I need to feed. I never understood Makayla's hunger before, but I do now."

"Your hunger will diminish after a while, you're still a

fledgling. For the first few months you will crave blood and have an unquenchable need to feed more often."

"How do you know? You're not a vampire."

"No, I'm not, but you have a big library, Xander, remember, and if you recall, I like to read. God knows there's not much else to do around here, other than cook and do housework."

Alexander chuckled. "Sorry, you were always an inquisitive child, even when you were hanging on to your mother's apron strings. Your mother used to frown when I'd encourage your curiosity with books. She'd wiggle her finger at me and say, '*Och, laddie, why ye be encouraging the child? All she need be knowin is how to be looken after ye and ye castle.*'"

Agatha chortled, tears glistening in her eyes as she grabbed her belly in laughter. "My ma believed a woman's place was tending to the lord of the manor and providing a hearty meal in the kitchen, not hiding in a library with my head buried in a book. She was old-fashioned, even back then."

"Aye, that she was, but I always believed, and still do, knowledge is power and everyone has a right to an education. I always wondered why you didn't follow your dreams but stayed on after she passed. You're a seer, Aggie; you could have done many things, especially with your extensive knowledge."

"I could have burned at the stake for witchcraft, too. I saw it, you know, in a vision. It was why I stayed, and I couldn't leave knowing what I knew. No, I had to stay to protect you from them."

Alexander angled his head. "Protect me from whom, Aggie?"

"Lilith and Tyron, I knew their intentions weren't good. I couldn't tell you, laddie. When I saw Makayla's arrival in a vision, I knew everything would be okay, but even then, I couldn't leave you. It was my duty to stay and protect you and your beloved. I was always protecting you in the background. I had to follow on with my mother's legacy – she made me promise on her deathbed to always watch over you and any offspring you were to have. I fear I may have failed in that respect. When you left, I couldn't follow. I'm sorry, Xander."

"Aggie, I had no idea. You gave up too much. You should have married, had a family of your own." Alexander brushed a hand through his hair, feeling a heaviness in his heart for all the things Agatha had given up for him.

"I'd do it all again, Xander, it has been an honour to care for you. A Druid should always have a seer at his side, they go hand in hand. It is the natural order of things, even if it was and still is one of your father's edicts. He made sure you were always protected, that's why he married Lilith, to shield you from her. She had her sights set on you even before your father married her. He knew she killed your mother and wasn't willing to risk your life so he married her to safeguard your future."

"Why have you never told me these things, and why are

you telling me now?"

"I was sworn to secrecy by my mother, it was part of the agreement she had with your father. We were to watch over and protect you, you weren't to know. I'm telling you now because I can no longer stand by and watch you suffer at Lilith's hands, and it was my mother who made the pact with your father, not me. You need to know what's at stake, Xander; it's the only way to guarantee your future, Makayla's future, everyone's future. This world is dying, there's no saving it. It's been on the cards for millennia." Agatha pulled out a chair and sat beside Alexander. "We're protected here in Corfe Castle; for how long is anyone's guess, but I have faith the ward will hold for many more centuries because it has protected the village surrounding Corfe Castle for centuries already. Everyone living here in this town will be safe as long as they don't leave. There will be other places in the world similar to Corfe Castle Village where no evil befalls them."

Alexander listened to Agatha intently, he'd always known there was more to her than she'd let on, but he could never have imagined the things she was now telling him. He felt relief knowing his father had known about Zobiana all along, but he also felt great sorrow for him having to align himself with the woman who had killed the love of his life. It was a lot to take in. Agatha's gentle voice soothed Alexander even when her words horrified him.

"After Makayla's arrival, I made sure the Village of Corfe Castle was protected from the outside world," Agatha continued. "Don't ask me how I achieved it, it was many years in the making. I will tell you this, though, after you left all those centuries ago, I vowed to myself to never let evil enter our village or Corfe Castle ever again. After what happened with Lilith, Tyron and Abigail I had great motivation. My visions are never clear and are sometimes indecipherable, but I understood something bad was coming. I could never have guessed the magnitude of what would happen and the great evil Lilith would do, but it isn't only Lilith we need to worry about. Something more sinister is gathering strength and I'm afraid it has its sights set on you and Makayla. I beg you, Alexander, your love for one another is your strength and, God willing, if you nurture that love and trust in it you will prevail. It won't be easy, it will test you both, it will try and tear you apart from the inside. It will try to devour your memories and lay you bare, but you must fight, Xander, you must fight. You may even have to sacrifice everything to win this battle – just don't lose your soul, please, I beg you, don't lose your soul. Never forget why you fell in love with Makayla in the first place. You will be safe if you remember, because the moment you forget you will no longer exist."

Alexander shivered; was Agatha speaking about the Dark One? Had he possessed his body? If so he couldn't sense his presence at all. Sure, he'd blacked out a few times, but he was still transitioning into whatever hybrid Makayla's turning had made him.

"Who, Aggie? Who will have won? Who are you talking

about?"

"It's not clear, Xander, darkness surrounds you. It's trying to take over your body, but is failing so far; you're too strong, you're protected by something." Agatha placed her palm on his chest, over his heart. "I can feel it here; your chest glows with green light, it surrounds and protects your heart, and it's so beautiful. It's more powerful than the darkness." Agatha removed her hand from his chest and looked up into his face. "Don't worry, she'll find you. She searches for you even now, but is having trouble sensing where you are. The Darkness is interfering with your blood-bond. Your bond is strong, but this darkness has latched on and masks you from her like a jealous lover, not even the bond you share can break through. Fear not, though, the powerful light protecting your heart will draw her to you."

Alexander rubbed his chest, knowing exactly what green light Agatha referred to. He drew in a deep breath, feeling the ever-expanding tightness in his chest. "It may be too late for me already. Aggie, this darkness you speak of worries me. When I was in the dungeon, Abigail and Zobiana planned to offer my body up as a vessel to the Dark One. Abigail is a powerful succubus like her mother, and has a knack for siphoning her victims' power, to weaken them. She said the Dark One would wear me like a jacket. I have this God-awful feeling they may have succeeded, and the Dark One now resides in my body."

Agatha's eyes rounded. "Do you feel his presence inside you?"

"No, I don't, but what you said earlier resonates with me, it's concerning."

"Does Makayla know? Have you said anything to her?"

"God, no, but she senses something's not right with me, she's not stupid. She keeps asking what they did to me in the dungeon. I can't tell her what I don't know. I keep having strange dreams, but what if they're more than just dreams, Aggie?"

"If he was inside you, Xander, believe me, you'd know it, you'd sense him. But if he is, something's protecting you from him. Makayla's the key."

"It's funny you should say that, she really is the Key, you know? The Key of Divinity, and I am her keeper. She has always been mine to protect, and look at me, I don't even know where she is. I'm not doing such a good job in protecting her now, am I?" Alexander stood, pushing the chair out with the backs of his knees; the chair-legs screeched as they scraped along the floor. "I'm sorry, Aggie, but I've got to go." He looked down into her worried face and brushed her cheek with the pad of his thumb before kissing it. "Thank you for everything."

"You say that like you won't be back, Xander."

Alexander had no idea what lay ahead, but he knew deep down in the pit of his stomach things would never be the same, not if Zobiana had her way. "I'm not sure I will be back, I'm not sure of anything anymore. The only thing I'm sure of is something's coming, something bad. I've felt it for a long while now. Zobiana has changed this world. She wants to control its gateways, and probably already does. She wants Evron, and she will do whatever it takes to have it, even if it means going to war. If I know Zobiana, she will not stop until she gets what she wants. She always gets what she wants." Alexander pushed his chair under the table. "Goodbye, Agatha, you have always been like a daughter. Know that I have loved you as such." Alexander swept the tears from her cheeks. "Please, no tears, this is not goodbye, and if it is, I'm sure we'll meet again in the next life." Alexander turned and walked out of the kitchen. He didn't look back; he had things he needed to do.

CHAPTER 30.

Zobiana pushed past the horde of Newbloods crowding the castle courtyard towards Abigail and Tyrone. Earth's gateways were hers; she'd received word from Nathanial. Evron was close, so close she could taste it. The Shadow Seekers hadn't seen her coming, they were too busy fighting the unfightable – V5, the Blakspor virus – and trying to figure out how to free the humans from the blood farms. They were all diversions, important stepping stones, but not her ultimate goal.

Zobiana looked up into the heavens and shaded her eyes with her hand, twenty or so seraphs darted by, too close for her liking. Seraph Guard flocked the skies, searching for her, searching for her base of operations. The Earth was a big place and one thousand seraphs was not enough to monitor an entire world. They were getting close, but with the powerful wards in place she was undetectable. She lowered her hand and continued walking across the courtyard. Abigail waved a greeting as she came to their side. Zobiana looked at Tyrone, she sensed his apprehension. Good. She wanted him to sweat. They'd spoken earlier, he'd explained his actions and she'd accepted his apology – she wasn't as unforgiving as the Dark One. She even understood Tyrone's actions, given the circumstances and his animosity towards Alexander; she may have reacted the same way. A smile snaked across her features as she smoothed her hands down her legs; it felt strange to be wearing trousers and armour, but she was going to war and couldn't do that wearing a slinky ball gown, more's the pity.

Abigail looked her up and down, a smile creasing her face. "I don't think I've ever seen you dressed for battle before, Mother. The black crown is a nice touch."

Zobiana laughed, touching the tip of a spike on her crown. "I thought so, too. Is everything in place?"

Abigail nodded. "Yes, we have control of all the known gateways here on Earth, except the Zoldarni gateway. There were Zoldarni warriors guarding it. We could have incapacitated them, but the less they know the better. We didn't want to bring a legion of Zoldarni guards down on our heads. We have enough to contend with at the moment."

"Let's worry about them later; there'll be time when Evron is ours. It's better they think they're in control. When they realise they've lost Earth and its gateways, things are bound to change, and it's only a matter of time before they realise their emissaries are dead, if they don't already," Zobiana said, looking about the courtyard. She'd amassed an army to be reckoned with. Her smile widened when she noticed members of the Vampire Guard among her ranks. "How many Vampire Guard do we have on our side on Evron?"

"I would say more than half," Tyrone responded.

"Good, it seems our alliance with Malachi has paid off."

"Yes, mistress, so it would seem." Tyrone bowed his head. "The Vampire Guards loyal to you have waited centuries for your return. From what I've heard there was considerable anger among their ranks when you were exiled after King Eridan's death. They were expecting Lord Sebastian to take his rightful place on the throne with you at his side. When he abdicated and refused to honour his betrothal to you, there was unrest and public outcry, more so when the senate was formed," Tyrone said, folding his arms behind his back.

"Yes, I remember. It was most unfortunate. I don't think Sebastian approved of me killing the seraph queen. How was I to know it wasn't Ambrosia? They looked so similar. She was the one I wanted dead, not the queen. What a shame my tactic failed and didn't push things to the brink of war, instead it got me exiled. Well, there's still time to remedy the situation."

"About that, Mother, have you thought about what we discussed?"

"We can't kill Ambrosia, Abigail, not now at least. She performed a resurrection spell on Alexander, I saw it myself. If we kill her, there's a possibility Alexander will die, and we don't want to release the Dark One, not when we have him where we want him. No, she must live, but it doesn't mean we can't do other things. Come, I have something better in mind, something far more interesting. Sebastian will have no choice but to take the throne, I'm betting on it; and what I have in mind will put me in a better position to be his queen."

Zobiana lifted her hand into the air and the wind picked up, funnelling around her. Dirt particles, dry leaves and small pebbles lifted off the ground and circled her ankles as she formed a gaseous ball in her palm. The ball spun until a black vortex appeared. It continued growing in size and power until it looked like a miniature black hole. The air was electric and crackled with the smell of ozone. The debris ceased spinning and dropped to the ground the moment she hurled the gaseous ball towards the inner curtain wall. It hit the barrier, sizzling like a live wire coming into contact with water. The ball flattened against the wall like a giant circular paint splat, and the sizzling sound grew louder as the rock disintegrated like acid eating metal. The hard surface of the circle dissolved in on itself until there was a spinning wormhole.

Zobiana nodded at Tyrone, who whistled to get the attention of the surrounding soldiers. He signalled them towards the vortex with a quick wave of his hand. The Newblood army began to move in the direction of the curtain wall in orderly lines.

Zobiana waited briefly before placing an arm around her daughter. "You will enjoy what I have in mind, Abigail," she said, guiding her towards the portal. She laughed. "I think

we're all going to enjoy this."

Shadows hadn't always bothered Augustus, but now, after spending an eternity in a dark dungeon, it bothered him more than he'd liked to admit. Shadows weren't necessarily shadows on Evron, or anywhere for that matter, not in his recent experiences. It felt like he was in a roomful of watchful ghosts waiting for the moment to strike and scare him senseless. He knew he was being paranoid. He shrugged, trying to relax the kinks that had formed in his tense body. Augustus checked the hallway before stepping out from the safe confines of his chambers. He closed the door and set off down the shadowed hallway.

After everything that had transpired, he felt sure Malachi and Zobiana had loyal followers here on Evron and conspired to overthrow the governing bodies so they could take control of Evron together. He hadn't a clue how they'd achieve their goals, but if he didn't speak with Uriel and warn him, God knows how bad things would become. If it was anything like the violent coup in the past then he feared this time would be far worse. Many innocent lives would be lost and a great deal more than the first time Zobiana had tried to usurp the leaders.

He looked over his shoulder when he heard a noise. *Was that a footstep? Stop being so paranoid.* He straightened his back and held his head high, he would never have cowered at the slightest sound years ago, but it was difficult to retrain thirty years of incarceration and reclaim the confidence of his youth. Augustus stopped walking and closed his eyes. He took a deep, calming breath and released it slowly, repeating the exercise until he found composure. He couldn't let fear rule him; if he did, all would be lost. Evron. Earth. The gateways. Everything.

When he heard approaching voices he straightened his collar, smoothed a hand down the front of his robe and began walking again. The voices grew louder as they drew nearer; he recognised three of his colleagues from the Vampire Council. His shoulders tensed as he clasped his hands in front of his robes; and waited for them to see him for the imposter he was. *You are not an imposter!* he reprimanded himself. The moment they saw him, their steps slowed and their conversation ceased.

"Chancellor Lagorias, how fare thee? We feared you'd met with foul play."

Augustus cleared his throat before speaking. "I am well, Lord Cavendish, I apologise for not contacting the council regarding my absence. I had pressing matters to attend to of a sensitive nature and am afraid I had to rush off. Unavoidable, given my position as chancellor, but all is well. As it turns out everything was in order upon my arrival and my concern was unfounded."

Lord Cavendish raised his chin, his eyebrow lifting in a manner that implied he wasn't convinced he was hearing the truth. "Keeping the peace is the council's main objective,

Chancellor Lagorias. We understand the immense pressures of sustaining peace here on Evron."

Augustus's skin crawled with an unsettling tingle. Lord Cavendish was lying. When Sebastian mentioned Ambrosia's blood would help unmask liars, Augustus had thought he was exaggerating.

Lord Cavendish continued speaking. "Next time it would be prudent to leave word of future absences, after all, Chancellor, we aren't exempt from council protocol. If all council members were to just up and leave without a word or a care, what example would we be setting? We must live by example if we want the vampire nation to follow and adhere to our laws."

Augustus bowed his head. "Yes, yes of course," he said, folding his arms behind his back. Emboldened by his extrasensory ability, he refused to grovel for forgiveness; it would oust him for the imposter he felt he was. He'd always been proud in his youth with an air of authority, if he didn't act the same way now he may as well yell to the rafters that his position had been compromised. "If you'll excuse me, I have much to catch up on due to my absence."

If they only knew just how much he had to catch up on. He bowed his head once more before taking his leave. He wished he had more time before he spoke to Uriel, but the more time he wasted dallying in the council archives, the less time he had to warn Uriel of Zobiana and Malachi's deceptiveness. He was certain she'd show, he just didn't know when. He prayed

Uriel would believe him and update him on the most important issues that had transpired in his absence.

The council members, Tydias and Selza, watched Augustus walk away before continuing down the hall in the opposite direction, Cavendish hung back before following his colleagues. Augustus could feel Cavendish's eyes lingering on him as he walked away. The sensation was unnerving, but an instinctual one he was familiar with. It almost felt like being back in the dungeon surrounded by hungry vermin ready to strip the flesh from his body. He'd never liked Cavendish; he suspected it had to do with his swaying loyalties in the past. Cavendish had always been a zealot, a fanatic of the most conniving kind. Augustus doubted he'd changed much; even if you removed a viper's tooth it could still bite.

Augustus walked for what felt like hours, but was mere minutes to reach Uriel's private chambers. Odd, usually there were Seraph Guards stationed outside Uriel's chamber door. The door was ajar. Augustus looked about, the silence invaded his calm, was he too late? He eased the door open further, the hairs on his arms spiking in alarm. The air rippled and seemed to stretch and pop as he stepped over the threshold into the room – a protective ward, he felt sure. That he was able to pass the barrier surprised him. He closed the door, moved further into the room and stopped by a dim alcove. Where was he?

"Uriel . . ." he whispered. No response. "Uriel, are you here? Please, if you're here, show yourself, it's Augustus, I need to speak with you. Sebastian sent me. He said to tell you all is not well in the realm."

The air rippled, and a hand appeared out of nowhere, hovering in front of his face like a severed apparition, it grabbed hold of his arm and tugged. Augustus lost balance as someone pulled him through the veil into what could only be the Seraph Shadow Realm. Uriel stood in front of him surrounded by Seraph Guard. Augustus wiped the cold sweat from his forehead with a trembling hand and gaped at his surroundings. He opened and closed his mouth, lost for words. He was struck by how warm he felt. The warmth comforted and dispelled the goose bumps covering his body.

"Where have you been, Augustus? You've been missing for a week."

"I've been missing longer than a week, Uriel; I've been missing for thirty-odd Earth years, held captive in one of Zobiana's dungeons."

"Lower your weapons," Uriel commanded, placing a hand on a Seraph Guard's sword. He eyed Augustus with tight-lipped interest, his face a mask of regal curiosity. "Come with me, Augustus, where we can speak without fear of being overheard."

Augustus relaxed when the Seraph Guards lowered their weapons and stepped back against the walls, allowing him passage. He followed Uriel through a white, narrow hallway decorated with swirling gold motifs. Augustus's footsteps staggered as he looked at the arched ceiling high above his head; everything glowed with an angelic brightness, blurring with white brilliance. If ever there was a place that appeared to touch heaven this was it.

Uriel stopped and looked over his shoulder then followed Augustus's gaze heavenward. The corner of his mouth curled. "Augustus, time is of the essence."

Augustus cleared his throat. "I beg your pardon, your royal highness, but I'm, I'm at a loss for words. I thought the Seraph Shadow Realm was a myth."

"Your royal highness? You haven't called me that in a long time, Augustus." Uriel's face softened, his features relaxing into a welcoming smile. "Come, we have much to discuss, I've suspected for some time you weren't quite yourself and now my suspicions are justified. There's much you have missed. We must plan – Evron is under siege. The great prophecy is at hand."

CHAPTER 31.

There was a crowd standing in Vasili's office when he opened the door. All the Shadow Seekers were there except Makayla, Ava and Freya. Gabriel, Bryce, Zack, Reece, Anna, Ashley, Jackson, Morgan and Darrius stood in a huddled group deep in conversation. They silenced the moment he entered. Vasili sensed a deep foreboding within the group as he closed the door. He traced a sigil on the door and waved his hand, manifesting a ward of privacy over the room. Vasili acknowledged the group, noticing the grim looks on their faces. He made his way to his desk, picked up a crystal decanter of port and poured himself a glass, filling it to the brim. He sat in his leather chair and took a deep draught of alcohol. The rich, fruity flavour soothed his nerves as the smooth alcohol glided down his dry throat.

What could he say that wouldn't cause unrest? It was

happening; the prophecy was upon them. He brushed a tired hand over his beard and looked into Gabriel's eyes. "Please, make yourselves comfortable, we have much to discuss," he said, pointing to the couches. Bryce didn't move from his position by the wall, and neither did the others who gathered around Vasili's desk. Vasili sighed at the tight-coiled tension in the room.

"Who wants to go first?" Gabriel asked.

"I'll go," Zack said. "I'm the only one here who has good news."

"Maybe you should go last," Reece said. "At least we could end on a brighter note."

"You could always tell one of your horrible jokes to end on a brighter note, Reece," Jackson said, trying to lighten the mood.

"I don't think my jokes will help, Jack. Not with the way things are at the moment." Reece rubbed his eyes and Anna grabbed his hand and squeezed it.

"I think we should go with the bad news first, sorry, Zack," Jack said. "Ashley and I did what you asked, Vasili, and can confirm Zobiana controls Earth's gateways. We managed to contact other nations with Zack's help, and the gateways in their countries have also fallen."

Vasili nodded. "Yes, I suspected as much. The Zoldarni gateways here in London are unaffected. I'm uncertain of the remaining Zoldarni gateways throughout the rest of the world, but have a sneaking suspicion they too remain untouched. It's anyone's guess how long it will remain like this, though. I had been trying to contact the Zoldarni emissaries here on Earth for some time now, but was unsuccessful in all my attempts. So I travelled to Cwonoth uninvited to make contact with Overlord Avinash; the leader of the Zoldarni. I came close to being executed for my indiscretion; luckily I was able to convince him of the Earth's dire position and Zobiana's treachery before he lopped off my head for insubordination. Captain Ecktar and a small contingent of Zoldarni guard accompanied me back to earth to find out whether the emissaries had met with foul play. They were dead when we arrived and had been for some time. Abigail murdered them in cold blood. It was the reason I was unable to get word to Overlord Avinash. Ecktar is trying to contact the other emissaries on Earth, but it doesn't look good."

The Shadow Seekers grew silent for a moment as they absorbed Vasili's words.

Reece moved closer and placed his hand on the tabletop of Vasili's desk, lowering his face to his. "He's free."

"Who's free?" Vasili queried.

Reece's eyebrow raised, his back was to everyone in the room, Vasili looked down as Reece traced a symbol on his desktop. "You know who," Reece supplied.

Vasili blanched. "What! How . . . how is it even possible? We made sure no one could free him."

"Alexander freed him, but doesn't remember doing it."

"Eh-hum, perhaps I can shed some light," Darrius said, raising his hand and throwing Reece a quizzical look.

Vasili looked past Reece as he stepped back next to Anna. "Shed some light, how?" Vasili said, glancing back towards Reece. *"What does he know, Reece, tell me he doesn't know the identity of the entity?"*

Reece raised his chin and shook his head. *"No, he doesn't, but he's suspects something's off and has a good reason for feeling this way,"* Reece responded telepathically.

Vasili relaxed back in his chair and focused his attention on Darrius. He could have just read his mind, but he'd stopped reading the Shadow Seekers minds a long time ago, it was invasive and disloyal. Trust was, to him, a code of honour he lived by. Interrogation, on the other hand, was a necessary evil.

Darrius cleared his throat and recounted the events that took place in the sewers when he and Makayla had followed Alexander. He told Vasili about Alexander's strange behaviour and how he'd led them to a Roman temple and disappeared through a wall inscribed with ancient writings. When he finished speaking he looked pointedly at Reece. "We figured someone would know what was wrong with Alexander, maybe someone would know about the Roman temple beneath London's sewers. It seems we were right, someone knew more than they led us to believe."

"I was sworn to secrecy, Darrius, I could not go against the brotherhood of Rahul and fill you in on the details of an ancient mission I'd taken part in centuries ago. I'm sorry, but I am bound by my word to the brotherhood. Vasili would agree with me," Reece said and looked towards Vasili.

Vasili nodded. "It's as Reece says, Darrius. He is bound by the holy sacrament of the Custodians of Rahul brotherhood. He cannot speak of missions, past, present or future, with anyone other than brotherhood members, or, if I give him permission."

"Well then, why is he speaking now?" Morgan pointed out, eyeing Darrius thoughtfully.

"He hasn't gone into the specifics or given you the name of the upper level demon who was entombed in the Skarskee temple, has he?" Vasili replied. "It's okay, Reece, you have my permission to speak freely regarding this issue." Vasili continued speaking silently, *"Just don't mention the demon's name, or his alias names, names are dangerous."*

"Upper level demon," Morgan gasped. "What, what the hell."

"Do you think it's connected to Zobiana's scheming, or could it be more sinister than we thought?" Reece continued speaking, ignoring Morgan's outburst.

Vasili took another gulp of his beverage, massaging his forehead with his free hand, the tension was a growing ache behind his temple. Alexander hadn't mentioned what had happened to him during his incarceration, and Vasili hadn't asked, not with Ecktar present. Alexander had said nothing about releasing an upper level demon when he'd spoken with him earlier either, not that he would have recognised the demon possessing the human he'd released from the spelled sarcophagus. Makayla had mentioned Alexander going AWOL, but they hadn't had the chance to mention specifics with Ecktar in the room needing proof of her identity. Things were happening that he'd not foreseen in any of his visions.

"I don't know, it could be, it certainly points to Zobiana, the question begging to be asked, is what does this have to do with Xander and what she did to him while she held him captive. I wonder if Xander was taken captive because he's a member of the Custodians of Rahul brotherhood? She wants the Trinian Globe, it's no secret she married his father to get closer to him and his secret knowledge regarding the artefact. This is pure conjecture, though, and Alexander is the only person who can answer these questions." Vasili rubbed his forehead again. He should have asked Alexander what had happened in the dungeon, but felt it was an invasion of privacy. If he'd wanted to talk about what had happened, he would have, unless he had no memory of what had transpired and had blocked it out. Vasili wouldn't tell the Shadow Seekers of Alexander's visit, not until he knew more. "I've yet to speak with him about Zobiana and what happened in the dungeons since his return, has anyone spoken with him besides Makayla?"

"No," the group shook their heads replying in unison.

"The whole time he was here, he's been unconscious," Bryce said. "One minute he was there and then he wasn't. I remember because I was in the infirmary at the time sitting by Freya's bed. He didn't just get up and walk out, he disappeared right in front of my eyes, like smoke he was gone. I searched for him. I came to tell you he was missing, Vasili, but you weren't here."

"He must have reappeared outside the compound, because that's where Makayla and I first saw and followed him."

"Where's, Makayla now?" Vasili asked. Knowing exactly where she was and keeping the information to himself.

"We saw Makayla a few hours ago, after she and Darrius returned from following Alexander," Anna said. "She was a little hyped."

"Just a little, humph, that's being kind, I'd say a lot," Jackson cut in.

"More like hysterical," Morgan added. "What she was rambling about made no sense at all. It's crazy, something about being transported back to the 14th century."

"She's wasn't rambling, Morgan, she went back in time, I know because I was there, in the past, I mean; both Reece and I saw her; she followed Alexander to a brotherhood meeting," Vasili said.

"What," Reece gasped, rubbing his eyebrow. "I had no idea that was Makayla from the future—" Reece stopped speaking and chuckled, understanding brightening his features. "Ha, no wonder she'd said the things she did."

Vasili smiled. "Hmm, yes, why do you think I separated you, we couldn't have her influencing past events any more than she had already by turning up in the past."

"Didn't you see her in the past too, Zack?" Ashley asked.

Zack grimaced. "Yes, I saw her."

"We digress," Gabriel said. "Morgan, while we're on the subject, I think now would be the perfect time to tell Vasili what you saw in the infirmary."

Morgan nodded. "I saw a stranger in the infirmary just before Xander disappeared."

"What?" Bryce stepped closer to Morgan. "I think I would have noticed a stranger in the infirmary, don't you?"

"I said the same thing," Darrius commented.

Morgan exhaled. "He must have waited for you to leave, Bryce, because I saw him coming out of the infirmary and when I checked to make sure you were okay, you weren't there. He was creepy though."

"Do you think Ava and Tess saw him?" Zack asked.

"Ava would have mentioned it to me had she seen stranger," Gabe said, folding his arms over his chest. "They keep the lab door closed at all times to keep the room sterile."

"Did you follow the stranger?" Vasili asked, leaning forward in his seat.

"Yes, I tried, but lost him deep in the tunnels, before I had the chance to get my bearings he'd disappeared, dissolved into fog."

Vasili looked at Gabriel. "Do you think it's Zobiana's watcher?"

"It's a definite possibility. I'm certain some of the Vampire Guard are loyal to Zobiana, but this stranger showing up doesn't sit well with me. How do we even secure the compound? Who can we trust? I fear we may have invited wolves into our midst."

"I fear you may be right, Gabe." Vasili leaned back and

looked towards the ceiling, deep in thought before refocusing on the Shadow Seekers. "Zack, do you think you could set up some hidden infrared surveillance cameras around the compound? Gabe, no one knows the compound tunnels like you do, could you help Zack position them in the passages and places we don't use regularly? With all the comings and goings in the compound, we can't lock it down tight, but we can see what's going on. We won't put cameras in our private quarters, but I want them everywhere else, and that includes the infirmary and the lab. It worries me a stranger entered and disappeared right under our noses." Vasili clapped his hands together. "Now, what good news do you have, Zack, God knows we need it."

"I may have found a way to access the computer mainframe for the human farms without having to enter the building. Makayla and I were talking, and she mentioned something I hadn't considered. I don't know if you're aware of my powers . . . Yes, I do have them, Morgan," Zack said, winking at Morgan. "Ever since Makayla healed me, my old powers have returned." Zack smiled, lifted his hand into the air and the crystal decanter near Vasili lifted into the air simultaneously, he twisted his fingertips and closed his hand. The decanter tilted and poured port into Vasili's empty glass. Zack twisted his hand again and moved it to the right, the decanter lowered to the table. "As you all know, I'm a telepathic technopath, I can move things around, but my specialty is technology. Theoretically, I should be able to access the computer mainframe with my mind. I've been practicing and can use my computer without actually touching it. The only downside is that I'd have to be close to the building where the computer mainframe is housed. The tricky part will be getting the humans out of the rectrobeds. I should be able to disconnect all the apparatuses connected to them with my mind, but I need someone, many someones, with the ability to teleport the captives to a secure place. There's just one, maybe two, problems: we aren't set up for an influx of hundreds and thousands of humans. They'll need hospital care until they've fully recovered, and we just don't have the numbers to undertake such a large endeavour. It will take years for us to free all the captives from the farms."

"I thought you said you had good news," Jackson said.

"I know, I know, we may have to start with the smaller farms first, but having said that, someone may notice on the mainframe computer something's going on. Not only that, we'd have to save all the captives at the same time, which is impossible. Shit, it's not good news is it?"

"I don't know how we could facilitate such a huge undertaking," Vasili said. "It would take immense planning; we may even have to abandon saving the humans at this stage. I know it goes against everything we stand for – as Shadow Seekers it's our job to protect humanity. But right now we're nowhere near ready to save the humans from the farms." Vasili shook his head and exhaled. For the first time in his life he didn't know what to do.

"Do you think the Vampire and Seraph Councils could help further?" Darrius asked.

"I think the Vampire Council may be compromised. We can't rely on anyone, so keep everything we discussed here today to yourselves. We need to be smart about who we tell. Right now, all we have are each other." Vasili rubbed his eyes. "We will have to think on it further and come up with a plan. Right now all we can do is help those who haven't been captured." Vasili stood, and rounded his desk, feeling the growing need to speak with Sebastian and see Marianna again. "We have much to think about. I need to speak with my superior regarding the issues we've discussed; maybe he can come up with an idea or two. Zack, could you put up those cameras and get a monitoring room running, and Gabe, ward the room to prevent people from stumbling on it. The rest of you keep your eyes peeled; continue watching the gateways and patrolling the streets. Save as many humans as possible. I fear the prophecy is upon us."

The Shadow Seekers bobbed their heads in understanding and moved towards the door. There was a whoosh and a pop of air as the door opened and the ward was broken.

"Vasili, could I have a word with you before you depart?" Reece squeezed Anna's hand and whispered in her ear, she nodded and left the room with the rest of the Shadow Seekers.

Vasili bowed his head, acknowledging Reece's request. When the last person left, Vasili closed the door and replaced the ward and sigil once more. He motioned Reece to the couch by the wall and they sat. "What else do you have to tell me, Reece?"

"It's Alexander. I think he may be possessed by the Dark One."

"How did you come to this conclusion?"

"Because no one but the Dark One could break the seal and free an upper level demon."

CHAPTER 32.

Shards of red sunlight danced on the cottage walls as Makayla rotated the Gem of Past Times within her fingertips. She clenched the ruby in her fist and sat on a nearby couch; Lazarus's words plagued her mind. She'd always wondered why Darrius had two wings instead of six, but had dismissed it as being because he was more vampire than seraph. What had Kraegan done, apart from the obvious? And what part had Lazarus played? Before she'd had time to continue the conversation with Lazarus, he'd up and left; claiming that something had happened to Tess and she needed him.

"You have more important things to worry about, like finding Alexander and the three remaining Trinian Gems," her nemesis reminded her.

Makayla rolled her eyes. "Well, well, well if it isn't my friendly neighbourhood pain in the—"

"Ask me a question."

"Ha, ha . . . you're hilarious

"Ask me a question, any question, I may be able to help."

"Why? All you do is berate, irritate and demand. Why would I ask you a question? What could you possibly tell me that I don't already know? I mean, technically what I see, you see, right?"

"What I see may be different to what you see; for instance, I may know where the Trinian Globe is located."

"Pray tell, where is the Trinian Globe?"

"Where do you think it is?"

"I have no bloody idea." Makayla closed her eyes and massaged them. "I don't have time for riddles, I'm tired and losing my patience, say what you have to say and leave me alone." She hadn't slept in over a week. Normally she could go months without sleep, but the longer she went without nourishment, the more fatigued she became. And lately, she was fatigued and hungry all the time.

"Think, Makayla, where could it be? You're linked to it now, you should be able to sense it, because you were the one to place the first gem into position. It bonded with you and will always return to you until all the gems are set in position – and then you'll be one with the globe, the Chosen One complete."

"You sound like the Oracle's ambiguous prophecies; you're not the Oracle, are you? I mean seriously, how do you know?" Makayla laughed sarcastically. "Okay, okay, I have a question for you: who the bloody hell are you and how did you find your way into my head?"

"You know who am, or part of who I am, you will figure it out."

"Enough with the fucking riddles! GO AWAY . . . If you're not going to give me a direct answer, leave me alone. I'm over you and your help. I liked you better when you criticised me, at least I could tell you to piss off and you would!"

"I'm here to help." Her nemesis sighed.

"Since when?" Makayla pocketed the ruby Trinian gem and stood. She navigated around the tree in the centre of her living room and yanked open the refrigerator, ignoring the sound of clattering glass bottles. She searched the interior for a bottle of blood; maybe if she drank something it would get rid of her nemesis's annoying voice. Her lip curled and her nostrils flared when the offensive odour of spoiled food struck her. There were no bottles of blood, instead there was a wrinkled, dehydrated peach, a block of mouldy cheese, and some rotten, black leftovers on a plate sealed in plastic wrap.

She picked up the plate, the peach and the block of cheese and tossed them into the bin along with all the other unidentifiable food remnants. She pulled out the crisper drawer and exhaled in relief when she saw the collection bags of synthetic blood. "It will have to do," she murmured, grabbing as many as she could hold in her hands. She pushed the fridge door closed with the heel of her boot and made her way back to the couch, dropping the blood bags on the coffee table before slumping onto the couch. The small box Vasili had given her sat on the table. She picked it up and lifted the lid. An unusual gateway key and a note were nestled inside. She removed and opened the note:

Makayla,

This is the key to the Zoldarni gateway here on Earth. It's the only one in existence, so protect it. I'm entrusting its safe keeping to you. Hide it well. Tell no one you have it, not even Alexander. Don't let it fall into Zobiana's hands.

Makayla folded the note, placed it back in the box with the key, and secured the lid. She figured Vasili had his reasons for giving her the Zoldarni key. She returned the box to the table – she knew the perfect hiding spot for it.

"Why won't you listen to me?"

Makayla scratched her head and raised her forefinger in the air. "Um, let me see . . . when have I ever listened to you?" She leaned forward, snatched up a collection bag and sank her fangs into the plastic, foregoing opening it the traditional way. "Ugh, this shit is disgusting." She grimaced, slurping it down until it was empty.

"Find the next gem and you'll find Alexander."

"What does that even mean? Enough with the cryptic innuendos." Makayla picked up another blood bag, stabbed it with her teeth and drank it too. Her nemesis continued talking, Makayla continued ignoring her. Each bag of blood she drank took the edge off her hunger and drowned out the unwanted monologue of her ever-present companion. Her nemesis's voice faded, not as quickly as it did when she drank Alexander's blood, but quickly enough given the circumstances. Makayla finished the last bag of blood, tossed the empty containers in the fireplace, and set them alight with a fireball she'd manifested in her hand.

"At last some peace and quiet." She rested her booted feet on the table, placed a cushion behind her head and relaxed back on the couch, feeling revitalised. Her thoughts were more focused since having fed. She glanced about her home and noticed the kitchen curtain fluttering in the light breeze. The musty air had been stifling when she'd first arrived. She'd opened every window to rid her home of the suffocating stale air. After months of being locked up tight, she'd expected it to smell worse. The chilly winds blowing off the sea had refreshed her home, but seemed to have got the better of her. Cold weather never used to bother her, but it had ever since her return from the past. She felt the cold seeping into her bones more so than usual.

The chests the Vampire and Seraph Council gave her caught her eye. She hadn't opened them since her return from Evron and had left them at her cottage because it had been the safest place for them. Not that anybody would have been able to wear or use the weapons. She closed her eyes and put her hand in her pocket and fondled the ruby gem, again spinning it in her fingertips. Was her nemesis right? Was she connected to the Trinian Globe? It responded to her commands. As much as she hated to admit it, her nemesis's words were always right. She'd grown to depend on her truths.

"Come to me," she whispered, trying to conjure the Trinian Globe to her. "Come to me now," she ordered in a resolute voice, wondering whether the Trinian Globe would hear her words. Where had it disappeared to after she'd travelled back in time? Makayla emptied her mind of everything and concentrated solely on the Trinian Globe, picturing its golden beauty in her mind's eye. She recalled the music she'd heard when she'd first set eyes on it. She remembered how it had made her feel euphoric and peaceful. How its warmth surrounded and invaded her body, threading through her veins and setting fire to her blood. She could almost hear the church bells, the whispering voices and the hypnotic angelic voice singing in the unknown language. The music had enveloped her with echoing symphonic orchestral tones. The angelic voice had reached inside her body and squeezed her heart as the music crescendo intensified, raising goose bumps all over her body. She sighed and rubbed her arms in remembrance.

Makayla snapped her eyes open and jolted upright in her seat. The music was no longer in her imagination, but was everywhere; surrounding her like it had the first time she'd heard it. She looked about the room and noticed the seraph chest aglow and hovering in the air. Brilliant light seeped from the cracks, highlighting the joins where the lid touched the lip of the box. The chest floated across the room and lowered to the floor in front of her. There were no chains securing the lid like there had been on Evron. Makayla leaned forward to open the lid, but stopped when the chest opened on its own. She watched the Trinian Globe lift out of the box and float towards her, where it hung suspended in front of her like a misplaced Christmas bauble. It was strange how the globe showed up whenever she needed it. It was almost too simple. Ever since she'd placed the first gem, the Gem of Sorrows, into position, she'd felt connected to the artefact somehow, like she'd bonded with it on a spiritual level and it had become a part of her psyche.

The globe wasn't as blinding as it had been when the Gem of Souls and the Gem of Sorrows were drawn into position. Makayla watched, mesmerised, as the globe rotated slowly; the yellow and amethyst gems catching the light as it spun, showering the room in a kaleidoscope of yellow and violet light. Makayla stood and withdrew the Gem of Past Times from her pocket. When her hand warmed, she uncurled her fingers. The ruby vibrated in her palm but it wasn't pulled into place as the other gems had been. The Trinian Globe stopped rotating, and an indent formed above the two gems already in place to form a triangle. Makayla pressed the ruby into position, the globe shuddered and red light flared, circling about her in fine delicate threads, stroking her skin with soft caressing touches. There was a sudden explosion of light and the familiar smell of ozone. The hairs on Makayla's arms stood erect from the electrically charged air. The room was bathed in red, yellow, violet and emerald green light. It wavered throughout the room like the great northern lights. There was a high-pitched whistling and then a loud pop and everything went black.

Alexander placed his hand on the wall to the left of his four-poster bed and recited an enchantment he'd placed there centuries ago. There was a hiss and the sound of grinding rock as the wall shimmered with electricity. The rock surface shuddered and an oval doorway appeared. Alexander stood before the opening and raised his hand to eye level; it tingled and he clenched and unclenched his fist and rubbing his thumb back and forth over his fingertips until the sensation subsided. Smoke tendrils curled about his fingers and he continued rubbing them faster and faster until the smoke was replaced with fire. He'd seen Makayla manifest fireballs many times and was a little taken aback that he seemed to have inherited her ability to create fire. He focused on his flame-ensconced hand and tried to create a fireball. The flame grew stronger the more focused he became. He clapped his hands together and drew them apart, trapping the flame between them, then he cupped his palms around each other until the flame was controlled and appeared more like a sphere. As a Druid, he could light torches and candles with a mere thought, but he'd never been able to hold a flame in his hands like Makayla. Alexander let the fire ball hover in his palm and smiled when he saw a torch in a nearby wall sconce.

"Here goes nothing," he said, tossing the fireball towards the wall sconce. The torch burst into flames the moment the fireball struck. "So that's what it feels like," he chuckled, shaking his head. "No wonder she throws them around so much."

Alexander looked about the cavern and melancholy settled in his chest, burning like indigestion. There were too many memories here in the cavern, memories he'd shared with his Makayla from the past. The roar of the waterfall masking the cave entrance was a soothing backdrop to his riotous emotions.

He rubbed his chest; the ache was getting worse. It was time, he sensed. The power was growing in strength. Agatha had no idea how right she'd been when she'd said something was protecting him, he knew what it was and if it was protecting him from the darkness, it meant Abigail and Zobiana had succeeded in their quest to free the Dark One. The Dark One wasn't in control of his body yet, but if he didn't circumvent the inevitable, he'd be lost – and so would his memories.

Alexander removed the torch from the wall sconce and passed through the makeshift doorway he'd manifested. He lowered his head and hunched his shoulders as he walked along the tight passageway, his arms rubbing against the walls as he navigated through the short tunnel into another secret cavern. He breathed a sigh of relief when he stepped into a small cavern. There was a solid oak desk to his left, a shelf laden with ancient scrolls and invaluable artefacts he'd collected over the centuries, and his leather-bound grimoire. A medium-sized podium stood between the desk and shelf. A large, antique sleigh bed was positioned on the opposite wall, and an altar sat along the back wall loaded with candles and vessels of various dried herbs and other paraphernalia. There was a large rug covering the floor, woven in warm earthen colours, and a protection sigil painted in white on the ceiling to keep evil at bay.

Alexander relaxed the moment he passed into the cavern. He snapped his fingers and candles lit throughout the room, warming the small space at once. Alexander inhaled the fragrance of sweet herbs and sandalwood candles and felt a sense of calm embrace him. He put the torch he held in a wall sconce and made his way towards the shelf to pick up his grimoire and place it on the podium by his desk.

The grimoire was a large, leather-bound book he'd had since he was a teenager. He ran his hand over the cover; it was smooth and dark with age. Even though it was over three thousand years old, the pages weren't brittle and the cover was still supple. The first spell he'd ever cast was on the book itself, an age-old spell to protect it and its contents from the ravages of time. Alexander traced his fingers over the dragon embellishment on the cover, his family's talisman. As a young boy, dragons had been an obsession. The dragon on the cover was mighty and strong, a symbol representing the strength of his family. The dragon lay on its stomach, its tail curled about its body with one giant wing extended outwards like the arched canopy of a tree. Its head was curved towards a young man who stood beneath his wing, sheltered from the elements and would-be enemies.

Alexander remembered when his father had first given him the book on his sixteenth birthday. It was a family tradition for a father to give his son a grimoire when his powers manifested. There were so many memories and life lessons attached to his grimoire. He opened and flipped through the pages of spells, looking for a specific incantation. He needed to protect himself from the Dark One – the artefact protecting him was awakening and would come to the surface soon and then he'd be defenceless. If only he'd known what lay ahead, perhaps he could have done things differently. But how does one predict their life being shadowed by evil incarnate itself?

Alexander rubbed his breastbone, feeling the discomfort increase, he removed his shirt and threw it on the nearby desk. There was a distinct lump the size of an egg in the middle of his sternum, he ran his fingers over the lump – it was hard and the skin felt warmer than the rest of his body. *Not long now,* he thought.

He turned his attention back to his grimoire. "Where the bloody hell is it," he murmured, skim-reading each spell as he went. Alexander stopped turning the pages when he found the protection spell he was looking for. He memorised the spell and moved towards the altar at the back of the cavern. He picked up a mortar and pestle and tossed in the ingredients to perform the spell. When he'd finished crushing and mixing everything together, he picked up a sacrificial dagger and a bottle of finely ground rock-salt and took everything back to the podium. Alexander placed the mortar and pestle near his grimoire, along with the dagger and the salt, and manifested a glass of water. He closed his eyes, breathing in and out, and when he found his centre he began chanting in Gaelic, reciting the spell. He opened his eyes and picked up the dagger, taking a deep breath before turning the dagger on himself. He hissed as he pushed the tip of the dagger into his flesh and took another calming breath as he carved a protective sigil over the lump on his chest. His fangs elongated the moment he caught the scent of his own blood, he drew in a shaky breath and gritted his teeth as he continued carving the sigil, blood trickling down his body in a sticky flow. When he finished the sigil, he put the dagger down and picked up the bottle of rock-salt, pouring it into the mortar. He mixed the contents once more before scooping out a glob with his fingertips and rubbing it into the wound. He gasped, biting down on his lip as he became lightheaded and his vision blurred; his wound began to throb and burn as he smoothed the concoction deeper into the wound. He read the incantation out loud three times and manifested a flame in the palm of his hand. He placed his hand over the wound and set the poultice alight. He screamed when the poultice caught fire, burning the sigil into his skin. Alexander fell to his knees and almost toppled to the floor as the sigil turned black. He grabbed hold of the podium table and pulled himself upright again, gasping for oxygen. He picked up the glass of water and poured it into the mortar, mixing the remaining poultice into a brew and then drank it. It burned a trail down his throat and he gagged, almost throwing up. Then he staggered to his desk and pulled out the chair, slumping into it. He lowered his forehead to the tabletop, a cold sweat lathering his body. Alexander started to shake and his chest burned. The wound throbbed, his mouth was dry and his tongue thick. He swallowed, the bitter taste mixing with the bile he'd almost thrown up. Curling his toes, he cradled his stomach with his arms as the roiling cramps had him gasping again. He stood, pushing up from the table with his hands, and lurched across the room to his bed, his head reeling and heavy. He fell onto the bed, landing on his back, and flung his arms over his face; the room was spinning.

"Don't you dare throw up," he mumbled and lost consciousness.

CHAPTER 33.

The room was dark with shadows when Lazarus materialised; he looked about, but couldn't find Tess anywhere. He switched on a lamp sitting on a bedside table. She wasn't in the bedroom. He looked in the bathroom; she wasn't there either. He moved towards the kitchen, it too was empty. He circled on the spot until he noticed something by the front door. Tess was curled up in the foetal position, staring vacantly at a wall. Her face was blotchy and her eyes swollen; she'd been crying. Lazarus crouched down and brushed hair out of her eyes, she didn't move. He sat down beside her and picked her up, gently cradling her in his arms; she curled into his body, seeking warmth. He stroked her hair and could feel her shivering. Now and then she'd take a gulp of air and shudder, warm silent tears streaming down her face.

"Tess, what happened?" She didn't respond. "You can talk

to me; please talk to me."

She shook her head. "You wouldn't understand."

"Try me, what have you got to lose?"

"I . . . I can't," she sobbed. "I don't want to do this anymore."

"What don't you want to do anymore?"

"Live without him; I wish I'd died too."

"Tess." Lazarus placed his finger under her chin and lifted her face so she looked him in the eyes. "Why would you wish for something like that?"

"If I was dead, I could be with him, we could be together."

"Who could you be with?"

"My husband."

Lazarus caught his breath; he remembered feeling the same way for centuries after his wife's murder. "I understand your loss more than you know. I felt the same way after my wife was murdered, so you see, we're not so different."

Tess looked him in the eye, "I'm sorry, it was insensitive of me to assume you wouldn't understand. I forget you're an immortal sometimes."

"I have lived a long time, you'd be surprised by the things I've experienced in my long life."

"I feel so alone sometimes ... no, I feel alone all the time, even when I'm standing in a crowded room full of people. That's why I get so caught up in my work – to keep my mind busy. As soon as I stop and think, the loneliness takes hold. My work is all I have left now," Tess said.

"I know what you mean; it can be unbearable. I find it harder at night; the darkness unmasks our deepest emotions, our deepest desires and brings them to the foreground. When I'm lying in bed with nothing but my thoughts, it's hard to sleep. Some days I can't get out of my head, I just wish I could fade away and the darkness would take me, swallow me whole," said Lazarus.

Tess twisted in his arms. "I know . . . you're right, I close my eyes and my husband's face haunts my dreams. I pray for oblivion, but it never comes. Don't get me wrong, I want to see his face, but when I wake up, I always feel worse afterwards."

"Tess, what happened to bring this all up now?"

Tess looked away. "Did you know Ava can see the dead?"

"Yes, I knew. . . but what does— Oh, she saw your husband?"

"I didn't know. She said Ryan was always by my side and made her promise not to tell me. I saw him again right before he crossed over. He's gone now; we said our final goodbyes and I couldn't even hold him, kiss him. He told me to live my life to find love again. How can I do that, Laz? Tell me how I can do that?"

"He wants you to find happiness again; it's the most unselfish gift he could give you."

Tess rubbed her chest. "I have an unbearable ache in my chest, Laz, I feel so hollow, so empty, and this new world we live in now is terrible. How can anyone hope to find a shred of happiness when it's falling down around our feet? I'm scared all the time and what's worse, I can't find a cure for the Blakspor virus, it's useless."

"You're not alone anymore, little bee. I'm here, I won't let anything happen to you, I promise." Lazarus smiled and pinched her cheek.

"What . . . what did you just call me?" Tess's face was ashen.

"Um, little bee," Lazarus said. "You know, like a little honey bee?"

"Why would you call me that?"

"What? I don't know, sorry; I didn't mean . . . I never . . . it just flashed into my head out of nowhere..." Lazarus stammered. He stood and helped Tess stand, then moved out of reach. What was wrong with him? He never could bear seeing a woman cry and there was a vulnerability about Tess that reminded him of his wife. "Um, did you need anything else, Tess?" He had to leave before things got complicated.

"Laz, how did you know?"

"Know what?"

"How did you know I was distressed?"

"I don't know, I sensed your turmoil," Lazarus said, pushing his hands into his pockets, stepping back to put distance between them.

"Is that normal?"

"Nope, it's not. I best be leaving now." Lazarus looked anywhere but at Tess's face. The last thing he needed was to become attached to a female, no matter how attractive and broken they were. The last time he was distracted by a woman people had died. Yes, he'd married her, but she'd died because of him. He would not, could not, let it happen again, never again.

"Well, good luck with the vaccine. Be careful – the compound has been compromised. Here, take this." Lazarus handed one of his daggers to her. "I'd feel better knowing you're not defenceless. I've gotta get back out there, bye." Lazarus dematerialised before Tess had the chance to speak.

Uriel led Augustus through several corridors, each equally as impressive as the first. They were like phantoms, mere shadows walking the hallways unnoticed. Augustus was mesmerised by his surroundings. The twisting corridor walls changed as they progressed further into the labyrinth. The solid walls with gold motifs became rows upon rows of slender trees stretching high above their heads. At first glance the trees appeared to be intricately carved, but upon closer inspection, appeared to have grown that way. Delicate branches formed decorative loops of woven patterns, intertwining latticework and arches. They'd stepped into a white forest carved of ivory-white wood and they were no longer in a corridor but a white-forested garden. It looked like a winter wonderland, only it wasn't snow that coated the trees and landscape, it was white leaves and flowers. The beauty, the serenity, the purity, was unlike anything

Augustus had ever experienced. There was a single circular gazebo-like structure in the centre of the garden – the only thing in the entire area that had colour.

Uriel climbed the steps into the heart of the structure. It too was made of fine, interwoven white wood, but green twisting vines with blooming white and yellow flowers covered the entire roof, twining down the columns and around the balustrade. In the human world, people would have held wedding ceremonies there. Augustus inhaled the scent of honeysuckle and a fragrance similar to pine trees and Uriel beckoned him forward before disappearing further in. Augustus nodded at the Seraph Guards stationed either side of the steps before following Uriel.

Uriel watched Augustus's approach. "Please, make yourself comfortable," he invited, indicating a cushioned seat that followed the circumference of the gazebo wall. The floor was uncluttered, no furniture, just open space.

Augustus sat on the edge of his seat, feeling out of place; Uriel took a seat beside him, folding his hands beneath the sweeping fabric of his robes. "May I offer you sustenance, perhaps a glass of our finest Leitanberry wine?"

"Thank you for your kind offer, Uriel, but I find I'm too uneasy to eat or drink at the moment."

Uriel nodded. "It's understandable given the circumstances of your arrival. Did you travel through the royal gateway?"

"Yes, I'm afraid Earth's gateways have been compromised. From what Sebastian has told me, Zobiana – sorry, Lilith – has complete control."

"It was only a matter of time before she gathered enough strength and followers to seek retribution. What news do you bring of my daughter and son-in-law, Ambrosia and Sebastian? How do they fare?"

"They are well, all things considered, given the loss of their youngest son, Adrian. Ambrosia has taken his death hard, as has the king."

Uriel slumped against the wall and cupped his forehead, rubbing his temple with his fingertips; he dragged in a trembling breath and looked towards the ceiling, the sorrow evident in his glassy eyes. Augustus watched the play of emotion on the seraph king's face and felt like an eavesdropper. Augustus's throat tightened as he thought about his own loss.

"I had yet to meet the youngest of my daughter's children, Adrian and Emily. I feel robbed. I've only just met Makayla. She has no idea who I am to her. She's so like her mother in looks and spirit – feisty and headstrong."

"That she is," Augustus murmured, clasping his hands in his lap.

"Augustus, how have you been missing for so long and held prisoner in one of Lilith's dungeons. How did she get to you when she has been in exile all this time?"

Augustus scrubbed a hand over his face. "I'm not sure, Uriel, but the night before I awoke in the dungeons, I met with Malachi in my private chambers to discuss border security. We wanted to find a solution to combat the dissent and secure our borders before it got out of hand and compromised the truce between the seraph and vampire Nations. Because of the volatile topic we would be discussing, I thought it best to speak somewhere private – hence my personal office. When he showed up with three Vampire Guards in tow, it never occurred to me he had an ulterior motive for the meeting. I should have realised something was amiss. Stupid on my part. I never considered for a minute I'd be in danger. What would he have to gain by abducting me? What a fool I was. I invited him and his companions into my private study to discuss the matter. I was going to come to you the following day to discuss it with you, but I woke up in a dungeon." Augustus shook his head. "I can only surmise they drugged my wine. I've spoken at length with Sebastian and we came to the same conclusion. If you recall, Lilith had many loyal followers before she was banished. Do you remember the public outcry at her hearing for your wife's murder?"

"It's not a day I'll forget," Uriel said, his eyes darkening.

Augustus sighed. "I don't think she ever lost her following, Uriel, maybe on the surface, but underneath, she was still issuing orders. We discovered she and Malachi have been conspiring for centuries. Even before she was exiled from Evron. There have been too many coincidences to rule it out. Malachi has always had his sights set on the throne, as has Lilith, and I believe their sights are still set on ruling Evron. They're unified in their goals.

"The only thing I'm sure of is my position as chancellor is

compromised, or was. Malachi was masquerading as me all these years. There's no telling what changes he has made during my incarceration." Augustus clenched his hands and rubbed the unshed tears from his burning eyes. "My son is dead because of her."

"I'm sorry for your loss, Gus, 'tis hard to bear the loss of a child. Lilith has much to answer for."

"That she has," Augustus murmured and nodded. "We share the burden of grief; my son and your wife died senselessly." Augustus shook his head, wondering how many more senseless deaths there'd be before Lilith was brought down. "I've missed your company, Uri."

"I've missed you too, old friend. I'm just glad you're back, because much has changed since you left."

"Uriel, I think she's planning a hostile takeover of Evron. She already controls most of Earth's gateways. She has built an army of Newbloods with the designer drug V5 and has brought humanity to their knees with the Blakspor virus. Those she hasn't destroyed, she has captured and placed in blood-harvesting farms. It's only a matter of time before she makes her move and takes over Evron's gateways and does the same here. We must prepare."

"I fear it may already be too late. We've noticed a lot of unusual activity near many of the vampire gateways. We haven't been able to do much about it because it's in vampire jurisdiction. We've got most of our territory locked down and have secured the seraph gateways. We've shut down fifteen of the twenty-five gateways in our control; no one can travel through them. Lilith sabotaged five of our gateways before we were able to shut them down. The five functioning gateways we have remaining are heavily guarded and in hidden, hard to reach places on Evron."

"Do you have any idea who may have been compromised on the Vampire Council?" Augustus asked.

Uriel shook his head. "Not a clue. As I mentioned upon your arrival, I suspected something was amiss with you, but had no idea you'd been compromised. Do you have any suspicions?"

"I've only seen three of the Vampire Council members since I returned; two of the three were okay, but I sensed Lord Cavendish was lying – we need to keep an eye on him. I'll know more about the others when I speak with them."

"Do you think it wise to approach the council members? It's dangerous, Augustus, I wouldn't risk it. If I were you I'd avoid contact with them altogether, seek them out if you must, but before making contact, watch them for suspicious behaviour, see who they meet with."

Augustus nodded. "You're right, and I will heed your advice. I will meet you back here as soon as possible."

"I'll be waiting. Here, take this." Uriel handed him a silver coin-like object. "Just press the button when you're in my chambers; it will allow you to pass into the shadow realm."

"Thank you, Uri, I'll be careful. I need to go to the council archives and get up to speed with everything that has transpired since I was abducted. If I don't, the other council members will suspect something's amiss – especially if Malachi has been orchestrating a hostile takeover with Lilith. I may be able to discover their plans and sabotage them. If Evron is to survive, I must make contact with my council members and fish out those who have been compromised. They may slip up and tell me something only Malachi would know, it's the only way. I've yet to search my private lodgings and my office in the council chambers. I may find incriminating evidence against Malachi and Lilith."

"Be careful Augustus, trust no one – much has changed since you were last here."

Augustus stood, rubbing his clammy hands down the length of his trousers. "I'll see you soon. Hopefully I'll have the information we need."

CHAPTER 34.

Blinding light exploded around Makayla as she appeared in a place she least expected. She rubbed the stars from her eyes. Welcoming warmth surrounded her, wrapping her in its familiar embrace. The fresh scent of salt water, rock, and a rich earthy scent permeated the air. The last time she'd been in Alexander's cavern was on their wedding night. The rumbling sound of falling water just outside the entrance was a welcome relief; she just hoped she hadn't returned to the past again. Makayla rubbed her arms, a moment of déjà vu prickling her senses. Why would the Trinian Globe transport her here of all places? She walked further into the cavern; it appeared the same as it had the last time she'd been there, only the four-poster bed looked much older. The Trinian Globe wouldn't have transported her here unless the fourth gem was nearby. So where was it?

There was a lit torch in a wall sconce near the front of the cavern, the flame flickered as a light breeze blew down the tunnel. A single candle burned in a candelabra on Alexander's desk – the same desk where she'd found his cryptic note about her inevitable demise. She traced a finger over a burn mark marring the surface; the note was long gone. The torch succumbed to the frigid breeze blowing through the passageway and the candle followed suit, its flame sputtering out with a faint sizzle as the wick drowned in the pooling hot wax. The cavern was cloaked in darkness. Makayla manifested a small fireball in her palm and walked towards the bed. It was then that she noticed a shimmering light and the faint sound of music coming from an unusual oval opening in the rock wall by the bed. Had it appeared in the wall when she'd set the Gem of Past Times in the Trinian Globe? Had the secret cavern always had another room attached to it?

The music grew louder as she approached the opening in the wall; it was a song she recognised, Civil Twilight's *'Letters from the sky'*; the same song Alexander had been listening to after they'd made love the first time. He'd been so despondent and lost in thought. Now she understood why; he'd longed to hold the woman he'd married, the one who had loved him unconditionally. He'd been thinking of her, the wife, the challenging spitfire who had provoked such uninhibited longing in him. He'd been thinking of the past and the woman she had yet to become. Makayla lowered her head and entered the passageway, the sense of déjà vu growing with every step she took. Goose bumps tickled her skin as the song's haunting words echoed about her.

Makayla closed her hand and extinguished the fireball when she came to the end of the passageway. She looked about the cosy chamber. She'd never seen a Druid's inner sanctum, but had heard of such places existing. All Druids had private hidey-holes where they kept their grimoires and most treasured possessions, and practised their incantations. It was a sacred place of solitude, prayer and magic. The chamber was simple, yet lived and breathed, Alexander. She could smell him, his sandalwood aftershave, his spicy blood and the exotic essence that was his alone, an aphrodisiac that set her blood afire. Makayla closed her eyes and breathed in his scent, feeling bereft. He was all about her, but nowhere in sight. She moved into the room and stopped dead-centre.

"Where are you, Xander? I know you're here, I can feel you; I can smell you, please, show yourself?" Makayla squinted as she searched the room for Alexander and the origin of the music. She noticed a mortar and pestle on the workbench and moved to pick it up. There were dried remnants of a dark paste in the bottom of the bowl. She lifted the bowl to her face and cringed, pinching her nose as she turned away and lowered the mortar bowl to the bench. The song ended and began playing again on a loop. Makayla looked over her shoulder and noticed the air rippling like a desert mirage. It glowed an iridescent emerald green, could it be the Trinian Gem? The coloured light started to palpitate; one minute it was blinding and the next barely discernible. She reached out to touch the strange spectre as it brightened and the air rippled again, the mirage disintegrating as her hand passed through the illusion and touched something warm and solid. Alexander. His hair was wet, hanging in his eyes, his face clean-shaven and serene, his body bare except for the black track pants he wore low on his hips. Beads of water spotted his chest as if he'd just stepped out of a shower. Makayla swallowed. He was no longer thin, but covered with well-defined muscle once more. He stood barefoot on the rug-covered floor. Makayla spread her fingers, curling them over his glowing chest. She lifted her hand and noticed a slight lump between his pectoral muscles covered in sigil scarring. She traced her finger over the lines, then glided her hands up his chest, tracing the contours of his body, feeling his steady heartbeat beneath her fingertips. She continued caressing up along the length of his neck to his face and cupped his jaw, revelling in the suppleness of his smooth skin. He watched her, the shadow of a smile lingering on his lips. She ran her fingers over the dimples in his cheeks and then glided her thumb across his bottom lip. Alexander's eyes darkened and his mouth opened, and she glimpsed the sharp tips of his incisors. She couldn't help but slip her thumb between his lips and into his mouth, nicking the tip on one of his fangs like he'd once done to her. He sucked the blood from her thumb, groaning in pleasure. The slick pressure of his mouth and the sensual feel of his tongue flicking against her thumb elicited a need within her that could only be sated with the joining of their bodies. Makayla withdrew her thumb from his mouth and palmed his cheeks. He opened his eyes and shuffled closer.

"Xander, what happened? Where have you bee——"

"Shhhh." Alexander placed his finger on her lips. "You found me, like you were always meant to." He placed his hand over his chest, tracing the sigil lines scarring his body with the tip of his finger and recited a Gaelic incantation. Ancient words Makayla couldn't understand. His chest glowed with green light that brightened and faded with every beat of his heart. Makayla watched the skin on his chest change, the fine hairs prickling; there was a flash of light and an emerald Trinian gem passed through the sigil and appeared in his hand, drawn out of his body. Makayla bit her tongue, the sting in her mouth reminding her she wasn't dreaming.

Alexander grasped her hand and placed the fourth Trinian gem in her palm. He closed her fingers over the precious jewel and squeezed her hand. "So, now you know how you were able to find me."

"How, how is this possible? How did you know?" Makayla looked up into his face.

Alexander captured the tail of her braid, twirling it about his fingers.

"Xander?"

He slanted his head, his brows furrowing as he focused on removing the elastic securing the end of her braid. He unravelled her plait and threaded his fingers through her hair, combing out her long tresses until it fanned about her body in copper waves. Makayla shivered, no one ever touched her hair. It was as much a weapon as the rest of her body; hot to the touch in the heat of battle; incapacitating those stupid enough to handle it – but Alexander was immune and the only person unaffected by the lethality of her hair. The act was so sensual.

"That's better," he said, looking into her eyes again. "I've always loved your hair wild, free and unencumbered. I remember the first time I saw your hair out. You were on the battlements standing on the outer wall, staring at the dark horizon. You took my breath away." Alexander's eyes darkened in remembrance as he traced her lips with his fingertip. "I was lost until you came into my life and set my world on fire. When you left, my world turned to ash. I realised what once had passed as living was not living at all but a mere shadow of a life I would never have."

Makayla gulped and placed her hand over Alexander's as he touched her lip with his fingertip, "Xander?"

"Mm-Hmm."

"Um, you didn't answer my question."

"Oh, sorry." He shrugged. "It took me a while to figure it out and a little longer than expected to find the fourth Trinian Gem, the Gem of Protection. I had nothing but time to kill after you left. I've waited seven hundred years to be with you again; a lifetime, many lifetimes – you were worth the wait." Alexander smiled and caressed her cheek. "When you showed up in the past, I thought it was destiny – your prophecy. Maybe it was, but there was more to it. I had to look at things with an analytical eye and see the bigger picture before me. I recalled you telling me about the Trinian Globe and how you'd placed the Gem of Sorrows and the Gem of Souls into it and were transported back in time. The Gem of Past Times brought you back. I knew I had to find the fourth gem if you were to find me in the future. It was the only way to be sure you'd rescue me from Zobiana's dungeon. Luckily, I had access to countless ancient scrolls on the Trinian Globe. Being the conqueror of all miseries and the higher mystic of the secret brotherhood the Custodians of Rahul has its perks."

"But I didn't have the Trinian Globe with me. How could you know the Gem of Past Times would transport me to you, to the dungeons you were being held in, in the future, in another dimension, no less?" Makayla opened her hand and saw multiple reflections of her face in the emerald gem's facets. "How did you even know that this was the fourth Trinian Gem?"

"I didn't know, I took a risk and gambled with my life and our future. It was the biggest gamble I've ever taken and it paid off. The scrolls led me to believe I had the right one. I figured when you cut your hand and Zobiana's ruby gem reacted with your blood it would be drawn to me in the future, you having sired me and all. Our blood-bond is rare, you said. I thought about why the Gem of Past Times reacted to your blood for years and years, and then it struck me the Gem of Past Times is a blood-stone. It's the only reason it would have reacted with your blood and why you were able to find me in the Rivulous

Dimension. Maybe I was destined to find the Gem of Protection. Maybe it's our destiny and part of your prophecy for us to be together, to do this together."

"You're forgetting one thing: I never told you I'd sired you when I was in the past."

"No, you didn't, but you said you and I were blood-bonded soulmates, and that I was different afterwards, I assumed you'd sired me, and I was right, wasn't I?"

"Mm-hmm, you were." Makayla rotated the gem between her fingers; green light reflected about the room. "Where did you find it?" she said, nodding at the gem.

"In a sacred place of worship; a Druids' circle in Scotland, the Callanish Stones within the chambered tomb, quite fitting really. My forefathers once worshipped there."

Makayla placed the gem in her trouser pocket. "I have so many questions, Xander. Where have you been? What did Zobiana do to you? Why do you keep blacking out, and what were you doing down in the sewers in an ancient temple? How did you get out?"

"I will answer all your questions, the ones I have answers to, but right now, I have more important things to tend to."

"What could be more important than answering my questi—?" Makayla gasped when her weapons and body armour disappeared and reappeared on a chair in the corner of the room.

Alexander pulled her into his arms and buried his face in her hair. "This is more important, we're more important. You have no idea how long I've waited to be with the same woman who loved me in the past, my wife, my lover, my friend, my life. God, I've missed you, Makayla. I've missed talking to you openly without guarding my words for fear of messing things up, messing up the past and the future. I almost blew it when I asked you to marry me after Tyrone's attack. I came close to telling you everything so many times, the only thing that stopped me was the possibility of losing you altogether. So I bided my time and kept the truth from you. I hated lying to you. You know what I'm talking about because you were in the same position when you travelled back in time."

Makayla wrapped her arms around his body and squeezed him, desire filling her with twisting anticipation. His muscles rippled as she ran her fingers down the length of his spine. She tensed when she felt the thick twisted scars on his back and tears pooled in her eyes; he'd suffered so much pain. "I'm sorry I didn't get to you in time, Xander, I'm so sorry." She sniffled.

Xander grasped her face between his hands. "You're not to blame; you found me, that's all that matters, we're together now." He brushed the tears away with his thumbs and kissed her cheeks, touching his forehead to hers. "We're together now," he repeated.

"I thought I'd lost you, Xander. I thought you were dead." Makayla couldn't look him in the eyes; the guilt was unbearable; too fresh. Alexander grasped her waist and lifted her off the ground until her face was level with his and her body flush against him. She looked into his gold-speckled amber eyes, they were so different to the last time she'd seen them. There was a world of emotion in them and they were focused on her. She licked her lips feeling self-conscious. Alexander growled and lowered his mouth to hers, kissing her with the pent-up hunger of seven hundred years. Makayla dropped the barriers between their minds and was subjected to the full force of his love, his hunger, and the centuries he'd waited for her, for time to be on their side. She saw him circling above her in his eagle form. She saw him transform from an eagle to a man and stand naked in her small cottage watching over her, protecting her while she slept by the fire. So much wasted time they could have spent together.

Sensation coursed along her nerve endings, prickling her skin with awareness – a twitching live wire of sensitivity. She wove her arms about his neck and plunged her tongue into his mouth, eager to soothe the fever burning within her soul. She tasted the minty flavour of toothpaste and the residual trace of her blood in his mouth. Her throat tightened when he wove his arms about her and crushed her to his body. His skin and hard sculpted muscles were hot to the touch, almost feverish. She dug her fingertips into his hair as the hunger flourished in her belly.

Alexander slumped to his knees, dragging her down to the thick woollen rug beneath them. He settled her on his lap, her legs either side of him, the hard length of his erection pressing against the juncture of her thighs. She ground her hips against him and the heat between them ignited further. Alexander grabbed her vest and ripped it apart. The sound of tearing fabric and popping buttons flying through the air made her smile against his mouth. She slipped her arms through the armholes in a rush to remove the damaged garment, breathing hard; her singlet was the next thing torn from her body.

"There's something satisfying about tearing the clothes from your body," Alexander mumbled against her mouth between kisses.

"More satisfying than making them disappear?" Makayla teased.

"Hell yeah," Alexander said, running a finger under the bottom edge of her bra. His cheeks dimpled as a seductive smile hovered on his lips. Makayla watched him lower his mouth to her chest as he grabbed the middle of her bra and ripped it apart. The sting and pressure of tearing fabric against her super-sensitive skin heightened the pleasure. Alexander kissed one of her taut nipples, sucking it as his free hand teased her other breast, reducing her to a limp, boneless mass. Makayla sighed and dropped her head, exposing the skin of her neck and arching her chest towards his mouth. Alexander's fingers caressed and pinched and circled over her tender flesh. She groaned in pleasure, all the while rotating her hips and grinding herself against him. Her skin was a prickly, shivering bundle of nerves as Alexander's hands caressed a path down her rib cage towards the top of her trousers. He undid the button and zip and slid his palm into her underwear twisting his hand until he found the prize he searched for. He dipped his fingers between her warm folds and stimulated her with his fingertips. He was still kissing her breast and the sharp tips of his fangs scratched over her flesh eliciting a surge of rippling shivers over her body. He bit down on her nipple and she screamed and bucked her hips as he began to feed. The erotic sound of his mouth slurping the blood from her body added to the heightened bliss of his masterful fingers. Her eyes rolled back, her toes curling as her own fangs elongated and pierced her bottom lip, drawing blood. A smile slid across her face as lethargy took hold. Alexander stopped feeding and licked the wound, healing it with his saliva. He continued a path up her chest towards her neck, all the while feathering warm kisses over her skin. Makayla opened her eyes and stared into his entrancing face, all the while gyrating herself against his stimulating fingertips.

Blood trickled from the corner of his mouth; she licked her lips and watched his tongue glide out, removing every trace of blood from the edge of his luscious mouth. Her stomach rumbled. Bloodlust and a tangible hunger consumed her with the need to consummate their love. Alexander slid two fingers into her, moving them in and out until she was on the verge of crumbling, his thumb massaging, fondling her with the expertise of one who knew the intricacies of her body by heart. He watched her face in rapt attention as he elicited gasps and groans from her mouth. Her movements became erratic, spasmodic as the tantalising beginnings of an orgasm built.

"Please, don't stop," she groaned in displeasure when

Alexander removed his hand from her underpants and sucked the essence of her from his fingertips. She was so close to reaching the pinnacle of fulfilment, so close to losing herself to the tide of passion encapsulating her body. So close.

"Uh-ah, not yet, I want you writhing beneath me and screaming my name before we're through here," Alexander murmured. He grasped her throat with his left hand and wound her hair around his right, pulling her face to his and kissing her fiercely. She tasted her blood as he sucked her tongue into his mouth. Their clothing disappeared; no more barriers separating them now. Their breathing became haggard, more desperate; his mouth was hot, wet and inviting. Makayla bit and drew his bottom lip into her mouth and felt a rumbling groan vibrate in his throat. Alexander broke the kiss, turned his head to the side and listened to the echoing music.

"Letters from the sky" started anew, the piano chords reverberating all around them, the singer's melodic voice making her shiver. The haunting words were not lost on her; she understood their meaning now, and why they resonated with Alexander. They were symbolic, almost prophetic of how he must have felt when she'd left him behind in the past.

Alexander grasped her jaw between his palms and covered her face with light kisses, feathering them down her neck and back up to her mouth. Searing heat pooled between her thighs and travelled down her spine as he explored her mouth with his tongue. Her skin tingled as he nibbled and sucked, teasing her mouth with gentle caresses until she pulled him closer.

Makayla slid her hand down between their bodies and grasped his erection, rubbing her thumb back and forth over the hard, silky tip of his manhood. She raised her body and guided him to the juncture of her thighs. They gasped in unison as he eased into her tense body; filling her to capacity. They moved in steady, drawn out strokes, all the while looking into one another's eyes. Their movements became wilder as desire took hold and all thought fled, their bodies falling into a lustful rhythm. Alexander's hands were everywhere, all over her body, in her hair, on her breasts, skimming the lengths of her legs, grasping her backside as he pounded in and out of her body.

Alexander flipped them so she lay beneath him. He slid his hands down her arms and clasped her fingers, drawing her hands above her head and pinning her to the floor with the weight of his body. She wrapped her legs about his waist as he began to move within her again. Her eyes meandered along his torso, watching the threads of muscle contract and strain as he moved above her. Makayla sighed, matching his every stroke, his every thrust. Their movements became erratic, feverish, frantic, turbulent, furious, wild, and violent. An intoxicating burn built within Makayla as she quaked in his hands. She was lost, the need all-consuming.

Alexander released her hands and trailed his fingertips down the lengths of her arms until he reached the sides of her breasts. He circled her nipples, pinching and teasing them into taut buds. He dipped his head and licked along her neck until he came to her earlobe, he took it into his mouth and nipped, sucked and licked it until she was incoherent of thought. Her heart raced, a thundering beat in her chest. Makayla grabbed a handful of his hair and jerked him towards her; he lowered his chest to hers and squashed her in a tight embrace.

Makayla inhaled his exotic scent, her mouth watering and pooling with venom, she couldn't deny the hunger any longer. She licked her dry lips and bit into his shoulder. His body bucked. Makayla's body trembled, the bloodlust triggering an animalistic urge within her. Blood flowed over her tongue and down her throat in thick, streaming jets. It tasted different now he was a vampire, sweet with a little tang. Alexander's breaths became short and choppy as she siphoned the one thing that was always forbidden to her: real blood. Makayla ground her hips against his in a passionate ferocity that matched the feeding frenzy taking hold. She groaned when she felt the answering stabbing pressure of Xander's fangs in her neck. The coppery smell of blood and the sound of their lovemaking was an erotic acoustic.

The intoxicating friction between them enhanced the feeding frenzy. Makayla felt as though they would combust into flames. The heat suffusing their bodies was unusual. She stopped feeding, licking the wounds on his shoulder to heal them, then looked up into her husband's face and gasped. They were literally on fire. Flames surrounded their bodies. The carpet they lay on was smouldering; they were a blazing bonfire, only the flames didn't affect them. Makayla manifested a shield about their bodies to prevent the flames from burning everything in the room.

Makayla gasped anew as Alexander's powerful body pounded into hers, his hot flesh sliding in and out of her faster and faster until there was no beginning or ending to their bodies or minds. They were no longer separate beings, they were one, their minds in sync. Makayla sensed Alexander's climax building, because it was her climax as well. They were sharing everything; the same sensations, the same orgasm amplified by their blood-bond connection. She was his maker, they were bonded physically and mentally, one being, two minds bound together through love and blood.

Makayla arched her back, running her hands up and down Alexander's body; she dug her fingernails into his hips, pulling him towards her. A wave of tingling sensations struck them, swelling to epic proportions, growing stronger, lasting longer than they'd ever experienced. Their muscles clenched as their bodies convulsed with an explosion of shivering nerves. Alexander threw his head back and cried out, they tensed as a pleasurable wave of tingling spasms crashed through their bodies, their flesh tightening, throbbing with their simultaneous climax.

Alexander slumped forward, his head resting on Makayla's shoulder. They were both heaving and gasping for air, the flames dispersing as they caught their breath. Alexander rolled off Makayla and lay next to her on the charred carpet remains.

She smiled and looked over at him. "Holy shit, that was intense," she wheezed. "You really do have the hots for me, huh?"

Alexander chuckled. "Woman, you are the wood that fuels my fire." He rolled to his side to face her and brushed the hair from her eyes, kissing her tenderly. "I love you, Makayla Uriel Drake. I have loved you from afar for seven hundred years. I have watched and protected you for seven hundred years. We've been separated by time. Separated by consequences. Separated by evil. No more. I will not be apart from you one minute more and if I die tomorrow, know that the times we've shared have been the happiest moments in my long life. I love you, Makayla; I love you with my entire being. My heart is full. You could kill me now and I'd die a happy man."

Tears streamed down Makayla's cheeks, her lips trembled and her throat constricted with emotion. She felt his love within her mind and within her body. She couldn't respond, the emotion of his words choking any response from her. She leaned towards him, took a shuddering breath and touched her lips to his. "My world was on fire when you came into my life, Xander; I was lost in the shadows, lost in the darkness of my broken soul. I never dreamed I'd meet somebody like you. I didn't want to fall in love with you, but I did. You smashed down my walls and turned them to dust and made me feel for the first time in my life. You made me dream of you, and gave me hope. Xander, you immersed me in love even though I was abrasive, jaded and hateful. You treated me with respect when I gave you none; your love was unconditional and patient. I was unworthy, or so I thought. You changed my view; you changed my perception of everything. You turned my world upside down, Alexander Drake. God knows I love you, and I will die loving you."

CHAPTER 35.

Ecktar was surrounded by the contingent of Zoldarni guards who'd all returned from their individual assignments. The only good news Ecktar had received: the Zoldarni gateways were intact and operational with no signs of tampering. As far as the Zoldarni Emissaries were concerned, there were no survivors. They'd met the same fate as Idgar, Tahlia, Nyshtar and Ensor. He had a terrible feeling it was only the beginning.

Ecktar motioned Illiyaird and Targul forward. He held three blue metal cylindrical tubes of correspondence. The tubes comprised two inter-joining sections and were secured with sophisticated seals. The silver seals were circular and very similar to a traditional wax seal in appearance, but that's where the similarities ended. Only the intended recipient could open the tube, and to ensure this a small needle was hidden in the centre of the seal that would take a blood sample when the recipient pressed their thumb to the seal to open it. A mere thumbprint couldn't open the seal, and even someone masquerading as another could only alter their appearance, not their blood.

"Illiyaird, I want you and Targul to return to Cwonoth and deliver these correspondences. Targel, give this to Lord Dinbouar." Ecktar handed him one of the cylindrical tubes. "Illiyaird, I want you to give this to Overlord Avinash," he said, handing Illiyaird the second cylinder. The third cylinder he attached to his weapon belt about his waist. "Do not let these correspondences out of your sight. No one must intercept them, it's of the utmost importance they reach their intended destination. I want you to hand the communications to the person directly. Do not hand them off to their secretaries, you are to deliver them personally. Do you understand?"

"Yes, Lord Commander," Illiyaird and Targul replied.

"Good, be on your way. Once you have delivered the cylinders, I want Lord Avinash and Lord Dinbouar to open the missives in your presence. If they don't, and they usher you out of the room without a response to my correspondence, I want you to watch them. Pay careful attention to their behaviour, their mannerisms, their every gesture, how they speak, how they act. Be alert. Don't raise suspicion, do it covertly. We must be certain they're not imposters. If Earth has been compromised, there's reason to believe Cwonoth will be next. It's only a matter of time before they target the Zoldarni, if they haven't already. It's vital we thwart any hostile takeovers We are the last defence. Do you understand?"

"Yes, sir," they said in unison.

Ecktar nodded, and they made their way back towards the Zoldarni gateway. Ecktar beckoned the remaining Zoldarni Guard to him, formulating a plan of action in his head as they gathered about him. His plan would take cunning and secrecy.

The last of the Newbloods exited the portal and spread throughout the shaded area. Zobiana looked about the shadowy forest surrounding Sebastian's property, Wigmore Castle. The silence of the forest was unnerving. There were no chirping crickets or birds, no crawling insects or snakes, all living creatures had burrowed deep into their dens or fled. The moment the electromagnetic energy of her portal invaded their territory they would have taken flight sensing imminent danger. The only sound was of her people moving into position.

She'd known Sebastian's whereabouts ever since she'd drunk his young son's blood and eaten his heart. It was the connection she'd needed to locate her betrothed. She smiled, it was time to seek retribution for his rejection.

There were still a few hours before the sun set; time enough for her Newblood soldiers to manoeuvre into position without being hindered or burned by the sun. She was happy to wait until the last rays of sunshine descended before seeking vengeance. The forest was the perfect cover, it surrounded the entire castle. Wigmore Castle would be rubble, a burning pile of rocks after she was done levelling it.

Vasili was lost for words. Marianna stood before him, young, beautiful, full of vitality. The way she'd been the first time he'd seen her on Evron so, so many years ago. She smiled shyly as she had in her youth when he'd stare at her unabashed.

"How? I've been gone a few days, how?" he asked.

"Makayla paid me a visit."

Vasili's mouth gaped, he snapped it shut and brushed a hand over his beard. "She's getting stronger. I knew she was powerful, but I had no idea what she was capable of." Vasili moved closer to his wife. "Are you real? Are you here or am I imagining you?"

"I'm as real as the sun and the moon." She smiled.

"I've searched centuries for you." Vasili stroked her cheek. "I've missed you, Marianna, I failed you, I promised I'd protect you when we took our vows, and I failed miserably. I should have seen the signs."

"How were you to know, Vasili? Nobody can predict their own destiny, it is, and has always been, this way. You knew, we knew this when we took our vows. There were no signs to see, you couldn't have known Lilith's machinations. She used me to get to you, it's what she does; she manipulates a situation to achieve her goal – ultimate power. It's what she has always done. You are not to blame, my love."

Vasili pulled Marianna towards him and hugged her tightly. "It's good to have you in my arms again," he murmured and breathed in her scent. She'd always smelled like gardenias, sweet and as sultry as a midsummer evening. His wife was as breathtaking and exotic as the perfume she wore. Marianna embodied a timeless femininity and elegance; her scent was burned in the memory of his soul.

"Vasili?"

"Mm-hmm." Vasili buried his face in the crook of her neck, kissing her skin.

"When was the last time you fed?"

"I can't remember." Vasili looked into her face. "I've subsisted on synthetic blood for some time now."

"Synthetic blood?" Marianna's face creased in confusion. "What is synthetic blood?"

"It's a man-made product with all the nutrients a vampire needs to live."

"When was the last time you fed on living blood?"

Vasili dropped his arms to his sides and looked up in thought. "Other than the blood of a Newblood I interrogated, your blood was the last living blood I fed on. I went for centuries without feeding. When I became weak and my body wasted away and my mind deteriorated, Sebastian intervened and forced me to feed. He'd been working with Aemma Pharmaceuticals to develop a human blood substitute. They'd had much success synthesising artificial blood. I refused to drink the synthetic blood, so he held me down and poured it down my throat, force feeding me every couple of hours until I revived. I was the guinea pig, the first to drink it. Sebastian saved my life." Vasili closed his eyes and sighed. "You must be so disappointed in me," he said, opening his eyes to look at her again.

She shook her head. "Never, I almost gave up the fight too." She grasped his hand, stroking his fingertips.

"I was in a state of mind where I didn't care if I lived or died, after two hundred years of searching for you I'd lost hope of ever finding you. I couldn't sense you; I thought you were dead, along with our son Benjamin. Nikolai had also disappeared in his search for you – it was like my family was ash scattered to the wind. After Sebastian revived me and I felt somewhat alive, I learned Nikolai had infiltrated Zobiana's inner circle of people and was masquerading as her apprentice, Beltizare. I began to hope again. We learned you were still alive. Lilith came demanding, blackmailing me to do things that went against everything I believed in. I did what she asked, to a degree. She wanted Makayla's blood and I gave it to her with the hopes of getting you back, but she always had more demands. I was a fool."

Marianna gasped, covering her mouth with her hand. "Vasili, no, not Makayla's blood."

"Lilith never got a pure specimen from me. I corrupted every sample of Makayla's blood I gave her, but she got her hands on a pure sample. The Blakspor virus has annihilated the Earth's population and the Newbloods are finishing the job. Makayla blames herself because the Blakspor virus was made from her blood. You don't know how many times I tried to thwart Lilith, but she's always one step ahead of us."

"Makayla's not the only one blaming herself, is she? It's not your fault, Vasili." Marianna touched her palm to his cheek. "Now, old man, you need to feed because you look like my grandfather and it just won't do." Marianna swept her hair over her shoulder, lifted her chin and angled her bare throat, drawing his face towards her neck. "Now feed."

Vasili lowered his mouth to his wife's neck, it had been so long since he'd fed from her he'd almost forgotten the taste of her blood. His mouth watered, filling with venom at the thought of feeding from her, he kissed her neck once more before his vision blurred with a flurry of white stars, his fangs descended, his gums burning with the wanting of her blood. He licked the tender flesh and felt her shiver. He could no longer hold back and plunged his incisors into the main artery of her throat, the skin popping around his fangs. His eyes rolled back as her sweet blood gushed down his throat. He growled low in his throat, feeling territorial. He tried to reign in the feeding frenzy simmering just below the surface and savoured the pure sweetness pumping into his mouth. He'd forgotten the pleasure that encompassed his body. He felt Marianna's body weakening, succumbing to the drugging power of his venom and retracted his fangs; he didn't want to take too much blood.

He licked the wound closed, repairing her skin with the healing properties of his saliva. Her eyes were wide with desire, her gasping breath fanning across his face as her pupils dilated; passion crossed her face as she lifted her mouth to his and kissed him. Vasili squashed her to his body and grasped her face in his hands and kissed her back.

A muffled scream.

They broke apart and looked towards the door. "Did you hear that?" Marianna asked.

Low guttural growling.

"Wait here," Vasili said, edging towards the door and inching it open to look out into the corridor. The growling increased in volume. Vasili felt Marianna's hand on his back.

"It sounds like Izador," Marianna whispered. "Something's wrong, Vasili, Izzy never growls. Not unless Emily's in danger."

"Stay here, don't leave this room, lock the door the moment I close it."

Marianna nodded. "Please be careful."

Vasili eased the door open again and was about to step out into the corridor when it flooded with Newbloods. He closed the door and locked it, pushing a nearby closet in front to bar the way. He tried to communicate with Sebastian telepathically, but he was shielding his mind. "I can't contact Sebastian." Vasili took Marianna in his arms and tried to communicate with Makayla. He couldn't get through to her either, something was blocking him from her and it wasn't her mind-shields. He tried

Darrius and made contact, he explained what was happening at his home and told him to gather the Shadow Seekers and whoever he could find to help fight the Newbloods, then severed the connection. "It's too late, the corridors are overrun with Newbloods. I've got to get you out of here."

"What about Emily? What about Ambrosia and Sebastian?"

"Izador will protect, Emily, he's a Sandalius wolf, she's better protected than we are. Sebastian won't let anything happen to Ambrosia. I'll take you to the compound and come back for them, I promise. Do you know if Tristan's here?"

"No, I haven't seen him since I first arrived at Wigmore Castle."

"Damn." Someone banged on their door. "We've got to go." Vasili grabbed his wife and dematerialised. They arrived at the compound in his private office moments later. "I've got to find Darrius and the other Shadow Seekers." Vasili opened the door – the corridor was empty. He turned back to Marianna and kissed her hard on the lips. "Lock the door." She nodded as he stepped out into the corridor and closed the door behind him. He heard the lock engage and exhaled; then he placed a ward over the door and said an enchantment before taking off down the corridor in search of Darrius and the Shadow Seekers.

CHAPTER 36.

The Sandalius mark on Danny's arm burned; he groaned and crashed to the floor, grasping his stomach as a sharp pain stabbed him in the gut. The scar on his arm where Izador had bitten him throbbed, the bone aching with a heart-pounding beat. He hauled himself up off the ground using the bar top to get his balance. Danny's sight blurred with premonition, his restaurant faded into obscurity as the vision took hold. He saw Emily curled up on the floor in the corner of her bedroom, hugging a teddy bear in her arms. Izador stood guard in front of her, growling, his head low, his hackles raised, saliva dripping from his shuddering maw, ready to pounce as three Newbloods approached. The hallucination disappeared as quickly as it had appeared. Danny shook his head, his surroundings coming back into focus.

Emily was in danger.

With his head spinning, Danny headed towards his private rooms at the back of his restaurant. He yanked the door open and went to his weapons cupboard, grabbing his daggers and strapping them to his thighs, and pocketing throwing stars in his vest as he strapped his favourite samurai swords to his back. He focused on Emily, picturing her and Izador in his mind's eye and dematerialised in a funnel of searing black ash.

Danny materialised behind the three Newbloods intent on doing Emily harm. His hands and forearms turned black, threads of hot lava-like veins marring the surface of his skin. There was no stopping the change when it took hold, he just hoped Emily wouldn't fear the demon he'd become and be traumatised by what he was about to do to the Newbloods. Danny angled his head from side to side as horns twisted and grew out of his head, curling back from the middle of his cranium. He smiled as his teeth lengthened to deadly points. He withdrew his swords and bent his knees as he prepared to dismember the two outer Newbloods. The middle Newblood he'd save for last.

They still hadn't realised he was there; he was the perfect predator, deadly quiet, not even his swords made a sound when he unsheathed them from their leather scabbard casings. He spun the swords in his hands before stabbing the Newbloods in their lower backs. He sliced the honed edges upwards, carving the silver blades through the centres of their bodies and out across their torsos in a zig zag motion – severing their bodies and decapitating them. Black blood sprayed in shooting arcs before their bodies disintegrated into ash. Emily screamed in full now. Izador's growls intensified as the remaining Newblood spun towards Danny. Danny crossed his swords in front of his body and scissored them across the Newblood's throat, lopping off his head. He watched the head spiral up into the air and hit the ceiling with a meaty thunk before raining down to the ground in a shower of ash. The corpse stood briefly before collapsing to its knees and exploding more ash over the floor. Danny flicked the blood from his swords and resheathed them. He cracked his neck from side to side as his fangs receded and his horns disappeared into his head.

Emily stared at him wide-eyed, her bottom lip trembling, tears pooling in her eyes as she squashed the teddy bear to her chest in a tight hug. Izador paced back and forth and circled back towards her to nuzzle her face with his snout, he whined and looked over towards Danny.

Danny lowered to his knees and held his palms up. "Emily, I'm not here to hurt you, sweetie, are you okay?" She didn't respond. "My name's Danny, I'm a friend of your sister, Makayla; I'm here to protect you."

Emily raised the bear to her face and peeked out from between the stuffed toy's ears. "I don't know you, you're a stranger."

Izador angled his head from side to side looking at her with intelligence that belied his animal status and then looked back at Danny.

"We can't stay here, Emily, it's dangerous. She's coming, Zobiana's coming." Danny glanced over his shoulder towards the bedroom door. He could hear people running through the corridors, no doubt they were Newbloods. What were they doing here? How had they infiltrated the castle? The hairs on his arms prickled, something terrible was about to happen. He looked down and noticed smoke filtering through the bottom of the door. "Emily, we have to leave now, the castle's on fire."

Izador grabbed a hold of Emily's sleeve with his teeth and tugged but she wouldn't budge. He whined again and let go of Emily's pyjamas and rubbed against Danny's leg. Danny grabbed a handful of his fur, scratching behind his ears and patting him on the side of his belly. "It's good to see you again, Izzy. Wow, you've grown."

Emily stood, her mouth gaping as she looked from Izador to Danny, the teddy bear hanging in her loose grip. "Izzy doesn't like people, only my sister, Makayla, and me. How do you know him? How come he likes you?"

Danny chuckled. "Because I'm the one who found Izzy for you. He's the last of his kind, Makayla asked me to find you a protector and I did, I found you a Sandalius wolf." Danny stood. "Come on, honey, we've got to go now." He held his arms out to her. The fear had disappeared from her face and Emily ran from the corner and jumped into his arms. Danny smiled and kissed her cheek before grabbing a fistful of Izador's fur and dematerialising them to safety.

Ambrosia smiled as she took a fighting stance and levelled her swords at Abigail and Tyrone. "If you've come for me, I will not make it easy for you. I'm not pathetic like your mother, Abigail, I don't hide behind my soldiers. I fight my own battles. I was the General of the Seraph Guard." Ambrosia noticed the look of surprise on Abigail's face and laughed. "Oh, you didn't know? Bring it, little girl!"

Abigail sneered. "If it wasn't for you, my father would be with my mother. If you didn't steal him away, he'd be—"

"He'd be what? Your daddy? You're as pathetic as your psycho mother, Abigail."

Abigail made to rush forward; Tyrone stopped her. He whistled and Newbloods filled the room, surrounding Ambrosia on all sides.

"You're more like your mother than I thought, hiding behind your soldiers like she does."

"Seize her," Abigail screeched.

Ambrosia's eyes darted about her as Newbloods closed ranks. Three moved towards her as two others came up from the rear, she looped her swords overhead and twisted on the spot, collecting all five as she spun. Screams gurgled out of the vampires as they were cut down, various body parts, legs, arms and heads, flying into the air, black gushing blood splattering her clothing as she dismembered the Newbloods surrounding her. More Newbloods kept coming at her, she spun her swords like the blades of a helicopter twirling them about her body in blurring circles and killing all who got in her path. Newblood corpses covered the floor in piles about her, disintegrating to ash as their bodies broke down.

Ambrosia stopped when there were none left to fight, then she slashed her swords down, removing the blood from the gleaming blades with the flick of her wrist. "Is that all you've got?"

Tyrone chuckled. "You don't disappoint do you, Lady Ambrosia? Now I know where the Golden One gets her attitude from."

Abigail stared at Tyrone open-mouthed. "Enough of this shit; don't compliment the bitch, do something, Tyrone, we need to get the hell out of here."

Ambrosia rolled her shoulders, her smile widening when she noticed the look of disbelief on Abigail's face. "Did you think I'd come peacefully, Abigail? Not likely."

"Where's Sebastian, Ambrosia?" Abigail smirked. "Oh, I forgot, Mother's having a lovely conversation with him as we speak."

"No, she wouldn't. She wouldn't kill him, he's the one she's always wanted. Without him she can't be queen." Ambrosia's voice trembled.

"That's right, Queen." Abigail laughed.

"Enough with the theatrics, Abigail, playtime's over, it's time we were leaving." Tyrone sliced his hands in the air and Ambrosia's swords were ripped from her hands; then he closed his palms and made fists. The air froze in Ambrosia's throat; she gasped for oxygen, her mouth working open and closed as she tried to breathe. She tried to move, but her arms wouldn't respond, she tried to step forward, but it was useless – she was paralysed. Tyrone smiled.

Abigail lifted a pair of shackles and shook them in the air. "Looks like you'll be coming with us after all." She cackled like a demented crone. "Oh, just so you know, these are spelled shackles. You won't be getting out of them any time soon."

Ambrosia watched Abigail saunter towards her, white stars blurring her vision, her throat burning – swelling, her chest heaving for oxygen. Abigail cuffed the shackles to her hands and tugged on the chains to make sure they were secure; she looked over her shoulder and nodded at Tyrone, who released the spell.

Ambrosia's body was suddenly free of its paralysis. A rush of air filled her lungs, and she could breathe again. She coughed and spluttered, then Abigail pulled on the chains and she lost her balance and stumbled to the floor, still gasping for oxygen.

"Not so tough now, are you?" Abigail taunted, hauling Ambrosia to her feet and dragging her out of the room.

A crisp breeze scattered leaves across Adrian's grave as the wind picked up with a sudden flourish. Sebastian stood staring down at the headstone with the engraved image of his son's face. The heaviness in his heart hadn't abated; it grew, weighing him down with each passing day. There was no reprieve from the loss. There was no reprieve from the guilt. His heart was missing a piece.

Sebastian picked up the toy motorbike Makayla had left by Adrian's grave. He spun the back wheel and inhaled a shaky breath, his throat tightening. He couldn't cry anymore and hadn't since the day he'd found Makayla by Adrian's graveside. The breeze gathered strength, spinning the leaves on the ground; it was an unnatural wind that chilled his bones with a presence he recognised. There was a soft crunch of leaves as she stopped beside him. He didn't acknowledge her; she'd taken everything from him. Sebastian turned his gaze towards the woman he'd thought he'd once loved. It hadn't been love at all. What he'd felt for her had paled compared to the love he had for his wife. He realised after meeting Ambrosia, the love he'd felt for Lilith was a love one has for a friend, nothing more.

"Why? You were my best friend, why would you do such a thing?" he asked

"Do you even need to ask?" Zobiana answered.

"What happened to you, Lil? You aren't this." Sebastian pointed at his son's grave. "This isn't you, this was never you."

Zobiana glanced down at Adrian's grave and her gaze faltered, her eyes shining. She straightened her back and held her head high, her gaze hardening. "Maybe not, but people change." She looked at him, her eyebrows arching.

"You once claimed you loved me," said Sebastian. "But it was never love you felt for me. I was a stepping stone in your mad quest for power. You're right about one thing, Lil: you have changed. The woman I knew would never have done the things you've done, the things you're doing. You've become twisted, so twisted, in fact, you've chosen to destroy lives, to destroy worlds, and for what? Revenge, power, control, world domination." Sebastian lowered his eyes to his son's grave once more.

"You forgot freedom."

Sebastian laughed. "Freedom? Don't make me laugh."

"It would have been different had you told me about her."

"I don't think so. I was the prize – correction; becoming queen was the prize – your goal from the beginning. You blackmailed my father into our betrothal and then you groomed me for years, but you overlooked one thing. ME. My choices, my desires, what I wanted. It was always about you, Lilith, my feelings were never part of your plan. When you realised it wasn't you I wanted or loved, your goal of becoming queen was threatened. So what do you do? You turn into something unimaginable. I mean I've heard the old adage, *'Hell hath no fury like a woman scorned'*, but you've taken it to a whole new level." Sebastian kicked a stone with the toe of his boot and sighed. He knew the kind, funny woman he'd loved once was still inside her somewhere fighting to break free – or he hoped she was – but by the stiff posture, the regal and confident attitude she portrayed now, he knew his words were falling on deaf ears.

"Are you finished, Sebastian?" Zobiana clenched her fists and glanced heavenward before focusing her eyes on him once more.

"I didn't conform to your every whim; you couldn't control me, that's why you're bitter. You're just like him, you know, your master. You take and take, until there's nothing left and then you get angry when you don't get your way. You sold your soul to the Devil and became his puppet, his handmaiden. I feel sorry for you, I thought you'd broken free of him, but you were never free, were you? I'm sorry I hurt you, Lil, I'm sorry I never told you about my feelings for Ambrosia, I should have. I'm sorry your dream of becoming queen was stolen from you, but I'm not sorry I fell in love, I'm not sorry I married Ambrosia. I hope one day you'll find it in your heart and learn to forgive, but I'm doubtful. You're on a path no one comes back from. You've killed too many people."

Zobiana glanced towards Adrian's grave. "What if I told you Adrian's essence survived. What if I told you there was still hope. What if I told you he wasn't really dead, just in suspended animation?"

"I'd tell you it was impossible because I saw his broken body. He's dead – gone."

"Not gone; protected from the harshness of this world, in between worlds."

"The harshness of this world." Sebastian laughed again.

"The harshness you refer to is your doing, Lilith. You brought it on; you're the harshness of this world." Sebastian returned Adrian's toy to the graveside and straightened, folding his arms across his chest and faced her. "Why are you here?" He looked her up and down, the black crown and armour she wore was a farce. "Oh, I see," he said, the sarcasm in his voice dripping like melted butter.

"What do you see?" Zobiana clenched her jaw, her eyes turning red as her face hardened once more – the mask back in place.

"I see you're still pining for something that will never be."

"What will never be?"

"You will never be queen."

"Oh, I don't know, it's a possibility now, more so than ever before."

"How so, Lil? I'm not married to you, they banished you from Evron if I recall, murdering the monarch's wife will not win you any popularity contests."

Zobiana smiled, flashing her fangs. "That's where you're wrong." She circled him trailing her hand across his chest until she stood before him once more. "I'd say I was in the perfect position." She looked at his mouth, touching a fingertip to his bottom lip. He shifted his head away from her touch.

"Stop playing games, I was never into your theatrics. I wasn't a fool then and I'm not one now. Why are you here?" he asked again.

Zobiana looked back towards Wigmore Castle. "I'm here

to bring you to your knees, Bastian."

Sebastian glanced towards his home, it was on fire. Black smoke spiralled up into the darkening sky, flames billowed in every window. How could he not have noticed? How could he have not smelled the acrid odour of burning flames or heard the shattering windows as they burst from the heat? He heard and smelled them now. He burst forward and tried to get past Zobiana, but she whipped her hand out and gripped his arm; she was stronger than he'd expected.

"It's too late, your wife is no longer there, my men escorted her to her new home. I think a dungeon is quite fitting for her, don't you? And your daughter," Zobiana looked down at Adrian's grave before looking back at him. "Well, I don't think she lasted long with my Newbloods, you may as well dig another grave alongside your son's."

Sebastian screamed in outrage, grabbed hold of Zobiana's throat and squeezed. Her eyes bulged in surprise. "I will kill you, do you hear me? I will kill you before this day's end."

"If. . .you. . .kill. . .me, you kill. . . your wife," Zobiana choked out.

Sebastian loosened his fingers, but didn't let go. "You wouldn't dare," he hissed.

"Wouldn't I?" Zobiana curled her fingers under his and removed them from her throat. "If I don't return within the hour, Abigail and Tyrone have orders to kill her," Zobiana panted, rubbing her throat. "You will cooperate, you will take the throne and you will make me your queen."

"The hell I will, the monarchy no longer exists. You'll never control Evron, Lilith, never!"

"I already do, Sebastian." Zobiana smiled and turned away from him, walking towards the exterior curtain wall of his burning castle where there seemed to be a swirling portal gyrating on the rock surface. She waved her hand in the air and Sebastian saw the horde of Newbloods standing near the portal – and recognised a few Vampire Guards among their ranks. "You have five days to comply, Sebastian, or your wife's life is forfeit. I'll be waiting on Evron, at our favourite spot." Zobiana stepped into the portal. Her laughter lingered, reverberating in his skull long after she and her army had disappeared.

Sebastian collapsed to his knees, his body sagging as he watched the inferno decimate his home. Hot cinders floated above him, black ash raining down, and the crackling roar of fire loud in his ears. Heat surrounded him, but he shivered, the chill in his heart expanding throughout his body. He covered his face and wept.

Chapter 37.

Fire surrounded Alexander. Everywhere he turned he saw raging flames; he was standing within them, unaffected. It was as though he stood in the fiery centre of a volcano – the centre of the Earth. He couldn't feel the heat, nor smell his surroundings, or hear the telltale sound of the crackling fire. It was as though he were in a vacuum with none of his usual senses – except his vision. He knew he was dreaming again, he'd had the same recurring dream for days, but this time it seemed different. Alexander was underground again in a cave system of sorts, with numerous tunnels leading off into the distance as far as the eye could see. He stood on a wide, thick-crusted ledge of rock. To his right a river of hot magma flowed down the main tunnel. Where it flowed mystified him. The remaining smaller tunnels were to the left of the river of magma and evenly spaced along the ledge wall near where he stood.

He had an innate knowledge that each tunnel had something to do with his past.

Alexander headed towards the first tunnel, his curiosity getting the better of him. What would he find? He stopped at the entrance and squinted, trying to see beyond the darkness. The flames were localised to the main cavern, the tunnels themselves were flame-free. Alexander stepped into the tunnel and stopped to look down. He wasn't wearing shoes or clothes; he always seemed to be naked in these dreams. He wiggled his toes in the powdery substance covering the ground. The silky texture was soft like wheat-flour and cool to the touch – it was as though he stood on a beach made of powder rather than sand. The air was fresh and smelled of the ocean. He breathed in deeply, trying to capture the salty scent in his lungs; funny how his senses weren't affected in the tunnel.

Even though the tunnel grew darker the further he travelled along, his sight was unaffected. He saw a pinpoint of light up ahead and hastened his step. The pinpoint of light grew larger with every step he took. It was the size of a basketball, and then the size of a manhole, the light kept increasing in size until he reached the end of the tunnel. His mouth dropped when he took in his surroundings. He was standing on the edge of a forest, watching a huge battle of warring soldiers take place. It wasn't until he saw Makayla lop the head off Bulan Tzul that he realised he was seeing his first memory of her. He experienced the same emotions and thoughts as the first time he laid eyes on her: his heart beat wildly in his chest, his breathing became erratic, he couldn't swallow, his skin tingled with precognition, the same intrinsic knowledge that one day she'd be his. She was awe-inspiring, the same spectacular six-winged seraph he'd seen as an adolescent. Could each tunnel represent a memory?

Alexander turned and ran back down the tunnel to the burning cavern of fire and made his way towards the next tunnel. He followed the second tunnel to the end and was similarly gobsmacked when he looked out. He saw Makayla's arrival in the 14th century, he saw her draw back her bow and let loose an arrow, he watched the arrow kill the bandit, intent on killing him. He watched as she kissed him that first time, his throat tightening in remembrance.

He heard laughter and turned to look back towards the cavern. "Who's there?" The laughter grew louder, it was all around him now. "Who's there?" he called out a second time – there was no answer. Alexander headed back towards the fiery cavern and stopped when he reached the rocky ledge. He saw a dark figure entering the first tunnel and followed.

"Why do you follow me, Keeper of the Key?"

"Who are you?"

"You know who I am," the dark figure said, not turning, but continuing on his set path towards Alexander's first memory of Makayla. Alexander followed the dark figure, all the while foreboding fell over his skin.

"Why won't you tell me who you are?"

"I am the end and the beginning."

Alexander almost fell, his steps faltering at the dark

figure's words. He wiped his forehead with the back of his arm, a cold sweat having materialised out of nowhere, his head spun, his vision blurring as he stumbled after the entity.

"Why are you here?" Alexander croaked, his mouth dry.

"I'm here to take what's most valuable to you: your memories of her. One by one they will be mine, I will take them all until you are but a shell and your body is ripe for the picking." Malicious laughter ricocheted in Alexander's skull.

"You can't, I did a protection spell."

"You should have kept the Gem of Protection within your body, near your heart; it was the only thing keeping me from you. Now nothing can stop me, not even your Golden One. You're mine and so are your memories." More laughter. "I will save your most treasured recollections for last, and savour the pain it causes you. Prepare to lose everything you hold dear, Druid, for I will burn them from your mind."

The dark figure stopped at the end of the tunnel and surveyed the horizon. Alexander dropped to his knees and grabbed his head in pain. He saw everything in rewind. Makayla picked up her sword and swung it backwards, Bulan Tzul's head reattached to his shoulders, the dead rose. He screamed until the memory was not even a glimmer of a thought in his head.

"*Nooooooo!*" Alexander jolted awake, screaming at the top of his lungs, his chest heaving, his body trembling and coated in sweat.

"Xander, it's just a dream, it's just a dream, baby,"

Makayla consoled, touching his shoulder. "It's okay, you're here now, you're safe with me now."

Alexander looked about, dazed; he was back in his secret cavern with Makayla in his four-poster bed. He grasped his throbbing head and closed his eyes, trying to get his bearings as he took deep, calming breaths.

"Are you okay?" Makayla grasped his cheek and guided his face towards her; he couldn't look in her eyes.

"Xander, what were you dreaming of?"

Alexander looked at the velvet canopy above their heads; a hollow feeling taking hold of his innards. It was a giant hand squeezing his guts, making his stomach roil. He swallowed the saliva in his mouth and gagged – he sat up and manifested a bucket just before he threw up the contents of his stomach. He felt Makayla's warm, comforting hand rubbing circles on his back. Bitter stomach acid burned a singeing path up his oesophagus, he swallowed again, his dry tongue sticking to the roof of his mouth. There was nothing but stomach acid to throw up, his body having already metabolised Makayla's blood. He lowered the bucket to the floor and slouched back on the bed, flinging his arm over his forehead and covering his eyes. "Sorry about that," he mumbled.

"Xander, are you okay?"

"I'll be okay."

"Were you dreaming about the dungeons?"

"No, it's a recurring dream I've been having."

"Do you want to talk about it?"

"I keep dreaming I'm being consumed by fire, only the fire doesn't hurt or burn me, and I'm always naked, it's just plain weird. I'll be okay, though, don't worry. Let's talk about something else." *Coward,* he thought to himself.

Alexander felt Makayla's timid touch on his chest, her fingers circling the healed scar left from the protection spell he'd carved into his skin.

"Xander?"

"Hmmm." He lowered his arm and looked at her.

"I've been meaning to ask, why have you never spoken of your father and home planet Avalon?" Makayla stopped circling her finger on his chest and looked him in the eye. "Did you ever tell your father of Lilith's betrayal?"

"I never got the chance. Avalon was destroyed and those of my people here on Earth were the only survivors. Most are scattered across Ireland, Scotland and England," Xander said.

"I'm sorry, I shouldn't have asked."

"It happened a long time ago, Makayla." Alexander turned towards her and rose on his elbow, brushing hair from her eyes. "It's all right, I made Earth my home."

"What of the brotherhood, the Custodians of Rahul, do they still exist?"

Alexander nodded. "Yes, we're not as active as we once were. The Dark Ages were a time rife with danger, much like now, minus the inquisition; we were necessary. The Shadow Seekers do the job we once did. Now the brotherhood protects Earth's hidden knowledge and mystical artefacts not known to man."

"How was your planet destroyed?"

"No one knows, it just up and disappeared one day."

"So Avalon could still be there, hidden from view?"

"It's possible, but doubtful, the gateway doesn't work anymore, and that means only one thing." Alexander lay down and stared up at the canopy once more." *How was he going to tell her? He had to tell her, she needed to know.*

"Are there many of your people here on Earth?"

"There weren't to begin with, not even a sixteenth of Avalon's population, but after many centuries living on this planet, our numbers have grown. We brought Avalon to Earth. Have you not heard the tales? My people are lost to the mists of time. The lost kingdom, the utopian paradise. Many of our people live on the hidden island of crystal, where our magic is strongest. It seemed fitting, it's where the gateway to our home world is."

"I hope to see it one day."

"I shall endeavour to take you there." Alexander rubbed his eyes and frowned. "Something's wrong with me, Makayla; they did something to me in those dungeons other than torture."

Makayla nodded. "I've noticed a change in you, but assumed it had to do with your transition. I've never sired anyone before, so I didn't know what changes you'd undergo."

"Yes, I have changed, but there's something else, something more. It's something Abigail did to me that I didn't want to believe was possible, but now there's no denying it.

There are way too many strange things happening. I'm missing time, I keep blacking out and have no memory of the things I do when I'm not aware."

"It's like you become someone else, or someone's controlling you, almost like you're a puppet," Makayla whispered.

"That's it exactly." Xander grasped a coil of her hair and twirled it around his fingertips.

"Xander."

"Mm-hmm?"

"Can I ask you something?"

"Sure."

"Why did you put the Gem of Protection in your body? How is it even possible?"

"Um, you're speaking to a Druid, anything's possible! It was the safest place to put it under the circumstances. How else would you have been able to find me? How else could I have kept it hidden from Zobiana in the dungeon? You said Zobiana was holding me captive in a dungeon in the past, remember. I figured it was the Gem of Protection and it would protect me, and it has. Until I took it out of my body."

"So this scar." Makayla traced her finger along the lines of the rune on his chest. "What is it?"

He had to tell her, he couldn't keep the Dark One a secret. "It's a rune of protection, it does the same job the Trinian Gem was doing until I removed it from my body."

"But why would you need it? What do you need protecting

from, other than the obvious?"

Alexander sat up and faced Makayla. "I put it there because of what Abigail and Zobiana did to me while they held me captive. I put it there to protect me from him."

"To protect you from who?" Makayla frowned, here eyes creasing with worry, her head angling as she looked at him in confusion.

"To protect me from the Dark One."

Tears filled Makayla's eyes as she covered her mouth with her hands and shook her head from side to side. "No, no, no, please no, it can't be, the Gem of Protection should have prevented—."

"He's inside me, Makayla, the Dark One's inside me, he possesses my body."

Makayla shook her head. "It's impossible, it can't be. How could it have happened?"

"Abigail. She siphoned my power until I was at my weakest and almost killed herself the first time she drained my life force, my anima, from my body. She was more careful afterwards. Even with the Gem of Protection within my body, it would be possible because the gem fed off my energy – I had none left after Abigail weakened my anima. I don't remember much after, but ever since my return I've been having strange dreams."

"We have to get him out, we have to get him out now!"

"That would be a mistake."

"Xander, we have to."

"No, it's dangerous. We have to figure out a way, we have to be wise. If we exorcise him, how can we be certain he'll return to hell? We don't know what will happen, what if exorcising him sets him free to walk the Earth? It's too risky. I have ancient scrolls about the Dark One here, I remember reading about his imprisonment. I need to speak with a priest or a theologian before I consider exorcism."

"Can you feel him inside you now?"

Alexander shook his head. "No, your blood keeps him at bay, but now the Gem of Protection isn't in my body he seems pleased. He talks to me in my dreams, says he will take all my treasured memories. I think he may have already taken one or two memories already, I just don't know which ones. He said he would start with the smaller memories and then take the more meaningful ones, one by one, until I'm nothing but a shell. The more he takes from me the less of me remains and the more control over my body he'll gain." Alexander rubbed his forehead. "The only memories I have that mean anything to me are the ones I have of you my parents and Aggie, but my most treasured memories are of you, Makayla. You're all that matters to me. I'm nothing without you. I've spent centuries trying to get back to you." He brushed her cheek, wiping the tears from her face. "Baby, don't cry, we'll figure it out." He pulled her into his arms and hugged her.

"It's all my fault, I should have found you sooner, I should have figured it out sooner."

"Hush, it's not your fault, I'll be fine, we've just got to find a way to exorcise him from my body without freeing him into the world or killing me. I kind of like being alive." He winked at Makayla. She chewed her lip in thought, not responding.

"Put the Gem of Protection back in your body until we can figure this out."

"No, we can't, Makayla, you need to find the other gems before things get worse. You'll need the Trinian Globe and its power if we are to defeat Zobiana and the Dark One. The Trinian Globe is the key to it all, you have to find the two remaining gems, and you'll have to find them without my help. I don't trust the Dark One, he could take command of my body any time. If I know anything, I know he wants to be free of his fiery prison. He wants the globe, Makayla, you must keep the artefact away from him and away from me. If he escapes, it's the only thing that can send him back. If he is free, it will be hell on Earth."

"Have you seen how it is out there, Xander? It's hell already, the Dark One doesn't have to lift a finger because Zobiana has already readied the Earth for his arrival."

"Something's been bothering me, though." Xander scratched his head. "I can't figure out why I was in the sewers. You say you followed me, but I can't recall anything other than the fact I woke up in a strange chamber filled with ancient sarcophagi. There was a man dressed in early 19th century clothing who I'd apparently released from one of the sarcophagi. He was creepy and wouldn't tell me who he was — said he'd have to kill me if he did. He disappeared before Reece found me. When Reece found out I'd released him, he was distraught. He'd imprisoned him there over two centuries ago, he also said he was an upper level demon. Shit, the Dark One was in control of my body."

"I thought Reece was acting funny when I told him and the Shadow Seekers what had happened, it all makes sense now."

"How long was I out after I lost consciousness in the cavern beneath the compound?"

"A week," Makayla replied. "It was touch and go there for a while, your organs were shutting down. We gave you a direct blood transfusion of my blood. It seemed to work; it stabilised your condition – you were in a coma. You should have woken sooner, but we figured after everything you'd been through and on top of it you were transitioning. We figured your body was undergoing a lot of changes and would eventually heal itself."

"How much time have I lost since I was taken, did you come back to the same point in time after you left the past?"

"It's close to a year since you were taken, Xander."

Alexander dragged a hand through his hair. "That long. No wonder the world has deteriorated so much."

"I spent months searching for you before I figured it out. I may have only spent six days in the past, but when I returned to my time, many months had passed. So much lost time. So much made sense, all the things you'd said to me became clearer." Makayla touched his face. Alexander's eyes roamed to the curl of her lips as she leaned forward and kissed him.

His stomach coiled with desire, he grasped her face in his

hands and deepened the kiss, she opened to him, and he slipped his tongue into her mouth, tasting her. He pulled her into his lap and drew his lips away from her mouth, trying to catch his breath. He brushed hair out of her eyes and ran his finger over her eyebrows, down the length of her nose, across her parted lips.

"When I was in that dungeon the only thing that kept me going was my love for you, I knew you'd find me, I knew you were looking for me. So many times I thought of you and the times we spent together in the past. I thought on all the strange things you'd said and remembered your tears for the man I'd yet to become, you were so determined to find me, that's what gave me hope. It must have been hard to leave me in the past knowing how uncertain things were in the future, I could have been dead already. That night on my balcony when you asked me why I'd been watching over you, I wanted to tell you everything, everything that was between us, everything you and I were to one another. The words burned on my lips, but you were confused and angry; it almost broke me to see you that way."

"It seems like a lifetime ago." Makayla sighed. "I'm sorry for being such a hard-arse bitch to you. It can't have been easy when we were first partnered together, knowing what you knew, how I was in the past. I was miles apart from the person I was then and the person I am now."

Alexander chuckled. "It's what I love most about you, and for the record you're not a bitch. You are the strongest, most inspiring woman I know and have had the honour of meeting. If I had to make the same choices again, I would in a heartbeat, I'd endure the suffering and pain a thousand times over just to be with you and have you as my wife."

"Such pretty words. Enjoy her now, Druid, soon the memories you have of her will be mine and so will she. She will be mine and you'll never know because you will have ceased to exist," the Dark One taunted.

Alexander grasped his head; a sharp pain arcing through his mind as the Dark One's words reverberated through his skull. "Get out of my head."

Makayla bit her wrist and held it up to his mouth, Xander's nose twitched as the coppery scent of her blood laced about him. "It helps with the voices in your head, believe me, I know, I've had one particular voice in my head for centuries. Your blood drowned it out and gave me peace."

Alexander looked into her eyes. "You have? Why didn't you say? I had no idea."

"It's not something I like to advertise."

"You should have told me, Makayla."

"How would I have broached the subject? Oh, by the way, I think I'm bat shit crazy cause I hear a creepy voice in my head. No, I don't think so."

Alexander frowned.

Makayla shook her arm in his face. "Come on, feed, you'll see." Alexander grasped her wrist and covered the wound with his mouth, he groaned as her sweet blood flowed down his throat and warmed his belly. He rolled his eyes in delight and bit down into her flesh, his teeth hitting nerves and tendons, he couldn't help it. He heard Makayla's pleasured gasp and her blood sweetened further; he sensed her desire as it coursed through her body, through her blood, through their connection. Their blood-bond was unlike anything he'd ever experienced, it was transcendental. He drew her face to his shoulder, encouraging her to feed too. He sighed in gratification when she stabbed her teeth into his flesh and began feeding. She was right, the Dark One's voice faded into nothing. The moment Alexander relaxed and savoured the silence, he was struck with a vision of Wigmore Castle on fire.

Makayla flung her head back, a guttural scream wrenched from her body.

"Noooooooooo, not Emily!"

CHAPTER 38.

Darrius stared at the smouldering shell of his ancestral home and grasped his father's shuddering shoulder. He concentrated on sending his father calming thoughts, dispersing strength into his psyche. It depleted his energy, but it was all he could do to comfort the man who'd always been there for him after Lorena's death. He was no stranger to grief, but even he couldn't switch off the sadness of Emily's death. He drew in a shaky breath and rallied his emotions trying to harden his heart against the numbing ache and piece his father's shattered emotions back together. His father's devastation poured into him, overwhelming him with sadness; Darrius's strength was all his father had now. Tears streaked down Darrius's cheeks, he straightened his back and brushed them away with a shaking hand. He gritted his teeth, the tightness in his chest a constricting pressure he recognised all too well; it was the pressure of loss, of sadness and utter desolation.

When Darrius had arrived at Wigmore Castle, he'd found his inconsolable father on his knees at the foot of Adrian's grave, rocking back and forth. He'd left the compound the moment he'd heard from Vasili and informed the Shadow Seekers of the unfolding events at his parents' home and advised them to ready themselves for battle.

"Makayla, come home, Zobiana attacked Wigmore Castle. Mother's missing and Emily's dead." Darrius sent the thought out to Makayla for the fourth time hoping she'd hear him; there was no sugar-coating the news of his younger sister's passing. He needed Makayla. He'd already contacted Tristan, and he was on his way, but how he wished Makayla were here to heal their father's shattered emotions Darrius could already sense his father's heart deteriorating; he wouldn't last long.

Morgan stood next to him, tears streaming down her face. She wound her fingers with his and he felt her strength bolstering his; her offering helped relieve the pain in his chest. He squeezed her hand in thanks and gazed about his surroundings.

Ashley stood next to Morgan, holding her sister's other hand. Jackson was leaning on a tree to Ashley's left, along with Anna and Reece. Gabriel, Bryce and Vasili stood off to the side, deep in conversation. Lazarus stood by himself on the fringe of the group staring at the curtain wall. It was the only part of the castle that hadn't suffered damage from the fire. His eyes were focused on a spot closer to the centre. What could he see that Darrius couldn't? By the grim expression he wore, something of importance had captured his attention.

Makayla's words had haunted him ever since they'd spoken about Lazarus on the rooftop; she trusted him because he'd saved her life countless times. Had he misjudged Lazarus's intent all these years? Had he been as much a victim of his brother as Darrius? Lazarus had maintained his innocence for centuries, his story never altering, and he had apologised many times for the part he'd played in Kraegan's act of revenge and barbarity. Had Lazarus's warnings about Makayla been born of genuine worry for her and Darrius's family?

Darrius studied Lazarus's features; the frown on his face emphasised the jagged scars more than usual – he wasn't masking them as well as he normally did, his concentration divided. It gave his face a lethal, hard edge. He was just as scarred as Darrius.

Lazarus noticed Darrius watching him, his eyebrow raised as he motioned him over. Darrius released Morgan's hand and moved towards him. Lazarus guided him towards the curtain wall. He looked back towards the scattered group of Shadow Seekers before focusing his attention on Darrius once more.

Lazarus pointed to some dark markings on the wall. "See here, and here," he indicated different portions of the wall. "See how the pattern swirls and arcs in a spiralling motion?"

Darrius focused on the unusual pattern. "What about it?"

"These markings were once a portal opening; these specific

markings are Zobiana's, like a signature – a thumbprint if you will."

"How do you know?"

Lazarus looked Darrius in the eye. "Because I've seen markings like these before."

"Where?"

"In our family crypt, on a wall where my brother's body used to lay."

"Where your brother's body *used* to lay? What are you saying?"

"Kraegan's body disappeared from our family crypt not long after his funeral, and similar markings to these—" he indicated the black residue on the curtain wall "—were the only evidence of his disappearance."

"Someone stole his body," Darrius choked out. "Why, why would they do that?"

"We don't know, his disappearance has mystified us for years; the black residue on the wall was the only evidence we had. Which basically means it was a dead-end, excuse the pun."

"So, what are you trying to say, Lazarus?

"Zobiana made this portal."

"Yes, we've established that, but what has this got to do with your brother's body disappearing?" Darrius queried.

"That's the thing; it has everything to do with it. The markings left behind in our family crypt are identical to this one. Now I'm certain the portal residue in our family crypt was made by Zobiana."

Darrius felt lightheaded and his breath caught in his throat at the mere mention of Kraegan. "Why would Zobiana steal Kraegan's body?"

"I don't know if you're aware, but my brother was once Zobiana's apprentice before Beltizare. On top of that, they had a special bond; my brother would often brag about her." Lazarus scratched his head in thought. "It's just more proof she's been manipulating everything from the beginning and has been conspiring with my father all along. I think they plan on overthrowing the senate and reinstating the monarchy. She's taking Evron or probably already has."

"And you have deduced this from a few black scratchings on a wall?"

"Who else could bring my brother back to life? Nobody but Zobiana."

"Kraegan's alive?" Darrius gasped. "No, it's impossible, vampires can't bring the dead back to life."

"We're talking about Zobiana; anything's possible when it comes to her. Why else would she steal his body? Makayla and I suspect he's alive, but we don't have proof yet."

"Anyone loyal to Zobiana could have helped her; it doesn't mean it was Kraegan."

"It's the only thing that makes sense. How else do you think Zobiana got her hands on Augustus's vault key? How else do you think she got the Trinian Globe? She had help. Someone who hides in the darkness, someone in disguise who can manipulate the shadows, who's supposed to be dead; someone who only ever wears black, hooded clothing to mask his appearance? He is the perfect, loyal soldier."

Darrius placed his hand on the wall for support.

"Are you okay, Darrius?"

"Mm-hmm." He shook his head, trying to overcome the terror rushing through him. If he couldn't conquer the living dread he felt every time Kraegan's name was mentioned then he'd be a miserable source of stability for his father, or for anyone he cared about.

"Darrius, are you sure? I know it's a surprise. I promise, if he's alive, I will finish him, I will end him even if it kills me. God knows the bastard deserves to die."

Darrius removed his hand from the wall and straightened his posture. "Morgan saw a man dressed in a black, old-fashioned, hooded three-quarter-length jacket leaving the infirmary."

Lazarus was about to say something when the wind picked up, scattering the leaves and lifting the dirt off the ground in a funnelling coil. Makayla materialised with Alexander in a flash of blinding light and the ground shuddered as Salomae landed nearby.

Makayla hugged Darrius and stepped back. "What happened?"

"Zobiana happened, Mother's gone, Emily's—"

"—Fine. She's with Danny. He arrived just in time and got her and Izador out. He killed three Newbloods in the process, but they're safe."

"Oh, thank God, we assumed she was dead. Baba was mumbling something about Zobiana taking Mother and Emily being dead. He fell to pieces after that."

"As soon as you contacted me I lost it too, but then I realised there was a chance she was still alive and got in contact with Danny. I made him promise to protect her."

"But how did he know they were in trouble?"

"He was the one who found the Sandalius wolf pup for Emily; he bears the bite mark of Izador like Emily – he's connected to them both, that's how he knew they were in trouble. He had a vision. Where's Baba?" Even as she asked, Makayla saw him huddled on the ground by Adrian's grave. She hugged Lazarus before moving towards her father.

Darrius shook Alexander's hand in greeting, as did Lazarus. "It's good to see you, Xander," he said, as they made their way back towards Adrian's grave.

"It's good to be seen, Darrius. You too, Lazarus." Alexander smiled in greeting.

Makayla bobbed down in front of her father and brushed the hair from his face. She swallowed the lump in her throat when she saw his haggard appearance. "Baba, are you okay?" He didn't respond. Makayla sat on the ground beside him and rubbed her hands together. They grew warm from the friction and glowed with gold sparkling light. The light threaded up her arms until it immersed her body. She placed her hands on either side of her father's face and he sighed and closed his eyes. The hairs on her arms stiffened as the warmth from her hands transferred into her father's body. His head tilted back and his back stiffened as her healing light bled into his convulsing body. Makayla closed her eyes and slid her hands down his face and throat until they rested over his heart. In her mind's eye she could see blue ice expanding from the middle of his chest as if it was freezing. His irregular heartbeats were worrying so she focused on sending the warmth of her love straight into the muscle, it shuddered for a moment before growing stronger. Makayla opened her eyes and noticed her father watching her.

"She's dead, Makayla, Emily's gone, and Zobiana took your mother."

"Emily's alive, Baba. Danny saved her, she's safe, and we will get Mama back."

Her father's eye's widened. "Emily's alive?"

Makayla nodded. "Yes, she's safe."

"Oh, thank goodness." He tugged her into his embrace. Makayla hugged him back, she understood him now, so much more than she'd been able to when she'd first met him.

"We need to leave here, Makayla. It's not safe," Vasili said, holding out his hand to her.

Makayla's mouth dropped. "Vasili, is that you, what, what happened, you look so young."

Vasili beamed. "My wife's back in my life, all thanks to you. If it weren't for you and Lazarus she would have been lost forever."

"I didn't do much." Makayla grasped his hand and he pulled her up from the ground. "Lazarus is the one who saved her, you should be thanking him, not me."

As she turned to help her father, she saw Tristan already helping him to his feet. Makayla dusted down her trousers. "When did you get here, Tristan? I didn't see you here when I arrived."

He flexed his hands and wiggled his fingers. "I got here when you were doing your magic act."

Makayla chuckled. "Where were you? I thought you'd be here."

"Ecktar contacted me." Tristan eyed Vasili. "It's bad news, I'm afraid. All the Zoldarni emissaries on Earth were murdered."

Vasili shook his head. "We feared the worst when we found the London contingent dead."

"Zobiana's getting all her ducks in a row," Sebastian said. "She controls Evron now, she said as much when I spoke to her. I have five days to return to Evron, a matter of hours by Evron's timing. She wants to reinstate the monarchy and take the throne and she's using Ambrosia as a bargaining chip."

"I feel like I should throw a joke in here somewhere, but for the life of me, I can't think of anything funny to say," Reece said.

"When have your jokes ever been funny, Reece?" Morgan scratched her head in thought. "Let me think, NEVER!"

"I don't think now's the right time for a joke." Makayla

shook her head and glanced about. "Hey, where's Zack? I thought he'd be here."

"Zack's testing his theory regarding the farms with Thomas and a few fledgling Shadow Seekers," Gabriel said. "He wanted to see if he could hack the computers at the small farm using telekinesis before he attempts hacking the mainframe."

The ground shuddered and everyone stilled, staring at Salomae who was mere metres from them. She was shimmering gold, the fire light from the burning remains of the castle reflecting off her scales like shot silk. Makayla looked up at her; Salomae moved closer and snorted before lowering her face to Makayla's. Makayla nodded, glancing towards the tree line circumnavigating Wigmore Castle and searching the murky shadows for Zobiana's spies. She glanced back towards Salomae and lifted her hand to her cheek. "We've got to leave, we're being watched, it's not safe here, Salomae senses danger nearby."

Vasili glanced about. *"Back to the compound now,"* he communicated into their minds.

Makayla moved towards her father, to help him.

"It's okay, I'll take him," Tristan said.

Darrius placed his hand on Tristan's back and nodded before moving towards Morgan and Ashley. He took their hands and they disappeared, Reece and Anna were next to leave, then Bryce, Vasili, Gabriel and Jackson.

"And then there were two," Alexander said, looking about.

"Sorry, Salomae, I meant three," he corrected.

"You can hear her now?"

Alexander caressed Salomae's cheek; Makayla heard the soothing rumble in the back of Salomae's throat as she purred, ten times louder than a cat.

"Yes, I can hear her." Alexander looked from Salomae to Makayla. "She's right, someone is watching us. Zobiana has her spies; she has always had her spies."

"Come on, let's go." Makayla grabbed his hand and thought about dematerialising to the compound. Nothing happened. She tried again, and again, nothing. "Xander, I can't dematerialise."

"What, why?"

"I don't know; looks like we're flying out," Makayla said, worry clouding her thoughts.

Alexander stripped off his clothes to shapeshift into eagle form. "You just wanted to see me naked again, right."

"Hah, seeing you naked is always a bonus, even under these circumstances, but sorry to disappoint, no."

"Your eyes say otherwise." He grinned, winking as he removed his shoes and then his jeans.

"Maybe, just a little." She rolled her shoulders, the itch prickling between her shoulder blades was nothing new and her muscles tensed as the burning sensation gathered. She breathed in and exhaled, sparkling light gathering about her as her wings manifested in a burst of showering sparks. She unfurled her six wings, stretching them out to their full wingspan and flexed her muscles, fluttering her feathers. She looked across at Alexander; he stood watching her with a soft smile curling the corners of his lips.

"That never gets old. You truly are the most exquisite thing I've ever seen."

"I think you're biased." Makayla smiled and shot into the air.

"Maybe I am," Alexander murmured.

Makayla looked down and sighed when she saw Alexander's body morph into the wedge-tailed eagle. It had been an age since she'd seen him in eagle form. Salomae flapped her own giant wings, disturbing the dust and leaves on the ground. Alexander spread his wings and both he and Salomae lifted into the air. Makayla jetted off and they followed; the icy wind whipped her hair about her face as she found her rhythm.

The landscape below had changed somewhat, there were no longer lights marking the way to London. The power-grid had failed months ago, plunging everything into darkness. There were buildings on fire throughout the area, and the occasional building with power – those smart few who had the foresight to install solar panels and go off the grid. She'd always gravitated towards the night. Things didn't seem so bad, so hopeless, even in the direst of circumstances. The darkness hid the ruins of a once bustling, healthy city. It was what she'd liked most about going back in time; no man-made light to hinder the stars in the night sky.

She glanced to her right, Alexander flew beside her, he looked different somehow, larger. He opened his mouth and a sharp eagle's cry cut the silence. He moved closer, and it was then she noticed what was causing the difference: flames curled off the tips of his outer feathers; the edges of his wings were on fire. He closed his wings to his body and dove in a spinning arc, the flames forming a corkscrew of intertwining orange lines like a plume of coloured smoke behind an acrobatic aeroplane. He opened his wings and orange cinders sprayed out about his body as the air caught and shot him back up on the wind currents. Was the fire a result of his transition? Had he inherited her ability to manipulate fire or was it the darker part, a side effect of his newly acquired passenger?

CHAPTER 39.

Ambrosia gritted her teeth as Abigail pulled her along by the chains attached to her shackles. Ambrosia had tried to melt the chains with seraph fire, but had no success. Abigail hadn't been lying when she'd said she'd not escape her bonds. They were back on Evron. She couldn't remember the last time she'd been there – it had been years. Ambrosia had missed her home planet; it was so different from Earth. On the horizon the sun was setting, framing the dark mountain peaks in striking shades of purple, reds and pinks. Where the Earth's skies were a cerulean blue, Evron's was a light shade of pink.

Ambrosia focused her attention on her surroundings. Peculiar shaped buildings towered above them, making them seem at odds with gravity. They were passing through a large courtyard. A monument sat in the centre of the open space with seats positioned around its base. Ambrosia looked up at the monument as they passed; jutting steel beams arched over their heads in decorative coils, an artist's labour of love. But what really surprised Ambrosia was the lack of people. She remembered the courtyard bustling with people at day's end but now it was like a ghost town.

Where was everyone? Where were her people? There wasn't a single seraph or seraph guard about. The seraph gateways in the vicinity stood empty and unmanned. Ambrosia squinted as she passed another gateway, looking for something, anything, and then she saw it. They'd deactivated the gateway with a black-stoned gateway key. Seraphs hadn't shut the gateway down, if they had, the stone in the centre of the gateway key would have been pure gold.

They were close enough to the council chambers and on neutral ground to expect at least one or two seraph councilmen wandering about. Vampires and seraphs usually mingled near the council chambers, but all Ambrosia could see were Lilith's people. When had she gained control of the gateways? Surely she didn't control the seraph gateways too? To have achieved such a thing on such a grand scale had to have taken years to mastermind. Lilith had been banished decades ago, millennia by Earth's time. It appeared she'd been busy.

Things were different on Evron, very different, and it worried her. Where was her father? He wouldn't have allowed such a thing to happen to Evron, not in the old days anyhow. Ambrosia ran into Abigail's back, not realising she'd stopped in front of an intricately carved red door. It stood ten feet tall and six feet wide – Abigail banged her hand on it. After a short time the door eased open. Two regal vampires, dressed in the black robes of the Vampire Council, stood blocking the entrance but they moved aside to allow them passage when Abigail acknowledged them. Ambrosia refused to take a step further and held her position, the chains pulling tight.

Abigail looked over her shoulder and sneered. "Get your arse in here."

Ambrosia looked her up and down and then focused her attention on the two council members standing either side of the door. "Deceivers, shame on you, your king will hear of this. Mark my words, your lives are forfeit."

Abigail yanked the chain and Ambrosia held strong, stumbling when Tyrone pushed her from behind.

"Move or I will pick you up by the hair and move you myself," Tyrone threatened.

"When the time is right, Lord Tyrone, your throat will meet my sword and sing the gurgling song of death."

"You're delusional, woman. It will take someone far stronger than you to end me!" Tyrone pushed her again.

"Betrayers, I will end you both!" Ambrosia yelled over her shoulder at the vampire councilmen as they dragged her away.

Abigail stopped walking and faced Ambrosia. "You'll end nothing, you'll never see the light of day again, the only thing you'll be seeing are dungeon walls and perhaps maybe a few rodents. I hope you're not scared of cockroaches because there are plenty of those little suckers where you're going. Well.

Evron's version of cockroaches." Abigail laughed and spun back the way she was heading, pulling Ambrosia forward again.

"After I finish with them I'm coming for you, Abigail."

"I don't see how that will be possible, have you heard a single word I've said?" Abigail said in a bored monotone.

Ambrosia fell silent and followed behind her children's former nanny. How had she and Sebastian been so blind to Abigail's obvious hatred of them? How had Abigail hidden her animosity so well? Ambrosia shook her head thinking of Adrian's small, shrivelled form, dead on the rug in his bedroom. Abigail had killed her son, of that she was sure; the bitch would pay. Ambrosia eyed the chains in Abigail's loose grip and smiled. Tyrone had lingered to talk to the council members behind her. She coiled her fingers around the chain to get a better grip and wrenched the chain free from Abigail's hand. With lightning speed Ambrosia looped the chain over Abigail's head and pulled until it was constricting her throat. She drew her up against her body and lowered her mouth to Abigail's ear. "I heard every word you said, but did you hear me?" Ambrosia pulled the chain tighter and heard crunching bones as the chains bit into the flesh of Abigail's neck. "Not so tough now, are you?" She threw Abigail's words back in her face. Abigail gasped for oxygen, her face turning red and her eyes bulging.

"There'll be none of that," Tyrone said from behind them. Ambrosia turned towards him, but couldn't move fast enough, not when Abigail was almost pulling her to the floor.

THUNK.

Bone-crunching pain lanced Ambrosia's skull, her vision blurred and then only blackness.

Uriel and Augustus stared down into the courtyard as Newbloods infiltrated the area. Augustus's head still reeled from what he'd learned. He'd found a secret compartment in Malachi's desk – not Augustus's original desk, but a replica. To the average eye, Malachi's desk appeared to be the same as Augustus's, but it had minute differences Augustus had noticed at once. His desk had been in his family for generations, handed down from father to son. Although it had secret compartments, the ones in his desk were magical, Unlike in Malachi's fake desk.

Things were far worse than either he or Uriel had suspected. The gateways in the vampire territory had been under Malachi and Lilith's control for some time. They'd deactivated most of the gateways, not all at once, but gradually. Malachi had implemented the closures during the years he'd masqueraded as chancellor. He'd maintained the gateways were a security risk to the vampire nation. Gateway keys were fashioned to lock the gateways indefinitely; keys with black, multifaceted hematite stones. The irony of it all wasn't lost on Augustus. When crushed to powder and mixed with water, the liquid residue of hematite stones resembled blood. Blood was the symbol of the vampire nation.

Uriel's gasp and the slap of his hand against the window brought Augustus back to the present. He rested his hand on Uriel's shoulder and cringed when he saw Abigail and Tyrone pushing Ambrosia, shackled, towards the Vampire Council chamber door.

"Where do you think they're taking her?" Uriel asked, his eyes never leaving his daughter.

"The dungeons, I would imagine."

"Dungeons? It's a council building, there shouldn't even be dungeons in there."

"There aren't, but there are passages hidden beneath the council building leading to the dungeons. The only way to get to them is by entering the council building itself."

Uriel frowned at Augustus. "Do you know of any other way to get into the tunnels without detection?"

Augustus smiled. "I do, Sebastian told me many things the day he made me chancellor. I was oblivious to the tunnels' existence before that." Augustus glanced out the window again just as the red door opened. His body tensed and he narrowed his eyes when he saw two Vampire Council members open the door and step aside for Abigail and Tyrone. The crack of his jaw echoed in his ears as he clenched his teeth together. "I knew it," he murmured.

Uriel turned his attention back to the courtyard. "How many is that now, Gus? How many council members have been compromised?"

"More than half; eight in all. Only four of us have stayed true – myself, Sebastian and the two councilmen, Tydias and Selza, whom I encountered when I first arrived."

"Have you contacted them? Do you think they'll help us?"

"They're afraid, and rightly so. I explained what happened to me and they were shocked and appalled by Malachi and Lilith's deception."

"But will they help?"

"Yes, I believe so."

"Good, we need to rally the Seraph and Vampire Guard loyal to us and save my daughter." Uriel brushed a hand across his forehead. "Do you think Sebastian's still alive?"

"Oh he's alive, Lilith wants to be queen and she can't do that without Sebastian; she'll have given him an ultimatum using Ambrosia as leverage. I'm concerned about Ambrosia. If Lilith removes her from the equation, we're in trouble. There's no telling how Sebastian will react, but—" Augustus held his finger in the air "—I don't think Lilith will kill Ambrosia. It's too easy. She wants to control Sebastian and the best way to do that is to hide Ambrosia away like she did with Vasili and Marianna. If we don't find Ambrosia fast, we may never find her. I think the council dungeons are temporary lodgings until they find a more secure place to imprison your daughter. We need to act now while there's still a chance of finding her."

"Vasili's rallying his forces as we speak, and Makayla will come for her mother along with her father and brothers." Uriel looked out of the window once more. "I worry, though, how many of the Vampire Guard on Earth are loyal to us and how many are loyal to Malachi and Lilith?" Uriel met Augustus's worried stare. "We need to stop Lilith once and for all, Gus. We should have executed her when she killed my wife all those years ago."

"You're right, Uri, but it would have caused outright war. We need to be smart; we can't go in with our guns blazing. We need to think this through, we have to come up with a plan. I'll meet you back here in an hour. Bring your most trustworthy men and we'll rescue Ambrosia before the end of the day."

Cold water shocked Ambrosia awake, a thousand ice-cold needles pricking into her skin. Her body trembled, the ice water was a river of hurt. She rolled to her side on the hard rock floor and regretted it. Groaning, she touched the back of her skull, trying to avoid causing more pain. There was an egg-sized knot at the base of her skull.

"Wake up, this isn't a leisure cruise," a gruff voice yelled at her. It echoed about the room penetrating her skull and sending spiralling pain through her skull. "Wake up," the gruff voice repeated as he threw more cold water on her.

"All right. . . all right, I'm awake, enough with the ice water."

"Oh dear, methinks she's cold," a feminine voice lilted.

Ambrosia recognised Lilith's voice immediately. She opened her eyes, little by little. Lilith was sitting in a gaudy gold throne opposite her, bedecked in black armour, a pointy black crown atop her regal head. She tapped her fingers on the arm of her throne as she eyed Ambrosia. Ambrosia laughed, ignoring the stabbing pain in her skull, her laughter echoed about the room; a room she surmised was a dungeon cell. Chains rattled as Ambrosia pushed up into a sitting position and leaned her back against the wall. She swept wet hair out of her eyes and angled her head as she looked Lilith up and down.

"A little overdressed aren't we, Lilith? Given our location, I'm surprised you'd bring a throne into these lowly accommodations. I must apologise, I'd offer you a cup of tea, but I'm indisposed at the moment." She lifted her hands and shook the chains. "You understand. Although I'm afraid if I *could* get you a cup of tea the temptation to lace it with poison would be too great. I see you're still harbouring the pathetic pipe-dream of becoming queen."

"Oh, I don't know, Ambrosia, the pipe-dream you speak of will be a reality soon. Sebastian will come around, I have your life to barter with, don't I? Before long Sebastian will draw up the divorce papers and make me his queen."

Laughter burst out of Ambrosia's mouth again. "That's hilarious; you don't know him very well, do you? Sebastian doesn't want to be king, he never did. You have the wrong brother; it was always Malachi who wanted that position, not Sebastian."

"Oh, I wouldn't worry, I have Malachi in my corner too. How else would I have been able to take over Evron? Evron has been mine for years," Lilith boasted.

"You're delusional." Ambrosia shook her head. "Take your throne, your crown, and your pretty little arse and leave me in peace. I have things to do, like sleep."

Lilith smirked. "As you wish. Rest now, you'll need all your strength for what's coming." She rose and nodded at the guard before leaving the room. Two Newbloods rushed in and picked up the throne, almost tripping over their feet as they carried it out. The Vampire Guard looked down at her for a moment before turning to follow.

"Pheleon, is that you?" Ambrosia asked before he departed.

He stopped in the doorway and looked over his shoulder at her. "Yes, your majesty." His voice was no longer gruff, but held warmth; he checked the corridor and then returned his gaze to her. "Sorry for the cold water, majesty."

Ambrosia saw the shame and worry in his eyes. "It's okay, Pheleon, you'd best be on your way." Ambrosia closed her eyes and relaxed against the wall. She jumped when the dungeon door slammed and calmed when she heard keys rattling as Pheleon locked the door.

Ambrosia laughed anew. She hadn't seen Pheleon in years, but felt comforted by his presence. Lilith was in for a surprise.

Pheleon hooked the dungeon keychain to his belt and leaned

against the door to Ambrosia's cell. He closed his eyes before sweeping his hand through his mussed hair and glancing in the direction Lilith had gone. Two Vampire Guards were heading away from him. He peered over his shoulder through the door grate; Ambrosia rested against the wall with her eyes closed and a radiant grin on her face. He exhaled and moved away; the two guards would return soon enough. He checked the passageway one more time, making sure no one was about before heading in the opposite direction. Time was short; he only had a small window of opportunity to do what he must.

CHAPTER 40.

Danny placed another log on the fire before turning towards Emily and Izador. Emily was asleep, curled up in his king-size bed, and Izador lay on the floor nearby. Danny sat on the edge of the bed. It was the first time he'd seen Makayla's sister in the flesh. She wasn't what he'd expected and looked nothing like Makayla, though she shared similarities with her father and Darrius. Danny picked the teddy bear up off the floor where it had fallen and placed it in Emily's arms before pulling the coverlet up over her shoulders. He brushed a long strand of dark hair from her eyes, noticing the burnished copper tones as he swept it behind her ear. Something had changed, he had a fierce need to protect her; it was a foreign feeling he'd never experienced. When he'd seen the Newbloods threatening her he'd lost control of the demonic vampire part of himself. The last time the demon had taken control he'd gone on a killing spree; he'd been ruthless.

Danny feared he'd traumatised young Emily by the way he'd dealt with the Newbloods, but she'd taken it in her stride and seemed unaffected by his brutality. Still, he believed Izador had been the sole reason behind her acceptance.

Moments after leaving Wigmore Castle and returning to his home, Makayla had contacted him. He'd quickly calmed her fears and reassured her Emily was safe and unharmed. Danny looked up and stared at the cracks in the corners where the walls met the ceiling. Small spiders crawled along finely crafted cobwebs that hung like miniature hammocks in the corners, collecting dust and the odd stray insect that ventured too close. Danny hung his head and exhaled the breath he'd been holding, staring at the shag pile carpet. He balanced his elbows on his knees and covered his face. He couldn't stay out of the fight any longer; as much as he wanted to remain anonymous, he couldn't ignore the atrocities being committed in the world by Zobiana and her followers. He couldn't ignore who he was and who he was meant to be.

He felt a fluttering soft touch on his arm and lowered his hands from his face to see Emily's small hand. "Don't be sad," she said.

"I'm not sad, sweetheart, just a little tired."

"You should get some sleep," she said in a matter-of-fact voice, patting the empty space on the bed beside her.

He chuckled. "It's not that kind of tired, honey. I'm tired of all the death, all the killing. I left that world and the fight centuries ago. I've been here in Greece hiding away, running my restaurant trying to separate myself from the atrocities that happen in this world and I nearly succeeded until—"

"Until me," Emily said, a sad look flitting over her face. "Sorry."

"No, no, don't be sorry, honey, it's not your fault, it's mine. I can't fight what I am anymore. I'm a monster. I've been in denial for the longest time and have to accept who I am, but I don't know how. I should never have left Makayla's side, but I, I . . . just couldn't stay. Our anger combined was not a great mix; it was eating me up alive and feeding the demon inside me."

"You're not a monster, you're beautiful. I've seen pictures like you before in books in our library. Please don't tell my parents, they'd be angry I was reading them." She smiled sheepishly.

Danny's mouth dropped. "When you say pictures, what type of pictures are you talking about?"

"What you were when you saved me. You're not a demon, well you sort of are, but not really. You're an incubus."

Danny opened and closed his mouth several times and then scratched his head in thought, how had he missed it? It took a child to see. He stood and moved to the centre of the room. "But how do you explain these?" Danny rolled his head from side to side and rolled his shoulders. He felt the familiar itch as the muscles bunched between his shoulder blades. The room grew bright as sparks of light flared from his body and six huge black wings sprang from his back. He extended them to their full wingspan, the gold-edged tips of his blue-black feathers touching the walls on either side of the room. He looked towards Emily.

Emily threw the bed covers back and sat up. "Wow, you're a seraphympire just like me," she murmured in wonder.

"Am I? I don't know."

"Yes, yes you are, you have six wings like seraphs do and you are a vampire. An incubus is more or less a vampire, just more evolved," Emily stated.

Danny bit his tongue. He was more than an evolved vampire. He was a demon predator who preyed on women in their deepest dreams, encouraging erotic dreams where he'd play out their deepest, darkest sexual fantasies. Emily didn't need to know about his baser sexual appetites; appetites he'd managed to control all his life.

Izador lifted his head and yipped. "See, even Izzy agrees," Emily confirmed happily.

Danny's wings disappeared into his body as he glanced down at the wolf and noticed his eyes had changed, one eye was violet, just like Emily's and the other was gold edged in black, resembling his eyes. *That's weird,* he thought to himself.

"How old are you, Emily?" Danny asked, sitting on the bed next to her.

"I'm twelve."

"You look much younger than twelve; I thought you were about eight or nine. If you're twelve why do you have a teddy bear?"

"It was Adrian's, my brother's. He died."

"Oh, I'm sorry about your brother." Danny fumbled to change the topic before he upset her. "How do you know so much about incubi?" Danny asked, changing the topic.

"Ah, did I mention we have a very large library?"

"Sorry, kids these days seem to know more than they did when I was growing up."

"I told you how old I am, but how old are you?"

"Oh, I'm an old man, too old," he chuckled and touched the tip of her freckled nose.

Emily's eyes widened, she grabbed his arm and pulled it towards her. "You have one too," she said, pointing at the scar on his right wrist where Izador had bitten him. She pulled back her sleeve and showed him a similar scar.

Danny nodded. "Yes, I do . . ." He snapped his mouth shut and almost bit his tongue when he realised what that meant.

BANG. BANG. BANG.

Danny glanced towards the back of his house. *Guard her with your life,'* he told Izzy, who yipped twice.

"Stay here, Emily." He removed a dagger from the leg holster on his jeans and handed it to her. "Just in case."

He crossed the room, removing one of his Samurai swords from the leather sheath hanging on a hook by the bedroom door. He edged his way towards the back door.

BANG. BANG. BANG.

"Danté Delacruize, would you open this bloody door

~ 475 ~

before I break it down?"

Danny relaxed when he recognised Makayla's impatient voice. He lowered his sword and leaned it up against the wall before opening the door. Makayla stood frowning on his back porch. Alexander behind her with a wide grin on his face, he pushed past her and grabbed Danny in a bear hug, lifting him off the ground as he walked inside. He lowered Danny to the ground and thumped him on the back a few more times before hugging him again.

Danny hugged him back. "Xander, it does me good to see you, old friend, how long has it been?"

"Too long; four hundred years too long."

Makayla shoved them out of the way as Emily came dashing into the room and bent down just as she jumped into her arms. "Hi sweet-pea, I'm so glad you're safe. You had everyone worried."

"Hey Makayla, are Mama and Baba okay? Did they get out?"

Danny turned towards Makayla and Emily and knew something was wrong.

"Baba's okay, but—"

"Makayla," Alexander said in a hushed tone.

Makayla glanced at Alexander, he shook his head. "I will not sugar-coat it and wrap her in cotton wool, Xander, she needs to hear the truth, she's not a baby." Makayla looked back into Emily's upturned face. "Sweetie, Zobiana took Mama, and destroyed Wigmore Castle. It was burned to the ground, there's nothing left but the outer walls."

Danny felt a tightness in his throat when he saw Emily's bottom lip tremble and her eyes pool with tears. The protective instinct kicked into gear, he was about to say something when he noticed Emily straighten her back and swallow down the tears. "What are you going to do about it, Makayla?" she asked in a trembling voice. She glanced at Alexander before looking back at her sister. "You saved Alexander, you can save, Mama too, I know you can."

"I will." Makayla nodded. "I will, honey, but sometimes things happen and we don't always succeed. I will do my best to bring Mama home, and if I can't, I will destroy everyone who gets in my way, and if I die, I will take as many of them with me as I can."

Emily lowered her head to Makayla's chest. "Okay, if you can't kill Zobiana, kill Abigail, she deserves to die for what she did to Adrian."

Danny snapped his mouth closed for the second time that day, Makayla's honesty and frankness with her sister was refreshing. People usually sheltered their children from the harsh realities of life, but not Makayla. He felt honesty and frankness was important too. He'd sensed a deeper maturity in Emily from the beginning; the death of her brother was, no doubt, the reason.

"You guys hungry? Do you wanna drink something?" he asked. "I know I could use a drink right about now."

Makayla lowered Emily to the ground. "It's past your

bedtime, sweetie. Come on I'll tuck you in." Makayla pointed towards Danny's bedroom, he nodded and watched her lead Emily towards his room, Izador following obediently behind. Danny watched the bedroom door close and glanced towards Alexander, who was propped against the door to his restaurant bar.

Alexander's eyebrow lifted as he indicated the bar area with the nod of his head. "We need to talk."

Danny looked towards his bedroom door once more before moving in Alexander's direction. They closed the door behind them as they passed into the bar area. Alexander plopped down on a barstool and pointed at a bottle of Jack Daniels on a shelf behind the bar. Danny grabbed the bottle of whiskey from the shelf and two glass tumblers from underneath the bar. He filled a bucket with ice and placed it next to the glasses. Alexander was already filling the glasses with whiskey and ice cubes by the time Danny sat.

"How bad was it?" Danny asked, as Alexander pushed a glass in front of him.

"Pretty bad. Zobiana and her army of Newbloods were gone by the time we got there. Darrius was the first to arrive and found Sebastian by Adrian's grave; he thought Emily was dead. How did you know she was in trouble?"

Danny pointed at the scar on his wrist. "It's the bite of a Sandalius wolf. After Emily was taken by Zobiana, Makayla asked me for help, I suggested finding a Sandalius wolf to protect her sister, they're great guards and loyal companions.

"Alexander whistled. "They're also very extinct, where did you find him?"

Danny smiled. "I went Off World and tracked down someone who deals with locating exotic species. Izador was very hard to find, I got lucky. He's officially the last of his breed. His parents were killed by trophy hunters; bloody idiots didn't realise what they'd killed. They were more interested in putting giant wolf heads on their walls. I paid a fortune for him, but what's money when you've lived as long as we have? And I'd do anything for Makayla; she's saved my life too many times to count."

"Has the wolf bitten Emily as well?" Alexander asked, taking another mouthful of whiskey.

Danny nodded before gulping down the contents of his glass. The whiskey hit his belly and the warmth radiated outwards. "Do you think Makayla will be pissed? I've only just found out Emily has a scar too."

"If the scar is on the same arm as Emily's you're in the clear, but if it's on the opposite arm to yours, well, you know what that means." Xander finished his drink and refilled his glass.

Danny rubbed his forehead. "It's in the same spot on the opposite arm. What am I going to do, Xander? I'm the last person Emily needs to be attached to. I had no control, and I never intended for this to happen."

"Never intended for what to happen?" Makayla said, pulling up a barstool and sitting next to Alexander.

Alexander chuckled.

Danny retrieved a glass tumbler from beneath the bar and filled it with ice and poured Makayla some whiskey. "We've been talking about Emily's Sandalius wolf."

"He's amazing, best idea you ever had, Danny." Makayla clinked her glass against his and skulled the contents.

"What was it you wanted to talk about, Xander?" Danny asked, deliberately changing the subject.

Alexander took another draught of his whiskey before speaking. "When I was held prisoner in Zobiana's dungeons I was tortured for information regarding the Gem of Sorrows and the Trinian Globe's location." Alexander went on to explain how they'd tricked Zobiana with the fake gem, and how he'd ended up possessed by the Dark One.

"Fuck." Danny stood up abruptly and paced back and forth behind the bar. "What are you going to do, how are you going to keep the Dark One from taking control of your body?"

"I carved a sigil on my chest, it seems to keep him at bay."

Danny stopped pacing and faced Alexander. "That won't work for long. The longer he's in your body, the weaker you'll become. Sooner or later the sigil will stop working and he'll slowly take away your memories until you no longer exist. No, we've got to get him out, you need to be exorcised."

"Makayla and I have spoken about doing an exorcism, but it's risky. I have some ancient scrolls and books regarding the Dark One, and they all say exorcisms are dangerous. I need to speak to a theologian or a priest who's an expert and deals with exorcisms." Alexander swept his hand through his hair and glanced at Makayla.

"Well, you're in the right place for an exorcism. I know a Greek priest who you could speak with who would be willing to do one for you. There's a small Greek Orthodox church not far from here where he preaches."

"You speak as though you've experienced an exorcism." Makayla eyed him.

"I've lived in Greece for a long time and I've seen a lot of strange things here that can't be explained. I've even assisted in my fair share of exorcisms. Pater Nikolao often asks for my help. I don't know why he chose me, but he came to me one day out of the blue and asked for my help, maybe he sensed I was different. I was curious and said yes. We've become good friends. The people here think of me as their protector. In a way I am, I mean I don't age and have always defended this small village against evil. They think I'm a demigod sent to them from Zeus."

"I'm game," Alexander said, looking at Makayla and shrugging. "What could it hurt? I'll try anything once. Do you think you could set something up as soon as possible?"

"Sure."

"I thought you said it was dangerous, Xander?"

"It is dangerous, but no more dangerous than leaving the Dark One in Xander's body," Danny said.

"Set it up, Danny. In the meantime, we need to find the remaining Trinian gems and get back to the compound,"

Alexander said, rising from his seat.

"Xander, you should stay here while I locate the two remaining gems, you said it yourself, it would be dangerous if you come with me. When I locate them, I'll come back and we can go to the compound together. I'll try to get back before the priest performs the exorcism, but I can't promise I'll make it back in time."

"Yeah, I think that would be best, Xander, we don't know how the Dark One will react to being near the Trinian Globe."

Alexander sat down again and looked at the ceiling before focusing on Makayla and Danny. "All right, how quickly do you think you can organise the exorcism, Danny?"

"It shouldn't take me too long, Pater Nikolao doesn't beat around the bush, and you can talk to him before the exorcism regarding any queries you may have."

"Okay, sounds good," Alexander said.

"What about Emily, will you be taking her to the compound with you?" Danny asked.

"No, she'll be safer here with you, nobody knows about you and this village seems to be unaffected by the Blakspor virus. I'll come back for Emily when it's safe, is that okay?"

"Of course, I was going to suggest it myself. Izador will guard her while Xander and I are with Pater Nikolao. She'll be protected here, I'll not let any harm come to her, you have my word." Danny came out from behind the bar.

Makayla nodded and stood, Alexander looked up at her, she grasped his face between her hands and was about to lower her mouth to his.

"Well, that's my cue," Danny said, walking to the back door.

"Wait for me outside, Danny, I'll be right there," Makayla said, looking over her shoulder at him.

"Righto." Danny closed the door, giving them their privacy.

Makayla returned her attention to Alexander. He stood and pulled her into his embrace. "I feel like this is goodbye," he mumbled into her hair.

Makayla shook her head. "This is not goodbye."

Alexander drew back and stared at her. "Why do I feel like it is?"

"It's not." Makayla brushed an errant curl from his eyes and palmed his cheeks. "Before you know it, this will be behind us and the Dark One will be back where he belongs: in the pits of hell."

"I don't know, Makayla, I don't think it will be easy to get rid of him," Alexander said, rubbing his chest.

"If the exorcism doesn't work, we'll figure out something else, okay?"

Alexander nodded. "Okay." He grabbed her hand and drew it to his mouth and kissed her palm. He swept his thumb over the scar on the inside of her wrist. He looked up into her face. "Be careful."

"I will, I mean, how bad could it be? I haven't had any trouble with the other Trinian gems."

Alexander chuckled. "Yeah, right. We nearly fell into a bottomless pit when we found the Gem of Sorrows – we could have been falling for decades. You were transported back in time and burned at the stake for the Gem of Past Times. I can only imagine what's next."

"Hey, don't be so negative, finding the Gem of Protection was pretty cool." She smiled and leaned forward to kiss him. Alexander pulled her to him, wrapped his arms around her waist, crushed her to him and deepened the kiss. She wove her hands into the thick curling hair at the nape of his neck. The warmth of his mouth, the hard contours of his body and his scent seeped into her, igniting a familiar fire within her body. Need overcame her and her heart was racing. She broke the kiss and slowly drew back from him, leaning her forehead on his.

"I wish we had more time, but I've got to go, Xander."

"I know, God, how I know." Xander untangled his hands from her waist and brushed her cheek with his fingertips. "I love you, Makayla."

"I love you too, Xander, I'll see you soon."

"Be safe and don't do anything stupid." Alexander winked.

"Hey, I'm always safe, most of the time, but stupidity, well, that's a whole different ball game. I'm afraid me and stupidity don't have a good track record." Makayla grinned and stepped back, pecked him once more on the mouth and turned to leave. She looked over her shoulder and blew him a kiss before passing through the doorway.

Danny was standing on the back verandah ogling Salomae

who had made herself comfortable in his backyard, her body taking up the entire space.

He noticed Makayla and smiled. "Hey, since when do you have a dragon?"

"Since Africa."

"Oh, yeah, I forgot." Danny smacked the side of his head playfully.

Makayla hugged him. "Look after them, Danny. I don't think I'm going to be able to make it back in time for Xander's exorcism. God, I hope everything goes all right, I have a really bad feeling, please keep in touch, I want to know everything. Oh, and don't worry about the Sandalius scars."

"What, you knew?"

Makayla nodded. "Of course I knew. You're her protector, the Sandalius soul-scar confirms it."

"Makayla, I'm not good for her, really I'm not."

Makayla palmed his cheek. "You're wrong, you're just the right kind of perfect for her. I love you, Danny, I don't think I've ever told you. I'm glad I blood-bonded with you first – you are more than just a friend, you are my blood brother."

Danny's mouth formed an O. "When did you realise we were blood-bonded?"

"My mother showed me a vision of when you, Alexander and she saved me. I bit you, drank your blood, and when I found and saved you in that alleyway and fed you my blood all those years ago I didn't realise I'd blood-bonded us. I'm sorry my anger drove you away."

Danny glanced up at the full moon before looking back at her. "I'm sorry for leaving."

"Don't apologise, I understand, really I do, I wasn't in a good place back then and I was dragging you down with me. Now, I have to be on my way, the Trinian Globe beckons."

"Do you know where it is? Danny asked.

Makayla nodded. "There's only one place it could be," she said, pecking him on the cheek. She sidled up to Salomae and raised her hand to her face. "I need you to stay here, Salomae, protect Emily, Danny and Xander. I'll be back."

Salomae snorted her assent and nudged Makayla gently with her snout.

"I'll be careful, I promise." Makayla's wings manifested in a shower of shimmering light, she unfurled them, waved goodbye to Danny, and shot into the dark sky towards her Greek island.

CHAPTER 41.

Ten trustworthy Vampire and Seraph Guards surrounded Raziel, Augustus and Uriel. They'd gathered in Uriel's rooms, devising ways to free Ambrosia from the dungeon.

"How are we going to get her out? We need a key to open the dungeon door," Raziel said, looking from Uriel to Augustus. "I'm strong, but I don't think breaking the door down will work, we need to get her out of there quietly. The locks aren't simple to open and can't be picked, they'll be booby-trapped for sure. We need the key if we want Lilith to be none the wiser."

"Any suggestions? Augustus, you know the dungeon she's being held in, what would you do?" Uriel asked.

"We need to find out who has the master keys."

There was a light tap on Uriel's door. Nobody moved. A rapid succession of knocks came again, louder this time. Raziel signalled the Seraph and Vampire Guards to take up positions around the room and moved towards the door. He planted his back to the wall nearest the entrance, removing one of his seraph daggers. Augustus moved to the left of the door as Uriel stopped in front of the door, Raziel nodded and Uriel disengaged the lock and opened the door. Before the door opened completely, Raziel grabbed the person on the other side by the throat and pulled him into the room, slamming him against the wall. He jammed his dagger up under his chin as Uriel locked the door.

"Who are you and what do you want?" Raziel said in a lethal voice.

"I'm. . . I'm . . . Um . . . I'm . . ."

"Spit it out man."

"My name's Pheleon, I'm here because I can't sit by and let her take control of Evron, not without a fight."

"Let who take control?"

"Lilith, Zobiana, the High Priestess, whatever she's calling herself these days."

"Why? How do we know she didn't send you?" Raziel put more pressure against his neck.

"Because Sebastian is my best friend and has been since we were children. I am loyal to my king. I refuse to stand by while someone threatens his wife's life. They plan on using Ambrosia as leverage. Lilith wants to be queen, she's unhinged; she will do whatever it takes to get what she wants."

Uriel and Augustus looked at one another, only a friend

would know Sebastian and Ambrosia's marital status unless Lilith had mentioned it.

"How do you know about Sebastian and Ambrosia's marriage?"

"I was at their wedding."

"I don't recall seeing you there," Uriel said, searching Pheleon's face, trying to place him.

Augustus moved to Raziel's side and placed his hand over the dagger he held to Pheleon's throat, encouraging him to lower the blade. "He speaks the truth."

Raziel stepped back and sheathed his dagger, folding his arms over his chest as he scrutinised the vampire. "How do you plan on helping?"

Pheleon unclipped a set of keys from his belt and held them up in the air. "I have the keys to Lady Ambrosia's dungeon door and shackles."

"That's convenient," Raziel said with condescension. "This is too neat, it's too easy; it has to be a trap." Raziel looked at Uriel.

"Does Lilith know your connection to Sebastian? She's known him all his life, surely she'd recognise you?"

"No, we've always kept our friendship secret. Sebastian and I used to sneak out of the castle and hunt together when we were young. He encouraged me to join the Vampire Guard with him when we finished our schooling. I had no great aspirations other than serving the future king, so I joined. What better way to protect him?"

"What better way indeed." Raziel folded his arms behind his back. "Why did you keep your friendship a secret?"

"Because of what he did for my sister; he saved her life."

"And what was it he did?" Raziel questioned.

"I cannot say."

"When something's too easy, there's usually a good reason for it. I think Lilith is baiting us. It's no coincidence. We were just speaking about getting the keys and here they are, like magic."

Augustus placed his hand on Pheleon's chest and looked into his eyes. "Who's your sister?"

Pheleon's eyes darted about the room before he spoke, "Malachi's wife."

"She's dead." Raziel stated, "and she has no siblings."

"I'm her illegitimate brother, 'tis why all the secrecy, and she's not dead, she's hidden."

Augustus nodded. "Do you think Lilith suspects your allegiance to Sebastian?"

"Not that I'm aware of, Chancellor Lagorias, but she's devious, anything's possible." Pheleon lowered his hand and the keys rattled as he hooked them to his belt again.

Augustus removed his hand from Pheleon's chest and looked at Uriel. "He speaks the truth, but we need to proceed with caution. We need to do this with the knowledge Lilith is watching us and may have laid a trap. One consolation: only a select few know about the dungeons where Ambrosia's being held. Zobiana may be overconfident in this knowledge alone.

She hasn't a clue we saw Ambrosia dragged through the streets. So, we may also have the element of surprise on our side, Lilith's arrogance is larger than life and blinds her to the little things."

"I think she dragged Ambrosia through the streets to get a reaction out of us; she doesn't do things by half measures or without purpose, she knows we were watching, of that I'm sure," Raziel said.

"I'd be willing to remove Lady Ambrosia from the dungeon myself, it's the least I can do. You don't have to take any risks, I just need backup if things go askew. They'll be moving her within the next couple of hours, so we must free her now. We could disguise Lady Ambrosia in a Vampire Guard uniform. I could trick one of Lilith's guards into accompanying me into the dungeon and knock him out. Lady Ambrosia could wear his uniform while we escape. There are two such guards watching the passageway, young fledglings who are easily manipulated."

"It could work," Uriel said, hope brightening his features.

"All right, Pheleon, we'll back you up, but we need to stay hidden. Are there places to hide along the passageway?" Raziel asked.

"Yes, there are hidden alcoves every ten metres, but we need to go now."

"Give the seraphs your hooded cloaks," Augustus said to the Vampire Guards present. They obliged, removing their cloaks and handing them to their seraph counterparts. The

Seraph Guards donned the proffered garments, lifting the hoods over their heads and looking to Raziel for direction.

Pheleon offered Raziel his cape. Raziel shook his head "I don't think your cape will cover much, by the looks of it, it will come up to my elbows. Thanks though. I have other means of remaining hidden." Raziel smiled, his appearance shimmering and his face changing into that of a nondescript Vampire Guard. They'd easily forget his plain face. "Lead the way, Pheleon."

Pheleon nodded and waited for Uriel to unlock the door before moving out into the corridor.

Raziel and the guards followed Pheleon towards the dungeons. The corridors were empty, unusually so. As they drew closer to the dungeons, Raziel signalled the guards to hide at various key points along the way until he and Pheleon were the only ones who remained.

Raziel glanced at Pheleon. "Has Ambrosia been harmed?"

"No, my lord, she's being treated as well as can be expected, but I fear that may change if the High Priestess doesn't get her way. For the moment she's safe. I overheard her speaking with Tyrone and Abigail. They plan to move Ambrosia to a more secure location, and that's what worries me. She has given Sebastion an ultimatum. He has five days to comply with her demands; if he refuses, Lady Ambrosia will be terminated." Pheleon stopped and pointed towards the end of the passageway. "The dungeon is up ahead. There's an alcove a few metres away, you can wait there. I'll go find one of the guards I spoke of, I won't be a moment."

"Pheleon, why aren't there guards about? It's a dungeon, there should be more guards?"

"These dungeons are empty, Sire Lady Ambrosia is here temporarily, and as of this moment, I am the only guard on duty aside from the two young fledglings. Zobiana doesn't fear the Seraph Guard, her forces are substantial. I don't know if you've noticed, Lord Raziel, but many of the Seraph Guard are missing."

"I had noticed. We sent a large contingent of our forces to Earth." Raziel would not tell Pheleon there weren't many Seraph Guard about because they were mobilising for battle and waiting for Makayla's arrival.

Pheleon stopped when they came upon the hidden alcove; Raziel slipped into the shadows and watched him move off down the passageway.

Pheleon continued down the passageway, his nerves getting the better of him. He stopped when he reached Ambrosia's cell and peered through the grate in the door. She stared at the ceiling, with a faraway look on her face. He rolled his shoulders and continued on his path getting more and more jittery. He heard raised voices and straightened his posture, gathering his emotions and hiding them behind an expressionless mask as he rounded the corner. The two young guards lazed near an alcove bickering. Pheleon stopped in front of them and they stiffened, coming to attention the minute they realised he was there.

He looked them up and down, eyeing them with disdain and a superior air. "You." He pointed to the smaller of the two guards. "Come with me. You—" he pointed at the other guard. "Stay here and think about your duties, rather than the piece of arse you were arguing over. The Priestess will hear of this, mark my words. We are here to do a job, not bicker about trivialities."

"Please sir, please don't tell the High Priestess, we promise it won't happen again," the smaller of the two guards grovelled.

Pheleon grabbed the larger guard by the scruff of the neck and bared his fangs. "See that it doesn't, because the High Priestess will not be as forgiving as I am." He pushed him back into the alcove where he lost balance, flinging his hands out as he hit the wall. Pheleon grabbed the smaller guard by the arm and dragged him down the passageway, all the while berating him for his uncouth behaviour. He jerked the guard to a stop when they arrived at Ambrosia's cell. Pheleon released the guard's arm and retrieved the dungeon keys from his belt.

"You will learn to be respectful," he said, invoking a fearful look on the young guard's face. Pheleon almost felt sorry for him.

"You're not going to tell the High Priestess, are you?" the guard asked, his voice quivering.

Pheleon ignored the guard's question as he slid the key into the keyhole, unlocking the cell door. He yanked the door open, the hinges screaming their disapproval as he pushed the guard through the door. The guard fell into the cell and landed on the floor in front of Ambrosia's feet. Ambrosia looked up in surprise, Pheleon shook his head slightly and she raised her eyebrow, but kept silent.

Pheleon put his hands on his hips. "Strip."

"Whaaaat?" the guard stammered, his face draining of colour when he saw Ambrosia watching him. He glanced back at Pheleon.

"You need to be taught a lesson in humility."

"But sir, our conversation meant nothing."

"Strip," Pheleon repeated, removing his sword from its sheath and levelling the blade under the guard's chin.

The young guard stripped off, unlatching his weapons first. When he'd removed all his clothing, barring his undergarments, Pheleon struck the back of his head with the pommel of his sword and the guard collapsed unconscious.

Pheleon squatted beside Ambrosia and unlocked her shackles, placing them instead on the unconscious guard's hands. Ambrosia's face showed myriad of emotions as she stood and rubbed her wrists. "Put his clothes on, milady, quickly now – Zobiana will return soon." Pheleon turned his back, giving her privacy and moved towards the door to look out into the passageway. He heard the rustling of clothing as Ambrosia undressed and garbed herself in the guard's uniform. She placed her hand on Pheleon's shoulder when she'd finished dressing. He returned to the unconscious guard and placed her cloak over his form, covering his head with the hood and masking his identity. He picked up the guard's weapons and handed them to Ambrosia. She slid a holstered dagger into the waistband of her trousers and slung the guard's sword belt about her hips.

"Come on, let's get out of here." He looked out into the empty passageway again then guided Ambrosia through the door before locking it again. They hurried towards the hidden alcove where Raziel waited. Someone came around the corner behind them just as they reached the alcove.

"Lord Pheleon, wait."

Pheleon pretended not hear. "Carry on walking, Lady Ambrosia, I'll catch up," he whispered.

"Lord Pheleon, the High Priestess is looking for you; she wishes to speak with you about the prisoner."

Pheleon stopped and eyed Raziel as he turned towards the person calling after him. He heard the soft metallic ring of Raziel's dagger as he unsheathed his weapon.

Pheleon crossed his arms over his chest and waited for Zobiana's messenger to reach him. Raziel grabbed the messenger the moment he stopped and pulled him into the alcove, covering his mouth and slitting the vampire's throat before he had the chance to scream. Pheleon gritted his teeth as the metallic scent of blood and the gurgling sound of the vampire's death accosted him. He grimaced when he noticed glistening blood splatters on the wall and watched mesmerised as blood oozed down the surface of the rock. Raziel lowered the man to the ground in the darkened alcove and clicked his fingers in front of Pheleon's face to capture his attention.

"Come on, let's go before someone finds the body," Raziel said.

Pheleon nodded, looking at the pureblood's corpse before following Raziel down the passageway to catch up with Ambrosia.

"Well, well . . . what do we have here?" Abigail said, eyeing them and blocking their path. She smirked at them as three Newbloods joined her.

"Mistress Abigail." Pheleon looked at her companions and then back at her. "We were just on our way to see the High Priestess."

"That's funny, because you're heading in the wrong direction, my mother's back that way." Abigail pointed behind them. "Come along then, we'll accompany you."

"I don't think so," Ambrosia hissed, grabbing Abigail by the throat and smashing her against the wall, her hand flamed with seraph fire.

Raziel threw two daggers and downed two of the Newbloods and jumped on the third.

Abigail gasped for oxygen and threw a punch at Ambrosia's face. Ambrosia swivelled her head to the side, narrowly escaping the blow. Abigail's clothing caught fire as she tried to dislodge Ambrosia's fingers.

"I have a score to settle with you, little girl!" A suffocating cloud of smoke surrounded them. The stench of burning hair and skin was overwhelming. Abigail coughed as her body spasmed; she slid her hand down to the dagger strapped in a sheath on her thigh and curled her fingers around the hilt, sliding the weapon out carefully. She sliced the blade across Ambrosia's stomach. Ambrosia hunched, a grimace flashing across her face as she loosened her grip on Abigail's throat. Abigail sucked in a mouthful of oxygen just as Ambrosia tightened her grip. Ambrosia bit her lip, ignoring the stinging wound on her stomach and squeezed harder. The dagger clattered to the marble floor, the noise ringing in their ears along with the sound of bubbling flesh and popping blisters.

Pheleon looked over his shoulder and saw Newbloods running towards them.

"We've got to leave, and now," he yelled.

Raziel glanced towards the advancing Newbloods. "Ambrosia, we've got to get out of here before it's too late. Come on, there'll be time to finish her off next time, right now getting out of here in one piece is more important."

Ambrosia looked over her shoulder and saw the approaching Newbloods, she let go of Abigail, and watched her crumple to the floor in a black, charred heap. "We'll finish this another time, sweetheart, perhaps on the battlefield. Until we meet again." Ambrosia threw a fireball towards the Newbloods heading their way and they barrelled into each other as they dodged the flaming projectile.

They took off running down the passageway. Pheleon was dumbstruck by Ambrosia's display of power, no one had powers on Evron, at least no one he knew, except the royals. He noticed Ambrosia clutching her stomach as they moved along the passageway.

"Are you okay, my lady?"

"I'll be fine, it's just a superficial wound, it will heal."

Pheleon bowed his head. No one spoke as they journeyed along the passageways. With each hidden alcove they passed their numbers grew, the Seraph and Vampire Guards returning to their sides as they jogged along in a protective formation. Pheleon kept looking over his shoulder expecting to see more Newbloods heading their way, but none followed.

They reached Uriel's rooms, Raziel knocked; three slow knocks, two rapid, one slow then four more rapid. The door eased open, they passed over the threshold and the door closed, shimmering as Uriel chanted an incantation. The room changed and they were no longer standing in a room, but in a gazebo-like structure in the middle of a white forest. Raziel lowered his hood and reverted to his original form. A smile crept across his face as he caught his breath.

"That was awfully easy; child's play," Raziel chuckled.

Ambrosia lowered her hood, laughing along with Raziel. "I haven't had that much fun in ages." She glanced at Uriel and bowed her head respectfully. "Hello, Father."

"Hello, sweetheart." Uriel's smile disappeared. "Ambrosia, you're wounded."

"It's just a scratch." She grimaced as she checked the shredded clothing exposing her wounded stomach. She peeled back the bloodied fabric to get a better look at the long gash that reached from one side of her stomach to the other. The wound gaped open, smiling up at her.

"That's not a scratch." Uriel frowned. "Here, let me heal you." Uriel placed his hand over the wound and she jumped, hissing in pain as white light glowed from his fingertips and transferred into her body, knitting the flesh back together. When he'd finished healing her, Uriel pulled his daughter into his arms for a brief hug, then stepped back, holding her at arm's length and brushing her hair back from her face, all the while studying her features. "I've missed you, it's been too long."

Ambrosia kissed his cheek. "It's been way too long, I'm sorry I haven't returned, but with everything that's happened over the years, it wasn't safe to come home to Evron."

Ambrosia glanced at Pheleon and grabbed his hand. "Thank you, Pheleon, you've always had Sebastian's back, ever since he was a child." She kissed his cheek.

Pheleon's face flushed with heat. "I'm just glad I listened to Sebastian; I've remained in contact with him all these years. He said if ever the chance arose to infiltrate Lilith's people to take it. I was a part of the vampire contingent sent to Earth to aid Lord Vasili and the Shadow Seekers in protecting the citizens of Earth. It was just blind luck. There'd been dissent in the ranks. I tagged along with a number of Vampire Guard who weren't happy and we happened upon Lilith's people and I found myself back here on Evron among her guard."

"Well, had you not been among them, I don't want to consider what may have happened." Ambrosia looked towards Augustus. "They destroyed Wigmore Castle, Augustus, is there a way we can get word to Sebastian? I need to know if he, my Aunt Marianna, and Emily are okay. And I need tell him of Lilith's plans, he probably already knows what she wants, but I don't want her to use me as a bargaining chip. I'm free now, but I fear that won't stop her from pretending she still has me in her custody, Sebastian needs to know I'm safe."

"I'll get word to him. Pheleon, come with me." Pheleon nodded and followed Augustus.

"My turn," Raziel said, lifting Ambrosia off her feet in a bear hug and spinning her around. "It's about time you came home, sister-mine, we've missed you."

CHAPTER 42.

Sebastian paced back and forth in Vasili's office and ceased only when Vasili entered and closed the door. He watched him walk towards his desk and stop in front of a tray of crystal decanters and glass tumblers. Vasili filled two tumblers with brandy and handed him one. Sebastian took it gladly, he needed to calm his roiling nerves and warm his insides from the creeping cold gathering within his body.

"How's Marianna? I was a worried about her when we gave her the bad news of Ambrosia's abduction." Sebastian asked.

"I calmed her down; she's asleep in my rooms now, but she's worried – which is only natural considering how long she was kept captive by Zobiana."

Sebastian looked down into his glass in contemplation before lifting it to his mouth and taking a long draught. "I'm going back to Evron, I've got to speak with Uriel and find Augustus, I can't sit here and wait, I must leave now."

"I understand, I'd do the same." Vasili swirled the brandy around in his glass. "Use the royal gateway, it's safer and likely the only one uncompromised by Zobiana and her horde."

"I suspect that's true; she wouldn't have destroyed Wigmore Castle and taken Ambrosia otherwise."

"I'll gather the forces, the Seraph and Vampire Guard here on Earth who are still loyal along with the Shadow Seekers and meet you in the cavern. Will you go to Zobiana's meeting place?"

Sebastian finished his brandy and placed the glass on Vasili's desk. "I will, but I need to speak with Uriel and Augustus first and come up with a plan. Vasili, she's not the woman I knew; she's bitter and angry and will stop at nothing to become the queen of Evron. She must be stopped before she kills more innocents like my son."

Vasili finished his own drink before coming around his desk to take hold of Sebastian's arm in a forearm handshake. Sebastian returned the gesture and clapped him on the back. "Godspeed, Sebastian."

"And you, Vasili, and you."

Sebastian released Vasili's arm, stepped back and dematerialised to his hidden gateway.

Pebbles rained down from the bunker's ceiling where the Shadow Seekers were stationed.

"It's getting worse; the humans have escalated the bombings," Jackson said, sliding throwing blades into the slots on his tactical vest and then strapping a sheathing pouch containing more throwing blades around his right thigh.

"There will be nothing left for us to save if they keep bombing everything. What do they think they're accomplishing? Bloody fools," Morgan said, slipping her moulded Kevlar body suit over her head and securing it to her chest. She picked up the double sword harness with her katanas and shimmied into it, buckling the straps and wiggling it until it was positioned comfortably on her back.

"I recall Makayla saying something similar recently," Darrius said, his eyebrow lifting as he directed his comment to Morgan. She glanced away and moved along the weapons shelf to collect a black tactical belt with small grenades and fasten it to her waist.

"I'm surprised there are still humans left to fly aircraft," Reece said, looking back down at the map on the table. He looked up again. "Has anyone seen Bryce?"

"I think he's with Freya, in the infirmary, he said something about moving her to a safe place. I don't know why, the compound's the safest place for her at the moment," Anna said, coming to stand beside him.

"What is it with you and Bryce? What did you do to him, Reece?" Morgan asked.

"I did nothing, that's the problem," Reece murmured.

The ground shuddered and more pebbles fell, Reece swept the dirt from the map and traced his finger along a line on the paper.

"That one was close," Ashley said.

Gabriel came stalking into the room. "Are we almost done here? We move out within the hour."

"I thought we had five days to get to Evron?" Morgan looked over her shoulder at him.

"We do, but we still have to plan our strategies first. Move your arses, people.

"All right, all right, we're moving."

"Has Zack returned yet?" Anna asked.

"No, we still haven't heard from him, Vasili will get word to him, I'm sure."

"What about Makayla?"

"Don't worry about Makayla, she'll find us," Gabriel said, turning to leave.

There was the dull sound of another explosion, and the ground rolled; one shelf of weapons crashed to the floor, scattering things everywhere. Everyone looked at the ceiling once more.

"What the bloody hell is going on out there, World War Three?" Jackson said.

"It sure sounds like it, but I don't think that came from above, it came from below." Morgan looked to the ground and then to Darrius.

Reece rolled the map up and stuck it in his pack, then grabbed Anna's hand before heading for the door. The others followed them out into the corridor.

"I have a few things I want to get from my room before we leave, I won't be a moment," Anna said, sliding her hand from Reece's and heading off down the passageway.

"I'll come with you." Reece jogged after her. "Meet you all at Vasili's office in five."

"I'm going to find Tristan," said Ashley, walking away.

"Ashley, no, we should stick together." Morgan reached out to her sister.

"She'll be okay, Tristan's not a monster, you know. Come on, let's find out what's going on up top," Darrius said. "Really, she'll be safe with Tristan."

Morgan nodded. "Okay, let's see what the humans are destroying now. If it is the humans. I still think it's coming from below."

"Humour me; I know a spot with a perfect view." Darrius grabbed her hand and dematerialised outside.

Jackson glanced at Gabriel towering above him. "And then there were two." Jackson eyed Gabriel. "Correction, one-and-a-half."

"Come on, let's find Vasili," Gabriel said, ignoring Jackson's comment.

Jackson looked at the ceiling once more before following Gabriel.

Bryce unhooked the IV from Freya's hand and picked her up, blankets and all.

"What are you doing? She needs that," Tess said from the laboratory doorway.

Bryce looked across at Tess. "It's not helping at all. I'm leaving, don't bother trying to stop me."

Tess stepped forward. "But, Bryce, she'll die."

"She'll die if she stays here, Tess. You need to find Lazarus and get the hell out of here, something's wrong. It's not safe anymore. It's not safe anywhere. Something's coming."

"I have nowhere to go, Bryce, nowhere."

"Find Lazarus, you're safe with him."

Tess watched Bryce disappear with Freya. There was a distant rumbling above Tess's head then the floor trembled like an earthquake. Dust and small stones trickled from the ceiling; Tess looked up; squinting as dirt fell into her face. "Yeah right, how am I going to find Lazarus? I don't have a clue where he is," she mumbled to herself, brushing the dust from her face. Tess stripped the sheets from Freya's empty bed and noticed something shining on the ground beneath the bed frame. She threw the sheets in the linen basket and returned to the bed, squatting to retrieve the object.

"Tess, come here, I think I may have found the missing component for the antidote, it's been under our noses all this time," Ava called.

"Just a minute, I'll be right there, there's something under the bed I want to get first." Tess stretched her hand out for the shiny object, but couldn't reach it. What could it be? She crawled further under the bed and grabbed the circular object. It looked like a remote control, but more evolved. Tess turned it over, rotating it between her fingertips. It was small and made of black glossy metal-like material, yet felt like plastic. Something clicked inside. "Ava I found something, it's really weird." Tess looked towards the lab door and saw a red light flashing in the top left-hand corner of the room. *"Avvvvvvvvvvaaaaaaaaaaaaaa take cover."*

BOOM.

BOOM . . . BOOM.

BOOM. BOOM. BOOM.

The ceiling crashed down, crushing Tess beneath the steel bed frame as multiple explosions went off throughout the compound.

Alexander splashed water onto his face, trying to wash away the weariness. He turned off the water and rubbed the knot in the centre of his bare chest. The skin was still inflamed and a little pink, but had healed. He traced the lines of the sigil, praying they'd hold longer than Danny had implied. Makayla had left a few hours ago and Danny had gone to meet with Pater Nikolao. Danny seemed certain an exorcism was the answer, Alexander wasn't so sure. He rested his hands on the basin and looked into the mirror at his reflection. His hair was longer, his face leaner, he still looked the same, sort of, minus the colour of his eyes, and his teeth, and all the scars marring his body.

"Just face it, Xander, you're different." He turned the cold water on again and splashed his face a second time. Was it hot? Alexander couldn't seem to cool down.

"Arghhhh." Alexander closed his eyes as a stinging pain scissored across his stomach; he gripped the edges of the porcelain basin and clenched his jaw until the pain passed. Opening his eyes, he looked down at his stomach. "What the bloody hell?" There was a twenty-centimetre gash across the middle of his belly, smiling up at him like the Cheshire cat from *Alice in Wonderland.*

'Hey, how YOU doin?' The edges of the wound said, moving like a mouth, thick with oozing blood.

"What the fuck?" Alexander rubbed his eyes and shook his head before looking back at the wound. "You're hallucinating, Xander, pull it together," he mumbled to himself.

Laughter echoed in his head. He could hear the Dark One's amusement now, the barrier between them was deteriorating. The laughter wasn't in his recurring dreams anymore, it was in his waking hours too. Alexander couldn't help looking about, though, looking for the owner of the laughter echoing in his head, hoping to find a real person toying with him.

Alexander picked up a face washer and shoved it under the cold running water, wetting it and squeezing out the excess water before holding it over the wound on his stomach.

He hissed at the pain. "Stop being such a baby, you've felt worse," Alexander mumbled to himself as he opened the mirrored vanity cupboard door and removed antiseptic cream, gauze and a bandage and set to work dressing his wound. He heard a gasp just as he was returning all the items to the vanity cupboard. Alexander closed the door and turned, Emily was standing by the bathroom door, half hidden behind the door frame. Her eyes were wide as she gaped at the scars on his body. Her bottom lip trembled, and tears streaked down her cheeks as she stared at him in shock. Alexander picked up his shirt and shrugged into it buttoning it hastily to hide the twisted whip scars marking his body.

Emily took off running back to her room and Alexander could only imagine how distressing the sight of his tangled mess of scars must have been for a child. He followed Emily to Danny's room and found her crying with her face buried in a pillow.

Alexander came to an abrupt stop at the bedroom door when he saw the Sandalius wolf near the bed, the formidable creature lifted his snout, his nostrils flaring as he sniffed the air. Alexander held his breath, waiting for the wolf to attack and rip his throat out, but instead the giant animal lowered his head, closed his eyes and nodded off to sleep again.

Alexander made his way to the bed and sat down on the edge of the mattress, rubbing Emily's back to comfort her.

"It's my fault," Emily choked out.

"What's your fault, sweetie?"

She sat up and faced him looking at him with tear-filled, pleading eyes. "The scars on your body, they're because of me. You took my place and went with Zobiana."

"Oh, honey, it's not your fault, don't go blaming yourself for something beyond your control. Let's lay the blame at the feet of the people responsible. Abigail and Zobiana are the ones at fault, not you, okay, never you."

"I'm sorry, *bràthair*."

Alexander's heart fluttered with warmth, Emily calling him brother in Gaelic was a surprise. "Don't be, if I had to do it over again, I would. You're worth it, sweetheart, never forget that, okay?" Alexander wished he'd shut the door and Emily hadn't seen his scars. Guilt was terrible enough for adults, let alone children. "Come on, let's tuck you back into bed, it's still dark outside." Alexander scratched his head in thought. "Did you need to go to the bathroom, is that why you were hiding near the door?"

Emily nodded shyly.

Alexander's mouth formed an O. "O-kay, the bathrooms all yours, I'll wait here and tuck you in when you return."

Emily nodded and threw her arms about his neck and squeezed him tight. "I'm glad you're my brother too, Xander." Alexander's mouth opened and closed. She let go and dashed off to the bathroom only to return moments later.

He settled her in and tucked the covers around her. Alexander sighed and closed his eyes, his shoulders slumping as he thought of all the darkness that lay ahead, all the battles yet to be fought. Would he survive? Would any of them? What kind of future lay ahead for Emily, for all the children left behind? Who would protect them? He felt Emily's hand on his cheek and opened his eyes.

"I see the fire in you, Xander. Don't be afraid of it, embrace it; it will save your soul in the end."

Alexander didn't know what to say, he felt the fire wasn't a part of him, but a residual effect of the Dark One's possession. How could fire save his soul? He swallowed the lump in his throat and swept his hand through his hair, shaking his head. "No, I don't think so, sweetie. I have a feeling it won't end well for me."

Emily placed her hand over his heart. "Makayla will not rest, she will save you, she is your destiny and you are hers. She will save us all. She will obliterate the destroyer." Emily stared up into his face. Her body stiffened, the violet of her eyes turning iridescent, her voice changing, as if a higher being spoke through her. "Do not fear the Dark One, he cannot hurt you. Makayla's fire burns within you, it surrounds and protects you. Accept your fate; it is your path, for you will be reborn from the ashes." Emily lowered her hand and laid her head on her pillow as her eyes returned to normal.

"What, what did you just say?" Alexander stuttered, taken aback by her strange behaviour. Why, how, was she full of such wisdom, she was just a child?

"Huh?" Emily's face was blank. "I. . . I don't remember."

Her eyes fluttered closed. *"Goodnight, Xander,"* she murmured, and fell asleep.

Alexander stood, confused by Emily's prophetic words. He turned towards the door and jumped when he saw Danny standing in the doorway.

"She okay?" Danny asked, nodding at Emily.

Alexander closed the bedroom door before speaking. "Yeah, she saw the scars on my back while I was washing my face in the bathroom, they're not pretty. I took her place when we were in Africa. She was the bargaining chip in Zobiana's twisted game and somehow she blames herself for my scars. I told her it wasn't her fault, but she's not going to let it go." Xander placed his hand on Danny's shoulder as they walked towards the lounge room. "You'll have to convince her otherwise, old friend."

"Are you okay, Xander?"

"No, not really, but that's nothing new. How did you go?"

"The exorcism is set for dawn."

CHAPTER 43

Green flashing light blazed in multiple beams about Makayla as she placed the emerald Gem of Protection into the Trinian Globe. A kaleidoscope of coloured light lit her cottage lounge room as the globe floated into the air. Makayla closed her eyes when she heard the familiar sound of chiming bells and the whisperings of a language she was yet to understand. Angelic voices sang, evoking a transcendent feeling of love within her. She stood transfixed as she absorbed the Trinian Globe's exquisite music. It was the sound of heaven and the feeling of coming home. It surrounded her, making the hairs on her body stand on end; she shivered in bliss and sighed, she'd never felt as close to her angelic heritage as she did when she was in the Trinian Globe's presence.

Makayla opened her eyes and glanced down into the open chests given to her by the Vampire and Seraph Councils. The light coming from the Trinian Globe seemed to be affecting the weapons and armour within the chests. Makayla shaded her eyes from the glare. Her Druidoynan armour buzzed, sizzling with an electrical charge. Her mouth dropped open when the gold seraph body armour disappeared and reappeared on her body, having merged with the Druidoynan armour she already wore.

She stared at her reflection in the full-length mirror by the wall. When she stood one way, she could see her Druidoynan armour; when she changed position she could see the seraph armour. She took a position where she could see both armours superimposed over each other. The eagle wings on the chest plate of her Druidoynan armour had merged with the six striking wings of the seraph armour. Feathers encrusted in pint-sized diamonds and etched with fine silver had intertwined with the feathers of the eagle's gold filigreed wings. Makayla moved her body back and forth multiple times: what she saw was magnificent. The movement gave the impression the eagle's wings were flapping and catching the last rays of sunlight as they moved.

Makayla was about to retrieve the weapons from the chest when they appeared on her body alongside the weapons already on her person. The red and silver coronet headpiece materialised on her head. The cool metal warmed and unfolded, transforming into an elaborate headdress. Cascading, paper-thin gilded feathers with microscopic veins of rubies laced the gold feathers, draping and moulding over her shoulders. Makayla's eyes widened at her appearance. No wonder everyone had looked at her in awe at the Vampire Council meeting. She looked like a Goddess come to life. The middle of her chest plate shimmered; the magical gateway key appeared on her armour, the gemstone colours alternating randomly. The last time armour had appeared on her body, she'd activated the Trinian Globe and was thrown back in time. Her anxiety peaked – where was she about to go now?

Makayla turned back towards the Trinian Globe hovering above her and looked up, mesmerised, as the globe spun. She raised her arm above her head and the Trinian Globe floated down into her palm. The moment it connected with her skin the room flashed with searing white light. Makayla closed her eyes and a strange sensation of falling overcame her. When she opened her eyes again she was standing in a dim subterranean cavern. She drew in a long breath, breathing in the fresh, briny scent of the ocean. The air was cool, but not freezing, refreshing and almost sweet.

Makayla still held the Trinian Globe; strange that it hadn't disappeared. The glow from the globe was the only light in the area. Makayla's hand tingled from the small shocks of electricity it was emitting. Sensing the globe was about to lift into the air, she let go and watched it levitate. Light flared again and Makayla saw the true vastness of the cavern. She was literally under the ocean encased in a bubble of stone with walls of translucent quartz-crystal. As the light decreased in intensity, unusual marine life took form, swimming about on the other side of the wall; it was like looking into a huge aquarium full of otherworldly exotic fish. Makayla stood in the centre of a fifty-metre-wide circular crystal platform surrounded by a ten-metre-wide moat. There were four rectangular podiums evenly spaced around the room positioned along the quartz-crystal wall with large crystal skulls sitting atop each one. An enormous angular archway with alien hieroglyphic inscriptions stood before her. Two giant crystal warrior statues stood either side of the gateway dressed in armour similar to ancient Spartans.

Makayla noticed shallow trenches circumnavigating the entire quartz-crystal wall behind the skull podiums. She turned on the spot, her eyes travelling the length of the walls; the trenches stopped either side of the statues standing by the gateway. She narrowed her eyes and saw an oil-like substance glistening within them. Makayla manifested fireballs in each of her hands and hurled them towards the pits by the statues hoping the oily substance would ignite. She smiled in triumph when the flames sizzled to life. She turned on the spot again, her eyes following the flame's circular path as the oil ignited and illuminated the underwater cavern.

Makayla caught her breath at the sheer beauty of the underwater oasis. The Trinian Globe had transported her to the last known gateway to the underwater city of Atlantis on Earth. Makayla knew of two other such gateways on Earth, but hadn't a clue where they were, and those were gateways to the planet of Atlantis not the Atlantean colony on Earth.

She'd never really learned about Atlantis, yet as she stood

here she concluded she had actually heard many stories about Atlantis and its people. Their history was shadowed in mystery and intrigue and had, over thousands of years, been relegated to myth and legend. She'd never met an Atlantean; but she knew, somehow, that they tended not to interfere with the mortals of Earth anymore. They had once, long ago, and were punished by the Zoldarni for imparting their advanced knowledge and risking it being used against them. The Zoldarni, she realised, had deemed it better for humans to advance at their own pace. Since then, Atlantis had become Earth's "lost" continent. They'd chosen to hide their civilisation and submerged their lands under the ocean.

"Are you just going to stand there gaping at everything or are you going to look for the Gem of Hidden Knowledge?" her nemesis berated.

"Is that what it's called?" Makayla realised the gem she was looking for was the reason she suddenly knew about the Atlantean history with the Zoldarni. "Feel free to help if you wish, some assistance wouldn't go astray."

"Just get on with it; those Atlanteans always have booby traps in place. The quicker you find the gem, the quicker we get out of here unharmed."

"Yeah, yeah, I hear you." Makayla ignored the condescending tone of the bane of her existence and checked the Trinian Globe. It was spinning fast; so fast, in fact, it looked as though it was about to slingshot into the ceiling. She hadn't noticed the gyrating vibration coming off it, having been so enthralled by her surroundings. The globe continued speeding up and then stopped. The gems positioned on the globe glowed, coloured light shooting out like laser beams targeting the crystal skulls on the surrounding podiums. Four skulls for four gems; the individual beams of light refracted off the skulls and were directed towards one spot on the gateway in front of her. Chunks of debris fell from the gateway as the light burned into the rock, revealing the fifth Trinian gem's location. The Gem of Hidden Knowledge lay nested snugly in the top point of the gateway's uppermost arch. The moment the gem appeared, the shafts of light died out. Makayla walked to the edge of the platform she was standing on and stared up at the blue sapphire. It gleamed in the fire light, beckoning her forward. Makayla moved back ten paces and took a running leap across the water separating her from the gateway as her wings jettisoned from her back. She flapped them and floated into the air, hovering in front of the sapphire. Makayla retrieved one of her daggers from her thigh holster and slipped the tip underneath the edge of the sapphire, carefully popping the embedded gemstone out from the gateway.

She held it up to the light and smiled. "Five down, one to go." She tossed it in the air and caught it before pocketing it and returning her dagger to its sheath. The gateway trembled, a terrible sound of grinding stone piercing her ears as cracks formed on its surface. Chunks of rock fell to the ground and splashed into the water surrounding the platform she'd been standing on only moments ago. Makayla looked down at the water; it was moving, churning and spinning around the platform. She looked over her shoulder when she heard a loud banging noise; a sea creature ramming the quartz-crystal walls. Makayla squinted, trying to figure out what kind of creature it was.

"Oh shit," she mumbled when she realised it was a leviathan. It looked like it had swum up from the depths of hell. Its mouth was a mass of gnashing teeth, its body at least thirty metres long. It had four jagged eel-like tails that moved individually and six arms, three on each side of its elongated body. Each arm had clawed talons with webbed membranes between them for cutting through the water at heightened speeds. The top of its head was flat with multiple jagged horns sticking out from the back of its cranium. Its eyes glowed phosphorus as it targeted her, readying for another blow to the wall. It slammed its head into the barrier again and the wall groaned, small cracks forming where the creature had connected. Makayla heard something behind her and looked back towards the gateway ruins, she almost bit her tongue when she saw the statues coming to life and looking up at her as she hovered in the air.

"What the bloody hell?" she gasped, as one statue grabbed her foot and pulled her towards him. "Yeah, that ain't happening, big boy," she said, whipping her seraph swords from her back and slicing them down in a criss-cross motion, cutting the statue's hand off. She shoved her swords back into their sheaths and tried to manifest a shield about herself, but nothing happened. "What the fuck?" she hissed as the other statue threw his spear at her, it narrowly missed. She flapped her wings and shot up to the ceiling towards the Trinian Globe. "It's time we left," she mumbled, just as the leviathan crashed against the barrier again. The crack in the wall grew and water sprayed through as he made another turn. One statue jumped across to the platform while the other kept throwing projectiles at her. She dodged right when a chunk of the gateway came hurtling towards her. The statue below her jumped, trying to grab hold of her, his height a definite advantage.

BANG. CRACK. The leviathan was determined.

Makayla reached for the Trinian Globe and it floated down into her palm. She dug the fifth gem from her pocket and looked towards the leviathan again. Water was spraying through the growing crack and filling up the cavern. He rammed again and the spraying water became a torrent. The crack fragmented up towards the ceiling, showering her in ice water. She slammed the gem into the Trinian globe just as the leviathan hit the wall again and broke through. Water surged through, washing the feet out from under the statues and knocking them over. They fell and smashed into crystal shards as they hit the ground. Makayla screamed. The leviathan's mouth opened, its long tongue lashing out and curling around her waist, drawing her towards its razor-sharp teeth. Makayla wiggled, trying to loosen its grip, there wasn't much she could do, though, not when one of her arms was trapped against her body and the other held the Trinian Globe. Just as it was about to chomp her, the Trinian Globe flashed, transporting her to the next Trinian Gem location.

Makayla landed on her stomach with a loud *oomph*. Gasping, she lay on the ground with her wings splayed out, part of the creature's tongue still looped about her waist. Makayla scrunched up her face when the rank odour of seared flesh enveloped her and recoiled when her fingers met wet, spongy flesh. She pushed the slimy remains off and flung it away.

Makayla retracted her wings and rolled to her back, the Trinian globe floating just above her head, its light unveiling her surroundings.

"Son of a bitch," Makayla swore in disbelief.

CHAPTER 44.

Zobiana kicked the guard's corpse and spun about facing her daughter. "How, how could she have escaped?"

"She had help," Abigail replied.

"Help? What do you mean she had help? Sebastian wouldn't have had time to alert his people here, so, enlighten me, dear daughter, I want answers!"

"We did parade her through the streets. Royal loyalists, the Vampire and Seraph Guard, Ambrosia's father, her brother Raziel, the Seraph Council, all of the above could have seen her. I thought that was the point, making a spectacle and provoking a response? I think we got the desired response, Mother, even if the result wasn't to our liking. What did you expect?" Abigail folded her arms over her chest, grimacing when the newly healed skin on her arms brushed against the fabric of her clothing.

"What did I expect?" Zobiana looked between Tyrone and Abigail. "I expected to have her in our custody a little longer, or at least until Sebastian came grovelling on his knees, begging for her release. I expected Malachi to be here waiting for us, but instead he's nowhere to be seen. I expected there to be more resistance, but Evron's suspiciously vacant."

"You should be happy, Evron is yours. Does it matter that there was no resistance and Malachi is a no-show? None of it matters, you don't need Sebastian or Ambrosia as leverage to become queen here, Mother. You have control of Evron, so what difference does it make how you achieved your goal?"

"I should be happy! What difference does it make?" Zobiana laughed. "You know nothing about Evronian politics, Abigail. The fact THAT Malachi isn't here alongside us is something to worry about. That alone should bother you because he wanted to be king more than I wanted to be queen!" Zobiana waved her arm around in the air. "It's because of him that this is even possible, he set the ball in motion. We may control the gateways here and on Earth, but the battle has yet to be fought and won. What concerns me, what I really want to know, is where all the Vampire and Seraph Guard loyal to Sebastian are hiding? Where is everyone? Did you fail to see the empty streets and the unguarded seraph gateways? This hostile takeover was easier than expected. No one takes control of a highly guarded planet this effortlessly. Yes, we fought our way here, we even fought a few Seraph and Vampire Guard upon our arrival, but Evron shouldn't have fallen so easily.

Aren't you at all suspicious? Don't you think it a little strange? The Seraph Guard just don't run off, they fight to the bitter end no matter the cost. I remember the fierce battles between the vampire and seraph nations. Evron can't have changed that much in my absence."

"Don't look a gift horse in the mouth, Mother."

"Arrrgh," Zobiana screeched. "Leave off with the tired old clichés, Abigail. Nothing in my life has ever been this simple, nothing. I've fought tooth and nail to get where I am today. I've had to do horrendous acts on behalf of the Dark One – believe me none of it was simple, which means we have yet to fight the end battle. The prophecy is at hand." Zobiana noticed her daughter roll her eyes and wanted to slap some sense into her. "Why aren't you listening? Where are the Seraph Guard, where are the people, where are the Danairian servants? They can't have just up and disappeared, this planet is empty, why, *whyyyyyy?*" Zobiana looked about the cell and then down at the shackled corpse of the Vampire Guard.

"You're repeating yourself, Mother; you sound like a broken record."

Zobiana gritted her teeth, her jaw cracking from the pressure. "Round up the guards who were on duty and find Pheleon. And get rid of this damn body." Zobiana kicked the corpse one more time before turning towards the door. "Rally the Newblood troops, prepare for battle. If I know anything, the Seraph Guard are assembling their soldiers, it's only a matter of time before they show themselves. Evron isn't ours yet, but by

God it will be."

The cavern appeared the same as the last time Sebastian had been there. Beyond the mouth of the cavern behind him was a misty forest, but he was focused on the hieroglyphs before him. He traced his fingers over the script of his daughter's prophecy that was carved into the walls, then turned his attention back to the gateway on his left and searched for the passage entrance. His shoulders relaxed when he noticed the hidden passageway markers leading into the castle. He straightened his back and made his way towards the entrance.

Lowering his head, Sebastian stepped through the opening into the passage. He rubbed his tingling nose; the familiar stale air and the damp, musty odour of his surroundings was somehow comforting. Shredded cobwebs thick with dust hung in ragged clumps, swaying back and forth like shredded curtains as he passed. He saw recent signs of movement through the passageway and prayed the footprints belonged to Augustus.

Sebastian hunched further as the dim, passageway narrowed; reining in the sense of claustrophobia and sighing with relief when he came upon the masked doorway to the secret compartment in Augustus's closet. He opened the door and stepped through into the closet. Opening the door a crack, he peeked through the gap, and when he felt sure no one was there he edged out of the closet and looked about his old chambers. He'd given Augustus his rooms when he'd abdicated. Augustus didn't know there were other hidden passageways within the chamber leading to Uriel's rooms. He and Uriel had built the passageways in secret when he'd wed Ambrosia. It was how they'd kept their marriage secret over the years when they were on Evron. Sebastian locked the door to his chamber and crossed the room to the fireplace. He checked over his shoulder before stopping in front of the white marble fireplace and placing his hands in the centre-front face panel below the mantel shelf. He slid his palms outwards until his hands were a metre apart and curled his fingertips under the decorative carvings until he found finger grooves. He pushed his fingertips into the grooves and pressed the hidden buttons. When he heard a dull click he removed his hands, stepped back and watched the fireplace slide backwards into the wall to reveal a concealed stairway. Sebastian placed his hands on the Corinthian column jams either side of the fireplace as he descended the stairs into another shadowy passageway. The moment his foot left the last stair the fireplace moved back into position. There was a hiss and a dull pop as gas torches ignited with fire. Sebastian hurried along the square passageway until he came to a set of stairs on the opposite side of the tunnel. He pressed a button on a nearby wall and heard the grinding of stone as the fireplace in Uriel's chamber moved out of the way. He climbed the stairs and burst out into an empty room similar to the one he'd just left.

"Uriel, where are you? It's me, Sebastian," he whispered. He was met with silence. "Uriel, where are you? We need to talk, Lilith has captured Ambrosia." Someone grabbed him by the shoulder and yanked him off-balance. Blinding white light seared his retinas. Sebastian shaded his eyes from the glare, blinking rapidly as he tried to see where he was. He flung his arms out when something barrelled into him, almost knocking him over a second time. Just as he was gaining his balance, the thing wrapped its arms about his body and squeezed. He recognised his wife's fragrance at once.

"Thank God you're here," Ambrosia murmured, feathering kisses all over his face as his vision cleared.

"You're. . .you're really here," he stuttered and kissed her hard, wrapping her in his tight embrace. "How are you here? How did you escape?"

"Pheleon and Raziel got me out of the dungeon."

"Pheleon? I don't understand, isn't he on Earth with the Vampire Guard helping the Shadow Seekers?"

"I was," Pheleon said, stepping into Sebastian's line of sight. Sebastian rubbed his eyes again and smiled at his old friend.

"Pheleon." Sebastian released Ambrosia and hugged him. "Thank you for saving my wife. How can I ever repay you?"

"No payment is necessary; I owe you a hundred times over, Sebastian. I was lucky and happened to be in the right place at the right time."

"Sebastian," said Ambrosia, "Where are Emily and Aunt

Marianna? Please tell me they're safe?" Her voice trembled.

"Yes, they're safe; Emily's with Danny and Vasili got your aunt out before the fire destroyed the castle."

"Fire. What fire?"

"Lilith torched our home, there's nothing left but the outer curtain walls. The rest is rubble."

"No."

Sebastian cupped Ambrosia's face in his hands. "It doesn't matter, we'll rebuild, you're safe, Emily's safe, your aunt's safe, that's all that matters." Sebastian kissed her gently.

"Lilith must pay for what she's done. She must pay." Ambrosia said with vehemence.

"And she will. Makayla's retrieving the remaining Trinian gems and Vasili gathers our forces as we speak, they'll be here soon. What of our troops here?" Sebastian looked around at all the white trees and flowers, then saw Uriel walking towards them along with Augustus and Raziel. A contingent of Seraph and Vampire Guard followed behind them.

"They're ready," Uriel said, coming to a standstill beside them.

"Lord Uriel, it's good to see you again." Sebastian bowed his head in respect. "I'm glad you arrived safely, Augustus."

Augustus smiled. "It's good to be back, although Evron has changed somewhat. Uriel has been appraising me of the situation here."

"Father, where *is* everyone and how did Lilith take control of Evron?" Ambrosia asked.

"Our people are safe in the Taskien dimension. We started evacuating after we gave the Golden One her armour and weapons at the council meeting. We've been preparing the Seraph Guard for battle ever since."

"That's a lot of people to evacuate, Baba."

"Yes, it is."

"Why did you let Lilith take control of Evron? We should have stopped her on Earth. Why hand our planet over to her when all we have ever done is fight to protect it?"

"We took heed of the Oracle's insight; the battle must be fought here, nowhere else. Earth must be protected even in its current state. We let Lilith take control for this reason alone. We want her to think she has won; her arrogance is such that she will go into battle overconfident."

"Don't underestimate Lilith, she isn't stupid, she'll figure out something's amiss if she hasn't already," Sebastian said.

"We know she's not stupid; we want her to think she has the upper hand," Uriel said. "Come, we must make haste and meet with our battalions at the temple in the Barrens."

"Uriel, you and Augustus should stay here. If things go awry, go to the Taskien dimension. You're the only ones who can protect the people you evacuated. Pheleon, I want you to protect them with your life," Sebastian said.

"Sebastian, no," Uriel protested.

"Uriel, you must do as I ask, please, I will get word to you after the battle."

Uriel nodded. "As you wish."

"There's something else, Lilith seeks to release the Dark One. If she breaks the ancient seal at the temple, the doorway to hell will open and the Dark One and his demon horde will be set free. His physical body has been trapped there for a thousand years, what if she frees him?"

"We must have faith in the prophecy. The Golden One will send him and his demons back for another thousand years, 'tis her destiny." Uriel said.

"That she will, but what of the remaining Vampire Guard? How can we trust them? I saw a number of them among Lilith's Newblood Army when I was captured?" Ambrosia said.

"We've kept them separate from the Seraph Guard so far and mostly in the dark about our plans. We don't know who's loyal to Sebastian or Lilith yet. We were hoping once they saw the Golden One on the battlefield in all her glory we'd be able to figure it out."

"You did the right thing," Pheleon said. "There's discord within the ranks of the Vampire Guard, better to leave them in the dark until the last minute."

"Easier said than done; they grow restless, the few here with us are loyal to Sebastian because they've seen the Golden One already. They too speak of the growing conflict within the ranks. The Vampire Guard believe the Golden One is a myth. Once they see her in the flesh, I believe they'll rally behind her and those who don't will suffer Lilith's fate," Raziel said, crossing his arms over his chest.

The door to Uriel's chamber smashed open, Newbloods

poured into the room. Sebastian could see shimmering walls of white trees leading up to the oasis they stood in, yet he could also see Uriel's chambers. They were among the Newbloods, yet they weren't. The white forest was superimposed over Uriel's room. It was as though they looked through a shimmering wall where they were invisible to all in the chamber. Ambrosia raised her forefinger to her lips and Sebastian nodded, keeping quiet.

The Newbloods searched the room, tossing over lounges, knocking chairs and tables and breaking crystal vases and figurines on shelves. Abigail and Tyrone strode into the room.

"Where the bloody hell are they?" she screeched.

Sebastian caught Ambrosia in his arms as she rushed forward.

"We've searched everywhere, Abigail; they'll not show themselves until they're ready."

"It matters not." She turned and looked out of the window down into the courtyard they'd dragged Ambrosia through. She smiled. "What time is it on Earth now?"

Tyrone looked at his watch. "Nearly dawn, why?"

"Oh, we've got a remodelling project underway." Abigail looked over her shoulder at Tyrone and laughed. Tyrone frowned before he too started laughing.

"Come on, let's search the other rooms, they've got to be here somewhere." Abigail whistled and circled her finger in the air then pointed at the door as she stalked out into the corridor, Tyrone and the Newbloods following her.

Sebastian, and the others watched the last of the Newbloods vacate the room in silence, and waited a further five minutes before speaking.

"How could we have been so blind and not see her evilness, Sebastian? She was so amenable when she first arrived on our doorstep," Ambrosia said. "What do you think she meant by the remodelling comment?"

"Who knows? You're right though, she's a special kind of twisted," Sebastian said. A terrible sense of foreboding settled in the pit of his stomach and he wished he could decipher Abigail's' comment.

"We need to leave, make haste," Uriel said.

CHAPTER 45.

The rooftop Darrius and Morgan stood upon rumbled and jolted; Darrius glanced at his feet, waiting for more to happen. Morgan shrugged.

"So, no planes, no bombs falling from the sky, what do you make of it? Darrius questioned.

"I thought it a little strange for the humans to be up at this ungodly hour; they don't come out after the sun sets." Morgan clenched her hands together, staring out at the horizon.

"Something's wrong," Darrius said, his legs buckling as the building jolted again.

"I don't like it, what if it's like I said, coming from underne—"

The building groaned and giant cracks split across the middle of the roof, the debris littering the surface shifting as large chunks of concrete broke away and fell through a growing fissure. The tinkling of shattering glass and steel building girders shrieking filled the air with the sound of destruction. Dust clouds ballooned in the air as the building fell from beneath their feet. Darrius watched Morgan drop, falling away from him, her hands flailing as she screamed his name. Darrius's wings burst free and he dived after her, dodging building fragments all the while praying she'd not be struck unconscious, or worse, killed. Just as she was about to hit the ground, he dematerialised and reappeared under her, catching her in his arms. He unfurled his wings, and the updraft jettisoned them upwards. Morgan flung her arms around him and curled her face into the crook of his neck. Darrius squeezed her trembling body closer to his. His heart was racing as he dodged projectiles and flew higher into the sky, circling until the dust settled. Darrius looked down and gasped at the devastation. The building they'd been standing on was nothing more than twisted piles of steel and rubble; the surrounding structures squashed by the unrecognisable remains. Billowing flames cast a malevolent orange glow over everything it touched. There were no sirens, no police or fire brigade to help, not any more. The destruction spread across three city blocks. Worst of all was the cavernous crater revealing the once-concealed bunkers.

"Take me down; we've got to help them, Darrius. Ashley's down there, the Shadow Seekers are down there, everyone who matters to us is down there. Take me down, Take me down now!" Morgan shouted, hysterical.

Darrius narrowed his eyes, searching for a safe place to land, then swooped down to an opening big enough for at least ten people to pass through. The stairs that once led down to the compound from the Devil's Pit were no longer there; only a few remained at the base. He flew through the gaping hole, making sure his wings were tucked at his sides; all he needed was to get caught on the twisted metal sticking out from the edges of the opening. Once he passed through, there was enough space for him to extend his wings and land. The moment he set his feet down his wings disappeared into his body. They were in a cavern of sorts near what was once the compound entrance. Burning debris lit the area, casting shadows on the flat slabs of rock barring the way into the compound where the ceiling had caved in. He waved his hand in front of his face, trying to clear the dust hindering his vision. He sighed when he felt the warmth of Morgan's body disappear from his side as she stepped away from him.

"What the bloody hell happened here? I leave for a few hours and everything goes to shit."

Darrius looked up and saw Zack, Thomas and a number of Shadow Seeker students peering over the lip of the gaping hole above. Loose rocks trickled through the opening as they volleyed over the edge and made quick work of scaling down the uneven ruins to where they stood.

"What happened, Darrius?" Zack murmured, when he reached his side.

"We don't know, we thought the humans were dropping

bombs again, so Morgan and I took a look from the Devil Pit's rooftop. The building collapsed from beneath us."

"We need to get in there, Ashley's. . ." Morgan's mouth opened and closed, her face ashen. "Something has happened to Ashley, I can feel it, something's not right, we have to get in there." Morgan rushed towards the chunk of rock barring her way and pounded her fists on it, it didn't budge.

"Move out of the way, Morgan, I've got this," Zack said. Morgan continued bashing on the wall. "Darrius, she needs to get out of the way, you all do, move over there." Zack pointed to their left. "I need space to remove the rock."

Darrius nodded and took Morgan's hand in his, coaxing her away from the barrier blocking their way. "Come now, Morgan, we need to step aside so Zack can remove the obstruction." His heart clenched when she looked up into his face, tear-tracks streaking her dusty face. "Come now, the quicker you move, the quicker we can get to Ashley and the others." Darrius guided Morgan away from the barrier and moved to the side where Thomas and the fledgling students stood.

Zack waited until the area surrounding the barrier was clear, then he closed his eyes, exhaled and inhaled a number of times before opening them again and focusing his attention on the rock barring the entrance. His brow creased and his mouth formed a hard line as he lifted his hands away from his body. He drew his palms together, twisting his hands until they formed fists, bending his elbows and bringing them to his chest.

Rock trembled, pebbles wedged between the rock and the passage wall fell to the ground forming dust clouds. The room shook as the rock moved. Zack swung his arms sideways and up towards the mouth of the crater. The rock shot through the opening like a projectile launched from a cannon. Dust and grit rained over them as it jetted past and out into the lightening sky. There was a loud crash followed by the shrill wailing of a car alarm as the rock hit the street. Darrius's forehead creased at the absurdity of the strident car alarm. How a car and its alarm had survived the current state of the world and the recent collapse of the building was almost laughable.

Zack lowered his hands to his sides as their group gathered before the unblocked passageway; they got their first glimpse of the tunnel beyond when the dust settled. Chunks of rock littered the floor, but not enough to bar their way into the compound. Morgan took off running, dodging debris as she raced towards her sister's lodgings.

Darrius, Zack, Thomas and the student Shadow Seekers followed her. The smell of burning plastic, live wires and acrid smoke was overwhelming. Blinking lights swung back and forth from wiring along the passage ceiling. They sparked and buzzed, casting an unnerving shadow of doom over everything. A rising sense of discord shivered over Darrius's body with every step he took along the light-sputtering passageway, and the bitter taste of premonition left him with tremendous sense of increasing dread. Darrius's intuition was his curse, and he was getting a dizzying dose so strong he knew without a doubt something terrible had happened. Darrius looked at the ceiling; that the compound hadn't already caved in was a miracle. The shifting rasp of rock moving had them looking at one another.

"We need to get everyone out, now, before the compound collapses on our heads," Darrius said, brushing dust and rock particles from his shoulders and looking in the direction Morgan had gone.

"Agreed; we need to find Vasili and the others," Zack said, dividing the students into two groups. He pointed to the first group of students. "Help Darrius find the other Shadow Seekers. You come with me." He pointed to Thomas and the second group of students. "Darrius, who else is down here?"

"Tess, Ava, Gabe, Vasili, Jackson, Tristan, Marianna, Bryce, Freya, Anna and Reece," Darrius counted off the remaining people on his fingers. "Oh, and possibly more students; the Vampire and Seraph Guard are out on patrol, there weren't many of us here, luckily. We were getting ready to leave for Evron before Morgan and I went topside to see what was happening."

"What about Lazarus, wasn't he with you as well?"

"He was, but after we returned from Wigmore Castle I didn't see him in the armoury when we were gathering our weapons, he said something about checking in on Tess at the infirmary, but I couldn't tell you if he did or not."

"Okay, I'll find Vasili and Gabriel first, are you going after Morgan?"

"Yes," Darrius said, looking in the direction Morgan had

gone for the second time, he just wanted to be on his way.

"Could you stop at the infirmary and see if Lazarus is with Tess and Ava? They may need help. I think Bryce and Freya may be there too. I'll see if I can find Vasili and Gabe in Vasili's office, I'm sure Marianna will be with them, and we'll meet you back at the infirmary," Zack said, nodding at Thomas and the students to follow him.

Darrius watched them head towards Vasili's office. There wasn't a great deal of damage in the direction Zack had gone. Darrius turned towards the remaining students who looked at him expectantly; he waved his hand for them to follow. His thoughts wandered to Ashley as they jogged a brisk pace. He hoped she'd found Tristan before the compound had blown; No doubt Tristan would have got her to safety if she had.

As they moved along the passageway, the damage became more visible. Sizeable pieces of rock blocked their way, debris growing thicker with every step closer to Ashley's quarters. They wove through narrow gaps, barely squeezing through. Darrius pushed larger debris out of their way. Many times Darrius wanted to dematerialise, but it was too dangerous; he couldn't see what lay ahead and could end up reappearing in the centre of a rock and killing himself and the students he'd teleport with him.

"NOOOOOOOOOO. . ." Morgan's heart-wrenching scream echoed down the passageway.

Darrius took off sprinting and skidded to a halt when he saw Morgan sitting on the ground, rocking back and forth near a mound of rubble. It wasn't until he drew closer that he saw her holding Ashley's limp hand protruding from the rubble. He dropped to his knees behind Morgan and wrapped his arms around her waist, lowering his mental shield and opening his mind to her, sending healing thoughts her way. Morgan's sorrow beat against him, filling his heart with a crippling ache. Ashley hadn't made it to his brother after all. A large part of the ceiling had broken off and pinned Ashley to the ground and the remaining rubble had buried her in gravel, suffocating her.

"Save her. . .her. . .Darr. . .Darrius, save her, pleas. . .please," Morgan sobbed. *"She's. . . she's all. . .all the family I. . .I. . . have, sav. . .save . . . her. . .herrrr."*

Darrius rested his forehead on the back of Morgan's head. "She's gone, Morgan, she's gone."

"No. . .No. . .sh. . .she can be sav. . .saved, hel. . .help her, where's Ma. . .Makayla, she. . .can save her," Morgan said, between hiccupping sobs.

Morgan's tears dripped on Darrius's forearms, she kept begging him over and over to save Ashley. "Oh, sweetheart, it's too late, she's gone." Morgan shook her head in denial.

Darrius looked up when the rock pinning Ashley to the ground moved. Tristan looked down at him, his face mirroring Morgan's sorrow as he rallied the students to help remove the rock from Ashley's body. The moment Ashley was free, Morgan dragged her into her lap, brushing the gravel from her face and shoulders, taking her hand once more, and flowering kisses over her face. "Wake up, Ashley, you'll be okay. I'm here now, I won't let anything happen to you."

Tristan squatted beside them and swept the hair back from Ashley's beautiful face.

"Where were you, Tristan? She was looking for you," Morgan said in a small voice.

Darrius saw the change in Tristan as his jaw tensed and his eyes glistened and then hardened; a determined look crossed his face as he lifted Ashley into his arms and stood. Morgan's arm stretched upwards, Ashley's hand still in her tight grasp.

"Wait, what are you doing? No, no, no, you can't take her from me, she'll be okay, she'll wake up soon, she's just resting, don't take her from me. *Pleasssse don't take her from me,*" Morgan begged.

Tristan looked at Darrius, Darrius nodded in understanding and sighed when he dematerialised. Morgan's hand clutched air as Ashley's hand disappeared from her grasp. Morgan curled into Darrius's body, sobbing into his shoulder. Darrius swept Morgan into his arms and lifted her as he stood.

He looked at the students. "Come on, we've got to find the others and get our arses topside before the roof comes down on our heads."

Tess groaned and opened her burning eyes, blinking the grit and dust from them until her vision cleared. She squinted as she looked about; all she could see were rocks blinking in and out of focus as the fluorescent ceiling lights flashed. She shook her head, trying to rid herself of the disorienting dizziness. Her head throbbed in defiance; she tried to get her bearings, trying to remember what had happened. The last thing she recalled was crawling under the bed because she'd seen something. Tess looked about for the object and found it lying near her fingertips. She stretched out and hooked it with her fingernails. She held it up to her eyes, it was no longer flashing.

Tess's eyes widened. "Ava," she yelled. "AVA!" she shouted louder, coughing as dust stuck in her throat, her chest aching. Still no response. "Ava, are you okay?" More silence. "Maybe she got out in time? Or she's unconsciousness," she said to herself.

Tess tried to roll over, but the squashed bed frame pinned her body to the ground. She strained to drag in a deep breath, and was rewarded with a sharp, stabbing pain in her ribs. Wiggling her fingers, she edged her hands underneath her chest and pushed upwards, her back hit the underside of the bed frame, but it didn't budge. She sagged to the floor and brought her knees to her chest in the foetal position. She squirmed, wriggling her body little by little until she was laying on her side. Thank goodness she'd crawled under the bed, otherwise she'd have been a red splat on the floor instead … but she was no better off where she was, neatly entombed in stone. Not how she thought she'd go. She prayed Ava had heard her warning and taken cover before the bomb detonated. "She'll be okay, she teleported herself to safety," Tess said reassuring herself

Ava was safe.

"Tess . . . Ava?" someone called. "Where are you?"

Tess tried to respond, but only managed a broken croak, the dust had settled in her throat, making her tongue thick. She swallowed, but it was useless, she had no saliva to wet her tongue. Pebbles trickled overhead as rocks were moved.

"Tess, can you hear me?"

Tess sighed when she recognised Lazarus's voice. "Laz. . . I'm here," she murmured, then cleared her throat. "Laz," she said with more strength. "I'm here, under Freya's bed, help."

"I'm coming, little bee, hang tight, is Ava with you?"

"She was in the lab, I think, I don't know if she got out."

The grinding of rocks being moved, pushed and thrown out of the way echoed about her, more pebbles showered overhead, filtering down through the cracks, weight shifted on the bed, the metal frame creaked, labouring under the heavy mass; the steel buckled as it gave way and crushed her to the floor. Tess pushed upwards, trying to slow the bed's descent, but wasn't strong enough to stop the vice-like pressure.

Her chest burned and white stars spun across her vision as she struggled to gasp in oxygen; no matter how hard she tried to breathe, more air was expunged from her body. She gulped in small amounts of oxygen, panting, hoping it would help stop the burning in her lungs, but it was getting worse. She tried to call out to Lazarus, but the strain on her chest and the stabbing pain in her ribs was too much. Her breathing became laboured and panic overwhelmed her; she scratched and pushed the bed above her in a frenzy, trying to free herself. Tess licked her lips and tasted dust and the metallic flavour of blood. She moved to her right, trying to find more space, if she could only get comfortable so she could breathe. A metal bracket snapped and stabbed her in the chest searing her with stinging heat, she groaned, too weak to scream out. Blood soaked her clothing and she sighed, finally she felt warm. *Dying wasn't so bad.*

"Laz," she whispered, wishing she could see his handsome face one more time before she died. She knew it was the end and didn't mind so much, she was numb; it didn't hurt anymore, now she could be with Ryan. *"Goodbye, Laz."*

"Hang on, Tess, I'm nearly there," Lazarus yelled. "Don't leave me, stay with me, little bee."

A soft smile formed on her face when she saw Ava. *"Ava, you're okay, I'm glad."*

Tess closed her eyes.

Lazarus could hear Tess's heart fading and smell the unmistakable scent of her blood. The hospital bed she was trapped under was compacted beneath some rocks. It looked as though a junkyard car crusher had squashed it. Most of the debris barring his way into the room he'd removed. He was so close to her yet so far. Tess was fading fast. Lazarus looked at the ceiling, hoping it would hold. There was a huge crater with a sizeable crack in the rock surface. If he didn't hurry, the rest of the roof would come crashing down. He glanced where the lab door should have been, the room was rubble from the cave-in. He exhaled in relief when he saw Ava standing nearby, her troubled face creased with worry, and looking towards the twisted bed frame.

"Hurry, she hasn't long to live," Ava said, coming to his side.

"Hang on, little bee," Lazarus yelled, tossing debris out of the way as he pushed through the rubble cluttering the floor. He made it to the bed and noticed the missing part of the ceiling had landed on top of the bed; he looked back up at the crater, worried more would fall. Lazarus grabbed a hold of the rock slab crushing the bed and lifted, but it wouldn't budge.

"Fuck." He directed all his strength into shifting it; it moved a little, but not enough to free the bed. He tried again, yelling out as he got it moving, but he still couldn't lift it high enough to free Tess.

"Come on, put your back into it," Gabe said, appearing out of nowhere.

Lazarus nodded. "On three: one, two, three!"

They lifted it enough to free the bed. "I got it, Lazarus, you pull her out, quickly now, because I don't know how long I can hold it."

Lazarus dropped to his knees and his heart jumped into his throat when he saw Tess's limp form. He gripped the metal bracket stabbing her chest and eased it out as fast as he could and then grabbed her shoulders and tugged her out from under the bed. The moment her body was free, Gabriel lowered the rock.

Lazarus held his fingers to Tess's throat, searching for a heartbeat, it was faint, she was still alive, but that wouldn't last, she'd lost a large amount of blood and was losing more from her injury. He ripped the hem of her shirt and bunched it up, pressing it to the wound on her chest to staunch the flow of blood.

He glanced at Ava. "What do we do, Ava, tell me what to do?"

Gabriel frowned and looked around the room.

"Ava, help, tell me what to do."

Ava crouched down beside him, indicating for him to show her the wound, she shook her head. *"The wound's too deep, she's lost too much blood, there's nothing we can do."* She looked around the infirmary. *"The infirmary's destroyed, Laz, I'm sorry."*

"No, I won't accept that, she can't die, you have to help her."

"There's only one thing you can do, Lazarus," Darrius said from where he was standing in the infirmary doorway with Morgan in his arms.

"And what's that?" Lazarus asked.

"Change her into a vampire; but you gotta do it now, she's dying."

Lazarus looked down at Tess, what if she didn't want to be a vampire, what if she hated him afterwards? "I've never done it before, what if I screw-up?" Lazarus said to Darrius.

"Do you want me to do it?"

"Hell no, she's my responsibility, I'll do it. Tell me what I need to do?"

"You need to drink the rest of her blood until there's barely any left and then feed her your blood."

"Are you daft, man, she's not got a lot of blood left, if I take the rest it'll kill her."

"If you don't she's dead anyway, hurry before it's too late. You need not take much, just enough to make the connection, you need to have her blood in your system to sire her. Hurry. She's fading," Darrius urged.

Lazarus lifted Tess's wrist to his mouth and bit into her flesh, his teeth popping through her tender flesh. He heard Tess's soft whimper as he drank her blood and groaned, his eyes rolling in his head as her sweet blood glided down his throat. He hadn't tasted human blood in centuries.

Tess's life flashed before his eyes: he saw her deliriously happy on her wedding day and felt a twinge of jealousy, but it was replaced with sadness as he saw Tess witness her husband's murder. Next she was standing at her husband's graveside tossing flowers into the grave as the coffin was lowered into the ground. He saw into every corner of her life from childhood until the day he'd rescued her.

"Lazarus, stop, you'll kill her."

Lazarus gasped and threw back his head as he detached his fangs from her wrist; he licked the wound, healing it with his saliva. He bit into his own wrist and dripped blood into her mouth; she didn't respond, so he lifted her into his lap and coaxed her, placing his wrist to her mouth. Her head lolled to the side. "Come on, little bee, don't leave me, drink and we'll be together forever, please drink, don't leave me."

Lazarus grasped the back of her head with his free hand and guided her mouth to his wrist. His blood smeared all over her face. He heard Tess gasp as she inhaled and watched her tongue flick out and lick her lips before she latched onto the wound at his wrist. Lazarus watched her wound heal as she fed. She drank slowly at first, and more heavily as she grew stronger. Lazarus shivered, his head dropping back on his shoulders, desire swirling beneath his skin as her lips worked a burning fire through his body, rewarding him with an instant erection. He groaned in delirium and looked into Tess's dilated eyes; she had a lusty appetite and a similarly lusty look on her face – much as he was sure he had. She stopped feeding and lifted her face, her eyes wide and searching, her mouth covered in his blood. She'd never looked more beautiful. She licked her lips and focused on his mouth, the hunger for more than blood evident in her eyes. Lazarus gulped, sensing her desire through their blood-bond connection.

"Ahem." Darrius cleared his throat.

Lazarus looked up and smiled self-consciously. "I guess it worked,"

Tess stiffened in his arms; she groaned in pain and grasped her stomach as cramps seized her body. She convulsed, her body twisting and contorting as a seizure overcame her. Lazarus grimaced, he'd caused her pain and he hated himself for that – but he'd have hated himself more if he'd just let her die. Tess screamed, her piercing shrieks cutting the silence as the transition took hold. Lazarus held onto her until her tight grasp relaxed and her fingernails no longer bit into his skin. The moment she calmed, her body slumped unconscious. Lazarus lifted her into his arms and stood. He glanced towards Gabriel who wore a questioning frown on his face. Lazarus looked to his side and smiled at Ava, who smiled back.

"I think we better be getting out of here," Darrius said. "Did you see Zack in your travels Gabe?"

Gabriel eyed Darrius. "No, Jackson and I were on our way to Vasili's office when the bombs went off. I never got to Vasili's office, Jackson and I were separated. I imagine Vasili's getting Marianna to safety. I came here to get Ava, has anyone seen her?"

Lazarus glanced at Ava. "She's standing right next to you, Gabe."

Gabriel grabbed a handful of Lazarus's shirt and pulled him close, until their faces almost touched. He glanced down at Tess before pinning him with his intense gaze again. "I don't know what game you're playing, Lazarus, but she isn't standing next to me."

"I see her too, Gabe," Darrius said.

"She's touching your elbow," Lazarus said, looking at Ava.

Ava shook her head and pointed towards the lab. Lazarus paled and looked in the direction of the laboratory. He shook his head. "No, no, no, she's in the lab, Gabe." Lazarus jumped up and flashed forward and banged his shoulder against the debris blocking the lab, but he couldn't do much with Tess in his arms.

"Help them," Darrius ordered the students standing nearby.

Gabriel's face went blank; he ran towards the blocked doorway and began to remove rocks, along with the group of fledgling students. There was a huge rock blocking their way and nothing they did could move the barrier. Gabriel screamed in frustration, he smashed his fists against it to no avail and then all of a sudden he stopped, his face resigned. An unnatural calm overcame him. Gabriel opened his hands and splayed them over the rock. He lowered his forehead to the barrier and recited an incantation, shouting out the last words in anger. His hands glowed white and there was a low-frequency humming from his fingertips vibrating against the rock so fast. The vibration coalesced to a high-pitched ringing and then the rock barrier exploded into dust, sizzling until there was nothing left to settle on the ground. Lazarus watched Gabriel stride into the debris-free laboratory, not one rock or dust particle remained. Ava lay on the floor, her body pulverised. The stool she'd been sitting on was the only thing holding her together, it had become part of her body the legs having been forced through her, stabbing her like a pin cushion. The only undamaged part of her body was her striking face, the rest of her body was crushed and bloody. Gabriel made not a sound, he crouched down beside her and brushed the hair from her eyes, silent tears streaming down his face. He touched his finger to the twisted remains of the stool and they too disintegrated with a single touch. Gabriel inhaled a deep breath and picked her up; she sagged against his body like a boneless rag-doll. He strode out of the room in silence. Darrius followed him out with Morgan in his arms, along with Lazarus and Tess and the group of students. They headed towards Vasili's quarters and there they found Jackson on the floor, propped against a wall, the lower half of his body crushed by a huge rock. He was unconscious. Gabriel touched the rock with his fingertip as they passed, it turned to dust, releasing him. Zack and Thomas came barrelling around the corner and slid to a stop when they noticed them, the students following behind crashed into them almost toppling them to the floor like bowling pins. Gabe continued on in silence. Zack took in their ragtag group and when he noticed Jackson lying unconscious, he hauled him up and swung Jackson's arm over his shoulder, Thomas looped Jackson's other arm over his own shoulder and they followed Gabriel.

"Did you find Vasili?" Darrius asked Zack as he came to his side.

Zack shook his head. "He wasn't in his office. I think he's in his private quarters with Marianna."

"Gabriel said as much."

"What about Reece and Anna?"

Zack shook his head again. "I didn't see them; they weren't in their rooms so I'm assuming they got out."

"Bryce and Freya weren't in the infirmary either, I hope they got out," Darrius said.

The mood was sombre as they headed towards Vasili's room and they stopped when they realised they could go no further; the whole section where Vasili's quarters were housed had come crashing down.

"Vasili, can you hear me?" Lazarus said telepathically, trying to connect with Vasili's mind. Nothing. He tried again and got no response.

"Do you think they made it out?" Zack asked.

"I hope so," Lazarus said.

"I don't know, this section of tunnel seems to have sustained most of the damage," Darrius noted.

The tunnel grumbled, the walls trembling as rocks and dust rained down over them once more. The group stopped and looked up at the tunnel ceiling.

Gabriel wore the dead expression of a shark, his hooded eyes cold and devoid of emotion as he turned to Darrius. "How did you get back into the compound after the explosions?" Darrius told him just as the floor rolled beneath their feet. "It's going to come down; everyone out now!" Gabriel's voice boomed.

"What about Vasili and Marianna and the others?" Zack asked. "We have to find them."

"Take a good look, Zack." Gabriel pointed down the passageway towards Vasili's chambers. "Does it look like we can get through? If Vasili can get out, he will, he's more capable than any of us, he's probably topside already and the others are most likely there. NOW, move your arses, we need

to get out."

Vasili sat on the ground in his chambers with his back propped against a small patch of wall unhindered by debris. The broken body of his wife lay lifeless in his arms. He hadn't got to her in time; she'd died alone, crushed by falling rocks while she'd slept. Vasili's tight chest burned as he looked about his chamber, there wasn't much standing now. Nothing but shattered rocks and destroyed furniture. He didn't bother sweeping away the tears pooling in his eyes and they streaked down his face to drip onto his shirt unguarded. He swallowed the lump in his throat and kissed Marianna's cool cheek, exhausted by it all. "I love you," he whispered. "I'm sorry I failed you." His voice caught. "I don't want to do this without you, I don't want to live without you, I ca. . .can't, not without you. Not again." Vasili looked up at the rock ceiling with a numb calmness and sighed as the sound of cracking rock echoed about the room. A giant fissure opened above them, the room shook, dust and small pebbles rained down. He'd not foreseen their fate and was grateful; he hadn't had a vision since Marianna's return – a welcome reprieve. He looked down at his wife and caressed her cheek. "Not long now, Agapi-mou, I will join you soon, my love." Vasili exhaled and closed his eyes. A soft smile hovered on his lips as he thought of his sons, of Nikolai in particular, who would take their deaths hard.

Vasili wished he could say one final goodbye to Nikolai in person, but it was not to be. *"Goodbye, Nikolai, I love you, son."*

"Father, what's wrong?"

"Our time has com—" Vasili was cut off as a large rock finally crashed down.

CHAPTER 46.

The large courtyard in front of the small Greek Orthodox church was shaded by the budding leaves of a thousand year old fig tree. There were benches with peeling blue paint built around the base of the tree so people could sit and escape the heat in the summer months. Alexander lay stretched out on one such bench with his arms beneath his head and his feet crossed, looking up through the tree canopy. A light breeze fluttered the leaves as the first rays of sunlight filtered through a dusting of clouds and the foliage. Winter was coming to a close and spring was just around the corner. Alexander heard the scraping of a stray leaf blowing across the ground; he snatched it up and twirled it between his fingertips. He narrowed his eyes, marvelling at his new-found vampire sight; he could see the intricate veins and texture of the dried leaf he held. He let go and watched it spiral off when the wind caught it in its invisible grasp once more. He rolled to his side on the bench and lowered his finger to the ground tracing a finger along the dirt. There was another world beneath their feet unaffected by the tragedies of the world they lived in. Alexander put his finger in the path of a line of giant ants and they altered their course and continued around his finger, trailing behind one another as they gathered food.

Alexander turned his attention back to the tree canopy; wrens flitted from branch to branch, their sweet song serenading as he waited for Danny to come back. He was speaking with Pater Nikolao, discussing the preparations necessary for the exorcism Alexander was to undergo. Alexander had thought about the questions he wanted to ask the priest beforehand, but sometimes not knowing the dangers that lay ahead was better – ignorance really was bliss. Alexander's thoughts strayed to Makayla; where was she? Was she okay? Was she safe? Had she found the next Trinian gem without encountering danger? Would everything work out? They were the questions he really wanted to know the answers to. Alexander sighed, the bad feeling he had was getting worse; he resigned himself to the fact things would be how they were meant to be. He swept his hand over his jaw and felt the rough sand-papery texture of his whiskers against his hand. He closed his eyes and savoured the cool wind against his face. The weather hadn't warmed but he welcomed the invigorating cool climate now his body temperature was running hotter.

A shadow came over him and he opened his eyes to Danny

staring down at him.

"We're ready for you now, Xander."

Alexander swung up into a sitting position and looked over his shoulder towards the church when the church bells chimed. He placed his hands either side of his legs and pushed up and stood.

"You ready?" Danny asked.

"No, but that's neither here nor there, let's get this done." Alexander massaged his brow. "Danny, if this all goes to shit, please take care of my wife."

"She's like my sister, Xander, I'll always take care of her. It won't come to that, though, come on."

"If it does, I want you to put me down; don't ask questions, just do it."

"It won't come to tha—"

"If it does, promise me you'll end me. I don't want Makayla to do it, it would kill her, the wilding will consume her forever. This battle can't be won without her."

"I won't kill you, Xander, so don't ask me to. I could never face Makayla afterwards. I promise I'll find a way to get the Dark One out of you, but I'll not sacrifice your life to do it. That's the only promise I'll make you today." Alexander nodded and followed Danny towards the church and turned down a small path that led behind the building to the back door.

"Xander, where are you going, you've got to enter through the front door not the back."

Alexander stopped when he felt Danny's hand on his

elbow; the last thing he remembered was their conversation and following him towards the front of the church. He frowned. "Sorry, I. . . I don't know what happened." Alexander rubbed his forehead, pressure building behind his temples.

"This way," Danny said, guiding him back to the front of the church.

Alexander stopped at the door, he didn't want to go in. Something crawled under his skin and a cold sweat sheened his face, he physically couldn't cross the threshold into the church. It wasn't until Pater Nikolao moved into the doorway and placed his hand on Alexander's chest that he calmed. Pater Nikolao joined the first three fingers on his right hand to symbolise the holy trinity, bowed his head and crossed himself. He did this three times. Pater Nikolao raised his head and lifted a brass goblet filled with blessed holy oil. He dipped his thumb in and traced a cross on Alexander's forehead anointing him all the while speaking Ancient Koine Greek; a Hellenistic biblical Greek Alexander recognised. Alexander looked up into the kind eyes of the priest, a tranquil peace overcame him and he was able to move again.

Pater Nikolao turned, facing the altar at the back of the room, Alexander heard the swish of his black robes as he moved down the centre aisle of the church towards the dais. Danny held his arm out, encouraging Alexander to move into the chapel. The moment Alexander crossed the threshold the smell of tree resin incense immersed him. It wasn't strong and overpowering like other churches he'd been in, it was a delicate, subtle, sweet-smelling fragrance that soothed his chafed nerves.

"Come, do what I do," Danny said, crossing himself in the same manner the priest had done moments ago. Alexander watched Danny light three beeswax candles and place them in a tray filled with white sand and other burning candles. "I lit three candles for the holy trinity: the father, the son and the holy spirit," Danny explained. Alexander nodded, he was familiar with the doctrine. Alexander crossed himself and lit three candles, copying Danny.

Danny crossed himself again before kissing an icon positioned next to the sand tray. Alexander knew Danny wasn't worshipping the image or the icon, but venerating it and showing special respect for the saints depicted on the icons.

Alexander mimicked Danny and then followed him down the aisle to where Pater Nikolao waited behind a small lectern where a golden bible lay open before him. Biblical paintings of angels and saints covered the dome ceiling of the church, which itself was small, with few pews to sit on. There were candles everywhere, placed along the side and back walls, behind the altar and hanging from the ceiling in what appeared to be a chandelier. Gilded icons were positioned around the room; images of the Virgin Mary with baby Jesus cradled in her arms, Saint George slaying the Dragon, and many others. There was a large wood carving of Christ nailed to the cross hanging on the wall behind the altar. Two candle stands stood either side of the lectern filled with more beeswax candles. Their wavering flames cast a gentle ambience over the entire area.

Pater Nikolao came out from behind the lectern and stood before Alexander, who bowed his head in respect and kissed the priest's hand when he held it out to him.

"Good morning, Alexander, my name is Pater Ioannis Nikolao, 'tis an honour to make your acquaintance."

Alexander looked up into Pater Ioannis's face. "Good morning, Pater, I too am honoured to meet you and thank you for your willingness to perform this exorcism at such short notice."

"Do you have any questions, my son?"

"I have questions, Pater, and many doubts, but I will forego voicing them. I fear knowing the answers would cause more harm than good, your holiness."

"As you wish. Please lower yourself to the floor and kneel so we can begin. I ask that you open yourself up to the divine spirit of the Holy Trinity and our Lord God and, where necessary, respond to any questions I ask."

"Yes, Pater, I will."

The priest nodded and proceeded to the back of the altar where a small podium stood with an icon of Jesus, a dish of holy water, the brass goblet with the anointing oil he'd used earlier and hundreds of candles. He said a blessing over his stole and kissed the cross embroidered on the front before looping it over his head and settling it on his shoulders and chanting. He crossed himself and kissed the icon of Christ, bowed his head and touched the floor. He did this three times, then lifted a three-chained thurible filled with burning incense from a stand and did three double swings as he circled the small podium three times.

The loud jingle of the thurible bells and the strong scent of resin incense filled the small chapel, clouding the area in thick smoke. Alexander closed his eyes and breathed in the purifying incense, shivering as the priest's chanting grew louder. There was a sudden silence. Alexander opened his eyes and found Pater Nikolao standing in front of him.

"Alexander Beiynon Drakeius, do you surrender thy self to the sanctity of the all-powerful God, the son and the holy spirit?"

"I do," Alexander replied.

"Let us pray." Pater Nikolao placed the edges of his stole over Alexander's bowed head and lay the palm of his hand on top and began the exorcism prayer in ancient Greek.

The moment Pater Nikolao began to pray Alexander felt the sigil he'd cut into his chest burn, the pain was bearable, just, but he knew in his heart the sigil was failing. Alexander could feel the Dark One growing stronger, his presence awakening within him, squirming beneath the surface of his skin and psyche. Alexander lost track of time, he was no longer in the Greek church, but stood in a dark void only he seemed privy to. The priest's voice faded until Alexander no longer heard him.

"Fool, do you think to exorcise me so easily?" the Dark One's malicious voice echoed. *"You'll not be rid of me, Druid, I will steal your memories and bend your body to my will until*

you no longer exist."

"You can try," Alexander replied.

"You will die, as everyone does, and I will live forever."

Alexander laughed. "If living forever means burning for an eternity, then I'd rather be dead."

"Soon you'll be no more."

"How do you figure?"

"While you're here with me, I have access to your memories; when your body awakens, I'll be the one in control."

"You underestimate me greatly, my power is beyond your control."

"We shall see. I am your end and your beginning, I am your destiny."

"Um, haven't we had this conversation before? I believe my response was, and still is, I have one destiny and her name is Makayla Uriel." Alexander smiled, his fangs lengthening as he rubbed his hands together, threads of electricity buzzing between his palms. He swept his arms in wide arcs, blue lightning circling about his body as he pushed his hands upwards and slammed his hands together. Blue pulsing waves of light blasted outwards, everything crystallised; ice covered every crack, every crevice, every object in the area. A thirty-foot mass stood frozen before him. Alexander moved towards the entity and formed an electromagnetic plasma ball in the palms of his circling hands then hurled it towards the entity. The giant mass exploded and shattered, small ice particles raining down over his head like snow.

Malicious laughter boomed around him, Alexander's smile faltered. He was back in the fiery cave again, standing on the rock ledge with the river of hot flowing magma to his right. The tunnels leading to all his memories appeared and Alexander swallowed the lump in his throat as the rock ledge disappeared and he flitted from one tunnel to the next. Alexander was an unwilling passenger on a carnival ride from hell and the Dark One was his tour guide. Alexander's memories flipped past like the pages of a magazine fluttering in the wind. The Dark One was shuffling his memories like a deck of cards and splaying them out for him to pick a card, any card – only in the Dark One's case, it was pick a memory, any memory. Which memory was the Dark One going to steal? Which memory was Alexander going to lose?

One by one his memories were stolen. When he saved Makayla as a young girl from being raped in her village. Makayla saving his life when she'd travelled back in time. Makayla standing on the battlements of Corfe Castle, staring up at the moon. Their first kiss at Cambridge university. Makayla in the elevator travelling up to his apartment. Sitting on his verandah drinking and chatting with one another. Flying the English channel together. When she sired him. The dance they'd shared in the Devil's Pit. The Dark One seemed to be taking the smaller moments first and saving the bigger events in his life until last.

Alexander screamed.

Danny looked down at Alexander's heaving body, his breathing deep and gravelly as if a beast were choking the breath from him. The moment Pater Nikolao recited the exorcism prayer Alexander's breathing worsened and became more laboured. Danny had seen it many times, but this time there was something different. Alexander yelled out and blue lightning circled about his body, buzzing and growing more vivid, electrolysing the air. When Pater Nikolao came to the end of the prayer, Alexander stopped yelling. A sonic boom exploded from his body extinguishing all the candles in the chapel. Danny looked up when he felt grit shower down from the ceiling. He glanced towards Pater Nikolao and watched him cross himself three times and remove the ends of his stole from the back of Alexander's head. The church shuddered.

"Do you think it worked?" Danny asked Pater Nikolao.

"Time will tell."

Alexander's body trembled and his irregular breathing worried Danny. When he started gasping and coughing Danny knew something was wrong. Great hacking coughs turned to gagging and dry heaving. Danny grabbed a bowl from a nearby table and squatted near Alexander, holding it under his mouth expecting him to vomit. As quickly as he'd begun coughing and gagging, he stopped, toppled forward and lost consciousness. The floor beneath Alexander's body cracked open; Danny grabbed his arm and pulled him back, watching the crack progress across the floor and up the wall to spread across the ceiling. The church shuddered as if an earthquake was shaking the ground. Fragments of the ceiling broke away, raining over them. Danny pulled Pater Nikolao to the ground where he and Alexander were. The moment the priest was close Danny's wings flashed out of his back. He unfurled and curled his six wings over their heads and threw up a protective shield to shelter them from the falling debris.

Danny glanced at Pater Nikolao, his fascinated bug-eyed expression as he gazed at his wings made Danny smile. Danny watched the priest raise his hand to the underside of his wings and glide his fingertips over the downy feathers in wonderment.

"I've always known there was something different about you, Danny, something special, but I never imagined you were a seraph."

"Well, I'm not exactly a seraph, I'm a seraphympire."

"What's a seraphympire?"

"I don't want to scare you, Pater, but if I tell you, you may end up fearing me, and I don't want your opinion to change because of what I am. I would never harm you."

"I see the good in you, Danny."

"I'm half seraph, half vampire."

Pater Nikolao's eyes widened. "I thought vampires were a myth?"

"No, not a myth. Now, take a deep breath and hold my arm, I need to get us out of here," Danny said, scooping Alexander into his arms and dematerialising them outside.

They reappeared in the courtyard beneath the giant fig tree. Danny dropped the shield and lowered Alexander to the bench, straightening before folding his wings behind his back. A crowd of villagers gathered in the courtyard staring at the ruins of the fallen church.

"Sorry about your church, Pater."

Pater Nikolao looked at the ruins, and then back at Danny. "God works in mysterious ways, my son."

One by one the villagers noticed them. There were many gasps, wide-eyed expressions and open mouths as their eyes fell on Danny and his wings. Danny lifted his hand and waved at them.

"Well, I think I better be going now." Danny heaved Alexander up into his arms again and unfurled his wings."

"Shouldn't we wait until Alexander is conscious to see if the exorcism was a success?" Pater Nikolao asked. Danny looked towards the villagers again, "I think it would be best if we left. Thank you for helping Alexander, Pater."

Pater Nikolao nodded. "You're welcome, my son, I too thank you."

Danny nodded, flapped his wings and launched into the sky, dematerialising midair.

CHAPTER 47.

Swirls of sparkling light spiralled about the Trinian Globe in glittering arcs as it floated high above Makayla's head towards the golden dome in the centre of the ceiling. Wafer-like filaments of light expanded and grew with intensity; illuminating more of her surroundings. She was back in the cavern underneath her parents' home. The place Tristan had referred to as her space before she'd travelled back in time. Things were coming full circle now and the Trinian Globe had transported her to the one place she felt the most at ease. All things considered, the situation, the destination she found herself in, seemed fitting. The last piece of the puzzle was yet to unfold, but she knew when it did, it would be momentous.

Makayla savoured the tranquillity and breathed in the clean, untainted air. The smell of damp earth and limestone was refreshing. Strange, though, that it didn't smell like other underground caverns. She closed her eyes and listened to her surroundings, dripping and trickling water echoed about her. The underground cavern she lay in was as awe-inspiring as the first time she'd seen it. To say she experienced a profound sense of belonging was undeniable, she felt at ease even when the world outside was crumbling and suffocating in ashes. Makayla opened her eyes and held her breath waiting for the Trinian Globe to touch the golden dome. Would the next gem magically appear like the rest had? The moment the connection was made, light travelled down the sides of the walls, electrifying the room in brightness. The true size and splendour of the room came into view as sparks showered over her in a dazzling firework display. She'd almost forgotten how enormous and magnificent the cavern was.

She felt dwarfed by countless rows of massive columns emerging from the rock floor were revealed. Buttress arches peeled off the tops of the columns stretching high into a ceiling covered in glow worms; aqua-blue radiance lit the space with a star-like quality. The mix of architectural mastery and resplendent sections of chunky, untouched rocks covered in sparkling glow worms was breathtaking. Makayla's gaze wandered along the left wall, taking in the underground lake snaking along its length and reflecting the ceiling's blue ambience.

The Trinian Globe drew her attention; it was pulsating and radiating beams of coloured light flared. The light revolved from one spot to the other in a kaleidoscope of colourful beams as if a band were about to step on stage. The light beams coalesced to form one multi-coloured beam of light and projected onto a specific point on the wall. Makayla sat up and leaned forward, trying to make sense of what she was seeing. The light projected on the upper point of her personal gateway carved into the wall. Makayla stood, brushed the dust from her trousers and walked towards the gateway carving. Gold and blue light lit the hieroglyphs like they had when she and Tristan had touched the wall, only this time neither of them were touching the wall. Something was pushing out and rising to the surface of the stone as if the rock was giving birth to new life. A diamond suddenly appeared and ejected from the gateway carving, floating towards the Trinian Globe of its own accord. A rainbow of colour reflected off its facets as it hovered in the air. Makayla knew instinctively that it was the Gem of Power.

Fibre-like strands of light stretched out like grasping fingers, curling about the gem and drawing it back into the Trinian Globe. There was an explosion of white light. Makayla was momentarily blinded, stars danced in front of her face. She rubbed her eyes with the heels of her hands as a transparent wave shimmered over the walls of the cavern like an illusion was dropping. Makayla blinked and rubbed her eyes again, and almost bit her tongue, what lay before her was no longer an empty cavern but an ancient city like something on one of her beloved Greek islands. Whitewashed, square buildings, with flat roofs, square windows and rectangular doors surrounded her as far as the eye could see. She stood in a small courtyard just below the golden dome at the edge of what looked to be an enormous bowl-shaped fire pit. A mosaic of decorative swirls and bright coloured patterns covered the surrounding floor. Narrow streets and stairs led to many of the abodes. It was as if she'd stepped back in time and was in an ancient city made of stone. She opened the door of a nearby house and was surprised to see furnishings; beds, tables and chairs, jugs, pots, pans, mugs and tableware, a wood stove, kerosene lanterns sat on bedside tables, a hearth, lounge chairs of simple design; there were no modern day appliances. The interior looked much like her home on her Greek island; simple, warm and inviting. Makayla closed the door and went back out into the courtyard. The Trinian Globe beamed down like the sun, its glowing light shining over everything from its rotating position above her. Had she stumbled upon a lost city? How was it even possible? What did it mean? Was this the last sanctuary on Earth? Was she meant to fill the houses with people? Why had the Trinian Globe manifested the city? Was it out of necessity or was something terrible about to happen?

Excruciating pain struck Makayla in the chest as if a sword had stabbed her. Her stomach cramped as if someone was twisting her body within giant hands; she dropped to her knees and screamed, agony searing through her body like a hot dagger. *"Noooooooooooo,"* she sobbed. She saw the collapse and destruction of the underground compound, and the deaths of Ashley, Ava, Vasili and her Aunt Marianna buried in rubble. Their deaths flashed before her eyes as if she were experiencing them herself. A crushing weight compressed her, her armour felt like it was squeezing the oxygen from her body. She couldn't breathe and gasped, dust coating her tongue and the sensation of pebbles filling her mouth and choking her. She began to cough and gag, her chest burning from lack of oxygen. Her vision blurred, the ceiling spun and turned black as she lost consciousness.

Zobiana paced back and forth waiting for Kraegan's arrival, she turned when she heard the door slide open. The pressure eased in her breast when she saw him hovering in the doorway. She wanted to run to him, but clenched her hands instead, digging her fingernails into her palms. He was much like her. She watched him close the door and make his way towards her with a smooth, confident gait. He stopped inches from her and gazed down with a look akin to appreciation, then slid a finger across her jaw towards her lips. She held her breath. Why couldn't she have what she really wanted? Like in the past, it could never be, she was doomed to die alone, tied to the Dark One, feeling the bitter bite of loneliness. She'd had two chances at love long ago, but arrogance had controlled her will to submit the first time. The second time they'd executed her lover. Zobiana looked at her feet feeling nothing but impending doom. The Dark One was too powerful and would never let her go.

Kraegan brushed hair from her eyes. "It is done, the

compound is destroyed as you requested."

Zobiana swallowed the lump in her throat. "Any casualties?"

"I would think so, I don't know how many were there; I left as the bombs were detonated. Time will tell. We must prepare, though, they'll be coming for blood now."

Zobiana nodded.

"I thought you'd be happy, I did as promised."

"I am. I am." Zobiana pasted a smile to her face. "Have you heard any news from your father?"

Kraegan shook his head. "No, Father's gone underground, we'll not hear from him until he resurfaces. It could be years before that happens."

"I thought he wanted to rule Evron?" Zobiana queried.

"I believe Father has set his sights higher and has left Evron to you," Kraegan said.

The door crashed against the wall and Abigail strode into the room. Kraegan turned, folded his arms behind his back and stood beside Zobiana. Zobiana expected him to pull the hood over his head and mask his identity, but he didn't, instead he raised his chin with regal arrogance. Abigail stopped mid-stride and eyed him openly before focusing her attention on her mother.

"Sorry for the interruption, Mother," she stammered eyeing Kraegan from head to toe. "I thought you were alone."

"Is that how you always enter a room, cousin?" Kraegan sneered, bringing his arms to the front and crossing them over his chest.

Abigail's face paled, her mouth working open and closed as she looked between her mother and Kraegan.

"This is your half cousin, Kraegan, Malachi's firstborn son and brother to Lazarus," Zobiana introduced.

"Cousin?" Abigail frowned. "Didn't Makayla kill you?" Abigail stepped back when Kraegan growled.

Zobiana touched his arm in a soothing manner. "I brought him back from death's door," she said, placating him with the gentle caress of her fingertips. "Why are you here, Abigail?"

"We found the seraph army; they're in the Barrens."

Zobiana looked at Kraegan; a lethal, predatory grin marred his features. Zobiana had always known they'd fight the final battle at the Dark One's temple where the doorway into the underworld was located and his corporal body was imprisoned. Without the Trinian Globe the Dark One wasn't getting free, unless …

The realisation dawned on her. Her heart hammered in her chest. The Dark One had wanted Alexander all along because he was the Key, not Makayla. How had she not seen it, how had she been so blind? Abigail was the one who had suggested using Alexander's body as a vessel for the Dark One's possession – had she known Alexander was the key to the Dark One's freedom? Impossible, unless it was the Dark One's plan from the beginning. Zobiana thought back to all the orders the Dark One had ever given her. He'd told her to kidnap the cryptologist after she'd retrieved the Trinian Globe; she'd thought it a solid plan because the Trinian Globe needed translating, but without Alexander the ancient hieroglyphs on the temple were also undecipherable.

Had her daughter and the Dark One played her? Zobiana narrowed her eyes on her daughter. "Abigail, how did you come up with the idea for using Alexander's body as a vessel for the Dark One to possess?"

"The Dark One came to me in a dream, it was. . . Um. . .very erotic." Abigail cleared her throat and blushed. "He, um, he—"

"No need to tell me more," Zobiana cut her off. The Dark One had played them both, he was the master manipulator. "Prepare the army, we go to war."

Abigail nodded, looked at Kraegan once more before striding out of the room and closing the door behind her.

Zobiana glanced towards Kraegan. "Will you stay and fight?"

Kraegan smiled. "I have old scores to settle, so yes, I'll stay and fight alongside you, my queen,"

Zobiana gasped when he yanked her into his arms and his eyes focused on her neck. She angled her head in offering and felt her skin pop as he sank his fangs into her throat and fed. Her eyes rolled back in her head, ecstasy shivering along her nerve endings as he drank his fill.

Gabriel stood topside with the others staring at the sunrise. He felt numb and as damaged as the jagged buildings lining the horizon. He ignored the hooded reapers with their skeletal hands, floating above them; they'd taken four lives and hungered for more. Guilt plagued Gabriel; he should have known something was wrong. God, he should have sensed her pain, felt her die; he should have felt something for fuck's sake, she was his soulmate. He looked up towards the heavens, his lip trembling, tears pooling in his eyes and flowing down his cheeks in silence. She was gone, just like that, she was gone. He would never see her smile, hear her laugh, hold her body against his or feel her tender kisses ever again. How was he going to carry on without her? He looked down; she was dead in his arms, covered in blood, light as a feather, her face untouched by her horrific death. Gabriel dropped to his knees and howled to the heavens. *"Why?"* He rocked back and forth with her crushed to his chest. Sorrow slithered through his body and squashed the remnants of his heart. *"Argghhhhh,"* he cried, brushing her hair from her face.

He watched the debris on the ground before him catch in a circle of wind, the dust particles crystallising and shimmering as a translucent form took shape within the wind-funnel. The wind stopped and Ava stood before him, dressed in the clothing of her Native American ancestors. She wore a long white doeskin dress and matching moccasins embroidered with turquoise beads. Her hair hung free down her back and swayed in the wind as she lifted her hand and waved. Gabriel shook his head, his face scrunching up in pain. He knew why she was there and he wasn't ready to say goodbye. He felt a gentle kiss on his cheek and heard her symphonic voice in his head. *"I'll love you forever, my husband. My time has come to an end, but yours has not, you must continue fighting. This world needs you, the Shadow Seekers need you, and Makayla needs you. You have much to do before we meet again in the spirit world. Yá'át'ééh, Ayóó'áníinishní,"* she said in Navajo. *"Goodbye, I love you,"* she repeated in English.

"I love you too, Silentwind; *Ayóó'áníinishní Doo Íits'a'í Da nilchi'i,"* he repeated in Navajo. He couldn't bring himself to say goodbye, though. A lump formed in his throat as she turned and walked away, her shimmering body disappearing like mist before his eyes.

Gabriel felt someone grasp his shoulder and squeeze; he looked up into Darrius's understanding eyes. "We need to leave, Gabe."

Gabriel nodded and stood, lifting Ava's crumpled body higher in his arms. "Do you have a place in mind?" he asked.

"I do, it's the safest place I know and Zobiana would never expect us to return there."

Gabriel nodded and looked out towards the sunrise once more before nodding again. "Okay, let's go."

CHAPTER 48.

Danny sat staring at Alexander, waiting for him to wake. He'd been mumbling in his sleep for the last couple of hours since their return. Danny looked up when his bedroom door opened and Emily came wandering out with Izador by her side. He smiled at her mussed up hair and unravelled appearance. She leaned on Izador as she rubbed the sleep from her eyes.

"Good morning, gorgeous girl, did you sleep well?" he asked.

Emily mewled as she stretched her arms overhead and nodded with a sleepy smile. She covered her mouth to stifle a yawn and almost tripped when Izador nudged her with his snout; she giggled and wrapped her arms about his neck, hugging him.

"Are you hungry? I can make you anything you'd like to

eat."

"Anything?" she asked, her eyebrow lifting in mischief.

"Hmm, maybe I shouldn't have said that. I can make you anything within reason, chocolate and sweets are out."

"Oh, poo, I was going to ask for an ice-cream sundae with strawberries, bananas, passion-fruit, whipped cream and chocolate topping."

"Yeah, I don't think that would be an appropriate breakfast, but I can whip up some cinnamon pancakes with strawberries, bananas, a little yoghurt and a drizzle of Greek honey. How's that sound?"

"Sounds good," Alexander said, sitting up and scratching his head.

Izador nudged Emily out of the way, positioning himself in front of her as he lowered his head and growled.

Alexander raised his hands in a non-threatening manner and glanced towards Danny. "Did I say something wrong?"

Danny searched Alexander's face for signs of the Dark One's presence, but saw nothing in Alexander's eyes suggesting evil intent. He squatted in front of Izador and lowered his forehead to the wolf's temple. Izador whined, Danny brushed his hand through the thick fur at his neck. "It's okay, Izzy, she's safe." Izador yipped once. "I'll not let harm come to her, I promise." Izador lowered to his haunches and whined, looking from Alexander to Danny and back at Alexander again.

Danny rose. "Come on, let's get that breakfast," he said

and held his hand out towards Emily.

Emily smiled at Danny before launching herself at Alexander; giving him a big hug and a sloppy kiss on the cheek. "Good morning, Xander," she said, giggling at the look of surprise on his face.

Alexander returned her hug and ruffled her hair. "Morning, sweetheart."

"Hey, no fair, how come you didn't hug me like that?" Danny said, chuckling.

"Xander needs it more than you do," she replied, taking Danny's hand.

"Is that so?"

"Uh-huh."

"If you say so." Danny glanced towards Alexander and baulked at the odd look on his face. Danny snapped his fingers in front of his face, Alexander jumped, and looked around his face blank. "You okay, Xander?"

Alexander rubbed the back of his neck. "Yeah, sorry, I think I zoned out for a minute."

"Ya think?" Danny frowned.

Alexander scratched and shook his head. "When did we get back?" he asked.

"We've been back a few hours now, do you remember anything?"

"The last thing I recall was standing at the church altar, the rest is a blur." Alexander rubbed his forehead.

"How do you feel?" Danny repeated. When they reached

the kitchen, he lifted Emily up onto a stool by the benchtop.

"That's the thing, I feel great, a little lightheaded, as if a giant weight was lifted from my shoulders. I wish I'd got the chance to thank Pater Nikolao. Do you think we could go back to the church and thank him before Makayla returns?" Alexander took a seat next to Emily and rested his elbows on the kitchen benchtop.

"Um, yeah, that may be a little difficult."

"Difficult how, what happened?"

"Ah, the church kind of fell down on top of us after your exorci—" Danny looked at Emily. "Um, afterwards. But if you're feeling better, maybe you could, you know," Danny lifted his hands and wiggled his fingers. "Do a little magic and fix the church."

Alexander's face paled, Danny clapped him on the back. "It's all good, Xander, no one was hurt. You can fix the church later, and I'll fill you in on all the details."

Alexander nodded. "Yeah, okay."

"How 'bout that breakfast, maybe you could help?" Danny wiggled his fingers again.

Alexander's face went blank for a second time.

"Xander, did you hear me?"

"Oh, yeah, sure, no problem, it's the least I can do." Alexander waved his hands over the kitchen benchtop and three plates appeared, loaded with cinnamon pancakes, strawberries, bananas and yoghurt drizzled with Greek honey.

Emily clapped her hands and picked up her knife and fork

and dug in.

Danny and Alexander looked at their plates and grimaced before looking at one another. Alexander smirked and waved his hand one more time; their plates disappeared and two large glasses of blood appeared before them.

"Now that's what I'm talking about," Danny said, clinking his glass to Xander's and guzzling down the warm contents. "Not as good as the fresh stuff, but good enough to stamp down the hunger pangs." Danny watched Alexander drink the contents of his glass before pointing at his empty glass for a refill.

"Have you heard from Makayla?" Alexander asked.

Danny shook his head. "No, not yet."

"What about—" Alexander clutched his head in his hands and fell to the floor. Danny bounded around the kitchen bench and crouched by him.

"Xander, what's wrong?"

"It's Makayla, something's happened. Something's wrong. *Ugh*," Alexander groaned, rubbing his chest.

Salomae screeched, Danny looked up at the light fixtures as they swung back and forth. The roof trembled, and the ground rolled, Izador howled. Danny held his arms out to Emily and lifted her off the stool and placed her on Izador's back. "Do you know where Makayla is, Xander?"

"She's underground, in a cavern, there are hieroglyphs carved all over the walls and glow worms everywhere."

"Come on, I know where she is." Danny helped Alexander

to his feet, and they made their way to the back door. Danny threw the door open and waited for Izador to dash through before he and Alexander followed. Salomae shrieked and stomped her feet, her talons churning the ground, she flapped her wings and lowered her head to the ground when she saw them.

"She wants us to get on her back," Alexander murmured. "She'll carry Izador with her talons,"

Izador howled. "Yeah, I don't think that's gonna work, Xander. I can teleport us there," Danny said.

Are you going to be able to teleport Salomae? Because she won't be left behind." Alexander said, making his way towards the Terrin.

"Ah, no, I don't have that kind of strength."

Alexander clutched his head again. "We need to leave, like right now. I need to get to Makayla, she's suffocating." Alexander climbed onto Salomae's back. "Do you think you can teleport Izador and Emily?"

"Yes."

"Okay, I'll meet you there, where's Makayla?"

"She's at Wigmore Castle, that's all I can say right now, get there and I'll show you where she is," Danny said, moving towards Emily and Izador.

"Wigmore Castle was destroyed, Danny, are you sure?"

"Yes, now go." Danny watched Salomae flap her wings and lift into the air; she gathered momentum and took off like a shot. There was a sonic boom and the pair disappeared.

Danny glanced at Emily. "Take my hand, sweetie." He twisted his hand into Izador's fur, grasped Emily's hand and dematerialised.

Seconds later they reappeared at Wigmore Castle and they weren't alone. There were Seraph and Vampire Guard everywhere. Danny sighed and took in the desolation; Wigmore castle was a burned-out shell, nothing but the curtain wall and black ruins remained. It felt as though the world had fallen down around them. Darrius was standing near a stand of trees with a ragtag group of people.

Danny patted Izador's head. "Calm down, boy, these guys are with us." Izador craned his neck, eyed Danny and quietened. "Emily, stay with Izador, I'm going to speak with your brother." Emily nodded and sat on a nearby rock. She patted the ground and Izador curled his body around her and settled beside her making sure she was nestled against him.

Darrius acknowledged Danny when he stopped beside him. "What happened?" Danny asked, looking at the Shadow Seekers sitting on building debris behind Darrius. They hadn't formally met, but he knew their names from Makayla's memories. Morgan stared at the ground vacantly. Jackson's legs looked like they'd been through a meat press and his face bore the telltale signs of excruciating pain as they healed. Zack was talking to Thomas and a number of fledgling vampires. Lazarus cradled an unconscious woman in his arms. Danny searched the area for Vasili and the missing Shadow Seekers.

"The compound was bombed."

"What?" Danny said; focusing his attention back to Darrius, no wonder the Shadow Seekers looked a little worse for wear. "How? That place is an underground fortress."

"We don't yet know, but lives were lost." They discussed the events that had occurred in the time they'd last seen each other.

A piercing screech sounded above them. Danny shaded his eyes; Salomae and Alexander hovered overhead. Salomae snarled, hissing at the Seraph and Vampire Guard as they scrambled out of the way. She settled to the ground, flapping her giant wings and kicking dust and ash clouds up into the air. Danny watched her fold her wings behind her and lower her head. Alexander jumped to the ground and strode towards them, oblivious to those around him.

"Hey Darrius," Alexander said, he nodded at Zack before turning his attention to Danny. "Where's Makayla? We need to get to her now, she's suffocating."

"I thought she was with you, Xander?" Zack said, coming to a standstill next to Darrius and Danny.

"She's in her space," Danny said, clenching his fists. The last time he'd seen Zack was just before he and Alexander had rescued Makayla from the dungeons. Danny had beaten the crap out of him and they still had issues to resolve. Danny reigned in his anger and ignored him. Makayla trusted him, but he was yet to be convinced Zack was trustworthy. Danny directed his attention back to Darrius and Alexander.

"What?" Darrius said, concern crossing his face as he looked towards the ruins of the castle. "How can she be down there?"

"We don't know, she was searching for the last two Trinian gems. How she ended up here is anyone's guess," Alexander said, looking about the crowded area. "Why's everyone here?"

"We've got nowhere else to go, the cavern's the safest place for us now. We've started digging, but it's slow going because it's underneath metres and metres of rock. Come with me, Xander, you're just the person we need to move the debris. Gabe's been down there alone since we arrived. How he's holding it together after Ava's death is anyone's guess."

Alexander stopped in his tracks. "Ava's dead? How?" he whispered, covering his mouth with his hands.

Darrius stopped, and brushed a trembling hand through his hair. "The compound was bombed. Ashley died as well; Morgan's a mess," Darrius's voice broke. "We don't know about Vasili and Marianna, we haven't been able to contact Vasili telepathically. So we're assuming they didn't make it, and we don't know if Reece and Anna or Bryce or Freya got out either."

Alexander fell to his knees, bowed his head and buried his face in his hands, choking back a sob. His chest felt tight, he rubbed it, trying to breathe through the shock. His heart ached for Gabe, for Ava, Ashley, Marianna, and Vasili; for all the lives lost. Surely Vasili had got out with Marianna? Alexander couldn't comprehend a world without Vasili in it, he'd known him for centuries. The prophecy was happening; the end times was a red carpet rolling out at their feet, daring them to autograph the pristine surface with their bloody footprints. *Find Makayla, or she'll be lost too.* The thought broke through his sorrow. He inhaled and exhaled several times before he pushed up from the ground again. "We need to get to Makayla," he choked out again. "She's suffering, I can feel her pain, we need to hurry."

"This way," Darrius said.

Alexander saw Gabriel standing in the rubble. Before Darrius had the chance to point him out Alexander took off down the incline, lost his balance and slid the rest of the way until he came upon some unearthed stairs. He rushed down the stairs until he reached Gabriel. Gabriel didn't turn or acknowledge Alexander, just continued lifting rocks and tossing them aside like an automaton.

Alexander grabbed his arm, and when Gabe looked up his face crumpled and his shoulders sagged, Alexander pulled him into a bear hug and held him tight. "I'm so sorry, Gabe."

Gabe patted Alexander's back, his body shuddered then he nodded and stepped out of Alexander's embrace. "We need to clear these stairs before we lose the light." Gabriel pointed at the pile of rocks and continued working. "My magic's depleted, my powers are gone."

"It's okay." Alexander examined the debris. "Step back, Gabe, I'll get rid of the rocks."

Gabriel nodded and moved behind Alexander. Alexander

knelt and placed his hands on the rocks blocking the way, he said a few words in Gaelic, his arms lit with blue-fire as he swirled his hands over the rock and slammed his palms down. The rocks shimmered and then disappeared altogether, revealing a winding stair that led down to a large wrought-iron double door.

Alexander straightened to his full height and looked at Gabriel. "Let's go, Makayla's down there and she's in trouble."

CHAPTER 49.

Dust and black smoke spewed out of the gaping black hole that was once a secret way in and out of the catacombs beneath the compound. Reece pulled Anna to his side, thanking the powers that be he'd been with her when the bombs had detonated. They'd only just got out. If he hadn't dematerialised when he had, they may have died in the cave-in.

"Do you think everyone got out?" Anna asked.

Reece tore his eyes from the tunnel opening and looked at her thoughtfully. "I hope so."

"What do we do now?"

"We find the others,"

"And how do we do that?" Anna asked, glancing back towards the catacombs.

"If I focus, I should be able to sense the Shadow Seekers' whereabouts."

"I'd ask you how, but I'm not sure I want to know the answer."

Reece grinned and wiggled his eyebrows and answered her question anyway. "I'm clairsentient, in other words, energy sensitive. I can sense the vibrational energy of a person from a distance. Every living being emits an energy vibration, sort of like a person's handwritten signature, a radio wave if you will – only it's energy orientated." Reece shrugged. "When I was younger, my ability wasn't as developed, but as I matured it strengthened."

Anna opened her mouth to speak, but closed it again and scratched her temple in thought. "So, you've always known where I am?" Reece nodded. Anna narrowed her eyes. "So what you're saying is, even if you weren't my maker, you'd still be able to find me?" Reece nodded again, a sheepish smile hovering on his lips. "Did you know where Alexander was? Please tell me you didn't."

"No, I didn't know where he was; he must have been in another dimension."

"Do you know where the Shadow Seekers are now?"

Reece closed his eyes and lifted his chin, angling his head to the side; he smiled and opened his eyes. "They're at Wigmore Castle."

"Why on Earth would they be there?"

"I haven't a clue."

"What about Vasili, can you sense him?"

"I can't sense him at all, I tried to contact him earlier, but

I'm not getting anything from him. If Vasili's masking his presence, it's normal for me not to sense his presence. Come on, let's find the others." Reece embraced Anna and dematerialised, reappearing moments later at Wigmore Castle.

Alexander's head fell back on his shoulders as he stared up at the enormous wrought-iron door barring their way. Its curving pointed arch swept three metres high into the rock face. The four-metre-wide double doors were set in a frame made up of large rectangular stones. Decorative beaten silver bands swirled about the contours and across the middle of each door. Alexander unlatched the locks and pushed the ancient doors inwards with Gabriel and Darrius's help. The moment the heavy doors screeched open, Alexander rushed headlong into the cavern and the darkness swallowed him.

"Xander, wait," Gabriel said, following him into the shadows.

Darrius chased after them. "We need to get these doors shut." Darrius Alexander and Gabriel were standing in a small beam of light filtering in from the entrance. "The cavern won't reveal its interior until the doors are closed. It's protected by magic, even if torches are lit, the room will appear to be in darkness because the illusion prevents it," Darrius said, trying to push the doors closed. "Hey, a little help, please!"

Alexander and Gabriel moved to help him close the doors.

As soon as the doors were secured, the cavern revealed its treasures: a magnificent ancient city.

"This isn't what it usually looks like," Darrius said in wonderment. "There were no buildings here at all before."

"Quick, do you see Makayla anywhere? We need to find her, we can admire the architecture later," Alexander said, moving further into the cavern.

"Over there, in the centre of the cavern." Darrius pointed. "The small courtyard just below the. . .is that the Trinian Globe?"

Alexander froze mid-stride and looked up at the ceiling. Warmth rippled beneath his prickling skin and circled within his body like a serpent. The sigil was on fire. He rubbed his chest and swallowed the knot in his throat and continued walking forward, his eyes mesmerised by the golden orb floating above their heads.

"Xander, watch out." Gabe grabbed his arm.

"Whaa-aaaat?" Alexander shook his head and stopped.

"You nearly tripped over Makayla," Darrius said, squatting by his sister.

"Shit, is she okay?" Alexander kneeled and pulled her into his lap, brushing the hair from her face. "She doesn't look good at all." He bit his wrist and held it to her mouth. She didn't respond. Alexander guided her head to the wound and pressed her mouth to his wrist. Nothing. He rubbed his wrist back and forth over her lips, smearing blood on her mouth until she roused. He felt the sting of her fangs pierce his flesh as she latched on. Alexander closed his eyes, the warmth of Makayla's venom working into his system, filling him with euphoria. He stiffened when he heard echoing laughter in his head and he was filled with dread; was the Dark One still trapped in his body, or had he imagined the laughter? Alexander looked down into Makayla's face and blanched when he noticed her black eyes. He tried to remove his wrist from her mouth, but she had his arm in a vice-like grip.

"Makayla, stop, you need to stop, now," he said, feeling lightheaded. "Darrius, do something, she's taking too much."

Darrius grabbed her face and placed one hand over her chin, the other on her temple and pried her mouth open enough for Alexander to remove his wrist. Alexander cradled his arm to his chest and noticed the blood seeping from the wound on his wrist wasn't a healthy shade of red but a dark, almost black-burgundy colour. *What the bloody hell*, he thought, eyeing his arm. What had he done? He sniffed his wrist – his blood smelled strange. He licked the wound to heal it with his saliva and recoiled at the taste. His blood wasn't tangy, metallic or sweet like normal blood, no, it was bitter almost sour in flavour. *Shit, shit, shit, please, please let her be okay*, he thought over and over as he waited for Makayla to revive.

"She all right?" he asked, trepidation warring within him.

Makayla groaned in response and sat bolt upright, her eyes wild. "They're dead, they're dead!" she screamed, her voice echoing throughout the cavern.

Darrius smoothed Makayla's hair out of her eyes

"Makayla, Makayla, honey, wake up." She didn't hear or see them, she began coughing and gagging.

She fell on all fours, groaning, clutching her stomach and retching; her body arched as she threw up the blood she'd just drunk.

"Breathe, Makayla, breathe," Alexander whispered, grateful she'd thrown up his blood, there was no telling the damage it could have done. He stroked her back. "Come back, wake up, baby."

Makayla's stomach burned, whatever she'd drunk tasted vile, she spat on the floor trying to remove the foul taste from her mouth. She shivered, a cold sweat beaded on her forehead and trickled into her stinging eyes. She coughed, opening and closing her watering mouth as she poked her tongue out and wiped it and her mouth with the back of her hand. She sucked in oxygen, trying to gather her strength. Makayla's vision cleared, her shoulders relaxed, and she looked up. "Gabe," she sobbed, her breath catching in her throat, her chest burning. She held her arms out to him and he fell to his knees and pulled her into his embrace. "Gabe, oh Gabe, where is she, where's Ava? I can bring her back, she can't be gone, I have to try, please, where is she? I can bring her back."

Gabriel shook his head, released Makayla and sat back on his heels and rubbed his red-rimmed eyes. "She's gone, Makayla, her spirit came to me and we said our final goodbyes," Gabriel choked out.

Makayla placed her glowing palm on his chest, sending healing thoughts into his shattered heart. When she felt him relax; she removed her hand and rubbed her throbbing temples. She exhaled and someone squeezed her hand. How had she not noticed Alexander sitting beside her? "You're here," she said, touching his cheek. "Are you okay?"

"Yeah, I'm okay," he replied. "What about you?"

Makayla scrutinised his face; he had black circles under his tired eyes. "I'll survive." She glanced towards Darrius. "How's Morgan?"

"How do—?"

"How do I know? I saw Ava, Ashley, Vasili and Marianna die. I felt the pain of their deaths." Makayla leaned against Alexander and he gathered her to him. Makayla felt a shudder go through his body and looked into his ashen face. His eyes were glazed.

Alexander gulped. "Are, are you sure, about Vasili and Marianna?" he whispered.

"Yes, I'm sure."

"I can't believe they're gone." Alexander rubbed his eyes, his voice but a whisper. "I felt your pain, Makayla, I thought you were dying too."

"What about Reece, Anna, Bryce and Freya?" Darrius asked.

"They got out," Makayla replied. "What about Jackson and Tess? How are they faring?"

"Jackson's healing, Tess still hasn't woken up; Lazarus is

worried she'll hate him for turning her," Darrius replied.

"She'll understand." Makayla pushed up from the ground and Alexander helped her stand. Gabe and Darrius followed suit.

"What's up with your armour? It looks different? Damn, girl, you look different, you're like an Egyptian Goddess come to life and ready for war," Darrius said.

"She's exquisite," Alexander murmured, biting his lip.

Makayla looked down the length of her body. "About that," she said, noticing Alexander's intense look as he studied her body armour, a thoughtful look passing over his face as he scratched his head. "It's not just one armour; I'm wearing two. The Druidoynan armour Alexander gifted me and the golden armour given to me by the vampire and seraph council."

"That's not possible," Gabe mumbled.

"I was just as surprised. Look." Makayla twisted her body one way and then the other. "You can see both armours in different positions.

"How?" Darrius went to touch her armour.

Alexander grabbed his wrist. "I wouldn't do that if I were you, Druidoynan metal will give you a nasty shock."

"Why wasn't Gabriel affected when he hugged her?" Darrius queried.

"I'm impervious to Druidoynan metal," Gabriel said.

"How's that possible?" Darrius asked.

"It's a long story." Gabriel said, giving nothing away.

Makayla looked up at the Trinian Globe hovering above

their heads, Darrius noticed.

"Why are you here, Makayla?" Darrius asked.

Makayla smiled. "I found the last two gems; one was at the Atlantean Gateway to their underwater colony here on Earth, and the final gem was here in this cavern, over there, to be exact." Makayla pointed towards the gateway engraved on the wall.

Darrius's eyes bulged as he looked up at the Trinian Globe. "Why do I feel like I just stepped into the twilight zone? Tristan has been raving about this place and its part in the final battle for centuries, but the buildings are a surprise."

"The buildings appeared when the final gem was set in the Trinian Globe. It was like a veil lifted, as if the globe knew we'd need somewhere to stay,"

BANG. BANG. SCREECH.

They glanced towards the door as it opened. Everything fell into darkness. Tristan stood in the light of the entrance, Lazarus stood behind him with an unconscious Tess in his arms, Seraph and Vampire Guard and the Shadow Seekers surrounded them. As Tristan crossed the threshold, he manifested fireballs in the palms of his hands and hurled them towards the fire pit behind Makayla and the others. Makayla wondered how he knew there was a fire pit nearby. He shouldn't have been able to see anything in the room with the doors open. The flames lit the cavern with ambient light. Makayla looked down into the fire pit; there was no accelerant to feed the fire yet a fire burned. The Vampire and Seraph

Guard filed through into the cavern in an endless, steady flow. Makayla couldn't help but notice the way they looked at her as they passed, especially the Vampire Guard. Their eyes were wide with surprise, their mouths gaping as they looked her up and down. Many had heard about her prophecy, few believed in her existence, though, and none of them had seen her wearing the Golden Armour. Makayla held her head high and rested her hands on the hilts of her swords, acknowledging each of them with a brief nod as they passed.

Makayla closed her eyes when Salomae's voice chimed in her mind. She touched the scar on her wrist and saw through the Terrin's eyes; she would never get used to seeing her parents' home in such a devastated condition. *"Yes, there's room for you down here, Salomae. No, I'd feel safer with you in here, though. I know you want to guard the door, but you can guard it from inside, at least if you're in here the Vampire Guard will toe the line. No, I don't trust them, GET YOUR ARSE DOWN HERE NOW! Sorry, I didn't mean to shout. Yes, I know it was disrespectful. I KNOW; OKAY! Stop nagging, would you just come down now? All right, all right, wait until Emily and Izador and the rest of the Shadow Seekers are down here."* Makayla looked around for a large enough space for Salomae. *"Do you see the space I'm showing you? Okay, I'll see you shortly."*

"Aren't you a bossy boots? You're taking this prophecy too far." Makayla rolled her eyes when her nemesis joined the conversation.

"Is there a reason you're here?" Makayla spoke to her silently.

"He's not who you think he is; be careful, guard yourself at all times." Her nemesis warned.

"Who?"

"You know who; you must end the deceiver or he will end you."

"Who's the deceiver?" Makayla asked, but got no response.

It wasn't until she heard the screeching hinges of the doors closing that she realised everyone was in the cavern. Everyone except Salomae, who appeared just as the doors closed and the ancient city reappeared. There were many gasps as the cavern's beauty was unveiled.

"Makayla," Emily called out, almost bowling her over as she came to an abrupt stop.

"Careful, my armour may zap you if you touch it." Emily threw her arms around her anyway; nothing happened. Makayla frowned when she noticed her armour was shimmering, an invisible barrier protecting Emily from the Druidoynan metal of her armour.

"Oops, sorry." As Emily stepped back and lowered her hands, the invisible barrier disappeared. "Wow you look like a queen," Emily said.

"That's strange," Alexander said, glancing at Gabriel. "I think your armour recognised Emily wasn't a threat and allowed her to touch you, Makayla, it must be the seraph armour's influence over the Druidoynan metal."

Makayla noticed Alexander and Gabriel's shared look. "It's not the strangest thing I've seen lately," Makayla said, tousling her sister's hair. "Where's Danny?" she asked.

"He's over there with the others." Emily pointed towards the Shadow Seekers standing off to her right.

"Thanks, sweetie, wait here while I speak with them."

Emily nodded and leaned against Izador as Makayla walked towards the Shadow Seekers. The first thing Makayla noticed was the vacant look in Morgan's eyes. Makayla squatted in front of Morgan, who sat on a small wall nearby. Morgan didn't acknowledge her. Darrius placed a hand on Morgan's shoulder, worry shimmering in his eyes. Tristan called out and jogged towards her.

Morgan looked up, anger bubbling in her eyes, the moment Tristan came to a stop beside them. Morgan lunged at him, grabbing his throat. "Where's my sister? What did you do with her?" She screamed, spittle flying in his face as she increased the pressure on his throat.

Tristan gasped and threaded his fingertips under hers, prying them open. "She's safe, Morgan," he gasped.

Morgan thumped her fists on his chest and clawed at him like a she-cat ready to shred pieces of flesh off his body. "She was looking for you, you're the reason she's dead." Morgan's voice cracked. Makayla looked at Tristan's face, remorse and sadness reflected in his glassy eyes. He grabbed Morgan's hands and held them away from his body.

Darrius hugged Morgan from behind, trying to pull her away from Tristan; Makayla moved between them and placed her hand on Morgan's chest. She settled immediately. Golden light ebbed from Makayla's fingertips into Morgan's body, soothing her shattered nerves and mending the heartache. Makayla closed her eyes and concentrated on Morgan's wild emotions, bombarding her with healing light and love. Makayla opened her eyes and looked into Morgan's eyes.

"It's okay, Morgan, you'll be okay; everything will be okay." Makayla lowered her hand, opening and squeezing it shut until her fingers stopped tingling.

Reece and Anna stood nearby, Bryce next to them. "Bryce you're here! Where's Freya, is she okay?"

"She's still unconscious, but alive." He pointed to a nearby building "She's in there sleeping, maybe you could do to her what you just did to Morgan. She hasn't woken since she drank your blood to cure the virus."

"I'll do my best to help as soon as I'm done here." Makayla looked at Zack and smiled; his eyes danced over her form, unmistakable admiration lighting his eyes. She exhaled in relief that he was alive. "Jackson, you look like shit, you all right?"

"I feel like a beef patty." He grimaced, rubbing his thighs.

Makayla squatted down beside Jackson, rubbed her hands together until they glowed again and placed her palms on his legs, his face calmed instantly. Makayla smiled when he nodded his thanks. She stood and glanced about. "Where's

Tess?" She asked Lazarus.

"She's unconscious, we put her and Freya together; she'll be out for a while due to the transition she's undergoing," Lazarus murmured, guilt lacing his words.

Makayla squeezed his shoulder. "You had no choice, Laz. It was change her or let her die.

"I couldn't let her die."

Makayla nodded, lowering her hand from his shoulder. "And Nikolai? Does he know about his parents?"

"We don't know where he is," Zack said. "They didn't make it, did they, Vasili and Marianna?"

Tears gathered in Makayla's eyes, her throat closed, she shook her head. "No, they didn't, I felt their pain. I saw their deaths as well as Ava's and Ashley's. There was nothing I could do, I couldn't stop it, I couldn't help them," Makayla's voice broke, tears streaking down her face as she swallowed the lump in her throat. "I'm sorry, it's all my fault, all the shit that's happening is my fault."

"It's not your fault, Makayla," Morgan murmured.

Makayla grasped Morgan's hand and squeezed it. "No, it's Zobiana's fault." She looked between her brothers. "Where's Father? I thought he'd be here too?"

"Father's on Evron," Tristan said. "He went to save Mother."

"What? Tell me he's not giving in to Zobiana's demands?"

"No, Grandfather sent word, Mother's safe."

Makayla relaxed. "Thank goodness."

"We're to meet them in the Barrens, within the hour."

"The Barrens? Sounds peachy, NOT," Jackson said.

"Why the Barrens?" Makayla asked.

"It's where the Dark One's corporeal body is imprisoned."

"Oh," Makayla said, assessing Alexander's reaction. He was staring at the ground, shuffling his feet. Danny wouldn't look her in the eye either. *What the bloody hell happened?*

"We believe Zobiana will make a play for the doorway beneath the temple and free the Dark One's eternal body from the underworld." Makayla glanced at Alexander. *What did it mean for him? Had the exorcism been a success?* Alexander and Danny were tight-lipped; first chance she got she'd confront them and demand the truth.

"So, what do we do now?" Anna asked.

Everyone looked to Gabriel, Gabriel looked to Makayla.

"We go to war," Makayla said.

Chapter 50.

Tristan and Makayla stood in front of the gateway carving surrounded by the Shadow Seekers and the Seraph and Vampire Guard. Makayla glanced towards her brother, and then at the dagger she held in her hand.

"Are you sure we will end up in the Barrens?"

"Makayla, this is your gateway. You control the endpoint, just think of the place you wish to go and the gateway will open a wormhole to that destination and transport us there."

"Yeah, but doesn't there have to be a connecting gateway on the other side for a wormhole to appear?"

"No, this gateway's different."

"What if we end up in the Sahara? I have no idea where the Barrens are on Evron."

"Oh my God, would you stop procrastinating?" Reece uttered with impatience. "Enough with the twenty questions already, time's-a-wasting!'"

Makayla frowned at him.

Tristan touched Makayla's forehead with the tip of his finger and planted an image of the Barrens in her head. "That's our destination, now picture it in your mind's eye and let's do this."

Makayla nodded. "Okay." With the destination fresh in her mind, she slashed the dagger across her palm and resheathed her weapon. She smoothed the pooling blood over the surface of her palm and held her hand over the indent to the right of the gateway, waiting for Tristan's signal.

"On three. One. Two. Three," Tristan said.

Makayla slammed her hand into position while envisioning the Barrens; praying it would work. The hieroglyphs on the wall illuminated the moment her hand connected with the barrier. Blood siphoned from her wound and flowed along the decorative grooves bordering the gateway. Weaving red filaments fluted in and out until they reached the uppermost point of the gateway where the Trinian gem had surfaced. Blood filled the hole and continued downwards until fine interlacing scarlet threads edged the entire gateway. Makayla removed her hand and stepped back from the wall when the sucking pressure holding her hand in place ceased. She looked over her shoulder when she heard the Trinian Globe's exquisite music echo throughout the cavern.

Makayla smiled at the wondrous looks on everyone's faces; they heard the chiming bells and the angelic voices too.

Her shoulders scrunched up as she shivered, goose bumps prickling all over her body. The Trinian Globe floated towards the gateway; coloured light swirling around it like Saturn's rings. The globe stopped and hovered metres above her. Threads of light reached out and touched the gateway, travelling the same path as her blood until the gateway exterior glowed. There was a thunderous boom and the medallion gem in the centre of her breastplate grew bright just as the Trinian Globe flashed down and smashed into her body. She crashed to the ground, landing on her hands and knees.

Lazarus yelled, "Don't touch her; she's one with the globe now."

Makayla shook her head, white stars blurred her vision and her ears rang as she pushed up from the floor. She rubbed her eyes, the light was so bright. She stuck her fingers in her ears and wiggled them trying to stop the buzzing. Her back itched, her muscles tensed and twitched, she shrugged and realised her wings had appeared. She unfurled and flexed them, stretching out her feathers and shaking out the kinks. When her vision cleared and her ears stopped ringing, she noticed everyone was on their knees, bowing.

She looked towards Danny, Lazarus, Zack, her brothers and Alexander; their smiles were contagious. "What the bloody hell's the matter with everyone? Get up off your knees!"

"Makayla, you're glowing," Alexander said.

"The prophecy is upon us," a Seraph Guard murmured.

"All hail the Golden One, the queen of two nations," a

Vampire Guard's voice boomed.

Makayla shook her head. "I'm no queen,"

"Turn around and look at your reflection; you look like a queen to me and everyone here," Lazarus said.

"How am I going to see my reflection?"

Alexander touched her arm and turned her towards the gateway, which was glistening with a rippling liquid silver surface. Makayla gaped when she saw her reflection in the mirror-like surface. The headpiece she wore had changed, and so had her appearance. Her armour was much the same as before, only now the two armours blurred with luminosity as if she were staring at the sun. Her headpiece had turned into a golden crown. Delicate gilded feathers formed the base of the crown, framing her face in paper-thin plumes. Four gold chains with feathers dangling on the bottoms hung from the crown base and tickled her cheeks. Seven triangular spikes of differing sizes circled the crown. The largest spike rested above the middle of her forehead in the centre-front of the crown. Makayla's hair flowed down her back in gleaming gold-copper waves falling well below her hips. Her weapons appeared the same, yet shimmered in the same manner as her armour. What struck Makayla were her luminous eyes: they were pure gold, it was as if a light shone from within them. Makayla held out her hand, twisting it back and forth as she spread her fingers; her skin glimmered in the flame-light. Her angelic heritage was more evident than ever before. Even the feathers on her wings glistened uncharacteristically. Makayla rolled her shoulders and morphed her wings back into her body.

"Well then," Makayla said, lowering her hand and turning back towards the crowd. She clapped her hands. "Please stand, it's making me uncomfortable. This here—" Makayla waved her hand up and down in front of herself "—is an illusion caused by the Trinian Globe. Just liken me to Cinderella's carriage; when the clock strikes midnight, I'll turn back into a pumpkin, or rather, myself." Makayla noticed the confused expressions on the Vampire and Seraph Guard's faces.

"I don't think they understood your analogy," Alexander whispered, bumping her shoulder with his.

"I think you may be right. I should have explained it better," Makayla replied.

"Seriously, woman, you're no pumpkin, you're a teenage wet dream! Just look at the fledglings' faces I think they'd agree with me." Reece winked.

"Humph." Bryce shook his head.

"You got something to say, brother?" Reece eyeballed Bryce.

"Our friends are dead and you're making bad jokes, as usual." Bryce crossed his arms over his chest, and raised his chin.

Reece glared at him, his expression hardening, his mouth a grim line. "Oh, you want to do this here, now? Well all right then. Where were you, brother, when our friends were dying, where were you, huh?" Reece pushed his face into Bryce's. "WHERE THE FUCK WERE YOU? You knew something was off, why didn't you warn us? Oh, I forgot, you do what you've always done. You tuck tail and run and desert those who love you, those who idolise you. You run, like you ran when I needed you the most. Why did you leave me with those monsters? Why didn't you take me with you? Goddammit, Bryce I needed you and you deserted me, you were all I had. You're my brother, I love you, but you're just like them, CRUEL." Reece poked Bryce in the chest. "CALCULATING." He poked him again. "COLD." He thrust his hands against him. "UNCARING. You succeeded, Bryce, you got what you've always wanted, to be alone!" Reece pushed Bryce once more.

Bryce pushed back. "I spoke with Vasili before I left and was returning, so back off."

Reece glanced at Bryce's clenched fists; white heat radiated from his hands as the black synthetic gloves he wore melted away. Reece leered, his fangs elongating "What are you going to do, Bryce? Zap me, obliterate me, turn me to ash? Go ahead, remove all your family obligations, then you'll get what you've always wanted: true freedom. It should be easy, brother, kill me like you killed them. God knows it would be a welcome relief from this fucked-up existence. There's one problem, though, it won't work on me, remember? Oops, sorry, I forgot, you don't know do you? You already tried that and failed. The night our father whipped you in front of their guests I was the one who stood between them and you. I took the lash for you, brother, I protected you, I stopped them, and I'd do it all again given the chance. I hated what they did to you, how they treated you. I got you to safety, but in your delirium you went supernova and I got caught in the crossfire. I learned a valuable lesson that night: I'm immune to your power." Reece glanced towards Makayla, who sensed his pain and anger and understood he needed to get the centuries of hurt off his chest. "Goodbye, brother." Reece eyed Bryce one more time and pushed past him, heading for the gateway.

Reece's outburst silenced everyone; Makayla had never seen him so livid. She grabbed his arm as he passed, but he shrugged her off. "Reece, wait," she yelled as he disappeared through the shimmering silver wall.

Bryce didn't give it a second thought and followed after Reece. Makayla grabbed Anna to stop her from following them, shaking her head. "Let them be, they need to work things out. Theirs is a shit-storm that's been building for millennia. Whoever runs into them on the other side will be sorry," Makayla looked over her shoulder at the gateway again. *What lay beyond it? How many more of her friends would die?* She shook her head and cracked her neck. Her muscles coiled tight with tension. It was always the same before a battle; there'd been a time when she'd savoured the feeling, not so much anymore. She had people she loved who she didn't want to lose.

Makayla noticed Freya standing among the Shadow Seekers and moved towards her. "How are you feeling, Freya?"

"A little lightheaded, but a lot better than when I first woke up, thank you, Makayla."

"You're welcome,"

"Do you think they'll be okay, Bryce and Reece, I mean?" Freya asked, looking towards the gateway.

"Yeah, I do," Makayla said, glancing towards Thomas and the Shadow Seeker students. "Thomas, I want you to stay here with the fledglings; protect my sister, Tess and Freya." Thomas nodded, his rigid stance relaxing.

"Makayla, I can hel—"

"Freya, you've been comatose for months, you're weak, your reflexes are slow and you're in no condition to fight, you need to gather your strength. I need you here, you'll distract Bryce. As it is he and Reece are distracted enough. You'll put yourself and the rest of us at risk. I'm sorry, but I need you to stay here with my sister, Tess and the fledglings."

"I understand," Freya said in a despondent voice.

"Salomae, protect everyone here and guard that door." Makayla pointed. "If anything gets through, lay waste to them." Salomae snarled, shook her head and snapped her jaws. "No, you stay here, we'll manage; I want you here," Makayla growled back.

Salomae shook her head and responded in kind.

"Do as you're told, I need you here!"

"I GO WITH YOU! 'TIS MY DUTY TO PROTECT YOU!" Salomae's guttural voice rumbled for all to hear.

All eyes turned towards Salomae, Makayla gaped. It was the first time she'd heard Salomae's physical voice, she glanced about; everyone was watching and waiting for her response.

"You stay here, I'll call if I need you, I promise."

Salomae extended her wings, snapped her jaws again and bowed her head, conceding to her wishes. Makayla exhaled the breath she'd been holding.

Emily stepped from behind Danny, Makayla knelt and pulled her into a hug. "Look after Freya and Tess for me."

Emily nodded, tears pooling in her eyes. "Please come back, and bring Mama and Baba home with you."

"I promise to do my best, but battles are unpredictable and risky, sweetie, I'll try."

Emily's bottom lip trembled. "I love you, Makayla."

"I love you too, baby girl." Makayla squashed Emily to her again, a lump forming in her throat; she released her and grabbed a handful of Izador's neck fur then lowered her forehead to his. *"Protect her with your life, Izador."* Izador yipped twice. She ruffled his fur, stood and glanced towards Gabriel, he nodded.

Makayla looked about the cavern at her friends and the Vampire and Seraph Guard. She sensed sorrow and anger issuing from the Shadow Seekers, her eyes fell on Gabriel and Morgan, their auras were grey, grief surrounded them, their eyes empty and despondent. The Trinian Globe had sharpened her senses – there were so many emotions radiating about the room: anxiety, sadness, apprehension, rage, anticipation, excitement.

Makayla held her head high. "We have lost our homes. We have lost loved ones. We have lost friends. The Earth is in ruins, we are in ruins, and humanity is in ruins. Zobiana has taken much from us, but while we live and breathe, there's hope. I know you're grieving, but we cannot let the deaths of our loved ones be for nothing. All the people who have died, their deaths must not be in vain, their deaths must count for something. We have to finish this; we must rise from the ashes and destroy those who dare to take freedom from us. We must fight until the bitter end, for we fight for more than ourselves, we fight for the souls of every living being in the Multiverse. If the Dark One escapes his prison, he and his demon horde will wreak havoc, the atrocities Zobiana committed in his name will seem like child's-play compared to what he'll unleash. I'm willing to die to stop him – are you?"

"YES," everybody shouted, their voices echoing about the cavern.

"Will you follow me into battle?"

"YES!" the crowd roared.

Makayla circled her hand in the air. "Move out. Vampire and Seraph Guard go first, two hundred at a time; you know the terrain better than any of us. When you arrive, spread out and secure the perimeter. Expect the unexpected. A word of warning to those of you who have never been to Evron, your powers may not work, you must depend on your fighting skills alone. Don't underestimate Zobiana's people – the moment you do you die."

The Vampire and Seraph Guard unsheathed their weapons and broke off into groups; twenty rows of ten seemed way too wide to fit through the narrow gateway. Makayla watched two hundred Seraph Guard advance towards the gateway. There was no way they'd fit through such a narrow opening. Makayla was about to tell them to walk through double-file when the gateway expanded, allowing them passage. Two hundred Vampire Guard were next. Seven rows had passed through the rippling silver gateway when five guards began screaming. Smoke spiralled off their bodies as the silver barrier barred their way and burned their flesh, shock-waves dancing around their bodies and shimmying down the line of Vampire Guards like a rock skimming the surface of water; skipping some and destroying others. It was as though the gateway knew who were true of heart and who were not. Seraph Guard drew their swords, watched and waited as the agonising death screams echoed about the cavern. Vampire Guard spies scattered every which way, abandoning the regimental lines trying to outrun the lightning arcing from the gateway. The cavern flashed like an electrical storm tickling the heavens before the downpour. There was no escape for Zobiana's spies; those who weren't zapped by electricity were picked off by the remaining Seraph and Vampire Guard loyal to Makayla.

The putrid stench of charred flesh and hair filled the cavern. Makayla pinched her nose, her stomach heaving and her mouth watering. She clenched her teeth, swallowing often, trying to stem the flow of saliva building in her mouth. *She was not going to vomit. She was not going to vomit. SHE. WAS. NOT. GOING. TO. VOMIT!* Makayla held her hand over her mouth, gagging. *She was going to vomit.* She dropped to her knees, her weapons clanging on the rock floor as she emptied her stomach on the ground.

"Makayla, are you all right?" Anna asked. "You're as pale as a ghost.

"Uh-huh, I'll be fine." Makayla shook her head, dry retching again, and spat, getting rid of the excess saliva pooling in her mouth.

Anna placed the back of her hand on Makayla's temple. "How long have you been experiencing these symptoms?" she asked, rubbing Makayla's back with her free hand.

"Not long. I was all right until I arrived in the cavern. I seem to be super-sensitive to everything. Ever since the last gem was placed into the Trinian Globe."

"You've been out of sorts since you returned from the past," Darrius said, shoving a bottle of water in her hand. "Drink."

Makayla unscrewed the cap and took a mouthful of water, gargled and spat it out again, she swallowed the second draught and felt a little better.

"How many?" she asked

"How many what?"

"How many Vampire Guard were killed?"

"About one-hundred-and-fifty, give or take a few," Darrius replied.

"Do you think they had anything to do with the compound bombing?" Anna asked.

"I wouldn't rule it out."

Makayla looked about. "Where's Xander?"

"Over there, speaking with Zack, Lazarus, Gabriel and Tristan."

Makayla nodded, Darrius helped her to her feet. Morgan stood soundless beside him, her eyes lowered to the floor.

"Any news of Nikolai's whereabouts?"

"None."

"Do you think he knows about his parents?"

"I don't know," Darrius said honestly.

"It will kill him. He's spent a lifetime looking for his mother only to lose her and his father a short time later. Come on, the sooner Zobiana and her armies are destroyed the better," Makayla said, making a beeline for the gateway. She wasn't wasting one more minute. She walked past the remaining Shadow Seekers, unsheathing her seraph blades from her back. She nodded as she passed them and ran towards the gateway. They stepped in behind and followed her as she screamed a battle cry and jumped through the opening.

"Yeeeesssssss, set me free, Makayla, make me whole once more!" her nemesis rejoiced.

CHAPTER 51.

Heavenly fire swirled about Ambrosia as she swung her seraph sword through the air and lopped off the head of a Newblood. She watched his head spiral through the air, mesmerised by the bewildered look in his eyes and the mouth-gaping expression of disbelief on his face. Blood sprayed in pumping jets from the stump of his neck, splattering her face and coating her armour in gore. His corpse dropped to its knees and listed to the side with a soft thud, dissolving into ash seconds after his body connected with the ground. Ambrosia marvelled at the differences between Purebloods and Newbloods. Silver affected Newbloods, turning their bodies to ash instantly. Purebloods had no such weakness. Ambrosia looked heavenward, unaffected by the horror of her actions; Seraph Guard filled the sky, swooping back and forth, slaying Newbloods effortlessly. Ambrosia's parenting sojourn was over, it was time to step back onto the battlefield. She should never have laid down her weapons, Adrian would still be alive had she not. It was a heavy lesson to learn and a mistake she'd not repeat.

Thousands of warring seraphs and vampires crowded the open plains. The Barrens had seen many battles through the ages; endless fights sharing similar motivations, the ultimate goal of freeing the Dark One. It seemed Lilith had not forgotten her oath; she was set on a destructive path with one of two outcomes – death or servitude to the Dark One. Death would have been preferable in Ambrosia's opinion. Lilith had yet to show herself, her untrained Newblood army was the precursor to her grand entrance.

Ambrosia smiled when she saw Raziel dive-bomb a group of vampires trying to break through the front line at the temple entrance. His wings were tucked tight at his sides as he torpedoed down, his flaming body spinning like a corkscrew, a trail of sparks spraying behind him like burning jet plumes. His wings unfurled at the last minute and he mowed down a line of vampires, setting them alight as he jetted past. He angled his body and zoomed past Ambrosia taking out a Newblood coming up behind her.

"Focus, Ambrosia, he was nearly upon you."

"I saw him, brother, never fear, my focus is fine." She threw her sword; it looped through the air end over end and found its mark in the chest of a rogue Vampire Guard. She whipped out her throwing-knives and hurled them at two more vampires sidling up to her. She noticed Sebastian out of the corner of her eye, he winked as he dashed past her, the daggers in his hands glinting as he leapt into the air and landed on the back of another Newblood, which lost its footing and crashed to the ground. Sebastian stabbed him in the ribs with both daggers, one from behind and the other from the front, twisting them for maximum damage. Ambrosia retrieved her silver throwing-knives, and threw them at two more Newbloods then launched into the air. She pumped her wings and grabbed the hilt of her sword, pulling it from the Vampire Guard's body as she zoomed by. She flew higher and noticed an odd patch of air wavering near the ground off in the distance. Fifty or so Newbloods noticed the disturbance also and moved towards the abnormality. Whisper-thin lightning zapped the air like the electromagnetic currents in a plasma energy ball. A formation took shape until a solid structure appeared out of nowhere. A rippling silver pool surrounded by decorative carved rock solidified. Ambrosia smiled again when she recognised the gateway carving from the cavern hidden beneath Wigmore Castle.

Reece felt the invisible force of the wormhole propelling him forward until it released its hold and he exited the gateway the same way he'd entered – running. He smiled when he saw a crowd of Newbloods approaching him. He unsheathed his sabre and leapt into the air; slashing his sword across the stomachs of three Newbloods on his descent and disembowelling them.

They howled in pain, their faces screwing up as they dropped their weapons and grabbed their wounds to stop their guts from falling to the ground. Reece spun on his heels, arcing his sabre back the opposite way and separating their torsos from the lower halves of their bodies. He jumped over their disintegrating corpses and barrelled into the next cluster of Newbloods, bowling them off their feet as he charged past. He heard someone yell behind him, but couldn't discern their words above the escalating buzzing in his ears. He glanced up into the soft-pink sky, marvelling at the beauty of such a harsh landscape. Seraph flew in formation with stern expressions on their faces. The battle raged, the smell of blood ripe in the air, Reece licked his lips and tasted the sour metallic tang of tainted blood. The sound of clanging swords, battle cries and death groans of warriors riled him further.

He inspected his surroundings, looking for Zobiana, Tyrone and Abigail, but couldn't see them. Someone grabbed his shoulder. Reece back-flipped through the air and landed in a squat behind the person who'd grabbed him. It was Bryce. Newbloods circled them, too many to count, Bryce opened and closed his hands numerous times.

"Why'd you follow me, Bryce? I left to get away from you!" Reece looked left and right as Newbloods closed in about them.

"Because I love you too, brother, and I couldn't let you leave without telling you so. I'm sorry for being an arse and treating you with disdain all your life, I shouldn't have, you didn't deserve it. I promise I'll never leave you behind again."

Reece swallowed the hard lump in his throat, he'd waited a long time for Bryce to acknowledge his feelings. Never in a million years had he expected to hear them. He clapped his brother on the back and smiled.

"Aww, how sweet, did ya hear that, boys? They love each other," a Newblood said, moving closer.

Reece stared at the Newblood who'd spoken. "Did mummy drop you on your face as a baby?" The vampire's nose was flat and bent to the side, his blemished skin covered in pockmarks. "Fuck, man, you look like you've been hit with the ugly stick one too many times."

Bryce smirked and folded his arms over his chest as he eyed the Newbloods.

"You ever wonder why nobody wants to fight you?" Reece questioned the Newblood eyeing him up and down. "Because ugly people have nothing to lose."

"What's that, pretty boy?" The Newblood cupped his ear with his hand, drawing Reece's attention to the hair sprouting from his ear hole.

"Um, if my dog had a face like yours, I'd shave its arse and walk him backwards."

"Why, you son of a bitch," the Newblood hissed and closed the gap.

"That's right, our mother was a bitch." Reece smirked and nodded, Bryce held his hands out, opening and closing them and frowning when nothing happened. "Looks like we'll have to go old school on their arses, brother, because my powers aren't working," Bryce said, shaking his hands.

"Fine by me, just leave hairy Harry to me, he'll never hear me coming, not with the earmuffs sprouting from the sides of his head."

"Me name's not, Harry, fancy pants," the Newblood said, charging forward, his fist flying at Reece's face.

Reece ducked and slapped him on the back of the head as he passed and tossing a handful of throwing blades at the other Newbloods rushing towards them. "Whatever, I don't care." Reece swung his sword and the hairy Newblood blocked the blow with a sword of his own, pushing him back. Reece lost his footing, but recovered in an instant, engaging the Newblood in swordplay. The gateway flared behind them. Seraph and Vampire Guard flooded the area, marching through the gateway and dispatching the Newbloods in the vicinity.

Reece looked up, distracted by a flaming female seraph flying above him. She was the spitting image of Makayla. She flew towards him and pushed him out of the way just as the Newblood he'd been fighting swung his sword. She grabbed the Newblood by the throat and he caught fire and dropped his sword, screaming as his flesh bubbled, and dissolved into ash moments later. It surprised Reece he himself hadn't caught fire when the seraph had pushed him out of the way. He looked about and lowered his sword; the Newbloods surrounding them were alight with celestial fire. Reece eyed his brother and their saviour. She'd moved away and was ordering the Vampire and

Seraph Guard to spread out, pointing in differing areas of the Barrens still under attack. Reece looked back towards the gateway just as Makayla jumped through, screaming a battle cry with her swords swinging and followed by the remaining Shadow Seekers. She stopped short when she realised there was no immediate danger and Reece watched Makayla embrace the female seraph who looked so much like her.

Makayla stopped the moment she passed through the gateway into the Barrens. Her mother was standing nearby dressed in seraph armour and shouting orders to the Seraph and Vampire Guard who'd arrived before her. She sheathed her swords and snapped her mouth closed, she knew she was staring, but couldn't help it. She had only ever seen the softer side of her mother, not the warrior.

Her mother's eyes widened when she saw Makayla and she touched a finger to her crown, wonderment lighting her face. "Makayla, thank goodness you're here," her mother said, hugging her. Makayla returned her hug, her shoulders relaxing in relief; the Trinian Globe and seraph armour seemed to be overriding the Druidoynan properties of the armour.

"Mother, we were so worried when we heard Zobiana had taken you, are you okay?"

"Yes, I'm fine, is Emily safe?"

Makayla nodded. "Danny got her and Izador out before they destroyed Wigmore Castle." Makayla shaded her eyes and looked towards the horizon. "Is that the temple off in the distance?" She pointed.

Ambrosia looked over her shoulder. "Yes, that's it." She looked back towards Makayla and smiled at someone behind her.

"Tristan, Darrius." Ambrosia hugged them as the rest of the Shadow Seekers circled them. Makayla made the introductions.

"Where's Zobiana? I thought she'd be here," Darrius said.

"No, not yet, she keeps sending her Newblood army to distract us. Just as we finish dispatching them, more appear out of nowhere."

"Where's Baba?" Makayla asked.

"He's further afield. Come we need to prepare for—" Ambrosia stopped speaking and smiled. "Xander, it's good to see you safe... but you look different, are you okay?"

Makayla shivered and turned to look at Alexander, all her deepest fears coalescing the moment she set eyes on her husband.

His body wavered as he grew taller. "Alexander's no longer present," he said in an unrecognisable voice. He eyed Makayla with black, fathomless eyes. His mouth hooked up, the dimples in his cheeks deepening as he touched her face and lifted a coil of her hair to his nose. "I see why he likes your scent, it's to die for."

He looked at Danny. "Commendable exorcism, Danny-boy, but I'm not easily evicted. Granted, the Druid put up a good fight and held me at bay right up until we passed through the gateway. He fights still, wiggling like a worm on a hook, screaming for freedom. Not long now, though." He looked at Makayla again. "All his memories will be mine soon and when they are, he'll be no more and, you—" The Dark One touched her breastplate with his forefinger. Sparks flew off her armour as his finger sizzled, catching fire. Makayla held her breath expecting the Druidoynan metal to render him unconscious but nothing happened. The Dark One smiled, removed his finger from her armour and angled his head, focusing his eyes on her face once more. "You and the Trinian Globe will be mine."

The Dark One turned away from her, flames dancing up his arms and covering the rest of his body as he walked towards the temple. He looked over his shoulder and winked, the corner of his mouth hooking up in Alexander's seductive grin; it was the smile that set Makayla's heart thundering with desire. This time her thundering heart wasn't beating with desire, but trepidation.

"Alexander will never be yours and neither will I," she called after him, her voice trembling.

"He already is, Golden One, he already is. Make no mistake, soon you will be too," the Dark One said as he walked away.

It was difficult to watch the man she loved being controlled like a puppet. Makayla's heart twisted tighter in her chest with every step he took away from her. Newbloods appeared from out of nowhere forming a shield about his body, bowing their heads as he passed. Makayla didn't know what to do, how was she going to free him? She'd never felt so useless in her life.

"To defeat the Dark One you must give up that which you love most," her nemesis said.

"What are you saying?" Makayla queried. Her nemesis had said something similar once before.

"You must give up that which you love most," her nemesis repeated.

"Surely you can't mean Alexander?"

"Yes. You must give him up."

"I will not give him up, he's my husband. He's still in there, I feel him, I feel his love."

"You must destroy the Dark One before it's too late."

"And how do you propose I do that?"

"You must kill that which you love the most."

"I will not kill my husband, there has to be another way."

"She comes, she comes now. She is, I am, we are, vital to your success."

"Who's vital?"

"Makayla, we need to stop him," Danny said, interrupting her internal conversation. "We cannot allow him to break the seal to the underworld, if he does, the Dark One and his demon horde will reign for a thousand years."

"I know, but how am I going to stop him? Alexander's still in there. Tell me how and I'll do it, I'll do anything except kill him."

"You may have to, Makayla; it may be the only way to free Alexander and destroy the Dark One."

"I will not kill my husband, I won't do it, I won't!"

Makayla glanced at her mother. If she killed Alexander she'd be killing her mother as well – the resurrection spell still connected them.

Her mother touched her cheek, Makayla noticed tears swelling in her eyes and shook her head. "No, Mother, I will not be responsible for your death, or my husband's, there has to be another way."

"Makayla, honey, I knew the risks when I saved Alexander. I knew it might cost me my life and I'm prepared to die to save the lives of billions. Hell cannot reign over the Multiverse. You know this, you must not hesitate; if it's the only way to bring down the Dark One, you must sacrifice us both."

"I will not kill him, or you. I can't, please don't ask me to. Xander's the love of my life, my soulmate. What about Emily? She needs you, and what about Father? He would not survive your loss. None of us would. I will find another way." Makayla gulped, her chest was on fire. *Breathe, Makayla, breathe, everything will be okay,* she thought, rubbing her throbbing temples. She shook her head, the pitying looks on her friends' faces was too much; she would find another way.

Zack moved to her side and touched her shoulder. "Tell me what to do and I'll do it, let me help."

Makayla almost lost it, she drew in a long quivering breath. "Thank you, Zack, but it's okay, I'll figure it out." She shook her head, tears streaming down her face; she brushed them away with the back of her hand and straightened her back.

"There's no other way," her nemesis said, sorrow lacing her words.

"There's always another way," Makayla said, looking off into the distance. "Come on, let's go, we've a score to settle." She started running, her wings burst from her back with a shimmering flare as she unfurled them and thrust into the sky.

CHAPTER 52.

The portal swirled before Zobiana, growing larger and gathering strength the longer she fed power into it. She waited for Abigail, Tyrone and the last of her Newblood soldiers to pass through before raising her hand to touch the outer edges of the portal. Her hand tingled as the colour drained from her fingertips, turning them grey. She lowered her hand to her side and stared into the black abyss. This was it, the end; whatever the outcome, whatever happened, she would be free either way. She straightened the black crown on her head and slid her hands down the length of her cool body armour then stepped into the maelstrom. Her hair whipped about her face as she walked through the blustery vortex. She'd waited a long time for this day. Zobiana smiled when she saw the light at the end of the tunnel. She'd planned the moment just right; grand entrances were her speciality. Clanging swords and the roar of battle grew louder as she drew closer to her destination.

The moment she exited the portal it closed behind her, disintegrating in a fizzing hazy spray of dark sandy particles. Zobiana had arrived inside the Dark One's black granite temple, which was encircled by narrow columns that reached the ceiling. She stood in the middle of the room on a solid round slab of gold, the seal; a lid of sorts, that covered the gateway into the underworld. Ancient writings were inscribed into the granite floor surrounding the golden seal.

Zobiana made her way to the front of the temple; a growing black cloud gathered about her feet floating along the ground as she crossed the threshold and stood on the top step to stare out at the Barrens. It was, as its name suggested, barren and inhospitable. Red dirt, rocky, flat terrain and the black twisted remains of dead trees stretching for as far as the eye could see. Three full moons cast a pink glow over everything, turning night into day. She descended the steps regally, the black cloud masking her feet as she glanced up into the heavens. Seraph Guard cluttered the sky, darting back and forth as they fought her army.

Newbloods bowed their heads and parted to make way for her as she passed; they closed in and followed behind, forming a protective barrier around her. The Vampire and Seraph Guard no longer surrounded the temple, having been forced back by the sudden influx of her army. Zobiana searched the field and spotted Abigail and Tyrone and headed towards them. She couldn't see Kraegan anywhere; he'd said he'd meet them there, but she had a sneaking feeling he wouldn't show. Abigail and Tyrone were discussing something and pointing further down the field, grim looks on their faces. Alexander was heading their way. Zobiana smiled, she would not make the same mistake a second time upon speaking with him.

"Mother, what do we do?" Abigail whispered, coming to her side with Tyrone. "He's coming, what if he burns us agai—"

"He won't, he needs us. Now bow and do as you are told." Zobiana lowered to her knees and bowed her head, Abigail and Tyrone followed suit. The Dark One stopped in front of them, his legs spread wide, his arms behind his back. "Rise."

Zobiana looked up into Alexander's face, he was long gone; the Dark One had complete control. She smiled as she rose from the ground. "My Lord, you are here."

"I am." He looked back the way he'd come and then towards the temple. "The Shadow Seekers are here; destroy them all,"

"As you wish, my Lord, and the Golden One?"

"Keep her busy; when the time's right, I'll seek her out, she has an integral part to play in all this. The seal must be broken first."

Zobiana smiled, knowing what part the Golden One would play because it matched her own agenda. "What of the Trinian Globe?"

"The Golden One has it." The Dark One angled his head scrutinising Zobiana's face. "It will be mine soon, as will the

Golden One. Do not let them breach the temple before the seal is broken or I'll have your head. I will be free of my prison and this body. I will reign and bring the Multiverse to its knees."

Makayla had lost sight of Alexander, she searched for him among the battling warriors, but he'd disappeared, swallowed by the river of bodies. She knew where he was heading. She shaded her eyes focusing on the temple in the distance as she flew along. It jutted up from the ground like a black smudge on the horizon. Something was happening; the Seraph and Vampire Guard were being pushed back by hordes of Newbloods flowing from the temple entrance.

Raziel drew alongside her. "Hello, my queen." He smiled, his cobalt eyes regarding her with interest.

"Hi Raziel," she said, glancing across at him and then back at the horizon. "Any idea on what's happening down there?" she said, pointing towards the temple.

"I believe your nemesis has arrived."

Makayla frowned. "My nemesis, do you mean Zobiana?"

"Correct." He nodded.

Makayla had never thought of Zobiana as her nemesis, more a thorn in her side. Raziel was right to call her that, but she considered the voice in her head more her nemesis than Zobiana, strange that Raziel would have chosen that word. Something stirred in the far reaches of her mind, a puzzle begging to be solved. Makayla glanced down and saw the Shadow Seekers and her parents far below her, she looped about and descended, landing among them. Raziel followed her down.

"See anything?" Zack asked.

"Something's happening at the temple," she replied. "Our people are being pushed back."

"What about Xander?"

"I lost him."

"He's heading towards the temple," her mother said. "Raziel, did you see anything?"

"Lilith's here, sister-mine,"

"Sister?" Makayla looked between Raziel and her mother.

"That's right; Raziel's your uncle, Makayla."

"What the fu—" Makayla bit her lip to prevent the expletive from slipping out. "Why didn't you say anything?"

Raziel shrugged. "I couldn't." He looked towards her mother.

"Bullshit."

"Makayla," her father reprimanded. He frowned as he looked about. "Where's Vasili? I thought he'd be here."

Gabriel's back stiffened. "Didn't anyone tell you?" Makayla asked, glancing at Gabriel.

"Tell me what?" Sebastian glanced between Lazarus and Tristan.

"Vasili and Marianna, along with Ava and Ashley, were killed when the compound was destroyed," Gabriel said. Makayla's mother gasped, tears glazing her eyes as she covered her mouth.

"What, no, that's impossible." Her father's face paled as he stopped and took her mother in his arms. "Gabriel, I'm—"

"It's okay, Sebastian."

"No, no, it's not okay, she has taken too much, killed too many."

"I'm just getting started, Sebastian," Zobiana called out. "Glad you all made it to the soirée." She smirked. "It's not exactly what I had in mind, but it will do."

Zobiana stood a good thirty metres away, a jagged black crown atop her head and bedecked in black armour surrounded by hissing Newbloods. How had they not noticed their approach? Abigail and Tyrone stood either side of Zobiana with smug looks on their faces. Makayla manifested fireballs in her hands and launched them. They hit Zobiana's invisible barrier and bounced into a group of unprotected Newbloods standing off to her right. The burning Newbloods screamed, patting themselves down in a futile frenzy to put out the seraph flames. Their body armour melted as their flesh disintegrated into ash. Zobiana laughed when the fireballs hit the barrier.

The Shadow Seekers spread out, surrounding Makayla in a wide circle. Danny moved to Makayla's left, unsheathing his dual swords. Lazarus to her right, twirling his daggers. Anna nocked in a lightweight explosive arrow in her longbow and took aim. Morgan swirled her katanas about her body in artful loops. Zack levelled his modified Glocks, sighting down the barrels at his targets. Reece, Bryce, Gabriel and Jackson pulled out various weapons, Raziel and Ambrosia manifested seraph fireballs. Sebastian twirled his sword, spinning it in the air as if it was an extension of his arm. The Vampire and Seraph Guard held their weapons aloft, ready for battle.

"Ready to play?" Zobiana baited, her eyes turning black and her red irises flashing.

"She's mine," Makayla hissed, her fangs lengthening. Power rippled over her armour as she took off running. The Shadow Seekers, the Seraph and Vampire Guard fanned out and stormed after her, battle cries roaring from their mouths.

Zobiana raised her hand in the air and sliced it down. "Destroy them," she screamed. Battle horns sounded as the Newbloods charged forward. The two forces ran towards one another and clashed with the clang of swords and roaring battle cries. Seraphs launched into the air, swinging their swords as they flew. The sounds of battle faded into the background as Makayla focused her attention on Zobiana. Zobiana lifted her chin, acknowledging Makayla with a playful nod and turned towards the temple. She slunk away, unperturbed by the destruction she'd set in motion. There was no way Makayla was letting Zobiana escape the battle this time. The bitch was dressed for battle and by God she would take part and taste the bitter bite of her blade.

Makayla's invisible shield flared about her body with blue-fire as a Newblood stepped in front of her. She didn't hesitate; she grabbed him by the throat, lifted him into the air and flung him at three Newbloods moving up behind Morgan. Morgan was a sight to see, graceful yet deadly as she danced about her opponents. Her blades were a blur of silver as she made quick work of the Newbloods, chopping them to pieces. She diced off body parts like she was dicing carrots.

Makayla pushed through the crowd chasing after Zobiana; every time she made a little headway, another vampire would step in front of her and waylay her. An arrow flew past her and struck a group of Newbloods coming at her from the right. The ground exploded; showering Makayla in dirt, blood, chunks of flesh and body parts. She glanced over her shoulder where Anna stood holding her bow; four Vampire Guard protecting her as she targeted and killed their enemies. Makayla watched her whip out an explosive-tipped arrow from the quiver strapped to her back and nock it in; she pulled the string back levelling it against her cheek as she took aim and let it loose. The arrow landed ten metres in front of Makayla with another ground-trembling explosion, clearing a blood-splattered path. Anna smiled at her, and nocked in three silver-tipped arrows at once, sending them flying in Gabriel's direction where he battled several Newbloods. Three were struck in the forehead by her arrows, killing and ashing them instantaneously. A Seraph Guard swept past Makayla, the updraft of air whooshing against her face as his wings worked the air. He slashed his sword left and right, hacking a row of Newbloods to pieces as he jetted past.

A body dropped from the heavens and landed at her feet; she looked up and saw Darrius jetting towards another Newblood. Seraph circled above her like gathering storm clouds on the horizon, diving in for the kill and retreating. Makayla retrieved her silver throwing stars from a pouch clipped to her belt and flung them into the battling horde. Newbloods dropped to the ground, their bodies convulsing as the silver burned their flesh and turned them to ash instantly.

Makayla unfurled her wings and ran, unsheathing her seraph blades from the scabbards on her back. She flapped her wings, gathered momentum and shot into the sky. She looked down at the battle below – they were making headway towards the temple, but no matter how many Newbloods they killed, the numbers never diminished. Makayla took in the scene below, Reece and Bryce were fighting back to back, synchronised in their movements. They swung each other around, kicking and slicing, maiming and killing as they flung one another from one side to the other. Anna covered all the Shadow Seekers, taking down any Newbloods who got too close. Lazarus, Zack and Danny herded Newbloods, grouping them together for Tristan and Darrius to take out as they flew past; Darrius would decapitate the Newbloods while Tristan hurled fireballs at their bloody remains. Jackson and Gabriel had paired up, Gabriel's height drew in Newbloods like a magnet; he toyed with them while Jackson picked them off with throwing-knives.

Then there were her parents and Raziel; they were a different kind of warrior altogether. Makayla had seen nothing quite like them – they were focused and in complete battle mode. Her mother was a sight to see, flipping and swaying left and right, waltzing around her adversaries as if they were dance partners at a ball. Billowing flames ensconced her mother and she twirled her swords as she took down Newblood after Newblood. Her father was the fiercest warrior on the battlefield, his face a mask of concentration. He didn't run after his foes, he walked towards them. One strike of his blade and they were dead. Her Uncle Raziel was also a force to be reckoned with. At nine feet tall he made Gabriel's seven feet look dwarfish. His wingspan was almost double his height; he was a huge weapon dropping from the sky, advancing to take out his enemies with the sheer power of his wings alone; they cut through Newblood bodies like razor-sharp blades as he flashed past.

Makayla lifted her gaze and focused on Zobiana; she was taking her time and hadn't yet reached the temple, Makayla dove; flying low as she skimmed the ground, slashing her swords in coiling arcs and cutting down Newbloods as she jetted towards her. Makayla landed just behind the enemy lines; soon the Shadow Seekers would join her. Zobiana stopped mid-stride and faced her. A lethal smile cut a harsh line across her face. Makayla cracked her neck moving her head from side to side as she spun her swords and studied her adversary. She took in Zobiana's countenance; her regal stance; her hip-length, thick blue-black hair swaying in the gentle breeze. She was a striking picture of beauty and arrogance. Zobiana intrigued Makayla, she wasn't like Abigail or Tyrone, she never engaged in battle, but left the fighting to others as she retreated. Makayla had to ask why. It was as if she wasn't invested in her end goal;

as if she had another underlying objective. Something was off, Makayla could see it in Zobiana's disconcerting gaze. Something had changed, shifted; she was different from the woman Makayla had met in the thirteen hundreds. Something lay hidden in the depths of Zobiana's eyes, buried deep within the shadowed recesses. Makayla couldn't put her finger on it, but knew deep down Zobiana was not who she pretended to be. She didn't quite fit the image she projected ... and then the shutter came down and the brief glimpse Makayla had got from Zobiana disappeared. The bitch was back.

"Have you come to play, Makayla dear?" she said, in a velvety voice that reeked with distracting familiarity, though they'd not spoken over twenty words to one another.

"I've come to do more than play, Lilith." Makayla flexed her wings, rolling her shoulders.

"Let's forego the pleasantries and get started, shall we?" Zobiana hissed, her mouth filling with multiple fangs as giant black, bat-like leathery wings shot out of her back. Red fire flared as she flapped her wings. Sparks zinged about her as she thrust towards Makayla. Zobiana's hand morphed, her fingers transforming into lethal talons, Makayla's shield flared as Zobiana swiped her claws through it and across her neck, cutting deep into her skin. Makayla blocked the severing blow at the last minute as Zobiana flew by. Makayla frowned. Zobiana shouldn't have been able to penetrate her protective shield. She spun into the air, her wound healing as she lifted off the ground. Zobiana raised her talons to her mouth and licked the blood off them, her eyes rolling back in her head as a euphoric smile slid across her face.

"I'd almost forgotten how delicious your blood is," Zobiana groaned in pleasure.

"Who the fuck are you? And how are you able to penetrate my shields?"

"I think you know the answer to that question already," Zobiana said, her face returning to normal. "Surely you must remember who I am? After everything we've been through together over the centuries. I have to say I'm a little disappointed you haven't figured it out yet. After all, you are the by-product of my creation; we've been together since your conception."

CHAPTER 53

Alexander was trapped, a passenger in his own body. He'd heard every word the Dark One had uttered to Makayla and Zobiana, powerless to stop the words passing his lips. The moment he'd crossed the gateway to Evron the Dark One had seized control of his body, rendering him useless. Alexander couldn't figure out how the Dark One had pulled it off.

"You'll never be free," Alexander said.

"I already am," the Dark One responded.

"You're trapped in my body, that's not freedom."

"Maybe so, but once I break the seal things will be different."

"We'll still be stuck with each other, even if you break the seal."

"No, we won't, I will barter a trade with the Golden One;

the memory of your wedding for the Trinian Globe. She'll agree because she loves you. If she doesn't, then you both lose and you cease to exist. Your body is a satisfactory vessel, I could do worse."

"She'll never give you what you want, I'll make certain of it!"

"How? Only I can hear you." The Dark One chuckled.

"I will find a way."

"You can try, but I am your end and your beginning," the Dark One said.

"Yeah, yeah, so you keep saying," Alexander grumbled.

The Dark One kneeled in the centre of the heavy gold seal, circling his body as he recited the inscriptions aloud. Once done, he traced his fingers over the carvings, searching for differences in the stone. Some letters were raised secret buttons, hidden within the code; he pressed them down in an ordered sequence and clapped his hands in delight when he felt the seal shift beneath him. The moment he stepped off the golden seal he crossed the room and stood in the doorway, waiting. The air rippled before his eyes as a shimmering wave of light blasted outwards whistling around the edges of the seal. As the pressure grew, the seal cover shuddered and lifted into the air. The ground trembled, shaking the temple foundations. The columns surrounding the ancient writings shifted and creaked, cracks snaking up their lengths growing deeper as the vibrations grew stronger. There was a backlash of air and the hovering seal lid was sucked back into position with a forceful bang, breaking into pieces. There was another bang as debris was blasted upwards like molten rock erupting from a volcano. The smell of sulphur permeated the air. Heatwaves and howling winds surged from the hole the seal lid had concealed, circling in the air and filling the room with a red, toxic haze. Flames issued from the opening and spewed along the ground, snaking a path across the floor and surging up the columns, coating them in black soot. The Dark One smiled and rubbed his hands together again. He walked to the edge of the vent and looked down into the cavernous hole.

"What are you looking for?" Alexander asked.

"I'm not looking, I'm waiting."

"Waiting for what?"

"You'll see soon enough."

"Oh look, the princess has arrived," Abigail said, twirling twin daggers in her hands.

"Wrong, I'm the fucking queen," Makayla replied.

A dagger flew past her head; Makayla didn't flinch, but looked past Zobiana at Abigail who was preparing to throw a second dagger.

"Really, why do you even bother? You'll just miss again," Makayla heckled.

Abigail's face flushed as she threw the second blade. Makayla lifted her hand and the dagger stopped and dropped to the ground. "You're pathetic. Give up while you're ahead." Makayla swept her hand up and jerked it sideways. Abigail shot into the air, her arms and legs circling in a spin-wheel motion as she was thrown away like last week's garbage. Abigail screamed in a rage as she hurtled through the air and struck a group of Newbloods. Tyrone watched Abigail struggling to untangle herself from the Newbloods, unfazed by her dilemma.

Makayla grinned at Abigail's predicament. "All that's missing is the clown suit, Abigail, and then the circus act would be complete," Makayla said, before eyeing Zobiana again. Zobiana's eyes were fixated behind Makayla.

"Nice one. There's hope for you yet, Makayla, your jokes are getting better," Reece chuckled from behind her.

Abigail found her feet and sauntered back to stand by Tyrone. Makayla winked at her and her face turned a deeper shade of red.

Makayla didn't acknowledge Reece's comment or wonder who had captured Zobiana's attention; she'd sensed the Shadow Seeker's arrival before Reece's comment. There was a notable change in Abigail and Tyrone's stances. Zobiana seemed unaffected by the new arrivals, in fact, she appeared happy. Her eyes brightened and her smile widened the moment her parents and the Shadow Seekers came to a standstill bedside Makayla. Makayla looked left and right and over each shoulder. Danny, Tristan and her parents were to her left along with Gabriel and Raziel. Anna, Morgan, Reece and Bryce were to her rear, along with a number of Vampire and Seraph Guard, while Lazarus, Darrius, Zack and Jackson stood to her right. Their weapons were drawn and at the ready; twirling, twisting, flipping and aimed at their adversaries. Makayla could feel the controlled energy emanating from the group; their emotions tethered, coiled tight, and ready to be unleashed at a moment's notice.

"Now that we're all here I believe we can proceed," Zobiana said, her exotic voice finally stirring the fires of recognition in the depths of Makayla's shoddy memory. *It couldn't be, surely not?* Makayla thought to herself, shaking her head.

"Why, Makayla dear, I think you're onto something," Zobiana's voice rang in her head. Makayla whipped her eyes towards Zobiana; Zobiana stared back, her smile turning to laughter.

How the hell was Zobiana able to penetrate her mind-shield?

"My capabilities would surprise you," Zobiana said, her voice eliciting an internal shiver throughout Makayla's psyche. *"Don't be so hard on yourself, dear, you couldn't have known, not really."*

"Couldn't have known what?"

"Oh, I'll leave it for my better half to explain it to you."

"Better half, who the hell's your better half? The Dark One?"

"Aren't you precious. The Dark One's better half, at present, is Alexander." Zobiana laughed and focused her

attention back to Makayla's parents.

"Sebastian, it seems my prediction is upon us."

"Don't do this, Lil."

"Don't call me that, Lil doesn't exist anymore."

"It doesn't have to be this way." Sebastian held out his hands.

"I'm sorry, Bastian, but you're wrong. This is the only way for me to be free; you know it better than anyone. One way or another, it ends today, no matter the cost." Zobiana regarded Danny briefly, her eyes softening before she looked away. Had Makayla not been watching her, she'd have missed the fleeting glance; what did it mean? Zobiana looked at the sky and then further afield, the battle raged on about them. The Seraph and Vampire Guard hadn't stopped fighting the Newbloods the entire time they'd been speaking with the High Priestess, oblivious to their momentary truce. The clanging of swords and the roar of bellowing soldiers seemed muted, the sound somehow lost to their present conversation.

"Hang on; I thought you wanted to be queen of Evron?" Makayla swirled her seraph swords for emphasis.

Zobiana looked at Makayla again, her eyes faltered, narrowed, then hardened, her fangs elongated, broadening and filling her mouth to capacity.

"As I was saying, I believe we can proceed now."

"Proceed, proceed with what?" Makayla queried, looking from Zobiana to her parents.

"With the reaping," Zobiana whispered.

"Mother, let's—" Abigail began to speak, Zobiana raised her hand silencing her daughter.

"Kill them; kill them all, except for her." Zobiana pointed at Makayla. "The Dark One wants her alive." Zobiana unfurled her wings and shot towards Makayla. Makayla lifted her seraph swords and prepared to fight. The Newbloods and the Shadow Seekers rushed towards one another. Makayla dematerialised and reappeared in the air above her earlier position, her wings flapping as she hovered overhead watching the battle unfold. Zobiana angled her head, looking for Makayla then manifested energy balls in her palms and hurled them at Makayla before tearing after her.

Makayla's shield flared with electricity and absorbed the crackling energy balls. "I thought you said the Dark One wanted me alive?" she yelled.

"He does, but he didn't say how alive he wanted you, I think I'll have my fun with you first," Zobiana said.

"Why are you doing this, Zobiana? It's not about being the queen of Evron, is it? You want something else!"

"Do I now?" Zobiana hurled another energy ball.

Makayla spun her body round and round like a spinning top, the energy balls caught in her shield's trajectory, revolving around her like orbiting planets. Makayla stopped spinning and thrust her wings forward, sending the energy balls back towards Zobiana. Zobiana smiled and held her arms out her sides as the energy balls struck the breastplate of her armour, which absorbed the power.

"Just the pick-me-up I needed," Zobiana said.

"Something has been bothering me, Zobiana, how am I the by-product of your creation? How could we have been together since my conception?"

Zobiana smiled. "I gave you a little pre-birthday gift while you were in your mother's womb and activated that gift when you were incarcerated in the dungeons."

Makayla frowned. "What are you talking about?"

"She speaks of me and the blood curse between you and Alexander," her nemesis said.

"I don't understand," Makayla said to her nemesis.

"Oh, come on, are you really that daft?" Zobiana tapped the side of her temple. "That little voice you hear in your head was a gift from me and the curse, well, that was a little something I concocted to sweeten the deal."

"No, that's impossible," Makayla whispered. "Why would you do something like that?"

"She wants freedom. And the curse was a sure way of getting what she wanted." Her nemesis whispered.

"That's right, I want freedom and you'll be the one to give it to me one way or another. Alexander is an unfortunate casualty!" Zobiana agreed.

"Who do you want freedom from?" Makayla asked.

"I'm sure you'll figure it out."

Makayla angled her head and narrowed her eyes. "Who are you?"

"Does *'she is, I am, we are,'* ring a bell?"

"What did you just say?" A cold sweat infused Makayla's body. *No, it's not possible,* Makayla thought.

"Isn't it?" Zobiana dematerialised and reappeared behind Makayla, grabbing the top edges of her exterior wings and dragging her towards the ground. Makayla spun her body, her swords glistening as she opened and closed her wings in quick succession, dislodging Zobiana's hold. She fanned out her wings and glided to the ground, landing behind three Newbloods. Scissoring her swords, she slashed outwards simultaneously. The zing of crisscrossing blades rang in her ears as she dismembered them, their bodies disintegrating the moment the seraph blades made contact with their flesh. Makayla looked about surveying the area; no one paid her any attention. It was like she was invisible to everyone except Zobiana.

Zobiana landed near Makayla's position and glanced back towards the temple, a curious look on her face, as though she was in some kind of trance or communicating with an invisible force.

Makayla took advantage and strengthened her mind-shield to exclude Zobiana from the conversation she wanted to have with her nemesis. She didn't want her to hear her questions. *Who are you?* she asked her nemesis.

"I am Lilith, the good part of Zobiana's soul. 'Twas I who placed my soul within you, not Zobiana, I did it to escape the Dark One's evilness and protect what good was left of my spirit. Zobiana is corrupt, she is the evil portion of my soul that

was left behind after our soul split," her nemesis said.

"All these years I've thought you were a figment of my imagination, an evil entity torturing my sanity. The things you said to me were hateful. Why, if you're good, would you say the things you did? Why irritate me so?"

"I'm sorry, but it was necessary, some days it was the only way I could get through to you, you were so angry. You responded to insults not affection. I had to distract you and alter your direction because you were heading down a self-destructive path I have already travelled. I needed to communicate with you by whatever means, even if it was to drive you crazy. Most days, my insults were enough of a distraction to divert you from a life lived in ruin."

"How can I stop Zobiana?"

"You cannot stop her, but I can. I couldn't before I merged with you, but my strength has grown alongside yours because you're the Golden One. Your power alone has revived and strengthened my spirit and the love you and Alexander share for one another has boosted my power ten thousand fold, enough to destroy the evil left within my body, within Zobiana's body."

Makayla was at a loss for words, she knew Lilith was being honest because she sensed the truth of her words deep within her being.

"But how will you destroy her if you're stuck in my body?"

"You must bite her; you must feed from her, make the connection through her blood so I can cross back into my

body."

"But if I do that, I'll be blood-bonded with her, with you, because she has my blood in her system."

"That's a good thing, without the blood-bond I cannot cross over into my body. I will let you know when to strike."

Makayla nodded. *"Lilith. May I ask you one more question?"*

"Of course."

"How can I save Alexander?" Makayla waited for Lilith's answer with bated breath.

"Alexander must rise from the ashes."

CHAPTER 54.

The ground trembled; rolling beneath Makayla's feet. Her legs buckled as the tremors strengthened. She almost dropped her seraph swords from the seismic activity jolting the ground. She looked about at the ongoing battle. When Zobiana ordered her men to leave her alone, Makayla had thought for sure there'd be a few who'd disobey her orders and seek her out, but no one had.

People were dying all around her, but none she cared about. Lilith's words clanged around in her head. *'Alexander must rise from the ashes.'* What did it mean? Lilith's cryptic words were baffling. Makayla was in the dark as to how to save him without killing him.

Danny stood to her left, his swords a whistling blur as he spun them about his body, the blades a silver haze as they swirled and sliced through rogue Vampire Guards and

Newbloods. His body danced about his opponents, darting and dodging left and right, his wings lifting him into the sky as he flipped through the air to avoid their weapons. Makayla circled on the spot, the Shadow Seekers formed a protective circle about her.

Gabriel held two Newbloods aloft, one in each hand, his clenched fists squeezing their throats. The Newbloods struggled, kicking their feet at him in an attempt to get him to loosen his grip. Their eyes bulged and filled with blood as they gasped for oxygen and scratched at his fingers. Gabriel's expression was devoid of remorse. Makayla saw a black skeletal entity hovering beside him, its grinding smile stretched across its bleached skull. Its hands were merged with Gabriel's, feeding his thirst for revenge. The reaper relinquished its hold, removing his bony fingers from the Newbloods' throats. The moment the reaper removed his hands, Gabe smashed their heads together, crushing their skulls to pulps. He dropped the corpses and moved on to his next adversary.

The ground jolted once more, Makayla shaded her eyes to see dark clouds gathered above the temple. A spinning halo of lightning flashed across the heavens and struck the temple roof. Makayla glanced about for Zobiana; she was speaking with Tyrone and Abigail, with her back to Makayla. It was time to bring Zobiana's reign to an end so she could concentrate on freeing Alexander before the Dark One broke the seal, if he hadn't already. Makayla feared it was already too late by the unnatural weather formations gathering over the temple. She resheathed her swords and strode towards Zobiana.

"Yes, 'tis time, she will fight, even though she too seeks freedom, be wise, you must outsmart her," Lilith warned. *"She's impervious to your armour; do not rely on its protection."*

Zobiana turned and saw Makayla heading her way; she unfurled her wings, stretching out the bat-like appendages before folding them behind her body once more. She whispered something into Abigail's ear and pointed towards the temple. Abigail nodded, black wings similar to her mother's manifested from her back and she flew off to do her bidding. Tyrone moved to Zobiana's side and crossed his arms over his chest. Makayla ignored him and looked over her shoulder at the battling Shadow Seekers one more time, Zack, Danny, Gabriel and Lazarus trailed after her. She indicated Zobiana with a flick of her head and they nodded. Makayla zeroed in on Zobiana; as she walked, she removed the crown from her head, it shrank in her hand, returning to its former state: a simple coronet. The coronet vibrated with power as she clenched it in her tight grip.

Makayla stopped in front of Zobiana. "Is the weight of the crown too heavy to bear Golden One?" she asked not taking her eyes from the coronet in Makayla's hand.

Makayla moved the coronet left and right, Zobiana's eyes followed the object like a puppy focused on its next treat. Makayla grinned and held the coronet out to her. "A crown was never part of my plan, Zobiana, but it seems it was part of yours," Makayla said, eyeing the black crown gracing her head.

"Take it, you want it, I know you do." Threads of gold light twirled about the coronet as it morphed back into the crown she'd worn only moments ago. It floated above Makayla's palm, its iridescence pulsing as it grew more brilliant. Zobiana's wings disappeared into her body as she lifted her hand towards the hypnotising object, her fingers curling and uncurling towards the glowing treasure. Zobiana's eyes were focused on the hovering crown. Makayla stepped back and glanced at Tyrone; he too was mesmerised by the shimmering crown. *It couldn't be that easy.* Makayla waved her hand in front of Zobiana's face and got no response, clearly it would be that easy. She looked over her shoulder at Zack, Danny and Lazarus, they too were affected by the hypnotising power of her crown, the Trinian Globe was weaving its magic.

Makayla's fangs descended as she dematerialised and reappeared behind Zobiana, and swept aside her hair. Makayla positioned her hands carefully, one below her ear and the other on the top of her shoulder and stabbed her fangs into her flesh. Zobiana screamed and popping skin echoed in Makayla's ears as her teeth punctured her neck. Zobiana jerked, struggling, but by the time she was fully aware of the situation Makayla's venom had already paralysed her into a meditative state. Makayla fed, groaning in pleasure as the coppery taste of Zobiana's blood flowed down her throat. The more she drank, the lighter she felt, and the more inebriated she became. Zobiana was old; the flavour of her blood was full-bodied, as rich and exotic as a well-aged wine, unlike any she'd ever tasted. Makayla's eyes rolled back in her head, as vision after vision flooded her senses.

Snippets of Zobiana's life flitted through her mind. Makayla saw Lilith reject Adam and leave the Garden of Eden. She saw her punished, cursed to walk the land as a vampire succubus living off the blood of man for an eternity. She saw her leave Earth and make her home on Evron. She saw a vampire king, with striking similarities to her father, give her the Gem of Past Times as a betrothal gift in a ceremony between Lilith and her father. Makayla saw her pregnant mother sleeping as Lilith placed a hand to her swollen belly. She saw Lilith kill a seraph who resembled her mother and saw her put on trial for the murder and banished from Evron. She saw Lilith escorted by a Seraph Guard to Earth. She saw Lilith give birth to a baby girl, Abigail. Makayla saw Lilith in the arms of the Seraph Guard who had escorted her to Earth, kissing and laughing with one another. She saw the same seraph put to death and Lilith giving birth to a baby boy. She saw Lilith holding a dagger to the babe's chest, unable to end the child's life. She saw Lilith leave the babe on the doorstep of an orphanage and walk away with tears streaking down her face. She saw the wilding overtake her and the Dark One bend her to his will, pressing her to commit many atrocities. Makayla saw herself in the dungeon with Lilith hovering over both her and Alexander. Makayla saw many more things, but they flitted through her mind so fast they became a blur, and when the visions ended she knew Lilith's spirit had left her body.

Makayla retracted her fangs and backed away from Zobiana. The coronet no longer hovered in the air, but lay on the ground, Makayla picked it up and fastened it to her belt. She moved to Lazarus's side and frowned, he looked behind her, dumbstruck. Zack and Danny wore similar expressions. Makayla turned and tripped backwards almost losing her footing. Fine cracks covered Zobiana's pallid skin, glowing light pulsing through them like the crust of moving magma. Her body expanded and decreased as if she were a giant beating heart. Her exterior shell swelled like a balloon and exploded. Ash residue burst into the air and floated to the ground. In Zobiana's place stood a golden-haired goddess. She had the same features as Zobiana's but her eye, hair and skin colour looked more like that of a seraph. She wore a white Grecian-like robe pinned at one shoulder, the soft fabric draping in soft waves down her curvy body.

The woman smiled and bowed her head. "Thank you, for freeing me, Makayla,"

"Lilith?"

"Yes, Zobiana is no more." Lilith turned to Danny and her smile widened. "Duranté, you look just like your handsome father." Lilith walked up to Danny and touched his cheek. Danny's eyes dilated, his mouth opened and closed and he glanced towards Makayla.

Makayla mouthed, "She's your mother."

"My mother," he repeated.

"Yes," Lilith confirmed, "I'm your mother." She pulled him into her arms and hugged him.

"What have you done? You stole my father, and now you've killed my mother, where's her body? WHERE IS SHE?" Abigail screamed and flew towards them. Lilith faced Abigail, Makayla looked up just as Abigail hurled a dagger. She raised her hand to stop the projectile.

"No!" Lilith cried out, and threw herself in front of Makayla and was struck in the chest by the dagger. Makayla caught Lilith in her arms and fell to her knees.

"Lilith why? My armour would have protected me from the dagger," Makayla said, tears swelling in her eyes.

Lilith smiled. "Do not cry, it has been an honour knowing you all these years, shine bright, Golden One," Lilith murmured, her breathing weakening.

"Let me help you," Makayla said, rubbing her hands together, Lilith stopped her. "No, my life was meant to end this way, 'tis a fitting outcome for all the atrocities I've committed."

"No, I can save you, let me save you."

"You already have, you gave me my freedom."

Danny slumped to his knees beside his mother. She touched his face once more, her breathing becoming shallow. "Do not grieve my loss, Duranté, my heart is full. Goodbye, my love." Lilith's hand dropped to her side, her gaze dulling as she took her last breath. Lilith's body shimmered and was replaced with small golden orbs of sparkling lights that circled about them and disintegrated into the ether.

"Where's my mother?" Abigail screeched.

Danny and Makayla stood and faced Abigail. "She's dead, you just killed her!" Danny said, dematerialising and reappearing in front of Abigail. He grabbed her by the throat and lifted her into the air. Tyrone charged Danny, but was intercepted by Gabriel who punched his hand into Tyrone's chest and ripped out his black heart, throwing it at his feet. Tyrone's face paled, he looked down at the gaping hole in his chest and gasped in horror before slumping to the ground, dead. Gabriel lifted his bloody hand and looked at his fingers before moving onto his next victim. The remaining Shadow Seekers had caught up and were holding back frenzied Newbloods as they tried to get to Abigail.

"I believe you owe a little girl an apology," Danny growled, spittle spraying Abigail's face.

"Fuck you," Abigail spat out.

"No, fuck you!" Danny slammed Abigail to the ground and pushed her face into the dirt, pinning her by the shoulders. Makayla jumped on her back, rammed her knee between her shoulder blades and curled her fingers around the base bones of her flapping wings. Abigail bucked and kicked her legs, flapping her wings harder trying to dislodge her, but failed. Makayla lowered her mouth to her ear. "This is for Alexander and Adrian." Makayla wrenched Abigail's wings back, ignoring the sickening crunch of shattering bones. The clanging of swords and the battling roar of warriors drowned out

Abigail's agonising screams. Makayla tugged again, the crunch and pop of bones breaking free from joints was sweet music to her ears.

Abigail's head flopped to the side, her eyes glazing over. Danny slapped her face and woke her. "You don't get to sleep, not after all the atrocities you've inflicted. You will feel every nuance of pain. This family reunion will burn in your memory and your hereafter forever, sister."

Tendons stretched and snapped, blood sprayed in Makayla's face as she tore Abigail's wings from her back. She jumped off Abigail's back and stared down at the gaping hole between her shoulder blades. The empty ball sockets where her wings had joined pooled with blood. The jagged ridges of Abigail's exposed spinal column floated like ice caps in a gruesome sea of blood, her torn flesh a mangled mess of red and white. Makayla felt no remorse as she threw Abigail's wings aside and set them alight with seraph fire. Makayla held her arms out, watching the seraph fire burn away the bloody gore coating her hands. Danny straightened to his full height and kicked Abigail in the ribs. Her body moved but no sound escaped her mouth. Makayla angled her head, taking in his appearance, his eyes were demonic black and his hands and arms were black to his elbows, his fingernails sharp, lethal talons. He noticed her staring and smiled, his teeth were sharp fangs, much like Zobiana's had been.

Jagged light fragmented across the sky as lightning flashed; seconds later thunder boomed and the ground jolted.

Makayla flung her arms out to gain her balance and looked towards the temple, Alexander was heading their way. She gulped and looked heavenward, the lightning wasn't coming from the sky, it was emanating from his body. His black gaze burned into her, unwavering as he strode towards her. Newbloods gathered around and followed him like moths to a flame. *It's not Alexander,* she thought to herself. He didn't even walk the same.

Makayla stiffened when the Dark One stopped in front of her and held out his hand, palm up. "Give it to me?" he said, his guttural voice grating.

"Give you what?" Makayla crossed her arms over her chest.

"The Trinian Globe."

Makayla laughed. "No, I don't think so."

The Dark One's hand flashed forward and grabbed her by the throat. "GIVE. IT. TO. ME. NOW!" His fingers bit into her flesh, the heat of his touch blistering her skin, she was defenceless against him, her powers rendered useless. She saw Danny unsheath a dagger from the corner of her eye and stayed his hand.

"NO!"

"Give me the Trinian Globe, or you lose him forever."

Makayla gritted her teeth, her throat burned and her vision blurred with white, spinning stars. Everything inside her said to bow to the Dark One's demands and save Alexander, but she knew he wouldn't want her to give the Dark One the Trinian

Globe. There was too much at stake. "NO."

"Give me the Trinian Globe now, I demand it!"

"You can demand all you like; I will not give you what you want!" Makayla grabbed his wrist with her left hand and his elbow with her right and pushed up, twisting his arm in a quick, fluid motion as she forced his arm down and behind his back. She slammed her knee into his back, shoved him to the ground and stepped away. Her powers may be useless around him, but her self-defence skills were not lacking.

The Dark One jumped to his feet, recovering quickly. "I'll make a trade; the Trinian Globe for Alexander's last memory. Say no, and he'll cease to exist. You'll lose him and his body will be mine forever." He smiled; it was not a smile of happiness, but one of spurned contempt.

Makayla stepped back from the entity wearing her husband's body. Her skin crawled as she swallowed the saliva pooling in her mouth, her stomach churned, she wanted to throw up. She looked over her shoulder, everyone she loved was standing in support behind her: her parents and uncle, her brothers and the Shadow Seekers. The Seraph and Vampire Guard gathered around her too, also waiting for her response. A pin could have dropped the silence was so fraught. No one was fighting, the battle had come to a complete standstill.

Makayla knew what she wanted, and what it would cost if she followed her heart, but she was no fool. Even if she gave the Dark One what he asked for, Alexander would not be free he'd always be a pawn used to barter a better deal, and they would all die, anyway. She looked down at her trembling hands and drew in a lengthy breath before lifting her face to look at the Dark One.

"What will it be, Golden One?"

"I want a blood oath from you before I give you my decision."

"Makayla, no, don't make—"

Makayla held her finger up in the air to silence her father.

"A blood oath? What is it you want for this blood oath?" the Dark One asked, his eyebrow lifting in curiosity.

"I want you to free Alexander."

The Dark One scratched his jaw, considering her proposal. "No."

"At least let me speak with him."

The Dark One studied her face. "No."

Makayla frowned. "Let me speak with Alexander and I will give you the Trinian Globe."

"NO, Makayla, no!" her father yelled.

Makayla looked at her father. "Trust me, Baba, I know what I'm doing."

Sebastian's shoulders sagged and he nodded.

Makayla looked back at the Dark One. "What say you?"

"As you wish." He nodded. "But I'll be listening, if you conspire against me, I will destroy him."

Makayla nodded in agreement. She would know when Alexander was in control and aware of his surroundings by looking in his eyes. Makayla watched his body morph and shrink to its normal size. She held her breath, the oxygen burning in her lungs as she waited for her husband to reappear. Alexander's head was bowed, his hair covering his face, Makayla moved closer to him and tucked a loose strand of hair behind one of his ears.

"Xander, are you here with me?" she asked, needing to see his eyes.

Alexander gasped and jerked his head up, gold-flecked honey amber eyes stared back at her.

He flung his arms out and grasped her face with his hands, drawing her mouth to his. Soft lips met hers, shattering her resolve and tipping her over the edge, she kissed him back opening to him. His tongue flicked into her mouth and she responded, wanting to take things further. Alexander framed her face with his hands, threading his fingers through her hair and broke the kiss to look into her eyes again. Makayla was bombarded with so many emotions; relief and love were the strongest of them all. He dragged her into his arms and embraced her. Her legs buckled, she'd have fallen to the ground had he not been holding her.

"We don't have long, Makayla. I fight him, but he's too strong," Alexander said, tucking Makayla to his side.

He acknowledged everyone. "The Dark One has broken the seal. As we speak, demons gather waiting for him; they can't breach the gates of hell until he summons them. It's why he's being so agreeable and letting me speak with you. Don't give him the Trinian Globe; I believe that's why he hasn't freed them yet, he wants the power the Trinian Globe will afford him; he wants the Multiverse and will not stop until he controls it. He'll not keep his word, he'll not honour the agreement he made with you."

"How can we stop him?" Darrius asked.

"You need to destroy the gateway and send the Dark One back to the underworld using the Trinian Globe." Alexander looked into Makayla's eyes. "Makayla will know what to do when the time comes."

"Xander, we need to get him out of you first. We can't destroy him until then."

Alexander shook his head, and glanced at her mother, she nodded at him and he focused on Makayla again. "It's too late for me, Makayla." He touched her cheek. "You must end this now."

Makayla shook her head. "No, there has to be a way to expel him from your body."

"There's only one way, you must kil—" Alexander's forehead furrowed as he buckled over, clutching his head in pain. *"NO, you can't. No, don't."* Alexander looked at Makayla. "He's trying to erase the memory of our wedding." Alexander dropped to his knees, gripping the sides of his head rocking back and forth.

Makayla knelt before him. "You are not dying today or any other day."

"I can't hold him at bay much longer, Makayla, if he takes my last memory of us, I'm as good as dead anyway. I will cease to exist and he will inhabit my body forever. Kill me before it's too late, kill me now, you'll not get a second chance, don't let him have me."

"Xander, I can't kill you," Makayla sobbed, her face wet with tears. "I ca. . .can't, *please don't ask this of me,* you're my everything, we were meant to have forever, not this, not this," she sobbed. "I. . .I can't end you, not like this. If I kill you, my mother dies too," Makayla choked out. Alexander's face blurred from the tears in her eyes, the knot in her chest ached, her head pounded, she was dying inside. How many more people would she have to lose? "I will not be responsible for your deaths."

"You must, Makayla," Ambrosia murmured, and looked across at her, nodding. "You must," her mother said again and looked towards Raziel, he nodded too and looked at his feet, his wings sagging.

Ambrosia looked back at her father and touched his face.

"What are you saying, Ambrosia?" Sebastian whispered.

"I performed the resurrection spell on Xander, my life is inextricably tied to his."

"No." Her father shook his head. "No, Ambrosia?" Sebastian's face paled as did Tristan's and Darrius's. "Makayla, no don't do it, please don't take her from me," her father pleaded.

Makayla covered her face with her hands and wept.

She felt Alexander's gentle touch as he lowered her hands, she looked up into his glistening eyes. "I don't want it to end like this either, Makayla. I don't want to leave you, I don't want to die, but I can't live knowing my body will be used by the Dark One." Alexander grimaced, his eyes closing as his jaw clenched. He wiped sweat from his forehead with the back of his hand. Makayla touched his cheek and gazed into his unwavering eyes, then she snaked her hand down her leg and removed a dagger from its sheath.

"I love you, I will love you for the rest of my life." Makayla looked across at her mother, tears streamed down her face as she mouthed, *"I love you, Mother."*

"I love you too, my sweet daughter, take care of Emily, she will need you more than ever," her mother's voice echoed in her mind.

Makayla felt the enveloping warmth of her mother's love surround her and looked back into Alexander's eyes. Her world was ending.

"I love you, Makayla, look after her,"

Makayla frowned "Look after who?"

Alexander smiled ambiguously and ran a fingertip down her nose and across her lips. Warmth filled her body as she was wrapped in his love and yet she was awash with sadness all in the space of a single moment. Makayla felt a ripple flash through her mind as Salomae roared her dissent. Makayla ignored her, cupping Alexander's cheek and touching her lips to his as she thrust the dagger into his heart and screamed. The heartache ripped through her and the sorrow numbed her mind as she drove the dagger in further.

Alexander's eyes widened and his mouth hooked up in a soft, peaceful smile. "Farewell, my love, this is not goodbye," he murmured. His eyes closed and his head lolled back, a black column of grainy smoke funnelling out of his mouth in a swirling noxious cloud and floating across the battlefield towards the temple.

Her father's howling scream rent the air as she laid Xander's body on the ground. She smoothed back his hair, crossed his arms over his heart and kissed his lips one last time. "See you soon, my love," she said, pushing up from the ground. She gritted her teeth. The ache in her heart was unlike anything she'd ever experienced, the pain was a black hole sucking her into its ominous depths. *'Hold it together just a little longer, Makayla,'* she thought to herself. Tears streaked down her face as she turned and saw her father rocking back and forth with her mother in his arms.

"Save her, Makayla, do something," her father begged. Makayla knelt by his side, rubbing her hands together until they were immersed in golden light. She placed her hands over her mother's heart and sent healing waves into her body. Nothing happened. She continued trying, but still there was no change. She lowered her hands with tears streaming down her face, and kissed her mother's cheek. Her father looked up into her eyes a broken man. Makayla ached with the sorrow of it all. She'd caused this. She'd done nothing but bring everyone heartache.

"I'm sorry, Baba, I'm so sorry. I don't expect your forgiveness. Just know that I love you, even if you hate me now." She stood, hugged her brothers, drew in a trembling breath and nodded. Angling her head from side to side, she cracked her neck and let go of the numbing pain. She closed her eyes, embraced the anger and surrendered to the wilding. "Let's end these fuckers."

Kraegan reclined against a boulder invisible to all eyes as he watched the Shadow Seekers. He'd seen the battle unfold, he'd told Zobiana he had an old score to settle and would join her in battle, but he'd not be settling any scores today. He'd seen the ancient scratchings of the Golden One's prophecy on the wall and knew things would not end well for Zobiana or her followers. He was there for one reason only: to bear witness. It was the last thing his father had ordered him to do before he'd disappeared.

Kraegan saw Abigail's broken body to his right, it wasn't until he saw her finger move that he realised she was still alive. He walked towards her, all the while keeping his eyes on the Golden One and the Shadow Seekers. He crouched by her and held his fingers to her throat and checked for a pulse, it was weak but she was alive. The moment he touched her, she was enveloped in his invisibility spell. He slung her up over his shoulder in a fireman's hold and walked back towards the boulder. He lowered her gently, not breaking contact with her body, he sat and pulled her onto his lap, careful not to cause her pain. Her back looked as though someone had carved her up with a chainsaw. He bit his wrist and held it to her mouth, rubbing the open wound back and forth across her mouth and smearing blood on her lips until she began to feed. Kraegan smiled when he felt her fangs dig into his flesh. Now he would be even with Zobiana; a life for a life.

CHAPTER 55.

Churning black clouds circled the heavens. A thunderous boom rent the sky and a twisted bolt of lightning struck the temple. The clean metallic scent of ozone imbued the air as the lightning struck again and again until the building took on a purplish glow and crackled with electricity. Cyclonic winds howled, stirring up the dirt and forming twisting wind funnels of ash, tree branches and mixed debris. The ground rumbled and quaked, cracks opened across the terrain forming deep ravines. The destructive wild weather escalated, growing more unpredictable with every passing minute.

Cracks spider-webbed over the exterior of the temple and another lightning bolt struck. There was a flash of blinding light and an ear-splitting boom as the temple exploded in a huge fireball. A shock wave of black smoke blasted outwards as the fireball expanded, setting the heavens alight with orange fire.

Pieces of stone jettisoned into the air and showered down in a hailstorm of debris. Violent tremors rolled along the ground as the cloud dissipated. The fireball didn't recede, but continued to grow, the flames swelling further until a shape within the monstrous fireball became more defined.

Makayla rolled her shoulders; bloodlust raged through her body. She felt the Trinian Globe now, within her – she'd not felt such unbridled power in all her life and it was a seductive energy she welcomed. It buzzed through her body igniting her nerve endings and energising her spirit. Her fingers tingled with power, the fine hairs on her body spiking with vitality. She closed her eyes and focused on the thundering power within her veins and tapped into it. She sensed the Shadow Seekers standing either side of her, but needed to be more connected with them. To defeat the Dark One and his demon horde they needed access to the Trinian Globe's power too. Makayla dropped the barriers protecting her mind from their thoughts and opened herself up to them. Her head flew back as a shock of jumbled thoughts flashed in her mind. The most predominant emotion was sadness with an underlying need for retribution. There was a unified gasp the moment she connected to the Shadow Seekers' minds, the Trinian Globe's power burst forth and flowed through into each of them. Makayla opened her eyes and glanced at her companions, a smile snaking over her face as she took in their appearances. Whatever they'd hidden of themselves was now laid bare, their true forms forced to the surface by the Trinian Globe's power. Danny had changed the most. Now she understood why he did the breathing exercises, it was to control the demonic beast within him. He was a seraphympire, but Lilith having been his mother made him an Incubus. Makayla chuckled, not knowing where to look. Small black horns threaded with gold curled back from the sides of his head, the whites of his eyes were black, his irises a shimmering gold, six huge black wings topped with lethal horns – the feathers edged in gold – opened and closed. His arms were black to the elbow with gold flashing veins, his fingers were lethal talons. His entire body was alight with demon-angel fire combined.

She winked at him. "I'm digging the new look, Danny. I knew you were hiding something."

He grinned and Makayla was treated to the sight of his shining mouthful of sharp teeth. "Yeah, I've kept the beast at bay for centuries; I guess you can never really hide forever, can you?"

"Nope."

Makayla looked at the others in her group; Bryce's albino skin pulsed with luminous brilliance. He was looking at his hands, mesmerised by the white light pulsing down the lengths of his fingers.

Zack hovered above the ground, weightless, floating debris rotating about him as he manipulated each object. Darrius and Tristan looked ready to destroy. What surprised her most was her father. He was no longer cradling their mother but stood among them with a snarling, feral look on his face – the sadness was no longer present, the wilding having taken over. That was the beauty of the wilding; it suppressed sadness and intensified anger making a warrior lethal.

Morgan and Gabriel wore similar expressions. Jackson was in his were-tiger form standing upright; his jaws open and dripping saliva ready to disembowel whoever came into his trajectory. His eyes focused on the space the temple had once occupied.

A number of Seraph and Vampire Guard along with Raziel stood behind her. Raziel was alight with seraph fire, his mouth a firm slash across his face. He looked beyond her, his eyes trained on the temple. Makayla faced the temple again; the fireball had morphed into a giant burning figure that stood thirty metres tall. The ground trembled and rumbled again as the entity hovering before them solidified and became more distinct. A choking sulphuric stench filled the air. The Dark One stood before them.

Broken chains swung back and forth from his wrists as he flexed the lethal talons on his hands and surveyed his surroundings. His bulging, muscular chest was humanoid in appearance and covered in thick, coarse hair. He stood on powerful legs; his meaty clawed feet flattened from his vast weight. His stomach and upper body were a mass of corded muscle. Jagged, razor-sharp, bone-like barbs protruded from his back, chest, arms and shoulders. Some were narrow spikes while others were similar to shark fins. His face was skeletal in appearance with curling horns on either side of his skull. He had holes for ears and empty black sockets for eyes. His thick arms with their long, bone-like fins and lethal, claw-like talons clenched and unclenched. A scaly tail whipped back and forth, disturbing the debris as he stomped his feet on the ground.

He continued stomping until the ground gave way. Chunks of rock fell into the hole near his feet, there was a low humming that turned to a shrieking and grew louder.

Makayla watched the Newbloods. They'd stopped fighting the moment Zobiana died and stood gaping at the Dark One in confusion. They seemed disoriented; their queen was no longer their master.

"Prepare yourselves, they come." Makayla finished speaking just as the ground shuddered, quaking beneath their feet. She felt her armour zing to life and the scar on her wrist burn with cold, she touched it and smiled, Salomae was on her way. Makayla got a bird's-eye view of the Barrens through the Terrin's eyes. Blood, ash and corpses blanketed the ground – there would be more before they were done. Makayla severed the connection and unsheathed her seraph swords; she twirled them and took off running, the Shadow Seekers following. Raziel and the Seraph Guards launched into the heavens along with her brothers. Salomae's screeching roar drowned out the shrieking screams coming from the pits of hell.

"GIVE ME THE TRINIAN GLOBE," the Dark One's voice rumbled.

"Come and get it!" Makayla yelled.

"*Arrrrrrrrrrrggggggghhhhh.* Bring her to me.*"* The Dark

One's massive hand swung up as he pointed at Makayla, the chains hanging from his wrists clanging as they oscillated back and forth. The wind picked up, fire swirled around the Dark One as the gateway to hell spewed forth demons.

Some crawled out slowly where others soared out, their jaws snapping. All were misshapen and deformed, their eyes black, empty sockets, their maws filled with jagged teeth dripping black saliva. Some were ten-feet tall, others were two-feet; some had multiple arms and legs while others had none; some flew and others ran on all fours. All had one thing in common: their bodies were grotesquely shaped and malformed. Their black talons dug into the ground as they raced towards them. Makayla saw hell-hounds that resembled flesh-eating zombies, their black lumpy skin hanging off their skeletal bodies, their craniums distended and abnormally large. There were thousands upon thousands of demons and they were all heading their way.

The Shadow Seekers moved in an arrow formation, Makayla the leading point; she focused her eyes on the Dark One, set on taking him down, all the while decimating those who got in her way. Her blades were a swirl of blurring silver as she lopped off heads, arms and other appendages. She didn't care what her future held, Alexander was dead and if that was her fate too, she'd happily join him, but not before sending the Dark One back to hell for eternity.

Makayla glanced to her left, Danny had unsheathed none of his weapons, it wasn't until a Newblood got close that she understood why. The Newblood's eyes rolled back in his head and his body seemed to shrivel in on itself, as if he was being sucked dry. Makayla watched, transfixed; Danny passed by the Newblood and the vampire turned to ash, his essence floating towards Danny and absorbed into his body as he walked along. He glowed for a short moment and then returned to normal. It was the same with the demons, they couldn't see him, because he was one of them, so when they came near him, they disintegrated into ash, the combination of seraph and demon fire a lethal mix.

Bryce was having a similar effect on Newbloods and demons; he'd lift his hands and douse them in UV light so they turned to ash before they got near him. Anna walked alongside Morgan, their swords swirling, decapitating and disembowelling whoever or whatever crossed their paths. Lazarus and Zack were on Makayla's right, Lazarus's facial scars were no longer hidden, making him appear a lethal, battle-worn warrior. He was flipping his daggers and tossing them through the air, they'd lodge in his victims' heads and throats, the silver metal ashing and killing them in an instant. Once his opponents were dead, the daggers would zoom back into his hands and he'd throw them all over again. Zack was using his telekinesis to rip his opponents limb from limb, body parts flying into the air all around him. Reece was doing much the same with his swords. Jackson was also tearing his opponents to pieces with his giant claws. Gabriel wasn't using weapons either, he was using his bare hands, and channelling the powers of the reapers who surrounded him like a flock of crows. Darrius and Tristan wreaked havoc with Raziel and the Seraph Guard, diving in and killing multiple foes as they jetted along. Her father took his time, he walked with a determined, detached air, his swords swirling and cutting demons and Newbloods to pieces.

A powerful gust of wind beat down from above as Salomae flew past, unleashing a jet of dragonfire, laying waste to the demon horde barrelling their way; she circled around coming in low behind Makayla and roared as she unleashed a second round of dragonfire. Makayla looked over her shoulder, and frowned when she saw Alexander's body catch fire, she screamed for Salomae to stop, but the Terrin continued blasting dragonfire along the ground and spraying out flames as she swept past the Shadow Seekers whose connection with Makayla protected them from the fire.

Salomae continued her air assault, while tears streaked down Makayla's face as she watched Alexander's body burn, waiting for him to disappear. Only he didn't disappear; instead, the flames flared and grew brighter. Makayla lowered her swords and watched as balls of gold light streaked about his body altering his physical appearance until he became the flame. The flame grew larger and brighter and then shot into the air in a spinning arc, the ball of flame hurtled upwards, morphing and forking as it sped up. The speeding fireball exploded like a star going supernova and a shock wave of fire boomed outwards like an EMP. When the flash of light receded, a phoenix uncurled its giant wings and hovered in the air before it hurtled back towards the ground, towards her. A loud squawk rent the sky as it picked up speed. It flashed past her, heading towards the Dark One; Salomae drew alongside the phoenix and spewed out dragonfire as they flew past the Dark One. The Dark One flung out his hands trying to bring them down. The dragonfire did nothing but antagonise him. The creatures split left and right and circled around again.

"Makayla, if ever there was a time to use the Trinian Globe, now would be it while Salomae and I distract the Dark One and the Shadow Seekers are keeping his demon horde at bay," Alexander's voice chimed in her head.

"Xander, is that you, are you the phoenix?"

"Yes, if I recall, I said this is not goodbye. NOW send him back to hell!"

Makayla resheathed her swords and smiled, her fangs elongating. She removed a dagger from her thigh sheath and then removed the multiple gateway key that controlled the globe from the breastplate in her armour. She slashed the dagger across her palm and smeared the gem in the gateway key with her blood. Makayla closed her eyes and concentrated, picturing the Trinian Globe in her mind's eye. She returned her dagger to its sheath and focused her power on the artefact, lifting it into the air. Makayla opened her eyes and looked up, the Trinian Globe floated above her head like a shining halo. She let go of the medallion and watched as it was drawn into the shining orb. The moment the globe was whole, Makayla was ensconced in power, an electric buzz flowed through her body. Her hands glowed, her skin, blurring from the brightness. Her armour was white, her hair a shimmering gold curtain floating about her like a flame. She touched a strand of her hair as it hovered in front of her face and let it slip through her fingertips. She waited for Salomae and Alexander to make another pass by the Dark One. This time the Dark One caught Salomae's tail and slashed her body with his lethal claws, hurling her towards the ground. Makayla formed a protective shield around Salomae and she hit the ground with a grunt, the ground shaking. Pain lanced Makayla's side as she too experienced Salomae's suffering through their connection. The wounded creature whined and Makayla looked over her shoulder; Salomae had three gaping slashes down her ribcage. Makayla hurled a healing fireball at Salomae's wounds, cauterising them to buy time while she finished off the Dark One.

Makayla watched the Dark One swat Alexander out of the way as if he were swatting a mosquito. Alexander spun through the air and dematerialised before hitting the ground. He reappeared in the sky above the Dark One, circling and waiting for Makayla to make her move. The Dark One focused on the prize, his eyes utterly mesmerised by the spinning orb above her head. Makayla looked at her companions, they still fought the Dark One's demon horde, hell was emptying fast and if she didn't do something quick, they'd have their work cut out trying to return all the demons to the underworld.

The Dark One held out his hand. "Give me the Trinian Globe," he growled.

She held her hand up and the Trinian Globe floated down, she grasped it in her palm. "Oh, I'll give it to you," she said. Her wings burst from her back and she jetted towards the Dark One faster than the eye could perceive, slamming the Trinian Globe into his body where his heart should be. The Dark One smiled, his teeth dripping black drool as he was immersed in power.

His smile faltered. "What have you done?" The Dark One grimaced and scratched at his chest, hunching over as the flames engulfing him sputtered out. His body shrank and turned black, his muscles withering as he became overpowered by the Trinian Globe.

"That's right, arse crack, I control the Trinian Globe because I put the gems into position." Makayla grabbed the chains hanging from his wrists and spun him up into the air then slammed his body to the ground. The Dark One tried to get up, but couldn't move, the power leeching from the globe incapacitating him. Demons screamed, their screeching grating on everyone's nerves as their bodies were sucked back into hell. Makayla unsheathed her seraph swords again and stood over the Dark One. Raziel, Darrius, Tristan, her father, Gabriel, Lazarus came to her side, as did the rest of the Shadow Seekers, their swords hanging loose in their hands. The ground rumbled. They raised their swords and stabbed the Dark One in the chest. Makayla aimed her sword for the Trinian Globe and as it struck, she absorbed the power. The globe exploded with a deafening boom and the Dark One's body disintegrated into black grainy smoke and was sucked back into the cavernous hole where he'd been standing.

The Shadow Seekers made a hasty retreat as the ground trembled violently before caving in. There was a sudden flash of light, and the Trinian Globe reappeared. It hovered above their heads spinning faster and faster as it rose higher into the air. A high-pitched whistling emanated from the artefact, the gems ejected from the object and floated away from the globe, coloured light flashing about them. The Shadow Seekers covered their ears from the piercing sound and curled their faces into their shoulders to protect their eyes from the extreme light burning their retinas. The Trinian Globe exploded in a firework display and disappeared with a sucking pop. A shock wave flashed across the Barrens, burning the field clean. They looked back up; all that was left of the gems were the coloured light paths they'd left behind and swirling ash drifts.

"Fuck, that was intense, but didn't it seem a little too easy? The Dark One didn't put up much of a fight," Jackson said, breaking the silence.

"Easy, you've got to be kidding?" Reece said, shaking his head.

"Why didn't he move, or come after us? I mean seriously, what a buzz-kill," Jackson continued.

"He couldn't move from the gateway entrance, he needed the Trinian Globe to break the final tethers imprisoning him.

And it seemed easy because we had the Trinian Globe. It is absolute power; whoever controls it is unbeatable. It would have been an entirely different story had the Dark One controlled its power," Gabriel said. "He will not stop until he controls it."

The ground jolted one last time, Jackson fell to his knees and was getting back up when a black tendril of grainy smoke curled around his ankle and jerked him into the shrinking hole the Dark One had fallen through. Before they had a chance to help him, Jackson was pulled into hell and the ground sealed up behind him.

The Shadow Seekers stared at the ground, dumbfounded.

"What the fuck just happened!" Morgan screamed.

They looked at one another. "Um, I think the Dark One snatched Jackson," Gabriel said, staring at the ground.

"We've got to get him back," Morgan said.

"There's only one way to get him back. Someone has to go into hell and bring him back," Gabriel said and dropped to his knees, digging at the ground with his hands. There was no moving the dirt – it was solid.

"I'll go, I'm the only one who can," Danny said. "I don't know how, but I'll find a way."

"We'll get him back," Makayla said, her shoulders slumping, the wilding having fizzled out the moment she'd seen Alexander's body catch fire. She sighed, feeling deflated. So many had died and now with Jackson being pulled into hell it all seemed so hopeless; without the Trinian Globe how were they going to get him back? It would never end.

Makayla had a feeling it was only just the beginning.

Salomae was still lying on the ground nearby. Makayla ran up to her and placed her hands over the long gashes on her rib cage; gold light flowed into the Terrin's body as the wounds healed. Makayla eyed her friends; they looked like they'd all bathed in blood. She shaded her eyes and looked out towards the horizon, the sun was rising and she saw the phoenix flying towards them and relaxed.

They watched him land and morph into human form. Alexander looked the same as he had before he'd passed through the gateway to Evron. Makayla threw her arms around him and hugged him and planted kisses all over his face and lips.

"I thought you were dead," she whispered, tears pooling in her eyes.

"I was. Salomae's dragonfire brought me back." Alexander looked at Sebastian.

Her father looked at Alexander and then back towards where he'd left her mother.

"I'm sorry, Sebastian." Alexander shook his head. "Ambrosia would have survived if I hadn't died, that's why she's. . .the only reason I lived was because of the phoenix. I was able to shape-shift into an eagle before my transition and I believe my eagle morphed into the phoenix as a result. I'm so sorry, it's my fault."

Sebastian nodded and gripped Alexander's shoulder. "It's

not your fault, Xander," he said and looked at Makayla before dematerialising.

Makayla shoved her hands into her pockets knowing what her father's telling look meant. He blamed her for her mother's death, and rightly so. Makayla felt something cold in her hand, her Zippo lighter. She searched her other pocket and pulled out a crumpled packet of cigarettes. She tapped the packet, pulled a cigarette out with her lips and lit the end. She sucked in a deep drag and held the smoke in her lungs before exhaling a smoke-ring. "God, I needed that," she moaned.

"Do you think you should be smoking?" Raziel said, crossing his arms over his chest, his eyebrow raising.

Makayla frowned. "If there was ever a perfect time to smoke, this would be it."

"I wouldn't advise it, not in your condition."

"Say what now? In my condition? What the bloody hell are you talking about, Raziel?" Makayla took another drag on her cigarette and looked around the group. Reece smirked as did Darrius.

"What?" Makayla said.

"Makayla, I think Raziel's referring to, um…" Alexander swirled his hand in front of her stomach. "Our unborn child. Smoking's not good for the baby."

Makayla's mouth dropped, and the cigarette fell from her fingertips. "Son of a bitch."

PERSONAL MESSAGE

Thank you for reading my book. If you enjoyed it,
please take a moment to rate and review it at:
goodreads.com & amazon.com

For more information about
The Guardians of the Gateways Series and
up-and-coming books please Visit:
www.reneespyrou.com

The Adventure continues in Book 4.

SERAPHYMPIRE ~ The Genesis Curse.

ABOUT THE AUTHOR

Renee Spyrou was born in Australia in a small town thirty minutes south of the Queensland border, to Australian and Greek parents. She studied Fashion in college and has worked in the rag trade since she was 20 years old. She loves creative arts and was sewing, knitting and crocheting from the early age of five. She grew up reading Greek mythology and always had a book or a paintbrush in her hand. She met her husband of 26 years in Greece when she was 22 years old on the small Island of Kalymnos where she'd been living for a year and a half with family. It was love at first sight; they were engaged after a month and married after two months.

Renee lived in Africa, the Democratic Republic of Congo, formerly known as Zaire, for three years. She was there when two point five million refugees crossed the borders of Rwanda into Zaire, during the Ebola outbreak, and when Mobutu's rule fell and the rebel leader Kabila overthrew the government. She's been held up at gunpoint, seen people shot; and seen the adverse effects of war, famine and disease.

Renee started writing when her son was diagnosed with a rare neurological disease called Adrenoleukodystrophy. Writing helps her escape the sad reality of losing her firstborn child. Sadly, her son died four years after he was diagnosed. She lives in Ocean Shores with her husband and daughter and their two Rhodesian Ridgeback dogs. She loves Sci-Fi, horror, paranormal and action movies and enjoys painting, reading, writing, drawing and sitting outside on a Friday night with her family near a small burn barrel watching the fire. If you would like to know more about Renee's up and coming novels, check out Renee's Facebook page, Twitter, or her website, www.reneespyrou.com. Happy reading.

www.ingramcontent.com/pod-product-compliance
Lightning Source LLC
Chambersburg PA
CBHW022142130726
47905CB00004BA/945